David Crackanthorpe was bor[n] [in] Westmoreland, where his fam[ily] include Richard Crackantho[rpe] mentioned by Sterne in *Tristram Shanay*, William and Dorothy Wordsworth and the notorious Daniel E. Sickles, a general in the American Civil War. Most of David's childhood until the start of the Second World War was spent on a Rhodesian farm. He studied law at Oxford University and practised as a barrister in London, where he married the Irish actress Helena Hughes, now deceased. He has written a biography of Hubert Crackanthorpe, a young writer of the 1890s associated with the *Yellow Book*. His novels, *Stolen Marches*, winner of the Sagittarius Prize, *Horseman*, *Pass By* and *The Ravenglass Line*, are all available from Headline. David Crackanthorpe now lives in France.

Praise for David Crackanthorpe's previous novels:

'A tightly woven thriller'   *Daily Mail*

'An ingenious novel'   *Sunday Times*

'The French background and the personalities are intelligently conceived and fleshed out'   *The Times*

'A fascinating glimpse behind the scenes in occupied France during the Second World War'   *Woman & Home*

'Beguiling . . . the ingenious and fresh plotting is matched by a fastidious and striking craftmanship in its use of language'
           Good Book Guide

'Unputdownable'   *Woman's Journal*

'A thoughtful and evocative reminder of how the mid-century upheaval of the war still casts a dark, foreboding shadow over France . . . Crackanthorpe's first novel, *Stolen Marches*, stood critical comparison with Sebastian Faulks' *Birdsong*; this might be compared with *Charlotte Gray*'   *Bookseller*

Also by David Crackanthorpe

Stolen Marches
Horseman, Pass By
The Ravenglass Line

This Time The Flames

David Crackanthorpe

review

Copyright © 2003 David Crackanthorpe

The right of David Crackanthorpe to be identified as the Author of
the Work has been asserted by him in accordance with the
Copyright, Designs and Patents Act 1988.

First published in 2003
by HEADLINE BOOK PUBLISHING

First published in paperback in 2003
by HEADLINE BOOK PUBLISHING

A REVIEW paperback

10 9 8 7 6 5 4 3 2 1

All rights reserved. No part of this publication may be
reproduced, stored in a retrieval system, or transmitted
in any form or by any means without the prior written
permission of the publisher, nor be otherwise circulated
in any form of binding or cover other than that in which
it is published and without a similar condition being
imposed on the subsequent purchaser.

All characters in this publication are fictitious
and any resemblance to real persons, living or dead,
is purely coincidental.

ISBN 0 7472 6667 0

Typeset in JansonText by
Letterpart Limited, Reigate, Surrey

Printed and bound in Great Britain by
Clays Ltd, St Ives plc

Papers and cover board used by Headline are natural, recyclable
products made from wood grown in sustainable forests. The
manufacturing processes conform to the environmental
regulations of the country of origin.

HEADLINE BOOK PUBLISHING
A division of Hodder Headline
338 Euston Road
LONDON NW1 3BH

www.headline.co.uk
www.hodderheadline.com

For Selina Hastings

Acknowledgements

I owe many grateful thanks to Elizabeth-Anne Wheal for reading the book in draft, and giving precious advice, and reassurance, about the credentials of the heroine.

One

IT'S A RETICENT-LOOKING landscape, as landscapes go, to spawn the myriad of vessels that have issued from it, like salmon smolt, surging over oceans to the ends of the earth. Flat green woods, and fields, and brown mud-banks exposed when grey tides are out. Enclosures. The open forest doesn't reach as far as the Solent. But the point of Hythe was that from there you could watch the Union Castle ships, purple-striped as an African sunset, heading off to the other hemisphere. That was what so appealed to Father in his retirement and why he bought a bungalow here, shaded from the Hampshire sun by spreading cedars of Lebanon in a garden forever damp, mossy, chill.

He would insist, by signs, on being wheeled along the slippery oak planks of the pier in the rain, out as far as the ferry, just to see the ships pass down the Test or Itchen on their way to Africa. He watched through binoculars, reciting the names when he still had a remnant of the power of speech. *Cape Town Castle. Edinburgh Castle* – fourteen days, those. The *Windsor Castle* with a single swept-back funnel, ten days. Wonderful, you get there sooner. He never seemed to stop thinking about Africa, but Briony has no memory of it, only a vague sense of the odour of fire. Father was so much older than a man should be, for an only child, and now he's at rest for ever under the cedars, within earshot of sirens from ships taking the tide out of Southampton Water.

Briony misses him, less keenly now but quite as much as he would have wished. Father was realistic about death and oblivion and a year's time heals a lot. He was a good man. A kind one, anyway. Never too possessive – a bit, of course, any less would have seemed like rejection. And almost never a cross word. He lived for her future, he wanted her free of the old ideas, most of all, he said, the racial ones. 'The surface of the skin,' he would say, 'the stupid pigment has so much to answer for.' Harting was an expensive school for a widower living on a missionary's savings, so he paid generously for her freedom.

Briony sheds some tears, like drops of rain filtering from the cedar branches overhead, whenever she thinks about Father and his dull, unselfish life, and the loss of faith that freed him too, in a sense, though it hurt him so. Once a widower he never thought of marrying again. Her education has taught her to think frankly on these subjects. Father probably only ever had one woman, her mother, in all his life. So it was natural enough, when he began to go downhill, that she should leave Harting at seventeen to look after him, wheel him along the pier; change him, in the end. He could hardly be guilty of selfishness with his faculties running out like the tide, leaving only mud-banks. Could he?

One must live in the present. She is free from all claims, she has some French and shorthand, the bungalow is for sale and there's an offer; quite soon it will be London, and rooms of her own, and a job. Goodbye cedars and oak pier, goodbye grey tides. On the Harting network you can generally find a quick entry and a good billet, somewhere in Bloomsbury perhaps. That, co-education and the open mind are the point of it. Not that she figures very brightly on the Harting network after all this time, but she has one friend who probably does because she always did, more or less by definition, as the emblematic Harting black pupil, the girl with the most pocket money in the school, daughter of a singer well known all over the world. Jo could be very helpful, Briony thinks, and once the bungalow's sold and she's free, she'll sit down and write to her.

The telephone rings indoors. Good. It's probably a confirmation of the offer. She can get out from under the weeping cedars. It's the fateful call.

But it's the solicitor, not the estate agent. 'Miss West? Could you drop round and see me at my office?'

Isn't that unusual? The solicitor generally writes a letter. A letter equals fees. 'Is there something special?'

'Rather special, Miss West.'

She wishes he would stop calling her Miss West. When she used to run into him in the Montagu Arms of an evening with Father he called her Briony and gave her looks. 'I'll come round on my bicycle right away.' Poor Father had no car to leave her; he despised cars, and in Rhodesia he was a horseback missionary, so he said. They seem a bit unreal to her now, all those Rhodesian stories to get her off to sleep. But there are some early memories, whatever she tells herself. If not, how would the stories get her off? The memories are of dust and heat, ants, sun; and of a sky that links you to another world than this one. The idea disturbs ... it stirs something ... a residue, far down.

'Thank you,' says the solicitor. He sounds defensive, as if aware of some professional error fatal to the winding-up of what little there was of Father's estate.

'I hope nothing's wrong?'

'Not exactly wrong, Miss West. Unexpected.'

Briony is shown straight into his office. He doesn't stand up, and he doesn't look up either. He probably disapproves of girls in trousers. There's a letter spread open on the desk.

'I am afraid we have been guilty of an oversight,' he says. 'Your late father, to my surprise, was something less than entirely open about his affairs. That has not eased the work of his executors.'

Briony's heart sinks. 'He wasn't in debt?'

'Not in material debt. We would have found out about that long ago, had it been the case. No. Debt of another kind, perhaps.'

'Is it what's written in that letter?'

The solicitor looks shocked. He stares out of the window at the rain falling heavily in the street and at the Montagu Arms opposite, then he rises and fetches a bottle from the filing cabinet. 'Perhaps a drop of sherry, Miss West?'

'Yes please.' She gives a smile which he doesn't return.

'Say when.' She lets him fill the glass to the top, noticing a light sweat on his forehead as he leans over it to watch the sherry go in. 'Your father made great sacrifices to do missionary work all those years. He was an able man. He could have done very well for himself in one of the professions. As it was . . .'

'He had memories.'

'Oh yes, I believe he had memories all right.' The solicitor wipes his brow and drains his glass. 'Which brings us to . . .' he picks up the folded letter and smooths it out, 'this.'

'Can I see it?'

'Perhaps that would be easiest in the end.' He sighs and hands it over.

West-Marimari Mission
Gatooma

Dear Sirs,

We were sad indeed to learn of the death of Reverend John West. Please convey our feelings of sympathy and solidarity in Our Lord to Mr West's daughter. He is still held in the highest regard here amid great sadness that due to problems of scruples

of conscience he felt it right to renounce his missionary work.
Our sons and daughters in Christ join us in expressing . . .

Briony's attention wanders from the page. Something insincere, unconvinced, seeps out of it. The solicitor is still watching the rain.

. . . duty to inform you of circumstances you may be unaware of. Miss West is almost certainly unaware of them too. The duty is a painful one, for any who admired Dr West as we did here at the Mission. The fact is, Mr West, before his marriage to Miss West's mother (well remembered with esteem here, poor lady) . . . taken advantage of by a woman of the Chifodya family, the reigning family here. The Reverend West was a young man, a fine-looking man, and we should not expect that women of native culture will have, before conversion, the same ideal of chastity as . . . in fact here they enjoy very wide freedoms.

Briony feels a bit lost. Insincerity doesn't seem to come into it any more. But chastity? She has never till now thought of it with reference to Father. He seemed above it, somehow.

In a word, there was issue of this unfortunate liaison. A boy, raised and educated in our Mission.

The solicitor is watching her now, with an unusual expression for someone normally so impassive. It's new to her, but she can read it. He is full of a kind of excited curiosity, and ashamed of it.

'The poor boy,' she says. 'Orphaned of his father.' She knows she says this as an echo of the kind of thing she can hear her mother's voice saying. Her mother was deeply religious and always put others first. Briony knows she is too young to do that, so her remark is a defensive gesture, like a hand raised to a cheek which has just

5

received a violent slap. The existence of this half-caste boy is a shock, a seismic shock. Father, apart from anything else, was not quite the man she took him for. In fact not at all. It seems he was a more begetting kind of man altogether.

'He will have had a far better education than other African children of his age,' the solicitor says. 'Your father gave him that at least. I can imagine, if I may say so, that no white man except a missionary fathering a black child could do it, out there.'

Whether or not he meant this to help her, it does. The sense of shock was selfish and unadventurous. She can feel herself slowly turning her back on it like the needle of a compass swinging round. She is young, this half-brother is young – the world is still young. 'I wonder how much good his education will do him in Rhodesia? Not much, I think.'

'After all, Miss West, you can really know nothing about it. And they don't say what has become of him in this letter.'

Briony calls to mind Father's photographs and his stories of the life. They included nothing of what should have been the most important, the most colourful part. It was as if he kept that secret even from himself. 'Perhaps they don't know where he is by now. He's a man and I think the Mission must be a long way into the forest. You walk out of it and you're in the heart of Africa. You disappear.'

'Well, with all the good will in the world, we are powerless on this side of the ocean. Your father didn't mention this boy in his will, as you know. In any case there was barely enough to make provision of any sort . . . even for you . . . However, one good thing is that the offer for the house has been confirmed. I have exchanged contracts. We will complete by the end of the month.'

It is September, and the rain is already bringing the oak leaves down. The long wet winter is just ahead. Briony thinks some more of those photographs and the burned land they show. 'Oh good,' she says. A ship's siren calls out somewhere in the Solent, a farewell, a sad sound. If the Montagu Arms wasn't in the way you would see the funnels from this window.

'Turn over the page. There's more you should know – on the other side.'

The title deed of the forest land purchased by Mr West in 1918 being held in our safe deposit here, we have notified the Land Bank of his demise as we believed the Land Bank had some interest. It appears the loan was paid off long ago. Kindly advise us what we should do, if anything. The land lies between the European and native areas and consists of uncleared forest with no roads or official habitation. But habitation in the form of villages can spring up . . . in a region to which there is no access except on foot or horseback. A stretch of empty land may support an invisible population of hundreds.

'Perhaps that's where he's gone to,' Briony says. The bare picture called into her mind by the description in the letter of the natural wilderness now includes the figure of a boy . . . a man . . . the brother she didn't know about and who is a man in some way belonging to her, black like Jo but not so lucky.

'I suggest we instruct the missionaries to take the necessary steps to try and sell this bit of jungle your father seems to have put some of his savings into. At least you will be a little better off – assuming it has any value at all.'

'I must think about it,' Briony answers firmly. 'May I keep the letter?'

'Who would have believed it . . . who would have believed it?' the solicitor mutters. 'And an *African* woman . . .' He has a faraway look and Briony has no difficulty reading that one either. She looks quickly at the signature before she folds it up – 'Douglas Cathcart (Rev)'.

There's no one to ask advice from, except Jo of course, and she hasn't seen Jo for more than two years. Just the occasional card, from New York, or Davos, or Cannes. But at Harting you're taught to think for yourself and not rely on traditional escape routes like seeking advice from the experienced. Experience is suspect because it's already over, whereas at Harting the future is all. And Briony has no family other than the unknown, new-found boy. Father was a solitary here in England. Therefore she was too, being so to speak wedded to Father and his care. He was out of place, he said so himself. One must sympathise, one must go on sympathising – loss of faith cut him off as if he had lost caste. There's the solicitor, of course, but when she thinks about it she feels sure that whatever he recommends, she will know to do the opposite. Well, in a way that would be useful, and the day before leaving the bungalow for ever, she requests another appointment.

'It is so personal a matter,' the solicitor says, 'that I doubt if it lies in my competence.' He pauses. Briony knows he won't take long to stretch that elastic zone, his competence, to fit his male vanity. 'But really I cannot urge you too strongly to put all this matter behind you. It is between your late father and his . . . "maker".' He smiles to show he is thinking the word in inverted commas, given the circumstances. 'The proceeds of the sale you should consider as being in the nature of a small dowry provided by your father.' He settles deeper into his chair, takes his hands off the surface of the desk and folds them comfortably at the point where waistcoat and trousers meet. A sartorial vortex, Briony thinks. 'Speaking as a family lawyer, I know from experience that unmarried ladies are at a certain disadvantage in the world. Even today. It is a situation which a wise one takes steps to remedy. And the dowry is small. On its own, it will soon go. Where do you think of living?'

'I had thought of London. Now I'm not sure.'

'London? A young girl like yourself? You could easily get a job as a secretary, in Southampton, say. Even Hythe. Have you thought . . .?' He leans forward slightly.

'No,' Briony says. No. She has not thought of working for the solicitor and becoming a small, helpless piece on the chessboard of his interests and fantasies. 'I've decided to go to Rhodesia.'

'Good God. Unaccompanied – there? A leap into the darkness – my dear Miss West—'

'It seems I have a relation; we can accompany each other. Until now, I was an only child.'

The hands are no longer comfortably seated at the trouser/waistcoat join. They are in the air, they're a judgement in themselves. 'Please stop and think. The situation in Europe is a hazardous one at the moment. Herr Hitler seems bent on trouble. Your situation too is hazardous, you are emotional, as is only to be expected. I realise your education might incline you to . . . but remember that your father was always there for—'

'I've made up my mind,' says Briony, doing so there and then. 'Europe doesn't need me.' That makes her feel a bit daring. 'When will the money from the sale reach my bank account, please?'

At the Marimari Mission, Douglas Cathcart wrestles with his soul. Oh, not just the ever-present temptations to which the late Dr West yielded like many others before and since – no, this is the mining of faith by the white ants of doubt. Dr West knew that too. It must be endemic among decent men who bring the Word to people so intensely vital that they have no need of it. The Word that kills.

It is Monday, and he has been to Gatooma for the mail. A mass of official envelopes from Salisbury. Missionaries administer large parts of Rhodesia where the government is more or less content to let them do its work. Douglas exercises, unwillingly, more authority in this part of the highveld forest than most of the headmen he has to deal with. He can protect, and he can withdraw protection. Faith, with such responsibilities and loves, is a crutch hard to throw aside. But when the white ants are tunnelling? You must learn to stand up without it.

There's one letter from England. Not from Mrs Douglas Cathcart, long since absconded, and Douglas wouldn't expect that even though he might yet hope for it. But Monday and the post from Gatooma are his usual date with disappointment. This is a typewritten page.

My dear Sir,

We are in receipt of your letter advising us of the late Dr West's extra-marital connection of which he had failed to inform us in his lifetime. We confirm that no testamentary provision was therefore envisaged for the resulting contingency.

However, Miss Briony West instructs us that she intends travelling to Southern Rhodesia in order to meet her relative and, it is hoped, seek to help him improve his present position suitably to his . . .

Douglas throws the letter on to his table among all the others that interfere with the work which for him is now the only labour of love. He doesn't want Dr West's legitimate daughter here. He has given his life to the boys in the Mission school and to the women who come to it for protection, some of them victims of patriarchy, some escaped prostitutes. Miss West from Hythe will be no use to them or to him; she may not even know what a prostitute is, and is surely ignorant of the necessities that can make a woman into one. He remembers the esteemed Mrs West, and she was everything that a man whose faith is turning to wormwood and ashes would wish to escape – correct, convinced, chaste with such conviction that you couldn't even imagine . . . No wonder Dr West's former relations with a daughter of the Chifodya dynasty were kept such a secret. Though the Native Commissioner must certainly have known. But the head of the Marimari Mission is above open reproach. And the West daughter will surely be of the same stamp as her mother.

But Douglas pulls himself together with an effort. These thoughts are unwholesome. He must prepare to welcome the girl, and look after her as she will certainly need looking after in a world she doesn't know, whose dangers nothing will have prepared her for. He will do his best to prepare her. Of course, the degree of danger varies according to the qualities of the individual – that is to say, of the individual woman and her . . . well, her appeal.

How wonderful to be on a purple-striped ship at last, after so often watching them slide along the surface of the water, from the slippery oak of the Hythe pier. This is not, unfortunately, the *Windsor Castle*, a bit too dear. It's the *Edinburgh Castle*, rather an old one, with three thin funnels aimed almost vertically up at the clouded firmament. Briony has off by heart her father's account of the stars of the African sky, and the *Edinburgh Castle* will be her passport to it. Now, in the late afternoon as the ship, stiff and swan-like, drifts down Southampton Water, she watches the shore. Beyond the cedars of Hythe the dark fringes of the New Forest, the beech and heath and pine, roll backwards and upwards, gently, towards the region of historic oaks. As a girl she loved the forest. Only yesterday, after all the packing up, she rode her bicycle up on to Beaulieu Heath to say farewell, looking out for a last sight of deer, mushrooms, ponies.

She checks herself. Farewell is a word Father might use but never thought, at least not where Rhodesia was concerned, because he believed he would one day see it again. He had to believe it. So she mustn't think farewell to the forest either. He probably did think farewell to her mother, though, with her undimmed faith, when his own was extinguished long since. Briony calls up a picture of them, in the bungalow over there under Beaulieu Heath. It is frankly not an encouraging vision – middle-aged people in middle-aged clothes saturated in a middle-aged smell – Briony is ashamed of herself, but realistic.

Hythe is drifting out of sight . . . the sun comes out for a moment between the usual clouds . . . a cedar of Lebanon lights up, on the gentle slope behind the little town . . . that little prison of a pretty town. Tears come into Briony's eyes and she feels a soft pain in the heart, but she knows she is doing what she must do; she's on the tide – the lazy throb of the engines, the following gulls, the steaming jets of water that issue from the side of the ship, white into the grey Solent, everything confirms it. There is Calshot Castle . . . Cowes further on the port side . . . soon, Gosport to starboard. The whole of huge Africa, next.

There's a boy called Jock Williams on the ship, also travelling alone; quite a nice-looking boy, if unfinished. He probably doesn't know it, but he sends urgent signals for help – from eyes, mouth and, come down to it, his entire person. They watch the violent turbulence of the wake together, from the rounded stern.

'Oh Briony,' he says.

There are at least two ways of dealing with this. No, at least three. Jock can be discouraged, kindly but definitely; he can be led on and pitched over the side, metaphorically, at his moment of greatest nuisance and weakness, and some Harting girls would do that, whatever the risk, for the fun of the thing; or he can be investigated further. Unfinished as he is, there doesn't seem much danger to it.

'The gulls . . . look at them. We must be hundreds of miles from land and they go on following. Just following . . .' she says. 'What is it they pick up in the wake?'

'Hundreds of miles from the nearest land, it's our scent.'

Briony senses an arm not far from her waist, then feels its arrival there. It's rather pleasant. An unfinished young man is like . . . well, it's an enticement. And the arm is warm and the evening cool. They are past the Bay of Biscay where everyone was seasick and the end of the world seemed at hand. She doesn't stir but she is aware of a current of response from her to him and back again. That isn't quite what she expected; she expected to be more detached than that. It's her body seducing her away from detachment. She leans into him a bit, not much, a mere suggestion of a lean.

Jock puts his other arm around her waist and presses himself against her. He is growing a moustache, reddish blond, and she feels it against her cheek, then on her mouth. She knows that Jock is going ahead faster than her, his pace is a different one. He may be a couple of years younger but what's at work in him doesn't respect age – from nine to ninety they all agreed, in comparative ignorance, as they discussed the boys at Harting.

'I'm feeling a bit sick still,' Briony says. 'I'm sorry.'

'Oh Briony, you're so . . .' Jock says again, and slowly lets her go.

Back in her cabin, shared with two other women, she thinks about it. The other women are already in their bunks; one of them reading her Bible, the other hanging on grimly to existence in this respite from seasickness. Spray dashes from time to time against the porthole, the cabin being fairly low down in the ship, where it's cheaper. Hot water in the bathroom down the corridor, but hot sea water, and miles to walk to the dining room, not that anyone much has been in a state to do that the last few days.

Has she been provocative with Jock? Done the very thing she thought she despised? Those things were often talked about at Harting, among the girls. Nothing upsets equality between the sexes faster than provocation, that's what was said, so if you're a serious person, be careful. Of course it was more dangerous for some girls than for others – girls like Briony, they informed her gladly, were not at great risk. She was a father's girl and she didn't send out, as far as anyone could tell, the signals of invitation that the less sheltered couldn't help. But it looks as if she did it with Jock, here on the Atlantic, with the sky warming up. Tomorrow she will keep out of his way; neither of them is ready for it. Well, Jock probably is, in a sense – but what sense? For her own part, she feels the time isn't ripe. She is only three days out on the journey to Africa and they haven't even reached the Tropic of Cancer. Ripening will speed up later, she already feels that, inside, somewhere. When they get to Madeira she will send a postcard to Jo – the experienced world traveller Jo will have light to throw on it all. And a postcard from Madeira is worth three from Cannes.

By the time they fill up the great canvas sack on the after-deck for a swimming-pool, Jock, mercifully, is paying her no further attention. He has attached himself to a married woman travelling alone, a Mrs van Breda, rejoining her husband who is a high-up South African official, so she has let it be known. Mrs van Breda looks to Briony as if she doesn't bother much with the equality of the sexes. She must know all there is to know about provoking, and Briony surprises herself with the thought that Mrs van Breda probably delivers, too. From a distance, Jock looks as if he thinks the same. There's a slightly ridiculous flush all about him, his skin, his movements, his eyes. He seems to be ripening by the minute, like a fig in an Indian summer.

Last night they sailed past another ship, going northward. They must have been celebrating something on board because the whole ship was lit up with coloured lights as it slid past them and some rockets were let off into the huge emptiness of the ocean. In a sky with no moon, the stars were as brilliant and hard as the lights; they were piercingly bright, almost blinding in the dark. Out on deck, watching the other ship diminish towards the horizon, Briony felt that she was at last about to reach another world. Southampton

Water was a universe away, lost to stern in the whipped creamy wake.

She is sunbathing. Father didn't like her to do that, it was a prejudice from his puritan past. 'I don't care to see it,' she remembers him saying, in a rough tone unusual for him. Perhaps, in a way, it was just what he did care for. Well, she's doing it now. And so is Mrs van Breda, on the First Class deck overlooking the canvas swimming-tank. Briony knows because Jock has only just gone from there, no doubt on some errand. Looking neither to port nor starboard, flushed eyes staring ahead. Now Mrs van Breda stands at the rail, looking down at her. Mrs van Breda smiles; a graceful figure, leaning forward.

'Come up, do,' she says. 'It's more comfortable here.'

What can she want? Well, nothing, probably. Women like Mrs van Breda don't have to want. Actual *want* doesn't come into it; what they do is take. Going up the scrubbed steps of the companionway to the First Class deck, Briony checks herself. She doesn't actually know that Mrs van Breda plans to take anything, she may just be friendly. Thinking about it between the first step and the last, Briony realises that she doesn't really know much more about other women than she knows about men. Other than Father, and look how wrong she was about him.

It's tremendously hot in the sun, as soon as you exert yourself. The ship must be near the Equator now and about to pass into the southern hemisphere, so time and place to learn. Mrs van Breda, who is lying on an upholstered deckchair very unlike the simple ones down on the Cabin Class deck, points to another beside her.

'Thank you, Mrs van Breda,' Briony says.

'That boy has gone off to play deck quoits with the Doctor,' Mrs van Breda says. 'I told him he needed some exercise. Do call me Babs.'

Briony sits on the edge of the deckchair. She feels a bit prim, perched like that, but she doesn't trust Mrs van Breda, not yet. 'Did you see that other ship last night, all lit up?' Briony asks. Close to, Mrs van Breda is younger than she thought, not more than thirty-five, about. It's her hairstyle that makes her look older from a distance, cut short behind and brought round under the jaw on each side in a studied arc.

'We were dancing in the dining room till quite late. What time was it?'

'Oh, you'll have missed it then,' Briony says. Dancing. In the First Class. And afterwards? What about the South African official? Perhaps he needn't be pitied. Men are not to be pitied. Probably he's busy on his own account, like the boys at Harting who were always busy as butterflies, lurching clumsily from stem to stem.

'Ships passing in the night . . .' Babs says. She hums some kind of tune, unknown to Briony. 'You have friends in South Africa?'

'I have a brother.' It's a first open declaration, even to herself.

'Whereabouts? It's my own country, I know it.' Babs is leaning a little towards her. Curiosity is to be read less in her eyes than in her mouth, which is moist and slightly open.

'I don't know exactly where he is.'

'So how will you find him? Africa's a big place.'

'I have the address of some people who may know where he is.'

'How very mysterious,' Babs says, sounding amused. 'You poor thing. Quite a babe in the wood. Wait till you get a sight of the southern continent. Not exactly a safe wood for straying babes.'

'I'm sure you must know all about that,' Briony says, ruffled.

Babs easily rises above this. 'I was born there. It's in the bones. I'd never lose myself because I never take risks I haven't worked out well before.' She unfolds her rather thick brown legs and stands up. Her bathing dress is made with a modest little pleated fringe or skirt in front, and Briony notices that below it, Babs doesn't shave those brown legs. Her hair is blonde, but not the fine down between knee and ankle. Briony looks upwards involuntarily. Nor in her armpits. Briony feels a shock which at the same time frees her from something. It seems that depilation is not such a female imperative in the southern hemisphere. 'I'm going into the bar here. It's eleven and I'm thirsty. No need to change. Are you coming?'

'I would love to,' Briony says. She feels light on her feet as she follows Babs, who is laughing as she goes along into the First Class bar just off the sunbathing deck.

'What would you like?' Babs asks.

'Some kind of fruit juice, I think.'

'You think, do you?' Babs turns to the barman, who is looking at her, so it seems to Briony, with hungry eyes. 'Give us a pair of Manhattans, Cyril. And one for yourself.' She sits immobile on her stool until the drinks arrive. 'Now listen to me, Briony. I'm a South African girl. Except you know damn well I'm not a girl and not your generation. I saw you couldn't handle Jock and I didn't mind taking him off you – for a day or two.' She laughs loudly and puts her glass back on the bar, already one third empty. Her bathing-dress is less modest above than below, and Cyril looks as if this has struck him too. Babs has rather ample breasts which to Briony's mind do not look as if they are there for nothing, like her own. 'But I'll tell you something, you don't want to cock-tease in Africa. You'd be asking for it, and when you get it, if you aren't just ready for it it isn't nice. Cyril! Where are you? Just now it's time for another.'

'Two, Mrs van Breda?'

'One would do it, I think.'

Briony watches Babs drink. Her upper lip trembles, pouts, and approaches the lip of the glass like a tropical orchid swallowing a butterfly. Anyway, that's the impression. Briony takes a sip herself. She likes the Manhattan, but feels cautious. Father, offering her the dry South African white wine he favoured, used to advise that alcohol spelled trouble for women; it was an agent of tutelage, not liberation, so he claimed. It doesn't look as if it's given Babs much trouble. The hand holding the glass flashes with jewelled rings and the way she wears them doesn't hint at tutelage. Briony already feels a bit light, as if she's been lifted off the surface of the canvas pool and thrown like a quoit across the bar of the First Class lounge. 'I think I would like another of those, please,' she says.

Cyril looks at Mrs van Breda, who is silently studying the sapphires in the ring on her third finger, the big single ruby on the little one. 'Sorry, miss. Can't take your order for drinks, not in First Class,' Cyril says.

Well, it's a lesson – stick to Cabin Class and fruit juice. Briony has a headache now but she feels no resentment against Babs, rather the contrary. She finds her refreshing; she isn't overeducated, which makes her easy to understand. She's a bejewelled animal, and if she scratches from time to time, it's only the way a big, spoilt cat scratches, without rancour. Affectionate, really, if you feed it, and with Babs you feed the vanity and the senses, the ones on the surface.

The ship surges on through the Atlantic emptiness, a mighty power guiding itself except for a few almost invisible officers in charge of all destinies but indifferent to the incidents of lives. Of course, the officers may be less invisible in the First Class dining room. Passing it one evening after deliberately taking the wrong companionway, Briony catches sight of the Captain, dressed in white with medals and braid, parading before Babs van Breda like a peacock. Briony doesn't see Jock anywhere. Off on an errand, no doubt.

Then, twelve days – or is it thirteen, you lose count – out from Southampton, Babs invites her to dinner. 'We'll be docking tomorrow night or next morning,' she says. 'I think you could do with a few words of friendly advice.'

'Oh do you?' Briony says.

'Don't get prickly with me,' Babs says. 'I'm old enough to be your mother's younger sister.'

Briony laughs. 'Far, far younger. My mother was forty when she had me.'

'A daughter of old parents. I thought so. You're that mixture of unripe and overripe we get in late-season Cape fruit. Look out for the bandits and frosts.'

'What time shall I come to the First Class dining room?'

'Meet me in the bar at seven.'

Briony knows they dress in the First Class, she's seen them. She has precisely one long frock – down to the calf, actually, and she has good ankles, much better than Babs's, which are sturdy as a donkey's – bought at Swan and Edgar's branch in Southampton on the eve, practically, of sailing. She hasn't worn it before. The other women in her cabin look on in admiration. 'Who are you after?' says one of them. 'Whoever it is, you'll catch him,' the other says, and they all laugh. It seems so unlikely and so harmless. She opens her suitcase again from under the bunk, and takes out her mother's engagement ring, kept wrapped in a strip of velvet. It is rather a grand ring for a missionary's wife, with quite a large, sharp-cut diamond you could draw blood with. Perhaps Father went to Kimberley to choose it, out of guilt because of the woman from the reigning Chifodya family. Briony puts it on. She has never actually worn it in public before, but south of the Equator she's going to be more showy, like Babs. She sees her reflection in the glass of the swing door into the First Class bar. She looks good.

Babs, unfortunately, looks better still, in pink silk trousers and a long-sleeved blouse like a Chinese clown; extremely daring. Shocking, actually. Cyril looks shocked, and excited. His eyes are starting from his head, Briony thinks. 'A Manhattan, Mrs van Breda?'

'A couple of double Bronxes, Cyril.' Babs winks at Briony. 'Let's get a bit tight,' she says. 'Our last night on board.'

It's a festive atmosphere in the First Class dining room, all the ship's officers are there; devastating in uniform, if you like that kind of thing. The Purser, however, no one could find devastating, he's like a verger or a bank clerk as he approaches Babs. 'Good evening. I've been looking through the passenger list for the passport authority, Mrs . . .'

Babs interrupts him, sails him down on a wave of self-assurance. 'Incognito, Purser. Incognito till we land, you naughty man. Colonel van Breda will be on the dockside to meet me.'

'I see. But the name on the passenger list . . .?'

'Leave the passport authority for the Colonel to deal with. They won't give us any trouble then, believe you me.'

The bearded Captain kisses Briony's hand when Babs introduces her. 'Welcome aboard, my dear,' he says, as if they had only just sailed past Spithead. 'What a pretty ring.' He runs his finger over it. 'Pussy claws.' Perhaps the Captain has had a Bronx or two as well and so holds on to her hand longer than necessary. Probably he's been lonely, up on the bridge. With Babs, his relations seem more hearty. He pats her silken clown's backside and she doesn't flinch. 'Easy as you go, Captain,' she says. Briony admires Babs's sangfroid even while deploring her vulgarity. Does she, actually, find it so deplorable? No. This is the southern hemisphere, where everything is different.

The band plays up. The soup is served. Dry South African white wine is offered, Briony accepts and it is excellent. She has two glasses of it and by the time the fish arrives she is on to the third and has passed beyond the zone of caution.

'Babs, I want to ask you, please,' she says, the words already sounding a bit thick in her mouth. 'Do you know Southern Rhodesia well?'

'Is that where your brother is?'

'I think it's where he is.'

'When did you last see this brother of yours?' Babs asks.

'I have never seen him.'

'He's a farmer? It's rich land out there. But no. He can't be a farmer or you'd know where he is. He must have gone out as a farm assistant. I know the type, I've met lots of those. Desperate and sex-starved.'

'I don't actually know what he is,' Briony says. 'I've never seen him.'

'Then what's your plan? For running him to earth? He knows you're on your way?'

'No.'

Babs laughs. 'He does know you exist, at least?'

'He may have been told, I suppose.' Briony hesitates. Having a secret is a lonely business. Besides, she is afraid – tomorrow she will be in Africa and reality will begin. 'I expect he doesn't know.'

'But you know about him. Is he a half-brother?'

'Yes, that's what he is.'

Babs is looking at her hard, her eyes sharp. 'Let me guess.' She is playing with the stem of her wine glass, turning it round and round as she watches Briony. 'He doesn't know about you because one of you two isn't exactly legitimate? Is that it? It's very common out here. It's an adventurous continent.' She laughs loudly and the Captain looks their way, perhaps wishing he was sitting between them.

'That's right,' Briony says and feels herself flushing, for no good reason.

'Well done your pa, is what I say. I'm on the side of liberty and life. I suppose she was a married woman?'

At this moment, an officer approaches the Captain at the head of the table and passes him a sheet of paper; as he reads it, conversation round about slowly dies down. The Captain's expression is solemn. Now there is only an occasional murmur or clink of glass.

'She was an African woman,' Briony says more loudly than she intended. The silence is complete. 'She and my father—' She breaks off. The Captain looks up from his paper. Briony experiences a mixture of feelings – she is nervously aware of being the focus of many eyes, her nerves make her impulsive and defiant, and she realises, looking quickly round her, that she thinks poorly of these rich people so eager to dine at the Captain's table in their best clothes. This is not what she is sailing to Africa for. She curls up her fingers to bury the diamond ring. She thinks of Jo. 'My brother is an African. A real one,' she announces. The Captain stands up with the paper in his hand as Babs's chair moves sharply away with a scraping of feet on the parquet.

'Ladies and gentlemen,' the Captain booms out. 'I have a signal here that you should know of without delay. The German storm-troopers have marched into the Sudetenland. What we have all feared may be about to happen.' He stops speaking, picks up his wine glass, then puts it down again. 'I served throughout the last Great War. We may be on the threshold of another. Let us hope and pray it's not so, but if it is, God help us, and our children, and their children.' He sounds emotional, for a captain. However, that's a passing moment of weakness. 'But come what may, remember that no stormtroopers can drive Britannia from the seas. I invite you to make the most of your last dinner aboard the *Edinburgh Castle* while I return to duty on the bridge. God save the gracious King,' he winds up rather lamely. The new king, after all, isn't quite the gallivanting one everybody looked forward to so much.

Briony's announcement seems forgotten in the general excitement and dismay and chattering and rattle of knives and forks. Except by Babs. Babs, staring at her, looks older, and above all, she looks strangely frightened. 'Get out of here, girl,' she says fiercely. 'Go back to the Cabin Class. Clear out.'

'I'm sorry . . .' Briony stammers.

Babs leans forward and takes the glass from Briony's hand. 'Don't make any fuss. If you have what you call an African brother, I don't know you and you don't know me. And you won't be at home in white society in Africa, believe me. Nor with blacks, come to that. The kaffirs won't want anything to do with you either. The races stay apart, it's better for us and better for them. Bastard mixtures are called coloureds and everyone despises them.' She stands up, pushing her chair away roughly, and moves to the other side of the big table. Soon she is chattering again with her neighbours there as if nothing much had happened, seated beside the Purser who looks too over-come by her sudden proximity to worry his head any more about the incognito mystery.

Too late, Briony recalls her father's good advice and what it meant. Keep quiet, was what it meant, don't trust yourself, beware of impulses, they're always dangerous. That's what he meant. But leaving the First Class dining room, Briony determines to pay no further attention to Father's advice. She and her brother – she doesn't even yet know his name – together they will find a way past the barriers; a slight swell moves the ship under her feet, the weather and the sea have been calm for days, divinely calm, you can throw a quoit and it passes through the air and silently strikes the deck in the same single plane as the surface of the water. But the Cape of Good Hope has a reputation for turbulence, gales, violent tides. For the first time on the voyage, Briony feels a bit sick, as after any shock. But perhaps it's the Bronx. Learn by experience, and avoid that kind of drink, and keep quiet, though that's less important. Keeping quiet implies respect. Which you don't – respect, that is. Not since Father with his soft, disappointed gentleness when what you wanted was something . . . oh, who knows . . . something harder, really, coming from him.

TWO

SPECK'S GRAND HOTEL – *All Windows Face The Sea* is the bold claim on the advertisement that hits you in the eye as you draw up at the platform, sooty, shaking, hot. But how can they? Gatooma is hundreds of miles inland and the hotel is surely in the middle of it. Some odd mistake. The sign has been brought from somewhere else where it would make sense, like Bournemouth or Shanklin. Thinking of those resorts after three days in the train, Briony laughs aloud with relief. This sign belongs here, nowhere else at all, and it is contempt for distance and measure that lies behind the message. That must be how life and experience are, in Rhodesia. Those days in the train have taught her something about distance and measure which perhaps only Africa can teach, that they have no more reality than you allow them. In the morning you see out of the train window, or from the little rocking balcony at the end of the coach, much the same vast landscape of savannah and rocky outcrops that you passed through yesterday, the same ostriches pacing the train, the same distant huts, and you condense days and nights and miles into a continuous, magical perspective where everything is possible.

So the owner of Speck's Hotel, Gatooma, decides to condense the four hundred miles from the sea by stating the obvious – one way or another, all windows face it. Briony is already in love with the idea. Holding on to the brass rail of the coach, with her small travelling bag in the other hand, she descends the steps on to the station platform. She had a big suitcase in the guard's van and there it is already waiting for her. A porter runs up, a small man with very white teeth and no shoes. Has he forgotten them? He speaks to her in what she thinks must be a Shona tongue, which she has been reading about during the days in the train. She doesn't understand a word he says but the sound of it attracts her at once. It's like an unfamiliar instrument playing a music you have never heard but which strikes into the musical sense you hardly knew you had. Smiling, she points at the suitcase.

'Speck's Hotel,' she says.

'Speck's. Yes yes,' the porter says, and lifts the heavy case on to his shoulder as if it were a child, then firmly takes her travelling bag. He starts off at once, almost at a run, on his bare feet across the dusty road outside the station.

'How far?' Briony asks, not because she minds how far it is; in fact the further the better, after all that time trapped in a boiling coach.

'There. Speck's big Grand Hotel.' The porter frees a hand to point at the largest among the small buildings in sight, fifty yards along the road. 'Very good hotel,' he promises her, hospitably.

Briony smiles again. When he speaks there is a frankness, free as the open ground. 'It looks good,' she says, following through the little low puffs of dust disturbed by his feet, padding soundlessly, rapidly along.

Actually, Speck's Hotel doesn't really look very impressive. There is a shanty-town air to it. The roof of the veranda running all along the front is of corrugated iron, painted red, and the hotel sign is both garish and run down, paint peeling in the brilliant sun of early morning, the second S of Speck's apparently back to front. Perhaps that was deliberate, part of the same idea as the sea-facing windows.

Briony continues to feel delighted. This is the kind of thing she came for. Carelessness, freedom from respectability, dust roads; she stops, leans down, and takes off her own shoes.

The porter has stopped in his tracks, watching her. He looks shocked, the white teeth have vanished. 'Madam put on shoes,' he says, and points at her bare feet with the hand holding the small bag.

'Why?'

'Snakes.'

'Oh no,' Briony says, laughing. 'Come on.' Snakes have nothing to do with it, she knows that. There aren't any snakes here, in the middle of a busy street. The porter doesn't approve of uncustomary actions; she read about that in the train. It isn't respectability that rules here, it's custom. She strides through the dust the last yards to the Speck's entrance and walks up the steps of the veranda. It is already roastingly hot under the tin roof, but not the enclosed, trapped heat of the train. It's the universal heat of Africa and she can feel it inside her, growing and growing and giving growth.

The small single bedroom looks out over the back – a garden with big unfamiliar trees, no grass, hedges of profuse, deep red, papery flowers. The sky is clear, pale with heat. Briony walks along the bare white corridor to the bathroom. Washing in the train was a haphazard business, in a compartment shared with three others, and a hand-basin lowering out of the side of the carriage when the bunks were down. She runs a bath and prepares her body for luxury.

In this temperature, you don't much mind that the water isn't really hot. It comes out in a tepid, pale rust-coloured rush but she's happy, wallowing in it. The ceiling is made of uneven plaster and through a gap in it you can see the roof, corrugated like the one over the veranda. You might think that in this climate, tin roofs were the thing to avoid; nevertheless, Briony accepts the corrugated iron with enthusiasm. It is a sign, like bare feet in the dusty road, of a totally different world, different from Hythe, for example. Did Father bathe himself like this under a tin roof? The thought of Father in a bath is enough to check the flow of simple pleasure. It is depressing, and she knows why. When he was here, his body was strong, young, functional, not the withered thing it became by the time she had the care of it. Strong and naked in his bath under the African sky before her day.

By the time she's dry and dressed in clean clothes, depression has evaporated. She goes downstairs hungry and in high spirits. After lunch she will walk round the town and get her bearings, and buy a map. She has an old one with her, creased and stained, showing the site of the mission (marked in red with a cross), and with a coloured-in area a few inches to the left of it. Not named, just coloured in with a transparent pink wash through which you can see contour lines, suggesting a hill.

'Can I have some lunch, please, or is it too early?' she asks at the desk.

The woman behind it looks down at Briony's feet. 'Glad to see you put some shoes on, dear,' she says. 'Only munts go without shoes.' She smiles in a kindly, instructive manner.

'Only what?'

'Natives.'

'I asked, am I too early for lunch?'

The woman behind the desk stiffens. 'In Rhodesia, you are never too early for lunch or anything else,' she says. 'The servants are there for that. Give an order, that's all you have to do. Shout if they don't seem to understand.' She turns away. She turns back. 'You'll soon learn the words.'

Lunch consists of a huge portion of very tough meat served with sweet potatoes and cabbage. Briony doesn't care about any of that; she washes it down with a bottle of cold ale and takes a coffee out on the veranda afterwards. The beer, in the heat, has made her light-headed. She watches the people pass on the road below, under the avenue of purple-flowering trees. What are they, those trees? Mostly women moving slowly, with children all round them and babies wrapped, strapped to their backs. She smiles at the women as they pass and they smile back, smiles full of satisfaction and fulfilment, in the hard light and dust.

And the children look happy, to Briony. Carefree and natural and unaware of the experience of pain as if . . . as if they have never known what it is. Or what it is to be without it. She waves at the children, but they don't wave back. One or two of them move a hand to clear the flies away from mouth or eyes, but it isn't a wave. Their eyes tell Briony that they have been taught how insolent it is to wave to a white person, woman or man, gender making no difference. Now the children have upset her. Until she saw them she felt accepted – by the landscape, by the porter, by her own desires. Did her brother have to walk barefoot under lines of purple-flowering trees, with flies settling on the remnants of food about his mouth, and big eyes afraid to signal greetings to white people? She stands and turns back inside the hotel. The refreshing bath refreshes no longer, its effect has worn off. She feels unclean, too hot, and also too cold; hot without, chilled within and lonely, all of a sudden.

In the big empty bar, the only public sitting space in Speck's Hotel, there's a small writing table with paper in a wooden stand. As soon as she sees it, Briony begins to feel lonely no more. She will write from Speck's to Jo and tell her the news. Jo, after all, is her one contact with the world beyond the seas that every window in the hotel faces from such a frightening distance.

Dear Jo,
Did you get my silly postcard from Madeira all right? Well, here I am in the middle of Africa now, in a crazy hotel where my whole life is about to begin. Actually, I'm not sure what to do to

get it started and under way. The thing is, there's something I really want to tell you.

Briony stops, and gazes down at the paper and the hotel pen nib and the ink-well with *Speck's* stamped on it. Should she go on? Without deciding the question, she dips the pen and continues writing. After all, Jo of all people should sympathise, and anyway the letter won't go off until there's a stamp on it. So she tells Jo about her African brother, and what Mrs van Breda had to say on the subject.

What I think is that we don't believe in any of all that, do we? It's just imperialist capitalism, really. Well, I'm not a member of the rich part of the world's population and when I find my brother I'm sure we'll feel we really belong together, always.

Reading this over, Briony is struck for the first time by the presumptuousness of her own expectations. Supposing her brother doesn't welcome her, wants nothing to do with her, wishes she had stayed far away in England, refuses to recognise any claim on himself or her? A bottomless pit seems to open up in her stomach at the thought of the distance she has come to meet that result. But she refuses to face it. She wills the pit to close, adds the words 'anyway honestly I do hope so', signs the letter and goes to the reception desk in the hall.

'I would like to have this letter posted and also use the telephone,' she says.

This time it's a young woman about her own age. 'Phone?' she says. 'It's there. Who would you want to phone to?'

'I want to find a number.'

'Hereabouts in Gatooma?'

'I'm not sure where it is.'

'Where what is, if you don't mind me asking?'

From her purse, Briony takes the address and name of the Mission.

'I want to talk to someone at this . . . someone here.'

This woman of about her own age looks at the paper, and laughs; a loud, a rather common laugh. Briony checks herself. What can 'common' mean, here in Africa? Nothing. That is one of the reasons she came, to escape the terror of the common. The image of the children, and the flies, comes back to her – that's why she is here, she thinks fiercely, because of the flies, because of the children.

'Oh, the missionaries,' the woman says. 'Those kaffir-lovers. You want to speak to them? Three long, two short, three long, it's a party line.'

'What do you mean?'

'You see the phone? That's a handle on the side. Like a winder on a sewing-machine? You lift the receiver. You put it to your ear. And if no one is talking on it, you wind the handle the way I said. Three long winds, two shorts, three longs. Out there at the Mission it could even be a kaffir answering.' Her accent is very strong. The R sounds are rolled gutturally, somewhere between the tongue and the back palate, and all the vowel sounds are flattened. It doesn't sound like any English regional accent, but it is English.

'I don't like how you spoke,' Briony says.

'Oh, I see. My Rhodesian voice doesn't please the young lady from London?'

'I mean I don't agree with what you said about the missionaries. Or what you call kaffirs.'

'Phone them up then. It's nothing to me. Give me your letter and I'll stick a Rhodesian stamp on it.'

The telephone is on the corner of the reception desk. Briony lifts the earphone, puts her mouth in readiness against the mouthpiece and turns the handle the way she was told. Nothing happens. She tries again.

'You often have to wait,' the other woman says. 'People can be out on the lands.' She doesn't seem unfriendly now, on the contrary, and perhaps she never was, only sounded it. Briony is reminded of school, where a person could seem hostile only because she did nothing to wrap up what she said or how she thought.

'Hallo?' The voice is gruff, abrupt, suspicious. There are several clicks on the line like someone tapping a pencil impatiently on a table top. 'Who is that?'

'I am Briony West.' No response. 'Briony West, the daughter of . . .'

'Oh, Miss West. You already. Where are you? How can you be ringing . . .?'

'I'm at Gatooma, at Speck's Hotel. I would like to come and see you if I may.'

There is a long pause. Indistinct voices are audible, female ones. Well, of course, nothing stops an Anglican missionary from having a wife; they're not Irish Christian Brothers. Her own mother, after all . . . not to mention the other woman. 'Your solicitor wrote that you were coming,' the voice says at last. It doesn't sound as hospitable as the voice of the porter who carried her suitcase like a child. It sounds wary, it sounds like someone wanting to give nothing away. 'I am the head of the Mission. Dr Cathcart. I succeeded Dr West. I first came out to be his assistant. Douglas. Douglas Cathcart.' Well, at least he's given his Christian name.

'Oh,' says Briony. 'If you knew Father, perhaps you saw me in my cradle . . .' Her voice trails off into another silence soon broken, however, by that dim twittering of other voices, several of them, somewhere along the party line, eavesdroppers and nosy parkers like birds sitting in rows on the telephone wire. 'May I call on the Mission?' She knows now to say nothing, but absolutely nothing on the telephone that could possibly feed curiosity. 'Whenever it would be least inconvenient for you and your . . .' His what? Staff? Colleagues? Wife?

'We will send the car in to fetch you. Perhaps you would lunch with us tomorrow. In fact I'll come myself. Does that suit you?' He is very formal but in his voice she can hear the note of shock that was in his letter. He is formal because of the party line and shocked because of the brother out of wedlock.

'That will be lovely. I'll wait for you on the veranda. It's so nice watching the people go by, I'll be happy all morning till you come.'

'Mind the African sun,' Dr Cathcart says drily.

The sky is hazy today and the air smells of burning brushwood. It's a Ford car with a canvas roof held up on a metal frame like something in a garden shed, and sending up a cloud of dust behind it from the naked surface of the roads. Soon they're out of Gatooma and the road becomes rougher still, with deep corrugations and potholes so the dust now is everywhere, thrown from the wheels of another car somewhere in front, going the same way. Briony is happy. She likes the dust on her arms, in her hair; she loves the heat, she adores the brown earth and the leafless trees and the savage forest without fences or tracks. And the smell of burning. From time to time they pass a cultivated space where the forest has been cleared, then, without apparent reason, the cultivation ceases and the forest marches along its fringes.

'How far away is the Mission?' she asks.

'We are thirty miles from Gatooma.'

'And what is it called?'

'The Mission? I thought you knew. It's called the West-Marimari Mission. We didn't change the name.'

'So Father is remembered.'

'Your father was a fine missionary and a good man. They called him the one with a hundred children.' The last part of this remark is spoken in a different tone from the first part. Dr Cathcart is a wiry, tall man, dressed all in khaki and dried up like the forest after the long winter. He can't be much more than forty so he must have been almost a boy when he came to assist Father at the Mission with his hundred children.

'Yes,' Briony says.

'It was a great personal sadness to me that Dr West encountered difficulties . . . in his faith.'

'He was sad about it too. But he couldn't help it.'

'We are very isolated, we missionaries, here in Rhodesia. Faith must be strong, very strong to survive. Sometimes I think the Irish Catholics do better. Once a man opens his mind to anything . . .' You would almost think Dr Cathcart wanted to talk, now he's seen her and got her in his car, but Briony is not comfortable with talk about faith. The word gets respectability from ages and ages of passive acceptance and active abuse, in her opinion. So she doesn't answer, even though not answering makes her feel, for some reason, that she is failing in her task as a woman.

'I hope at least your own is secure, Miss West,' Cathcart says, as the car bounces ever more fiercely along the merciless corrugations, with mechanical bangings and squealings from underneath. Held together, you might think, after so many thousands of miles across roads like these, by not much more than shaky faith alone.

The Mission house is surrounded by some of those lovely purple-flowering trees and there are children everywhere, more familiar and encroaching than the children at Gatooma. Briony is not in any way against children as such but she usually tries to give them a fairly wide berth. They demand skills which she doesn't feel sure she has, but these children don't seem to know what a wide berth is. They crowd round, they frighten her. 'I suppose there are some women here,' she says, looking at the children playing, or in some cases just lying, on the dusty ground among the purple trees.

'Of course . . . the mothers over there.'

'I meant . . .'

'Oh, I see, you meant white women. No, I fear we have no white women.'

Fear? Shouldn't he say 'regret'? Briony looks hard at Dr Cathcart and Dr Cathcart looks back at her. His expression is calm, defensive. The calm is studied. She is an intruder, young, female, inquisitive. But the defensiveness, Briony believes, is against something in himself and she feels alerted to that something, whatever it is. She wraps her arms about her breasts like a shawl. 'The trees are lovely,' she says. 'What are they?'

'Jacarandas,' Cathcart replies shortly, and turns away, towards the house. 'Come in. This way, Miss West.'

The roof of the Mission house is thatched and it is cool inside. Looking up, Briony sees the underside of the thatch. It looks unused, untouched, both dense and withered, like Dr Cathcart's skin. She tries to check herself. He is a decent man who wishes her nothing but well. Why invent disobliging comparisons? 'Did my father build the house?' she asks, thinking of the Hythe bungalow where he looked so diminished and ill at ease.

'It would be before my time, but I believe he did. *Homo faber* – he was that above all, Dr West.'

The inside is austere but comfortable with its raftered space, the thatch is far away above your head, the floor is like a hard, com-pacted, smooth brown plaster. There are rugs scattered about – not animal skins like at Speck's, Briony is glad to see – woven, geometri-cal, Asian-looking rugs. There are no chairs.

'This is our . . .' Dr Cathcart fails to complete the sentence. He is looking about him, searching the spaces under the thatch like someone besieged by doubt. 'Our gathering place.' There is a pile of hymn books on a table in one corner of the room, benches and hassocks heaped up in another. Briony feels a great pity for this gathering place created by Father and looking now so unused. She knows there was a monotheistic religion here before ever these colonising Christians erected houses like this, ten times, twenty times the size of any native dwelling such as you see from the train window. There – unconsciously, you already distinguish between a house and a native dwelling.

'I understand,' she says. 'I should perhaps tell you . . . it may make it easier . . . I am not a believer.'

'In what?'

'In anything.'

'I think you mean you don't believe you are. Belief is native to the human mind. Without it we wouldn't get up in the morning.' There is something in his voice that makes her wonder if it might be himself he's trying to convince.

'That isn't what I mean, but it doesn't matter,' Briony says. She must not get into an argument about faith. It would take them back to Father and his apostasy, and she doesn't want to hear what Douglas Cathcart thinks about that. 'I saw your letter,' she says, plunging ahead.

'Yes, I know.'

'Where is he?'

Dr Cathcart is considering her, weighing her up. Not the way men usually do but more, so it seems to her, as if he really wants to know what she's worth. It's an uncomfortable feeling, yet flattering in a way. She can feel herself advancing her own value in silence, like a jeweller uncovering a stone. 'My friends will soon be in from the school and the dispensary. We can go into my office,' he says. He leads the way through into a small room behind the big one and shuts the door, a heavy door of dark reddish wood. Carved on the inside surface are the words *Spred Holliness over the Lands*. The carving is crisp, deep and confident. 'Sit down,' Dr Cathcart says. It is a bare room, whitewashed, with no floor covering and a window through which Briony can see the kind of space she is beginning to get used to. Dry earth, dry air, trees approaching the house without purpose to shelter or ornament or invade. Just trees, just there, growing. The state of things in a land where space is endless, unowned, unmapped.

'I want to find my brother, I want to see him and tell him – explain – who we are for each other,' she says.

'Yes. I know that's what you want. Most natural.' Dr Cathcart pauses for a long time. He is looking at her, through her, as if the area behind her eyes is an open book.

'Then you know I want you to tell me where to find him.'

'Of course. And I will.'

'Well?'

Dr Cathcart smiles for the first time. He looks still sadder when he smiles, and more attractive, in a way, because you can't really be sad without love. Otherwise sorrow is just rage. 'I think a glass of South African white wine would do us both good,' he says.

'I'd like that very much. Father swore by it.'

Dr Cathcart takes the bottle out of a wall cupboard. It looks as if it has been broached, recorked, rebroached. The cork is obviously tired from all these operations. The two glasses, however, are clean, whole and quite large. 'Some of my colleagues disapprove of European drinks because our Africans are forbidden to buy them. My colleagues are right, no one feels it more, but . . .'

'Thank you. Forbidden? Even African wine?'

Now Dr Cathcart laughs, showing his teeth and the pink end of his tongue, a high-pitched laugh like a boy with a voice only recently broken. 'I promise you wine isn't what they'd want to buy. Whisky or brandy, yes. Or gin. Wine wouldn't be worth the government forbidding, there'd be so little demand for it.' He laughs again, but less heartily. 'They would think it a weak drink for women, and their women don't drink anything. In fact they may not drink anything.' He has picked up a wooden ruler from the table and holds it between his hands.

Their women offends Briony as if the women were cattle under discussion. But naturally, here, women are all owned by someone even if the space of the forest, the infinity of the land, is unowned. Ownership begins at home. So offence is not the right attitude; the right attitude is tolerance, flexibility, patience. 'Poor things,' she says.

'Poor things indeed. In the tribal lands it is the women who do the work. They hoe and stump and carry water from the wells in pots and tins and gourds.'

'What do the men do, then?'

'They hunt and drink. And beget children. And invent fights.'

'That sounds like what you read about the life of the English country gentry.'

'You're right. And those gentry feel very much at home here, as you will see.' There is a noise of voices in the main room. Dr Cathcart rises and shuts the door. 'Which brings me to the delicate matter of our brother Mathew.'

'Our brother?'

'Dr West's . . . your relative.'

'You mean *my* brother?'

'May I give some advice, not as a churchman, but knowing the ways of the world here?'

'Please do, Dr Cathcart, I know I need it.'

'Don't flaunt your connection to Mathew. I believe it would bring even more trouble to him and his people than to you. Be discreet. Those people – his own people – they've almost forgotten he's the son of a white man. And the younger ones never knew it. Nothing in his appearance shows it. He takes after the Chifodya, a long line of kings. He was raised in the Mission as an orphan. The more people are reminded of the facts, the more they'll talk; word spreads like wildfire, and then the Native Commissioner will come here prying . . .'

'But why should he pry?'

'Do try and understand, Miss West. Half a Chifodya and half English – for the Commissioner that's trouble, and trouble is dynamite under the foundations.' He raises one hand and lets it drop back in a despondent gesture. 'It's probably too late anyway. Just your name will be enough. If you hadn't come . . .'

Well, she has come. And who built this Mission, after all? 'You say Mathew's own people. Aren't we his people just as much?'

Dr Cathcart snaps his ruler against the table top. 'That's what I've been explaining to you. Apart from the administration, whose interest would not be a benevolent one, Europeans would want nothing to do with him. Or with you, but I think that's much less important because I'm sure you won't stay long here, in a hard land of hard people. You don't know yet how it is here. Africans are barely seen as part of our species. I am one of the very rare Europeans to take a black man's hand in mine, I live with his hand in mine, it's an honour to me that he gives it. And the white women are the worst of all, with their stupid fears.'

Dr Cathcart is paler and out of breath. 'The respect the people still have for your father from all those years ago would make it all the worse. You understand what I'm talking about? I mean the black people. The white people don't care for missionaries and they love to see one of them brought down by his own sins.'

Sins? What Father did was surely just what any lonely man might do, but the thought of it seems to upset Dr Cathcart more than mere sin should. Briony, until now, has felt out of tune with Father's memory over this indulgence, leaving behind the pieces for others to pick up – herself, Cathcart, Mathew – but now she rallies to it. She sees it as part of his refusal of all prejudice. He wanted the alliance of races, not fear going back and forth between black and white, men and women, that's how to think of it now.

'I shall certainly never do anything that could be against Mathew's interests if I can help it.'

'I'm glad,' Dr Cathcart says simply. He goes back to the cupboard in the wall for the wine bottle. 'I don't usually have another,' he says, 'but I think today . . . rather special, in a way?' His face, from being pale under the brown mask of wrinkles and authority, is suddenly flushed. Briony watches him pour. Hovering like a hawk above this Mission house as far as the first circle of forest is the spirit of 'sin', and hovering between the thatch and the desk in this office is the same sense of doubt that Briony recognised in Dr Cathcart's letter all those ages ago in Hythe, and knows well, better than anyone, from experience with Father. If wine helps, let it be poured.

'Where can I find Mathew?' she asks. 'And his other name, is it Chifodya from his mother's family?'

'He's called Shitofo and so is she, because of him. It's the name the boys gave him because he lacks one of the most important things, a patronymic. Shitofo means loose earth. They say Mathew is just a handful of earth.'

'Aren't we all?'

'We are God's ground.'

'All equally? Even a Shitofo?'

'Certainly,' Dr Cathcart says. How hard it must be for him to believe that. 'Certainly.'

'Mathew isn't here with you any more, is he?' Think of the miles and miles of forest they passed through, trackless, waterless, lifeless – except for all the beings great and small that you can sense swarming unseen in that wilderness without end, crouched, waiting there to grab and swallow you. Would they grab a missionary boy and drag him back into the dark? But Mathew, wherever he is, is not just a boy any more, he is older than she is. Still, she must think of him as a boy, the black and white boy with no patronymic. If not, what did she come to Africa for? She wishes she had Jo's answer to her letter now instead of in a month's time.

'Mathew was a first-class pupil,' Dr Cathcart says. 'On that score, more than the equal of any . . . he is remarkably quick. If only we had a university for African students in Rhodesia . . .'

'Just for African students? Isn't a university for everyone?'

Dr Cathcart laughs, showing irregular but healthy-looking teeth. If they weren't a bit irregular, the laugh wouldn't be so unexpectedly endearing, softening, but it is. 'I can see where you're going,' he says. 'You're a proper daughter of Dr West. He was so . . . what is the word, one gets out of the habit. Polemical, that's it. Dr West loved to argue, especially with slower wits. A born teacher, of a certain kind.' He looks at Briony as if he thinks he is beginning to take her in, that oddity, a woman. She can tell that he didn't much care for Father, not in his heart of hearts. Above all, he doesn't care for argument in his Mission house, a no-man's-land in the forest which tomorrow could be wiped out by fire, invasion, the tide of the surrounding bush. Naturally, in the circumstances, Dr Cathcart has no time for polemic; he's up against nature. 'But not everyone would go as far as your father to prove an argument.'

He means as far as begetting Mathew, of course. Of course he does. He means that Father intentionally got Mathew to prove . . . no. Father surely got Mathew to *show* that God's ground is all one. The trouble was that quite soon after that, he lost faith in God. Perhaps Africa was too much for the God he brought out with him, like the clothes you pack in your trunk and unpack when the Union Castle ship has docked and the train has dragged you across the Kalahari Desert and delivered you to Speck's Hotel. They don't convince you as they once did. You rather wish you hadn't invested in them before sailing. 'I do really want to find Mathew,' Briony repeats. Suddenly, and without warning, tears wash up and overflow easily from her eyes. She hates that ease of tears, she despises it, but it happens, the easy tide, come to betray her.

'Of course, of course, I know you do.' He is softened, now he looks ready for tears himself. How fast the emotions are in response to this land, like the small shadows of clouds, rapid as birds, that pass over the earth without easing the temperature or watering the drought. His embryo tears, not like tears in the English climate, will evaporate faster than they came. 'I will help you.' He is trying to find the right words. 'You feel alone. You're forlorn, I can see it.' He stretches a hand across the table to touch hers, but she has seen the gesture coming and withdrawn it in time. Dr Cathcart is a friend – at least she hopes so, she needs one – but physical contact with him is no part of what she is here for.

'How kind of you.'

He stands up. 'While you're here, perhaps you should see Mathew's mother.' His voice has changed. There's a rougher note in it now. 'Conversation may be limited. She will speak some words of English if she cares for the company, but none if she doesn't. Of course, Dr West was fluent in Shona as well as Ndebele.'

'I've come with a full heart,' Briony says, feeling the tears rise again.

'Remember that your mother took her place.' He says it without a trace of censure.

'She still lives at the Mission?'

'She will die here.' Not waiting for Briony to accept the offer, Dr Cathcart goes ahead out of the inner room and into the large one under the thatch. Two boys in clean, ironed white shirts and shorts are laying the big table for a meal. 'You will have lunch here with us,' Dr Cathcart states.

'Where will the lady sit?' asks one of the boys. He smiles at her, a smile of hospitality as limitless and possibly deceptive as the land.

'Next to me, Peter, and you can sit on her other side.'

'Thank you, Doctor, I like that,' Peter says in his light, high voice that sounds as if it will soon break. If it wasn't for the white shorts and the startling black skin you could take him for a Victorian schoolboy, a purified, disciplined, Anglican black boy. But he probably still has his black thoughts. His eyes are bright with them.

'And don't waste all the mealtime making those jokes of yours,' the Doctor says. 'You need to eat properly. You're growing fast.' He adds something in one of the languages that Father spoke so well, and both boys rock about with mirth, looking at Briony as if they hope she will join in even if the joke is on her as she suspects it is. 'This way, Miss West. Outside.'

When she arrived, Briony hardly noticed the immediate surroundings. Everything looks temporary, half abandoned while only half begun. That earth, that tree, that other dead tree, they don't seem to notice the presence of a Mission. In England – anywhere in Europe, as far as she knows – nature has learned its lesson. It is obsequious even at its most rampant, like among the feral rhododendrons in the New Forest. But not here. Here, it is hungry, unappeased, and the hard, hot, scattered earth gives life to what it wants to live, what it permits to live on it; and kills as it likes, when it likes. Man has nothing to do with that. Oh yes, Briony thinks, the heat of the soil under her feet reaching through, making her into a tree herself – that's the way, the right way.

'Don't walk on those army ants, they sting,' Dr Cathcart says. The huge black ants, marching in column of fours, are heading for the live tree from the dead one. Scouts run ahead of them, and others, outriders, dash back and forth at the double beside the column. You can almost hear their tread, thousands of infantrymen in unbroken step. Presumably there are some disorderly female ants, camp followers for ever out of step, somewhere or other, otherwise the whole ant regiment must die out.

'I'll follow you,' Briony says, and falls in behind him, lengthening her pace. Beyond the trees is a line of low brick buildings, like on the outskirts of a barracks where you would hardly dare wonder what went on inside. A line of doors too, with some human or other animal shut in behind each of them.

'This is Mother Shitofo.' Dr Cathcart opens the upper half of a door, without knocking on it, and gestures Briony forward. She doesn't move. 'Come, Miss West. Come. After all . . .'

Looking in over a half-door is like viewing a foal or calf, love for the young thing excusing the captivity. But not when it's a woman huddled in a corner on what may be her bed; where your father – oh, no doubt on a quite different bed, or in the bush, or even on his own bed in the comfort of the Mission house – begot a brother. 'I don't think I want . . .'

'But I think you should.' Dr Cathcart is behind her now, blocking her retreat. His close presence, his firmness, urge her forward in spite of herself. She peers into the relative darkness of the window-less cabin like a loose box. In the far corner is an old woman, curled up on a heap of blankets. She looks perfectly composed like that. Probably this is her siesta. There was no need to feel so sensitive about it; the woman is asleep. Dr Cathcart says something in the unknown language, loudly. Briony picks out the word Shitofo. The old lady stirs but does not sit up.

'Good morning. I hope you're well,' Briony says, to excuse her presence.

Now the woman stirs and raises the upper half of her body, supported on a shrouded elbow. 'I am well if you are well,' she says, articulating the words clearly, not mumbling them, speaking more like a Welsh woman than an English one. Briony's sight is getting used to the darkness and she can see Mathew's mother more clearly now. A strong emotion from a past she has not known, from out of the dark, takes hold of her. Mother Shitofo, on her pile of blankets, is the remnant of a beautiful woman; Briony can see that from here, even in this light. How she rests on that elbow – the line she makes of herself – that shows a woman who knows her own beauty. A kind of self-confidence and knowledge which Briony doesn't have. What must she have been like when Father first caught sight of her? Briony remembers her own mother like a half-erased drawing which was once full of detail, realism, life. Her mother was a bright English-woman with sharp eyes and a pretty face of the kind they say doesn't last long. Mother Shitofo's beauty has lasted; it looks made for ever. The high bridge of the nose, the narrow jaw, the great eyes – they will never fade.

'This is Miss Briony West,' the Doctor says.

'Yes it is.'

'She is looking for Mathew.'

'Mathew forgets. He go away and he forgets.'

'He will come back.'

Mother Shitofo looks upwards at the tin roof of her enclosure, her eyes seem to roll back, the upper part of her body sways lightly from side to side. 'One time just,' she says. 'Mathew will see me one time more.'

Dr Cathcart speaks again in his rapid Shona, the liquid vowel sounds like a kind of spoken laughter. But he is not laughing and neither is Mother Shitofo. She answers him in a monotone, heaves her flank off the blankets, falls back again and groans dramatically. 'It's lunch time, Miss West,' Cathcart says, takes her arm and turns her away. Briony disengages herself as soon as she politely can.

'Go well,' the old woman calls out behind her.

Briony knows now how to answer that. 'I go well if you go well.'

Dr Cathcart marches along, a pace ahead of her, silently. 'Why does Mathew's mother live here? Has she always lived in the Mission?'

'No. I brought her in a year ago. She was ill. She is ill. She needs care.'

The sun is fierce on Briony's head, yet the air is crisp, she isn't sweating. Discreetly, she raises an arm – nothing. She looks upwards. The sun is almost vertically overhead. 'Where did she live before?'

'Do you mean, where did your father find her?'

'I meant until a year ago.' Even to herself, she sounds – oh, so much primmer than she is inside. But the good Doctor, supposing he is good, seems to have something in mind that makes him push against her reticence like a man against a jammed door.

'This afternoon I'll show you where she lived. You should know about it, in fact you must see it, you're the supposed landowner now. And owning Rhodesian land is something particular, as you'll find out.'

'You mean . . .'

Crossing the last bit of open ground between the forest and the Mission house, Briony realises abruptly that she needs to know the whereabouts in this male domain of the lavatory. It is suddenly too late to find out what Douglas means about landowning. This is a down-to-earth requirement. Who do you ask? Certainly not those boys in the dining room. Suddenly, a young girl flits out from among the trees like an antelope and runs across their path; she turns and smiles at Dr Cathcart, swivelling on her ankles, her knees showing already plump below the rag of her dress. He moves a hand as if to sweep her gently aside, for her own good. Something about her smile may have been out of place – so willing. But here, what is in or out of place? A notable detail in England, the smile of a girl, here it's like a leaf off a tree. Briony lets Douglas draw ahead and then approaches the girl. 'Please,' she says in a low voice. The girl stares at her, questioning, uncomprehending. Briony points inward at her crutch and smiles too, makes a strained face. It doesn't work. She makes an agonised face. The girl breaks out in laughter, all her teeth showing. She points behind her at the forest, the bush, the shadeless branches. 'Here,' she says.

'Where?'

'Everywhere free.'

Three

THE SKY OF afternoon is pale with smoky haze, and there's a smell of burning so strong it seems to come more from your clothes and hair than out of those distant invisible fires. The whole world is hot, still and silent, the only movement an occasional spiral of air that sucks up a smattering of dust from the ground and disperses it twenty yards around, while hawks circle in the rising current far above.

Lunch was sparse and pretty silent too, preceded and followed by prayers in both English and Shona. The boy sitting next to Briony, made known to her as Peter, and obviously the leading boy here, has spent most of the meal watching her eat, as if she was performing for his special benefit. She knows that if he'd been a white boy she would have told him to get on with what was on the plate in front of him; as it was, she kept on smiling at him and feeling uncomfortable and guilty. Now she manages to be still hungry and too full at the same time.

'We'll take a walk over the lands before I return you to Gatooma,' Dr Cathcart says. 'But first we'll go into my office and talk about Mathew.' He leads the way into the back room as if he's a head-master, which of course he is, in a sense, and a kindly one as far as the children of the Mission are concerned. To Briony, he seems rather sterner. He seems to disapprove of her. She shouldn't have smiled so much, perhaps, or else smiled more at him. 'What do you think of our children?'

'They seem happy. I expect they're fortunate.'

'They're more than fortunate. They are baptised Christians.' Again, Briony hears that little defensive echo in his voice.

'I meant lucky' – she thinks of the endless bush and the half-naked children with flies round their eyes – 'to be so well looked after while they're growing up.'

'Growing up to what?' Dr Cathcart shifts and groans. 'Their own country offers no future to an educated black child. They're hungry for education and we give them what we can. Mathew could take all our education and more, far more . . . and look what he became.'

'What has Mathew become?'

'He's a servant.'

There's nothing unexpected about that, surely? The stewards on the train from Cape Town were easily the smartest and most self-assured Africans Briony has yet seen, and no doubt the best paid. So why does she feel so shocked? 'Where?'

'On a farm owned by one of the English gentry we were talking about. A real one. Mathew will never know ill treatment there. It's easy to act like an equal with those below you when you're so far above their heads.' In his voice is a mixture of resentment and admiration. Why wonder? The gentry rule the world. Briony's thoughts switch suddenly to the dinner in the First Class dining room, and the Captain's announcement. How much longer will they rule, Dr Cathcart's admired and resented gentry? She shakes the thought away because whatever happens, the rulers who follow on won't be young women adventuring into Africa in search of half-brothers, nor women of any kind. It will be an even worse kind of man, that's who it will be. Not that she knows anything much about the world of men. They are apart, odd, hankered after. Until, that is, something happens to help you know them better and then, presumably, the hankering stops. Even the presence before her of Dr Cathcart now arouses a certain wondering curiosity.

'What sort of servant? A gardener?' She has seen some of those, at work in front gardens on the outskirts of Gatooma, tidying up a free wilderness better left to itself.

'No. He's what they call a house boy. People here don't have women servants in their houses. African women seldom get into European houses. Except, of course, Mission houses.'

'Like Mother Shitofo.'

'Like Mother Shitofo.'

There is a silence. How did it begin, between Father and her? And when? Suddenly Briony is struck by an obvious fact she hadn't considered before. Mother Shitofo cannot possibly be as old as she looks. 'How old is Mathew, Dr Cathcart?'

'He must be thirty now.'

'His mother seems . . . she can't have been a young woman, not exactly, when Mathew was born.'

The Doctor looks at her hard, without sympathy. 'She has syphilis. That's why I brought her in. It has an ageing effect. She's far gone.'

Another shock; so close, in a way, to home. 'Surely she wasn't a . . .?'

'A prostitute? No. She was queen of a hive.'

'So Father wasn't the only one?'

'Monogamy hasn't the same value, the same deadly weight, here.'

'Does a doctor see Mrs Shitofo?'

'I see her.'

He must have meant it to come to her like that, raw, unwrapped, and Briony rises to it. 'Are you a qualified doctor? My father wasn't. I don't exactly know what kind of doctor he was. Divinity, I suppose.' Through the small window at the back of the office she can see the smoky sky and the purple-flowering crown of trees, and beyond that, the endless brown bush. 'Father must have seemed a strong man here, forty years ago, bringing magic medicines in his missionary bag.'

Dr Cathcart is looking at her with a warmer expression in his eyes. There is an admiring light behind the spectacles. She hopes he isn't about to lean forward and touch her hand again. 'He couldn't save them from syphilis but he taught them a lot about the care of children. You're a cool young woman, Miss West. I wish there were more women with character in our white local world. They don't want anything to do with the Africans except as servants. They hide from them. They play tennis and bridge and they down sundowners at sundown. But we in the Mission, we work for Africans, we work for love and the people deserve it. They don't hate the settlers enough, some think. Perhaps one day they will – I could tell you stories . . .' At the word love, a secret inner light comes on behind his features; he looks younger, he looks as if he still has something to hope for. Just as sad, though. 'But I do want you to believe that your father, whatever he did, he worked as best he could . . . we're all half slaves to the flesh . . .'

'The best for Mathew?' Briony asks, taken aback by this statement.

Dr Cathcart sighs and she can guess what's on the way. She is going to be told, however wrapped up, that a woman, and above all an inexperienced one, cannot understand, and so cannot judge, the action of a man under certain pressures. Those pressures supposed to excuse so much. 'Do you smell the burning? That's the true scent of Africa. Grass fires, usually. Anything sets them off – lightning, cooking embers, a broken bottle chucked away by white men drinking beer out in the bush, hunting for their sport the animals Africans need for food. But a grass blaze hardly ever sets fire to a forest. It lasts an hour or two, a day or two, a week. There are always some victims but fire like that is natural here. Dr West was burnt up by a grass blaze yet he lived to marry your mother and bring you into the world.' Dr Cathcart smiles, though not with his eyes, as if this was the happiest of all possible outcomes as long as not looked at too closely. The lecture is finished.

Politely, Briony smiles too. 'I do understand,' she says. And she does. She believes that excuses for what Father did are irrelevant here. No African would need them, nor think that Father needed them. 'I wonder if my mother ever knew about the grass blaze?'

'Not unless he told her himself. No one else here would.'

'So how does Mathew know? If he knows?'

Dr Cathcart is writing something. 'This is Mathew's employer. Here they say "boss". They call him "Inkos" or "Nkosi". I can introduce you, naturally.' He puts his pen away and folds up the sheet of paper. 'In fact I shall have to.' He is visibly struggling with some difficulty. 'If I hadn't told Mathew he was Dr West's son and if ever he'd learned of it in some other way, he would never trust me again. I wish I could feel . . . I can't feel . . . that you quite trust me yourself, Miss West.'

This is another surprise; he is almost pleading with her. 'Please, Dr Cathcart, please call me Briony, it makes it so much more comfortable.' Apparently not to him. A faint flush appears under the brown, parched, lined skin. 'I know no one else in Rhodesia. I've no one else to help me. So of course I trust you completely.' She thinks about the day so far, rapidly casting her mind over their conversation, the failures of communication. She is to blame. She hasn't given enough; women are there to give, that's what her mother always said. She extends a hand across the desk in front of her, palm uppermost, and Dr Cathcart stares down at it.

'Well, Briony,' he says in a voice to which some of the male assurance has returned, 'I think we need each other – Briony and Douglas.' He lays his hand on hers, cautiously, just for a moment. The effect of its removal is chilling. Briony feels angry with herself – would she be less chilled if he had let it rest there?

She gives herself up in despair. The grass fires haven't touched her yet. Perhaps they never will. 'Can I see, please?'

Douglas looks up, uncertain. 'Oh of course. Here you are.' He passes over the sheet of paper. 'I thought, for a moment . . .'

'Thank you.' Here before her is Mathew's address. Address, in what they call the bush? Does a house boy in the bush have an address, as such? She isn't sure but she doubts if any letter ever reaches him. She could send one and see. 'This Commander Chance – what is he? A naval officer?'

'Yes, he was in the War. He was at the Battle of Jutland as a boy of sixteen. One has to remember that and try to make allowances.'

'Allowances for what?'

'I think Commander Chance is still under fire, behind all his arrogance. Mathew steadies him, he humours him. In fact I think they humour each other and that's the best thing I know about Commander Chance.'

'And now he's a farmer?'

'He owns thousands of acres of the best territory and he doesn't just shoot animals over them. He doesn't spend his time out in the bush tracking elephants and buffaloes. He's a serious farmer who knows the land, his own, and the other land around it.' Douglas, as she must now think of him, hesitates. Clearly he doesn't like Commander Chance but fears something in him. His hands move nervously in front of him, short, jerky movements with no purpose. Then he takes a packet of cigarettes from a drawer of the work table. *Cape to Cairo*, it says on the packet. 'Do you smoke?' Briony shakes her head. He looks as if he wishes she did, and lights a match. 'The Commander being a serious farmer makes a problem for us.'

'For us?'

'I mean it may.'

'What exactly do you mean, Doctor . . . Douglas?'

'I mean regarding the part of the forest your father bought and which is now yours.' Douglas looks relieved. The nervous movements have stopped and he is inhaling the smoke of his cigarette deeply, thoughtfully, blowing it out towards the ceiling. And Briony begins to see a glimmer of light at the end of the tunnel of misunderstanding where their conversation seems to have been trapped up to now. Father's precious piece of land is somehow at the bottom of all this.

'Where is it, this land he bought?'

'It lies here . . .' He opens the drawer again and takes out a map, which he unfolds and pushes across the table at her. 'Just here, look. You can read a map? Some unkind folk say that women . . .' He doesn't finish the sentence. 'Between the Mission – that's Mission land, there, shaded in – and that area' – his forefinger traces out the limits of a neighbouring tract of uninhabited bush, presumably, nothing much being marked on it – 'which is Commander Chance's estate.'

'Where is the house?'

'The house? There's nothing you would call a house on your land. Oh, you're thinking of Mathew. You want to place the Chance house. It's here, more or less.' Douglas indicates a point at the heart of the forest. 'There are roads, but the map doesn't show them. Tracks, really, as you've seen on the way here.'

'Actually I love maps,' Briony lies, 'but I much prefer the ground.'

Douglas leaps up. At last she has found the right thing to say to him. He is an exterior man – perhaps men are better outside anyway, even missionaries – and he is unhappy shut in an office. He prefers the ground too. 'I'll show you and then you'll begin to understand things here much better,' he says, and stubs out his cigarette, half smoked.

The track they take is even rougher than the last part of the one approaching the Mission. Where the Mission's clearing ends and the bush begins is a tall carved post of the same red wood as the carved door of Douglas's study, a great fanged head ready to strike on an arched neck, erect on a corkscrew serpentine coiled tail, the whole thing standing the height of a man.

'I do like that,' Briony says.

'The god Nyami-nyami. He was here before ever the Mission was built.' She looks at Douglas in surprise but says nothing. 'If we destroyed the image of their god just so the one we fear could live in its place, they would be orphaned. Besides, in the end . . . what real difference?'

They bump along in low gear through the long coarse grass, sometimes higher than the car windows, engine roaring, neither of them attempting to speak. Douglas, seen from the side, looks comparatively happy now, with the ends of his mouth turned up as if he's humming to himself. Maybe he's a man who doesn't really care to talk with women. Not so unusual, even in Briony's short experience, and from her point of view it is, in this case, a bit of a relief, for the time being. When she wants information she will ask for it. Information, not talk, is what she's here for.

After a long time of jolting through the grass they reach a river bed. The only water in sight lies in green, unwholesome pools among the rocks and tree stumps. 'We have to walk from here on,' Douglas says. 'Don't touch the water.'

'Why?'

'Bilharzia. It gets into the liver. Also crocodiles. Not unknown, even dried up like this.' He sounds so much more brisk that you'd think his real calling was to be a guide or hunter, and so it is, in a way. His eyes look keener too. He smiles at Briony again. 'Keep near me.' He looks down at her ankles. 'You'll need a stick. Your calves are unprotected. The grass is full of insects and some of the plants can sting. Here.' He breaks off a leafless, dry branch from the first tree and gives it to her, allowing himself another quick look at the ankles. 'Beat the undergrowth as you go.'

They follow a wandering, rising path among the trees and scrub and high grass and stinging plants. Briony wonders about snakes. But she is sure he would despise her if she asked. Why should she care if he despises her? No good reason, and she doesn't ask. In a sudden, startling explosion some small partridges burst out a few feet in front and skim away among the trees, round the side of the hill. 'Francolin. Should have brought a gun,' Douglas mutters crossly. He will put the blame for the oversight on to her, just as Father would when he discovered, halfway along the rumbling planks of the pier at Hythe, that he'd left his binoculars at home.

'Why didn't you?'

'At the Mission – I don't like the boys to see me. They're a hunting people and the children respect me more – they believe my teaching more – if they don't see me hunting. They admire self-sacrifice.'

'Like not keeping a host of wives.' It comes out before she has time to stop it – her old fault. 'Your tongue, Briony, your ever-ready tongue,' Father used to say, so regularly she gave up hearing it.

'Not even a single solitary one,' Douglas says.

'I'm sorry.'

'You needn't be.'

They continue the walk in silence. Briony is again annoyed with herself; she ought to be making sure of Douglas as an ally, not teasing him in the dangerous way Babs van Breda warned her against. But he is after all a kind of clergyman and can be relied on for restraint. Unless like Father . . . If she doesn't want things to get personal, she must be more careful, that's all.

A gang of baboons swings from tree to tree over and in front of their path, keeping ahead. She knows they're baboons because she saw one drinking from a fishpond in the gardens of Speck's Hotel and the girl there told her. A lascivious-looking animal with an insolent expression – she checks herself. If you can think an animal's expression is insolent, isn't the next step thinking the same of people, the way women like Babs, and other European women here, think, and talk? The baboons are barking at them. Douglas stoops, picks up a stone, hurls it, and the baboons distance themselves. 'You want to sling something before they do,' he says, and laughs.

Looking back across the river bed and the forest top you can see the fires from up here. Miles away, a line of sharp little red points and a mounting cloud of grey and white smoke going straight up and then spreading open, thinning out, dispersing as haze. There is no wind. If there was, it wouldn't just be the grass that burned but the trees, the snakes, the baboons and all the rest. It doesn't bear thinking about. And the people too, of course. It is hot, terribly hot, walking uphill in the airless bush. Briony feels out of breath because of the unaccustomed heat and the effort of beating the undergrowth with Douglas's stick. She throws it away while he is on the other side of a tree round a turn in the path. He will have forgotten about it, anyway. Men quickly forget exactly what they told you to do because they're for moving on, ever moving on.

'This is where your land starts, by this big mopane tree.' The tree is one of the few in sight with early, fresh green leaf on it, and there are some stripped, smashed branches on the ground. 'Elephants love the mopane,' Douglas says happily.

Quite distinct from the enveloping heat, a secret warmth creeps up from the earth and into Briony's mood. She hadn't fully believed it until now, that story of Father's purchase; of her part in the African land where, they say, all things began. And here it is, under her feet. She will never be the same woman again, she's sure of that. She is on her own crust of earth. 'Does it go all round the hill?'

'It does indeed,' Douglas says. 'In fact that's it, the hill. Quite a big area, a thousand or so acres of rock mostly, not fit for the plough. And a thousand more on the far side of rich red earth. Under the stumps and the bush, that is.'

'Virgin land,' Briony says.

'Not quite, actually.' She waits. She is getting used to these silences of his in which he decides how much to tell her. 'There's a village.

They call it a kraal, if it's Africans who live in it. It's a Portuguese word, in origin, meaning a stable.'

'And they do?'

'Oh yes. A couple of hundred of them.'

'Is this where Mother Shitofo lived?'

'Yes.'

'They're her people – Mathew's people?'

'Half his people,' Douglas says, obviously relieved that she worked it out for herself. 'Living on what their tradition and law says is their land.' He is staring hard at her.

'You mean they've always been here?'

'For as long as anyone knows.'

'And did my father offer . . . did he buy it from them somehow?'

'He bought it from the government.'

The idea of government merges with an early idea of Father in her mind. He must have done it when he still believed in God, the governor of governments. Later on, he wouldn't have. Doubts would have sapped his purpose. 'Why did he do that?'

'One reason was to protect the natives from enforced population movement by order of the Commissioner. Come on. We've got to go round the hill. You must see the village, and them.'

'See them? May I not meet them?'

Douglas, already ahead on the path among the trees, turns back to her, takes off his hat and wipes his brow. There is a red line across it as if some wrong item has been discovered there and ruled out. 'You have to be very careful. They surely already know you are Dr West's daughter. To the Land Registry in Salisbury you're the owner, but to them you may be just a threat.' He looks around cautiously, as though every tree or rock could be listening. 'They can react suddenly in ways you don't expect. Stay close and keep quiet.' It isn't a word of advice, it's an order.

'How can they know who I am?'

'Word flies where there's no telephone wire. Or the birds pick it up and sow it wherever you don't want it to go, like the seeds.' Douglas lets out a brief laugh. 'That boy Peter knows how to make word fly a good distance, so they'll know all right.'

On the flank of the hill, dome-shaped boulders grow from the ground, mysterious and menacing, sometimes in groups like a huge bunch of poisoned fruit, sometimes in isolation. Douglas skirts them widely, keeping watch. The path dies out, is born again from nothing, wanders off downhill and backward. He pushes branches out of his way, not always holding them back for her as she follows close behind. As close as that, whether you want to or not, you find yourself thinking of the physical life of the figure in front of you, in other contexts. Does Douglas ... like Father ... have connection with African women? He's quite young, yet she doubts it. He seems too dissatisfied and anyway, now she thinks about it, there was always something a bit erratic about Father, like a marsh light. It was part of his appeal, in a sense. She looks again at Douglas's back; she's not sure now that he is quite without all appeal of his own, here on the hillside among the granite boulders.

'There's a chief in this village,' Douglas says, turning. 'It will be very formal. Behave as if you haven't seen him. Try and forget the law that says you own the land his village stands on. Don't let him see you looking at him. African chiefs are very old-fashioned, in remote country.' With a rush of noise from the stillness around, an animal the size of a big dog but more compact, more brutal, charges across the path in front of them and crashes on through the scrub and bush, making a high-pitched squeal like an ungreased axle. 'They don't care to be spoken to by a woman or seen by one till they say so.'

'What was that thing?' Briony has stopped in her tracks.

'Warthog. Timid creatures.'

Briony trudges on among the branches, hot and scratched and the skin of her face feeling tight under the overhead sun. The sweat marks on Douglas's shirt a couple of paces in front of her are the sign of his enjoyment. Heat means nothing to him in his joy at being released into the forest. Like the shy, alarming warthog, he crashes on through the undergrowth, clumsy and unheeding. And what if they meet a leopard, or something? Shouldn't he have brought a rifle at least, never mind the opinion of those annoying boys at the Mission?

'Look, there, between the trees. Down there. The village.' They have come round the hillside and now they have a view across level brown forest, on and on, full of violence, and desire, and fulfilment perhaps. The village is more perfectly part of its surroundings than any other Briony has ever seen – a wide, irregular circle of thatched roofs the same colour as the trees, the earth and grass. About twenty roofs in this circle, and now she notices another, smaller one a hundred yards off, related like a geometrical figure. There is no sign of life.

'Where are the people?' she asks nervously.

'Probably inside. They're waiting.'

Briony's nervousness increases. The extraordinary, dry beauty of the forest seen from this hillside, the tan and ochre world without end, makes matters worse. It feels indecent to own any part of it. The age of ownership doesn't belong, it hasn't reached here yet. All around is the low, regular buzzing of bees going about their work freely among the arid shrubs.

Now a figure appears from under one of the thatch circles, diminutive from here, looking up at them. He waves. Douglas waves back. The man begins to run towards them, up the hill, not varying his pace as it gets steeper but running with long strides. As he approaches, Briony sees that he wears sandals made of tyre tread tied with wire to his ankles, khaki shorts and an old tunic, unbuttoned over his thin chest. Douglas holds out an arm and the man takes it, gripping it between wrist and elbow. They smile and speak, still holding on to each other in this confident manner, as if playing a game with rules well known to everyone. Not to Briony, though. The man doesn't look directly at her, but she knows that from the corner of his eye he is gathering impressions. She does the same. This man who speaks to Douglas in such a familiar, easy way is laughing, his eyes turned upwards and his hands raised in front of him. His whole face, which at first she thought ugly, is lit by the charm of his laugh and the liveliness of his movements. And Douglas seems greatly improved in this company, he seems at home. The man has helped him to feel at home, that's how it is. It comes to her that Douglas needs these people, probably more than they need him. Did any of them need Father? Is any white person *needed* here, where the human seed first broke ground?

The two men are walking downhill side by side, paying her no attention, and she follows at a careful distance. She understands she must appear unnaturally respectful and not inquisitive. She doesn't mind this; she feels respectful – of the village, of the man who has come out to greet them, of the life they lead here on her so-called property which they, the possessors since for ever, have sold to no one. How do they live? She must ask Douglas about that. The land isn't ploughed up, the trees aren't cut down but encroach, wrapping the thatched huts round in their branches; there are no animals in sight, no women, no children. Three or four elderly men stand before the huts like statues. Briony noticed some men in Gatooma doing that – a disciplined stillness. And then, without warning, explosions of movement, just as disciplined. The whole country is a theatre, it seems to her. A thought comes from the blue – something else to ask Douglas – do these people *pay* something to go on occupying? Briony is ashamed of the thought but it presses forward, proving that the law of white parliaments and courts and solicitors' offices is an ingrained habit. Face to face with freedom like this, you must work against it. Habit and freedom are like oil and water.

They have reached the edge of the village, a place where the dry,

dense grass underfoot gives way to bare earth, trodden by many feet.
There are some goats tethered beyond the circle of huts, and audible
from far off, breaking through the chatter of Douglas and the no
longer ugly but now rather beautiful thin African man, a faint
irregular sound of animal bells out of the forest of branches, like bird
call. The man turns and smiles at her for the first time. She feels his
smile absolves her from the sin of landowning and she is too
delighted by it to respond before he turns away.

'Stand here by this tree,' Douglas says in a low voice. He walks on
into the dusty arena between the huts with his arms half outstretched, speaking a loud greeting. One of the statuesque figures
breaks the pose and comes forward. This is a more formal meeting
than the one on the hillside, with no grasping of forearms. Then a
still older man emerges from one of the huts; a couple of hunting
dogs come out after him, followed by a couple of women. While
women and dogs keep a safe distance, one of the men advances with
a box on which the old man sits down. The dogs then repose their
backsides on the dust, make a half-turn and curl up while the women
remain standing. The man who carried the box speaks to Douglas,
who answers volubly, then another box is brought out for him to sit
on. It's the ceremonial of customs.

Presumably that is the chief and those are wives. They look
perfectly satisfied, to Briony, and they look as if they have been
satisfied since they were her age, and probably long before. Douglas
is seated, and between him and the chief there is a formal exchange,
each speaking loudly in turn as if at a dinner. For an instant, she
thought the chief looked her way, she felt it like a dart. But that's all;
he doesn't look again and no one else, not even the man who
accompanied them down the hill, pays her any attention at all. This
doesn't make you feel you don't exist. You are intensely aware that
they are aware of your presence. You don't not exist, but to go on
existing you must observe the customs and the ceremony.

The chief rises. Douglas rises. The chief speaks a word to one of the men standing behind him, who passes the order to one of the women, who disappears into a hut, reappearing almost at once with a pot held before her like an offering. She shows it first to the chief, without speaking. He moves his head from side to side as if he disapproves. But this woman approaches Briony, holding the pot towards her, walking in a way Briony feels she could never walk, with a freedom, though the woman isn't young, she must be quite an early wife, a freedom drawn up from the hot brown dust under her feet.

The woman says something to her and makes a little bow, fluid as a wave. She wears a cotton dress which is hardly more than a rag, past rescue by mending, but spotlessly clean. The colours in the pattern are dazzling in the sunlight. Briony bows back at her, feeling clumsy. The woman pushes the pot towards her and Briony leans forward, lowers her head towards the pot, breathes in. Honey. A stronger, headier honey scent than you could believe possible, as if the essence and idea of honey were concentrated here in this earthenware pot. Honey from the boundless forest, except that it isn't boundless, unless for the bees. What did Douglas say? The estate of Mathew's employer is the next land lying across the map after hers. The open forest, for the Land Registry and the law, has its boundaries, inscribed on their maps. She feels chill from the pot of honey which is now between her hands, as she smiles and bows again, even risks a smile in the direction of the chief, but he isn't looking her way. Having ordered the honey for her his interest is at an end. Perhaps it's to be regarded as a form of rent, not a gift, forgotten as soon as paid. Still, she will take it as a gift.

The chief turns back into the shade of his hut, the wives following. Or are they daughters? As a former daughter, Briony thinks they must be wives. Daughters would somehow give off an air of unrest and sedition which is absent in these women.

'We have a good hour's walk in front of us,' Douglas says, 'and out here night falls very suddenly. Would you like me to carry that? It must be heavy.'

'No thank you.' She holds the pot against her stomach, both arms wrapped round it as they might be round a child.

'Well, just tell me if you change your mind.' He sets off in front at a smart pace, smarter than she can follow without breaking into an undignified trot, along the way they came. She has offended him again by accepting nothing from him. He seems to expect rejection, to court it, and to show anger when it comes. Once more Briony feels she has failed in the sphere of female sensitivity. You must, you really must, be ready sometimes to pretend.

'Actually, it is quite heavy going uphill.' It's so easy, after all. Douglas turns with that apologetic, assertive smile of his and takes the pot from her in brawny arms. 'You're very kind.'

'Not at all. We have no time to waste. As the light fails the animals come out and it can be risky. You don't make out the path so well in front of you.' They are climbing among the rocks and for a time neither speaks. Then Douglas stops, turns, facing the sun, which is huge and red and dangerous over the western horizon and the inflammable forest. 'I want to say something important to you, very important, about Mathew.' He hesitates, standing there like a beacon in the red light. 'You've seen where he comes from. His people. He's not really, in the end, half a white man, you know. So be careful, think of Nyami-nyami.' Douglas smiles uncertainly at her, not sure of her, unsure what she can take in. 'You won't change Mathew. I say it to you on this hill where he came from. And there'll be things in him you won't ever understand.'

The rest of the walk back to the Mission passes mainly in silence, but for the snapping of branches and cries of birds and, from time to time, the sound of drums from deep in the forest.

'Are they dancing to those drums?' is Briony's only question during the walk.

'Sending messages,' Douglas answers shortly.

'What about, do you think?'

'About the landlord's visit, I imagine.'

Douglas sees her safely into Speck's Hotel and watches the door close behind her. Now he turns away. She didn't ask him in for a cooling drink and if she had, he would have refused. He must get himself out of her presence – what the eye doesn't see the heart won't grieve for. Well, not for long, not for too long, only till work and responsibility resume their dominion. She is so young and insolent, with the insolence that doesn't count the cost, not knowing how insolence is a perishable luxury. If he could just protect her from what must happen – but she wouldn't want a missionary's protection. Under her thin cotton frock, she is hard, and hard inside her head.

The vibration of the engine and the jarring of the chassis along the lonely return road, and the vision in his solitude of the thin cotton frock, combine to take their toll of Douglas's resistance. He pulls up at a place deep in the forest and drives off the track and under the trees. Onan's so-called sin really cannot, to a reasonable, independent, adult mind, still be accorded the status of sin. It is only like washing away a fearsome thirst, after all; just obedience to a necessity that dreams, in their own sweet time, would have their own way of dealing with. But this time necessity won't wait.

Four

THE DRINKS BAR in Speck's Grand Hotel is a leather-padded counter at one end of the big room. A club-like atmosphere – leather armchairs, full ashtrays, men everywhere before long. White men, of course. And the walls painted chocolate brown. But veined with gold lines that run erratically, capriciously, across the surfaces like contours in a quarry. Briony enquires about them from the barman while ordering a shandy before lunch. Apart from her the bar is still empty, though there are loud white men's voices outside under the trees.

'Plaster cracks, miss,' he tells her. 'The boss puts gold.' He seems satisfied with the explanation. 'Gold mines all round Gatooma, miss,' he adds as an afterthought. 'Little bit everywhere.' He grins widely at her from the other side of the leather-padded barrier. 'Gold – gold – white bosses love gold.'

The bar is starting to fill up. Briony knows she must either go somewhere else or let one or several of these men buy her another shandy. It is not a difficult decision. There is nowhere else to go and the men here, like the woman in the kraal who presented the honey, have an air of freedom that draws her on. She finishes her shandy. These men are large, suntanned, noisy and muscular, and she feels her heart – if that is where the sense is coming from – endorse them.

Her heart says yes, to these loud, free men. Not individually, as a pack. There are no other women in the bar and they make her feel like a whore in a Western; it's quite a new sensation. If they treated her as one she knows she would bolt like a rabbit for her bedroom and lock the door.

'Hullo, hullo,' one of the younger ones says. He leans forward over the armchair she is buried in. There is a button missing off his khaki shirt. 'So who have we here?'

Briony gives him a prim smile and says nothing.

He empties his glass, still leaning forward. Whisky, by the smell. And tries again. 'Are we perhaps waiting for our colonial uncle?' he asks jocularly. That whisky may not be his first – thirsty work, being a white master in a black land.

'No, we are not,' Briony says.

'And what are we drinking, this fine morning?'

'Shandy, as a matter of fact.'

'Shandy indeed. Allow me.' He takes her glass and surges off in the direction of the bar, not steering an absolutely straight course. Some of the other men standing around with their drinks, one foot propped on the furniture, have dropped their voices and started watching. Briony stops enjoying herself. Being appreciated is one thing; becoming the target of loose imaginations is another. The chocolate walls and the throbbing gold veins seem to close in as one of the men comes towards her.

'Young Alan's a bit tight,' he says. 'Don't let him bother you. He's harmless.' There's a hint of a stammer and a suggestion of contempt in his voice. Briony looks up at him. Is the contempt for Alan's youth, his being tight, or his harmlessness? Actually, Briony has rather taken to Alan, probably just for those reasons. And this man, she doesn't take to him at all. He is very dark and he doesn't look harmless. His hair, pitch black, is sleeked down on either side of his parting, across a high forehead; he has strong, prominent teeth and a pushing-forward jaw that together give him an alarmingly sardonic air as if nothing is to be taken seriously except the demands of the will; and he's tall, taller than any of the other men in the bar, though not heavily built. His long legs are enclosed in trousers, not shorts like the others. Big dark eyes slanting slightly upwards and eyebrows unusually far apart suggest an innocence at the centre of things. No doubt an illusion. All the same, she doesn't take to this appearance, though in an uncomfortable way it moves her as if she is seeing in the flesh the original of some violent, autocratic character portrayed in the National Gallery by – Goya, for example. 'My name is Harry Chance,' he says.

Alan returns with the shandy and his own large whisky. It's a relief to have him back; she takes the shandy and smiles at him, more encouragingly this time. Harry Chance, the very man she needs to meet, frightens her. 'Bottoms up,' Alan says. He laughs innocently, harmlessly, and takes a big gulp of his whisky.

'Clear off, Alan, will you, so I don't have to put my boot in yours,' Harry Chance says, sounding careless but as if he might well do it.

'Bugger it, I got here first, Harry. Findings keepings.'

Briony sits frozen with her new shandy held in front of her. She looks at Alan, then at Chance, rapidly. They appear equally unruffled, their assurance riding over these exchanges. Maybe this is the flavour of men speaking normally to one another, a crude flavour, really, but being men, with a salty tang to it. She issues a warning to herself about that tang – be careful, out here, even of what you think, let alone do. And she has no plans for anything wanton.

Soon, casual as before, Harry Chance strolls back to join the other friends he came into the bar with. By now, drinking fast, they are making a tremendous braying noise accompanied by immoderate laughter. You can tell they're talking about some woman or other, you can see it in their eyes, and when one of them goes up to the bar to order a drink you can see the same expression – the women they were

66

talking about, the servants all around, the barman, are there to serve without question whatever they require at the moment. Alan looks over at the group as if he wished he could join them. Well, he can.

'No need to stay,' Briony says, pushing the glass of shandy away across the low table in front of her.

'I'll just see what Harry . . .'

As Alan turns away, Briony rises from the leather armchair. You hear a lot on the news about leadership and Empire, it's in the papers every day, it's on the newsreels at the cinema. Briony is not in sympathy with leadership or with Empire; what she likes is running hard into the future with eyes open, not being led into it in a squad. She looks over at the group of men on her way out of the bar – how they stick together, even their cohesion expressing rivalry and rank! They burst out of khaki shirts and shorts, their arms and thighs and whatever else demanding, ordering the freedom of the space around them. Well, they can't have all of it equally because, as Mrs van Breda graphically explained on the ship, women are in a small minority here. Which gives leverage. 'Never forget for a moment, Briony, that in Africa the white woman is at a terrific premium,' Babs had said, and she must have made the most of it, to judge by the rings on her fingers. On the way to the dining room Briony realises that she is starting to think coarsely, in this overheated land which already seems part of her.

She decides she needs some clothes – something lighter than she's got, or a dress without sleeves, or . . . something; anyway, after lunch she goes off to take a look at the Gatooma shops. Not necessarily buy anything, just take a look to see what there is. Her eye may light on just exactly what she needs, then she will know at once how she needs it.

The dusty street is full of cars and carts at a standstill, with impatient farmers in them. Two men on horseback ride by at a trot, calling out to friends as they go. Briony is aware of being watched. A man on horseback watching you is somehow different – both further removed and more alarming. A black policeman in khaki uniform and cap, all his buttons and badges gleaming, is running ahead towards the front of the line of cars, the long black whip that hangs from his wrist swinging back and forth as he goes. The sight of the whip shocks Briony, and she watches it swing as he runs. Someone starts blowing his horn, then others join in; there's a lot of laughter and some jokes that she doesn't make out but which may be about her. The farmers in the cars look less impatient now that there's something to amuse them. She keeps walking, conscious with a twinge – but only a twinge – of guilt that she is swaying a little more than she did when she came out of the dining room on to the street under the purple-flowering trees. Jacarandas, that's what Douglas says they are. When she tried out this piece of new-found knowledge on the girl at the desk the girl laughed.

'Jacky Randies, we call them,' she said. 'And there's plenty of those boys around, so look out.'

She can see now what it is that's holding everything up. There's a huge cart, laden with sacks and drawn by six oxen, blocking the street ahead, half turned to go back the way it came but stuck across the space between the lines of trees. The driver of the oxen is off his cart and at the head of the leading animals, pushing, cajoling them to shift their hooves the right way, into reverse. Briony can see he isn't getting anywhere, that the road will be blocked for ages, and the horsemen are just behind her. Here, fortunately, is a dress shop, quite a decent one, no cheap garish African frocks hanging outside. As she climbs the three steps on to the veranda in front of the shop she knows she should not have let herself think that. She didn't think it, it popped up. It's important to press down relentlessly on things that pop out from the background where they ought to remain until cauterised by the African sun.

She finds nothing convincing enough in the shop to be quite sure she needs it. The design and stuff of the clothes seem a bit – no, she won't even think the word. After allowing garish, she can't make it worse, here in this shop obviously for Europeans only, by having the word common so much as form up again in her mind. But it does all the same.

The blockage in the road is not resolved, in fact it's got worse. One of the oxen seems to have broken partly free and is now facing the wrong way and bellowing angrily, sadly, hoarsely, in fear or thirst. The rest are stamping and backing and jostling forward while the black driver, in despair, does his best to control the ox that got away. Briony is standing in the dust of the road quite near him and he looks close to tears; his face is a caricature of distress, his nose is running and his eyes are panic-stricken, signs which do nothing to calm the oxen. They are getting a bad message from this frightened man they must depend on, obey, and trust in their own way.

Now one of the impatient farmers marches over from his car, a big man, red in the face with fury, his rolled-up sleeves revealing arms like a butcher's. He strides towards the African cart-driver, shouting a few violent repeated words, over and over. Nothing like Douglas's polished Shona. Briony feels suddenly sick with apprehension as if she knows what is going to happen next. She steps backwards into the shelter of a tree as the white man breaks into a run. When he reaches the cart-driver he punches him in the chest with one fist and on the cheek with the other, then again on the same place, beside the mouth. The African makes no attempt to defend himself. He stands there, helpless in the face of white anger and summary white justice, his arms hanging by his sides. There is a trickle of blood at the corner of his mouth. Briony looks about her. No one is doing anything to stop this, no one seems surprised, the black policeman is looking away, moving off. Behind her she sees Harry Chance, watching not the scene in the street but her; she guesses that he has followed her.

Now the cart-driver is wrestling with his ox, his back to the attacker; this man, still shouting the same words as if his fury could be satisfied by nothing, grabs the ox whip from the cart. Briony turns to Harry Chance.

'Stop him. Stop him.' Her voice is high, her throat tight. She hears a shrill sound, and a squeal like a hurt dog following it. She turns. The man with the whip strikes again, hitting the African on the legs.

'Stop that, Joe, ladies present,' Harry Chance shouts from behind her. 'Leave him now.' He takes her by the arm, above the elbow, steadying her. 'It's hard, but it's what these fellows understand, you know. Shouldn't do it in front of women, though. Joe's an Afrikaner. Not a gentleman, you see.' His hold on her arm feels dry and firm. She makes no move to shake it off.

'That man's bleeding,' she says. It's all she can think of to say, trembling now as though from a fever.

'Oh, that'll soon dry up in the sun.' The poor ox-driver is managing to get his animals to draw the cart the right way at last. The hooting stops. 'You see, it hasn't really taken a feather out of him. He's got on with it. This isn't southern England; you have to be tough, they're tough too. Very tough indeed with each other, believe me.'

'It was horrible,' Briony says. Commander Harry Chance has withdrawn his hand and he's looking down at her in a way that might be amused and therefore patronising, waiting to hear the next priceless thing she has to say, or might just be the natural expression of a man whose cast of face is sardonic. His voice is quite unlike the booming voice of the captain of the *Edinburgh Castle*, far lighter and coming from the head rather than the throat. Perhaps it's the difference between the Royal Navy and the Merchant kind. Farther out of reach, perhaps. Briony's hackles rise.

'I think you need a drink,' the Commander says. 'You're shivering, you poor girl. We'll go back to Speck's for a stiffener.' Now he puts his arm through hers, holding it against his side, and starts walking back in the direction of the hotel. What can she do? He is so much taller than her. She goes along unwillingly, and willingly; angry, but curious. After all, this strange man is Mathew's employer, isn't he? He is Mathew's master and, according to Douglas, a man under constant fire. That arouses a kind of elemental sympathy.

'Tell me what you're doing here.' They're on the veranda outside the bar, on deckchairs in the long shade of the jacarandas. The drink she has been brought is gin with angostura, a mixture she has never tried before – astringent and explosive and enjoyable. Commander Chance's long legs reach from his chair as far as the balustrade of the veranda, on which he rests his feet. Briony has an awful feeling that these long legs, like a spider's, are ready to fold themselves round her, not eat her up, wrap her up. 'Most women don't travel alone, and if they do, they're on their way to Salisbury. And even in Salisbury they don't go into Meikle's bar on their own.'

'I don't care what most women do.'

Harry Chance laughs. 'I like your being cross like that, and bloody-minded.'

Oh of course. He's delighted because he thinks she's bloody-minded and so she must be easy. Briony looks down at her arms, her dress, her legs visible from the knee. Fresh as a daisy, and dim as a fifteen-watt bulb, as Father used to say. Well, he'll see about dim, this commander with the firm grip she hasn't forgotten. There's still an imprint of it on her arm, faint pink against the white skin. She must get more into the sun, then that sort of thing wouldn't show. She wonders if there is a Mrs Chance, and what she might be like.

'Actually,' she says on an impulse, 'I'm here to take possession of some land I own.' That should give him something to think about.

Apparently it does. He says nothing for a full minute. Or perhaps he's thinking about something else. He has a faraway expression, the dark eyes fixed on a point in the sky, above the buildings across the street. 'Have you bought it? I didn't know there was any for sale.'

'My father bought it a long time ago. He was a missionary at the Anglican Mission.'

Now his eyes are concentrated on her. 'Where is it, this land?'

The question is abrupt. If she wasn't alarmed by this tall naval man she would avoid answering, or say that the whereabouts of her land was her concern. But he does alarm her, with his black hair and drilling black eyes and slight hesitation of speech that seems to hammer the question home like a nail. 'Beyond the Mission land, on a hill.'

'South of the Mission?'

No good trying to remember where the sun was. It was overhead – no, wait; on the way back, when she and Douglas were almost running round the hill looking out for snakes, the sun was to their left. 'Yes.'

'You're sure? How do you know? Have you got a plan?'

'No. But I know which is south of the Mission because I know which is west.' She will give no more information and answer no more of his cross-examination. He is a rude man and he's too interested. Not in her, which would be – well, it would be what you might expect, and try to take in your stride and fend off; but just in the land, presumably because it's the next bit to his. Well, so much the worse for him.

'Then we're next-door neighbours now,' Harry Chance says, and grins at her. It isn't a warm smile to smooth the way for a man and a woman not yet at ease. This grin is a challenge. 'Welcome to the Rhodesian landed gentry.' Is he being sarcastic? She thinks not. Calling people next-door neighbours because their far-flung territories adjoin, and regardless of who may be living in between, comes straight from the world he belongs to. 'We'll drink to it. Being new, you may not know that here we drink to anything and everything. It's part of the joy of this great colony.' He gets up and goes off towards the bar.

There is something about him, actually, which you notice as soon as he isn't there and she knows what it is. He has an overheated personality to match the land. Excitement comes out of him like spray from a waterfall. Hearing his step behind her on his way back from the bar, she feels touched by it herself. Better take care with the drinks – Plymouth gin in this temperature . . .

'I'll tell you what we're going to do,' Harry says – there, the gin already makes her think of him as Harry – 'we're going to run you out to my place for the night. Or for just as long as you like. My wife will be delighted to see you. She gets bored on her own. Pack your bags, come on. You can't stay on in Speck's. It's not meant for people like you to stay more than a night, you'd get taken for something else. And taken's the word. After sundown fellows like me all go back to their farms and Speck's fills up with a very different class of chap – commercial Afrikaners, mostly.' He takes a gulp of his drink, which, Briony notices, is a lot bigger than hers. 'Do you ride? On my place I ride everywhere. It's the only way to get about the lands. It's the real freedom of Africa. It's what I love.'

'I've done some riding in the New Forest.' This is true. She used to canter on a pony along a well-trodden path between beech trees and heath, with some other inexperienced girls, every Saturday afternoon in the good weather, and then jump hurdles in the paddock. Not quite the same thing, though, as the lands under this sky.

Harry looks pleased. He leans forward so the space between them seems to heat up. 'Good. My wife won't ride with me any more. I bought her a horse but she's terrified of it. A nice quiet little mare, it'll suit you down to the ground. I bet you have a good seat.'

Briony, despising Mrs Chance for being frightened of the mare, draws herself back into her chair and crosses her legs the other way. Harry is looking down at them and he laughs. 'You'll need trousers to ride in. I hate to think of weals from stirrup leathers marking that white skin anywhere.'

It is a big blue American saloon car and it careers along the rough roads, throwing up mountains of red dust into the air.

'The faster you go, the less you notice the corrugations,' Harry says. He sounds a bit wild; there's something violent in his voice as if the car were a ship and the corrugations great waves into which he punches the bow. Anyway, that's how it seems to Briony, watching his arms wrestle with the wheel. Some men roll back their sleeves neatly as soldiers. Harry isn't one of those. His untidy rolled-up sleeves make her think of sheets hanging from the side of a bed.

'I can notice them all right,' she says, holding on to the leather handle beside the door.

'That's the hell of it.'

They turn off the road on to a track still rougher and narrower, plunging blindly ahead into the darkening forest like a mole in a tunnel. Harry turns on the headlights.

'Is this your . . . estate?' Briony asks.

'It's my farm.' He sounds serious and respectful for the first time, like a virtuous man mentioning his wife; only when he mentioned his, he didn't sound much like that at all.

'What do you grow on it?' Briony asks, rocked about as the car crashes on through the trees, the unrecognised form of some animal caught from time to time in the headlights or flitting past in twilight. The best plan for calming any man is to get him to talk about his work, even if, like Father, it's a long time since he did any.

'Maize, tobacco, cotton, and maize. To feed the men and their families.' It has worked. He slows down and sounds solemn. 'Some

74

cattle – Herefords – and sheep. Of course water's a problem – every drop comes out of wells. When I bought this land there wasn't an acre cultivated. I had to stump the lot.'

'Yourself?'

'With a couple of hundred black hands. Willing or unwilling. The unwilling, you encourage them as you can.'

Why is it she doesn't revolt against the implications of this answer? She should. Everything in her education and make-up tells her she should. She owes it to Father to take umbrage at the least hint of oppression against the native people. And to Mathew, too, certainly. But Harry's arm is there, the strong movements are there beside her as he takes them through the darkness and the bush. She isn't really quite in charge of herself. She can feel a current drawing her along.

'There's the house,' he says. They bump slowly, noisily across a cattle grid made of tree trunks. 'See the electric light? Home-made. That took a bit of doing, I can tell you.' He sounds quite joyful. Perhaps it's the prospect of soon seeing Mrs Chance, waiting for him under the home-made illuminations.

It seems quite a big house, with a steep roof, bigger than the Mission, spread out in the headlights with more buildings indistinct among the trees to left and right. The sky behind them is dark but for a thin blood-red line on the horizon. Briony feels nervous and strangely guilty at the thought of meeting Mrs Chance. She hardly thinks about Mathew at all, though his presence here is supposed to be the reason for hers. She can see a broad veranda in front of the house with steps up to it, and beyond that, faintly lit windows and doorway, with the Chance home-made current burning dim and irregular as a candle behind a curtain. There's a dark figure on the veranda, dressed in white. Mrs Chance must be a tall woman, nearly as tall as her husband. It makes Briony feel still more nervous. The figure doesn't move, as the car stops and they get out on to the earth. As far as Briony can see, there's no garden, no sign of water.

Everything is still and dry as the night – trees, earth, house, and the white figure. There is a sound like the howling of a dog but more hopeless, wilder and as if in a language not meant for human ears, coming from somewhere far off in the forest, and then answered from closer, among the trees beyond the cattle grid.

'Only hyenas,' Harry says reassuringly. 'Come on.'

Briony follows him towards the steps of the veranda. It is so dark now she can hardly see the ground in front of her. The sky over the house is black, with stars so close above you and brilliant you would expect them to light the way, but it's a black light they send out into the black sky. 'Please wait,' she says as Harry with his long stride moves ahead of her towards the figure on the veranda. He stops and turns.

'Here.' He holds out a hand which she can just see in front of her. How can she possibly take it, with his wife twenty yards away and waiting for them?

'It's all right. Just don't go too fast,' she says, and regrets the dry, hard feel of the hand she might have had in hers.

They are near the steps; Harry is on the first of them, towering above her now. What is Mrs Chance's reaction going to be to the unannounced arrival of a young woman from a hotel in Gatooma? Presumably even a town as small as Gatooma has tarts, professional or amateur; in fact especially a town like that, in a country of so few white women, with so many obviously licentious males. Harry will explain, but will the explanation be good enough? Briony pulls herself together. She hasn't done anything to hurt Mrs Chance. Hardly even an idea at the back of her head, other than taking against Harry at first sight. She climbs the four steps behind him, and looks up, determined to show a confident, pleasant, smiling front. In the dark, unseen, slowly, her smile freezes. The figure in white, still as a statue, is a man.

He doesn't speak. No one has spoken. She is not introduced to this man for the obvious reason. He is black, he is part of the night, only his white shirt and trousers make him different from those animals that howl out there, not for white men's ears. Briony stops when she reaches the veranda, as if out of breath. Her stomach, her heart, have given a lurch and swerve like a car at night when a fallen tree is sighted across the track ahead. The man in white holds the door open, waiting for her to pass in after Harry. Light from inside floats over the veranda floor, a dim ochre segment of electricity in the African darkness, its extremity just showing the feet of the man in white. They are bare.

'Starry night, Nkosi,' he says. This must be what she crossed the ocean for. He must be Mathew, this tall statue in the dark.

Five

RHODESIA IS A high land near the middle of the Earth where spring, in the European sense, doesn't happen. At the end of winter the heat grows like the tobacco plant, that's all. And even after a hot day, nights can still be cold. This is a cold one, the dining room is unheated and Briony is not wearing enough clothes. The table, on the other hand, is dressed up to the nines. Harry's wife's name is Anne, a take-it-or-leave-it name. She is beautiful in a willowy, languid, nerveless manner, with a narrow face framed by wings of shiny blonde hair, as if she were peering forth between drawn curtains in a theatre. She looks out of place, here in Africa. Briony can imagine her better in London, in a smart house with a lover a good deal older than herself. No wonder she has no taste for riding in the bush with Harry. She wears a long plum-coloured velvet housecoat, which should keep her warm enough.

'I do so admire those missionary people,' Anne says. 'Living among the Africans practically cheek by jowl like your father.'

Is there an insinuation? After all, Anne herself lives among Africans; well, perhaps not among them – above them. Briony glances upwards at the man who must be Mathew, standing erect behind the chair Anne is about to sit in. He has no expression at all as he slides it in under her bottom. His eyes are cast down, his mouth sternly carved into the mask of his face. Briony looks quickly away, afraid of the moment when their gaze will meet. What will he read in hers? What prejudice, what error of interpretation on one side or the other?

'I feel cold,' Anne says. Her voice is thin and sharp, between a complaint and a command.

'It's perfectly warm in here,' Harry says. He has lost that urgent cheerfulness he showed earlier on, a headlong drive into the next excitement or pleasure only half believed in; he has become a sultry, glowering figure at the end of the table, fiddling with his knife and fork.

'I'm frozen. You should have built a fireplace in this room. A dining room needs a fireplace.'

'You're in Rhodesia. Do you want a rose garden? You can't have one. This is the highveld.'

'Bugger rose gardens,' says Anne. 'Daddy has fires lit in every room at Billing.'

'Of course. Billing's a big house for idle people with nothing to do except—'

'They go there for the shooting.'

'And rogering about. This is a farm. If you work, you don't feel cold.'

'You don't get cold if you do enough of what you call rogering, though there is a better word.'

Briony feels out of her depth. Things have moved too fast and these two are squabbling in a vocabulary strange to her. Still, you can make guesses and her guess is that Harry is less at ease in the rich settlers' world surrounding him than you would expect, at first sight. No doubt he is in conflict about social right and wrong as any intelligent man should be. She looks at him with new understanding. He broods, there at the end of the table; he looks splendid, really – sullen, sombre, vulnerable.

Anne turns to Mathew. 'Go and get me a coat.'

'What coat madam?'

'Any coat. And hurry, I'm shivering.' She smiles up at Mathew. Just a formality. The smile says that she has been brought up to smile when giving orders because you can afford to be pleasant when there's no risk of not getting what you want, and right away. Mathew moves in an unhurried manner towards the door into the sitting room. It seems to Briony that his expression is contemptuous and indulgent, as if dealing with someone else's tiresome child. Perhaps she's wrong. That may be just how Mathew looks when he's on duty in the dining room. Men, in her experience, tend to be actors, especially men connected with missions. They may act less when there are no women around, but how would she know?

Suddenly there's a commotion from the other end of the table. Harry is on his feet and his chair is overturned on to the floor behind him. 'Come back,' he says, far louder than necessary for the size of the room. Mathew turns at the door. 'Forget coat. Fetch sticks and wood.' He is starting to shout, not particularly at Mathew; his voice has just risen as irritation flares into temper. 'Run.'

Mathew, unperturbed, proceeds at the same pace towards the opposite door. He seems to be laughing silently, but Briony is frightened. She has no experience of male anger or the violence you hear about. Father never shouted. So she is frozen into her place among these willingly violent people from another world, waiting to see what happens next, and a bit excited, she is ashamed to admit, in a not totally unpleasant way.

'I only wanted my coat,' Anne says, not moving. It seems she is frozen too. Her voice sounds like a little girl's, but fatalistic rather than afraid. Scenes, if endemic, are there to live through.

'You're not going to need a coat,' Harry says. He's tearing up some sheets of newspaper by the time Mathew returns, untroubled as before, with a small pile of brushwood. He looks as if he's been asked for valued advice and help and is now delivering them. 'Put it next to madam. Pull the carpet back.' All a game for both of them, two men, black and white, showing what male decision can do in the hearth and home.

On the cement floor, within seconds, a blaze of paper and twigs is created, the flames only a few feet from Anne, the smoke going up into the high vault under the beams and thatch.

'Mind fire, boss,' Mathew says, looking up at the thatch. Now he is laughing out loud. Perhaps he doesn't like Anne, or perhaps he hates them all and would be happy if the house burned to the ground. Briony studies Mathew's head as he amuses himself with the wood and sticks and flame. He has a high bridge to his nose like his mother's, and a narrow face with marked cheekbones. She finds him handsome, unique, wonderful, part of her. His mouth is generous and mobile when he laughs, showing teeth which seem made for laughter – bright and sharp. As Douglas said, he doesn't look like half a white man. He is good with fire, that's obvious. Under orders, he soon creates what Harry presumably wanted, a small, glowing hearth close to Anne's chair. Quite enough to subdue her.

'You didn't need to do that,' she says, just above a whisper, wiping her face and eyes with a napkin. She may be in tears. Briony feels truly sorry for her and guilty for entertaining unkind thoughts about her behaviour. Anne's sharpness must be a defence against bullying and the chronic fear it produces. The room smells of wood smoke and burning newspaper, and particles of hot ash float across the table and land in the plates.

Harry is sitting down again. He looks as if his former cheerfulness is back, a bit of action, however absurd, having relieved whatever it was that was building up in him. 'You'll be all right now, Anne darling,' he says. 'No more complaints about being frozen. All quite easy in the end. You thought you couldn't have a fire in a room

81

without a fireplace, but you know the regulation – no such word as impossible in the Navy.'

Mathew brings in a dish with a chicken on it and puts it in front of Harry. 'Killed yesterday,' he says. 'Dogs.'

'You can go, we'll look after ourselves,' Harry says. 'Go on, go back to women.' They both laugh and Harry waves a hand towards the outside world. Briony wonders where Mathew sleeps; she wonders about the women without necessarily believing in them, anyway not in the plural. After all, he's a Mission boy.

Now Mathew has stopped laughing, as if his laughter was something deliberate, like speech. His face is a mask, carved, cold, severe. He withdraws – that's the only word for it, it isn't just a man leaving a room. It's – what exactly is it? – it's the departure of someone leaving behind enough of himself to be a witness of the right. And of course she knows where that comes from. Even after he lost faith, Father could never go out of a room without doing just that; in fact he couldn't even depart from life without doing it. The land, the hill with the village on it, is the witness left after him. What Mathew leaves, padding away on tennis shoes, is the impression – there can be no doubt about it – of a conscious superiority. He serves them, he may receive their abuse, but he's a cut above them. Briony is glad. Hanging over the sideboard in this dining room of an African farmhouse, flanked by heads of slaughtered antelope, is a painted shield of a whole lot of coats-of-arms. The Chance family, she supposes. Well, Mathew wouldn't care about any of that; he bears the arms he needs, within him.

Briony is hungry. The chicken, hacked into three portions by Harry, is tough but tasty, there is a bottle of red wine and a rice pudding afterwards, like at school but with more cream. Anne appears to eat like a bird, pushing the food away from her across her plate and wearing an expression of injured distaste. All the same, when Briony looks again, most of it has gone. Harry wolfs down about half of his and then stops, as if his mood of ravenous appetite has abruptly changed into its opposite, leaving him stranded. He stares into the space above the table in front of him like a man reading his awful future there. It seems an age since anyone spoke, while from beyond the door where Mathew went in and out – presumably the kitchen – a deep liquid chattering of voices and laughter runs across their silence.

Briony knows she should make an effort. She has been made to watch Anne's humiliation and should somehow make up for that as if it hadn't happened. She feels hopelessly uncomfortable, now that hunger isn't any longer the pressing problem it was. 'Do you have children?' she asks Anne, as though, if the answer's yes, they'd be hers more, much more, than Harry's. As if he shouldn't have children, is in some way unfitted for it, being a man who is still a midshipman under fire.

'Oh God, yes,' says Anne. 'Such a worry, poor little things.'

Briony turns to look at Harry. It's a reaction she regrets as she makes it. If he's not fit for children he should be kept out of it. But he seems still absorbed in the blank space before him. His mouth is set, as closed as a locked door. It isn't a mean or secretive mouth, it's generous as though always just balanced on the point of laughter, even when locked and set like that. 'How many children?' Briony asks.

'Two,' Anne says. There is a silence. Where are they, these neglected two? As if she anticipated the question, Anne begins to cough. Her cough is deep-seated, hoarse and repetitive, musical too, as a natterjack in the night. 'There were three but one died.'

'And then there were two.'

'Yes.'

'Malaria, that's what it was,' Harry says, returning suddenly to earth. 'Don't forget whatever you do to tuck your mosquito net in firmly into the sides of the bed. Well in. Old Ian lost an offspring too, the same way. Not legitimate, actually, so it didn't matter so much.'

'Ian Mull,' says Anne, as if the name explains everything. She opens a big blue enamelled cigarette box on the table in front of her and takes one out. 'Give me a light, darling,' she says. Briony has no light to give her and so says nothing and doesn't stir. 'Ian has to get a boy or it'll die out,' Anne explains, leaning a little towards her. 'He's my cousin,' she announces, vaguely but firmly, 'but somehow he doesn't seem to marry anyone. Hasn't anyone here got a light?'

The bonfire has died down. It was a St Elmo's blaze, leaving nothing but a flicker in the mind and a guilty headache – as if one was responsible, by association, for Anne's complaints. Women complain, they provoke and make difficulties. 'No,' Briony says. She doesn't smoke and she feels unapologetic about it though knowing that one should, really, smoke to show that one is alive and well in the 1930s. In this day and age it is a signal to be sent out without ambiguity. But Father disapproved, and even with him safely under-ground she hasn't yet got round to it. 'But I would like a cigarette, please.'

'Do,' Anne says, pushing the blue enamelled box towards her. It has a design in diamonds on the lid. 'Passing Cloud,' she adds.

Harry, unpredictable as ever, is out of his seat and reaching forward with a cigarette lighter, already lit. Briony places the slightly flattened cigarette in the middle of her mouth and draws the smoke in, a bit uncertain what to do with it next. Some of it catches in her throat and she blows the rest out urgently. She feels she may not take to this.

'The children are at school in England,' Anne explains. 'There are no schools here.'

'There are,' Harry says, 'but they don't turn out gentlemen.'

'I thought gentlemen were born if they're real,' Briony says.

'Discipline comes into it. And a sense of honour.'

Well, if he says so – both of them must have been necessary at Jutland.

'At least they aren't here any more to annoy you,' Anne says.

'I miss them.'

'You were always knocking them about. George specially. It was better they went away.'

'Not knocks – he has to learn.'

'You beat him with a cricket bat for not playing the game. Anyway, school will teach him, don't worry.'

Briony is feeling desperately sorry for these children, George and . . . Anyway, what's their age, to be sent off to England on their own to get what for? 'What's the name of the other . . . your other child?' she asks.

'Caroline. After her daddy's dear mummy,' Anne says.

'How old are they?'

'Caroline is nine and George is six.'

'The one that snuffed it was in between,' Harry says. He wipes his eye with the back of the hand holding his cigarette. One shouldn't go by appearances; he may be truly distressed about it. Briony believes she is beginning to understand him. He is a man with volatile moods, but all of them, however contradictory they may seem, are perfectly genuine, like the swing of a barometer in a mad climate. She isn't so sure about the moods of Anne.

'They're awfully young to be . . .' Briony stops herself in the middle of this accusation.

'It's only ten days away by sea,' Anne says. She has her eyes fixed on Harry. Her head is lowered and she peers at him short-sightedly from between the blonde curtains, along this needlessly big table dressed with silver and cut glass, here in the heart of the highveld. Briony studies the expression as far as she can see it from the side. It isn't what you might expect, from the incident with the fire. Briony is not experienced but she has intuitions where other women are concerned. Anne's eyes are inviting Harry, they are urging him, Briony thinks, to wind up the evening as soon as possible and get to bed.

'We'll go out on to the veranda now and have a look at the stars,' he says. He turns to Briony. 'Care for a brandy?'

'No thank you, I'm not used to it,' Briony says.

Harry laughs, watching her to see what absurd answer she will come up with next. 'Oh come on. Try it. Brandy keeps the mosquitoes away.'

'She doesn't want it,' Anne says crossly. 'And it attracts them.'

Harry looks at his wife with that unnervingly level, distant gaze of his, as if he were the sole representative, here, of a race from another planet where things are ordered differently and no one hides motives since anyone can read them wherever they are. He stands up. 'You go out. I'll bring the glasses,' he says.

Briony finds herself alone outside, waiting for him to arrive. Anne has disappeared without saying good night or anything else, slipping away somewhere between the dining room and here. She's neurotic, Briony decides, not bad-mannered, just not quite answerable for what she does. All that business with the fire was a game between them, supposed to end in bed. Briony sits in one of the deckchairs. Insects buzz around the paraffin lantern which hangs from a beam at the edge of the veranda. Outside it is pitch dark with no moon yet, though on the horizon is a glow of bronze, spreading by the moment.

'Here you are. I didn't take you at your word,' Harry says, holding out the glass with a good inch of brandy at the bottom. 'Your first ever, a virgin brandy.' He raises his own glass. 'Long live Rhodesia and liberty and love.' The stars are enough to make you lose your head without any help from the brandy you're not accustomed to. They make you feel drunk, so sharp and close, like nails hammered through the sky. 'And the King, who between you and me was a bit of a wet at Dartmouth,' Harry says, almost to himself, gazing down into

86

the balloon of his glass. 'Stuttered and slept on a rubber sheet. Still had to be addressed as sir, even at thirteen years of age.'

'The King?'

'Emperor, poor chap.'

'You know him?'

'I wouldn't say that. You don't know people in the Navy, you serve with them.'

Perhaps that explains something impersonal in Harry. He can be intimate, familiar, impersonal. He knows the monarch, despises him, pities him, served with him and if war comes will serve again. Harry spoke as if he and the King were members of the same . . . what? Class gang, and of course they are. Yet Harry, whatever his character and however bad some of it may be, still doesn't seem to her really to belong in that world and she can't quite think where he does belong. There's something permanently displaced about him, as permanent as the Jutland fire he's under.

She takes a sip of brandy. Jolly good, it ignites in her throat, then lower down; a benign but intense burning. The stars seem suddenly nearer home, closing in. She has another sip. After a moment the whole of Africa seems to be hers, with its fecundity. 'Does your butler live with his wife . . . somewhere else?' she asks. She must be extremely cautious. Douglas warned her. The question was not planned, it popped out.

'Mathew isn't a butler. I do my job and he does his. He's the best friend I have here.' Harry, standing beside her chair, puts a hand on her shoulder, then withdraws it. The contact was in a way comforting, warming while it lasted. 'Live with a wife? I have no idea. They're not the same,' he says. 'Wives are computed in terms of cows. You have to understand. It used to be like that with us – wives and acres. Listen – the drumming's started. I love that. Once it starts it goes on all night. You wake at three or four and you don't feel alone. He has a woman, of course, probably a different one every night, Mathew does what he wants, he's from a line of kings. Real ones.'

Briony listens. At first it's a regular tapping from the horizon, then the sound comes much nearer. Now it's irregular, like a code. Impossible to imagine that such a rhythm of tapping, with such a rise and fall and complex interval, has no literal sense. This is a message, elaborated, rehearsed. 'What does it mean?' she asks.

'God knows, and as far as I'm concerned their god carries as many guns as ours did.' He drains his brandy glass and turns away to a side table where the bottle is. 'I've chucked him, such as he was, you'd better know that.' Why should she trouble herself to know about his dealings with God? What are they to her? But she doesn't ask. He is back beside her and looming between her and the paraffin lamp and the sky. She finds it disturbing but stays still, hoping he will move away, while part of her – the truer part – treacherously hopes he won't. 'I don't believe anything any more,' he says in the voice of a man convinced that his disbelief is something that really matters. A woman might not think that, she might feel it more as a secret loss. Men don't seem to know how to let belief and doubt sink quietly away as women do; they make pronouncements about them like Father, and now Harry. 'Mathew has a hut here next to the house but he goes down to the compound to wash. They're very clean men, you know, cleaner than us. Only ever wash in running water.'

'Is there a stream in the compound?'

'I built a wash place with a wall. We pump the water up from the well. There are wells everywhere here, the water table is constant. You just have to reach it and pump it, sweet clean water out of the African earth.' His voice is low and warm, a man in love. 'Most white people don't understand about Africa, but I believe you might in the end, I don't know why.'

Briony calls to mind Mathew's physical presence, glowing in white shirt and trousers, his skin cleaned by sweet African water. She looks at her own, on her arm. It glows too in the paraffin and starlight. Now from the other side of the house comes a loud sound of voices, rising and falling. Excited voices, one above the rest, then all at once, then silence.

'They've brought news of something,' Harry says.

'A message from the drums?'

'Exactly.'

Now the voices are receding into the night. Back to the compound, presumably, wherever that is. 'Is the compound a village?' Briony asks.

'It's a bit like a village a long time ago.'

'All the people in it work for you?'

'All the men. The women just cook and . . . they brew the beer. We've spoiled their way of life but they still have their beer. And by God they drink plenty of it. There are fights every night. If you get woken up, pay no attention. When a man gets knifed, they come running to us for iodine and bandages. The iodine produces more screams than the knives but you'll get used to it.'

Harry is speaking as if he knew she was going to stay for a long time. In fact he often speaks as if present and future were not as separate for him as for other people, as if he knows, being somehow ahead of time. It's annoying, but interesting too. Whether you actually like Harry or not, it attaches you to him, in a way. Your own future is already there in his mind.

'Did you enjoy the brandy?' he asks. She has forgotten about her glass, which is on the cement floor of the veranda beside her. His question draws her attention to the internal glow she has been enjoying for some time now; the answer must be yes. 'I didn't mind it.'

'Mind it? It's very good brandy, let me tell you. I think you liked it more than you know. You'd better have some more.' He leans down and picks up her glass. When she first noticed him today in the hotel, and felt a kind of fear and revulsion, who could have thought that by night time this atmosphere of intimacy would grow up? His hand holding the refilled balloon glass touches hers as she takes it from him and the contact is quite easy, familiar, comfortable. Like one flesh, already. What is happening to her usually well-ordered maiden thoughts? *Already?*

There is a slight sound behind them, from the doorway into the house. Briony pulls her hand with the glass back away from Harry's hand and the forearm below the rolled-up sleeve. She doesn't look round but supposes it must be Anne, come to remind Harry of her legitimate wifely wishes. But it isn't.

'Electric boy goes home now,' Mathew's voice says. He is holding two paraffin lamps high up, at shoulder level, to throw a sharp light on to the veranda.

'Who told him to?' Harry asks.

'I,' Mathew says.

'Right,' says Harry. There's something not questioned there, a thing between men who know each other well. 'The current takes a lot of pumping and stoking,' he says. Behind him, in the house, the electric light flickers, fluctuates, fades. 'That's what happened in the middle of a dinner party when the last boy was attacked by a leopard. He killed it, with his dogs. Brave chap. I installed the electrical system myself, very proud of that. Oh, I told you.' Funnily enough, he doesn't sound proud of it any more. His mood has changed.

Mathew is still there, the light from the lamps swaying gently across the cement floor. Briony turns her head and looks up at him. He is looking at her too, but impersonally in the swaying light, as if she were some sort of domestic animal, a woman belonging to someone else. Clearly, Anne is not coming back. She must have gone to bed alone. Briony feels less comfortable now that the electric current has died down completely and she's out here with Harry and

Mathew and the brandy and the lamps. It sounds fun, but it isn't. It's rather frightening. She stands up.

'I think I ought to go in,' she says.

'I will show Miss West her room,' Harry says.

'But I've been there already, before dinner,' Briony says. She puts her half-full brandy glass on to the table with the bottle. She can feel herself swaying gently with the rhythm of the lamps. The pleasant fuddling warmth has turned into something else, something stealthily alight between want and fear.

'Miss West take this lamp,' Mathew says.

It's a statement or order. Briony is facing him now, a couple of feet distant, so she can read his expression better. He is looking straight into her eyes and the expression is hostile, as if the sight of her injures him. Enough to make you turn away, normally, to avoid seeing it. But the moment is not normal. The brandy glow makes everything more fluid and airy. And apart from the expression of his eyes, Mathew's features are as calm and still as ever. So fine, Briony thinks, so remote that you want to hold out your arms to him and say—

'Thank you,' is what she does say.

'Yes,' Mathew says. His features are serious, without signs of the desire to please you usually see on men's faces – but now the eyes are quite different from a moment ago. They seem to wrap her in a tender feeling unlike any she has ever known, more enveloping, accepting, even than Father's.

Briony takes the paraffin lamp from his hand. 'Good night, everyone,' she says. She has got this far and scored this small victory; this acceptance, it seems.

'I'll bring you the key of your room; all the keys hang in the office,' she hears Harry say.

'An' you turn that key damn well,' says Mathew.

The mosquito net is tucked into the mattress but of course the lamp is outside it, hanging from the beam. The light comes through the net like a pale milky wash, but enough to read by if your eyes are good. She is leafing through *A Guide to Rhodesia 1924*, much thumbed, published by the Mashonaland and Rhodesian Railways. There is a lot of stuff aimed, it seems to her, at the sort of young Englishman likely to arrive here hoping to become the salt and lord of the earth, as he could not possibly have felt at home. That certainly wouldn't include men like Harry. He probably felt all right at home. He is a commander; he's all right everywhere, at home everywhere on land or sea. She smiles, under the mosquito net.

Then she comes on a passage that makes her think the *Guide to Rhodesia* is to be taken more seriously.

Occupation of land by unmarried women, or without adult male relatives, is for many reasons undesirable . . .

Why? Undesirable? What reasons? They are not given. A hush seems to fall over the page as if things were buried there not to be spoken. She reads on till she reaches the words that finally make her throw the book outside the mosquito net, get up and turn out the lamp, get back in and struggle to tuck the net under the mattress, giving up in despair in the dark.

The native servant has to be carefully watched . . . especially as concerns the women of the household.

Her room is in what they call the cottage, a few steps along the veranda and separate from the main building. There's no bathroom but there is a chamber pot in a cupboard beside the bed. It has been explained to her that the only lavatory is a short walk away from the house, in a little thatched building all of its own, not to be attempted after dark. She hasn't seen it yet but she knows that it is not a water closet. She rather dreads it, actually, but there you are. If Anne can get used to it, she can too.

'Lock the door behind me,' Harry had said, handing over the heavy key. Briony remembers his words now but she doesn't get up to obey them. She is not going to give in to the spirit of *A Guide to Rhodesia*. She lies in the dark, her hand touching the surface of the mosquito net where it joins the sheet. The net feels harsh but yielding, like a rough pitted skin on a soft animal. Where, she wonders, is Mathew's sleeping place? What woman has he in there with him? The thought has returned and it makes her smile, but it also makes her sad. They couldn't be worthy of him. And what about Harry and Anne, in the privacy of their married quarters? For some unknown reason, she has difficulty in thinking of them sharing the same bed, they seem so unlike each other, so odd, so alien. But perhaps that's how the relation of the sexes usually is. Her eyes close. There is a faint, distant humming in her ears, but whether it's mosquitoes or the brandy she doesn't know, or care. She will quite soon drift off and everything else is for tomorrow. With any luck, she won't have to use the chamber pot. A young bladder is full of elasticity . . . the future stretches happily on . . . she is where she wants and needs to be for the future to take possession of her, and vice versa.

There is light in the room. A swinging light outside the net, giving the sense of motion inside it like in a ship's cabin. Someone is there with a lamp. Briony isn't frightened, but surprised. The various possibilities pass across the half-wakened surface of her mind without leaving as much as a ripple of panic.

'Who is it?'

'My *Gott*, is a white woman in my bed at last,' says a man's high voice, rising sharply in pitch as he speaks. Briony peers through the net to make him out. The lamp is held up beside his face, showing it in the same moving, faint, untrustworthy light as falls on to floor, walls, bed, and on Briony herself, so they all shift about each other like currents in troubled water. She can see the face well enough, though, since the lamp is right next to it. It is a narrow, long face with a rosebud mouth, and down all the length of the cheek on the side where the lamp is held are two deep parallel scars, still faintly purple.

'They didn't tell me it was your bed,' Briony says stupidly.

'These English think of nothing.'

'In fact they didn't tell me there was anyone else staying here. I'm awfully sorry.'

'Awfully? Please, what does this mean?'

'It means extremely.' The question and answer make her feel a fool.

'So. You are awfully sorry.' He sounds pleased about that. Briony looks furtively at her watch in the lamplight – it is three o'clock, about. She listens for the drums, faintly audible inside the mosquito net. This man has turned up from nowhere at three in the morning and he sounds pleased with her apology for sleeping in his bed. Well, that doesn't take much working out, even for her with her ridiculous inexperience.

'Commander Chance told me to lock the door but I forgot. Is there somewhere else you can spend what's left of the night?'

'Oh, so awfully sorry,' the visitor says. 'Awfully bad form to wake you up.' Briony wonders if he is drunk, and feels alarm for the first time. What do those scars on his face mean? Has he been attacked by a leopard, like the electric boy? Or does he get into fights? 'From your *mädchen* beauty sleep.' Suddenly it comes to her. They are duelling scars.

'Please, let me go back to sleep. You go to sleep too, somewhere.'

'There is no need to be frightened. I am Werner, the farm manager for Harry. I manage whatever in this bad organised farm can be managed. I will leave you now and sleep on the veranda. We will meet again soon in the morning.' He approaches his lamp to the net and peers more closely at her, for what seems a long time. 'Yes. In the morning. I am a baron, you should know this. Goodbye for the moment.'

'Goodbye,' Briony says, and remains stiff and tense under the sheet and the net while his footsteps recede, the door closes behind him, and sounds of dragging furniture come from the veranda. She thinks he is perfectly harmless, in the end, when the noises stop: in fact almost rather sweet, with those curious scars. To think of men still duelling. Would it be over a woman? Duelling has died out, surely . . . She can't think of Harry in a duel; the mood that set him on would change long before the first stroke was slashed.

The morning light fills the world so fast that you have the feeling it's a direct continuation of yesterday after no more than a pause, like the end of the reel in a cinema. Briony is at the window of her bedroom and she can see the little thatched building about fifty yards away at the end of a path bordered by red-flowering shrubs. She puts on her dressing gown. She is going to be brave and go down that path to find out about the lavatory arrangements. Anything, almost, would be better than the chamber pot, a thing she has never in her life used. At Hythe she had her own little bathroom and Father had his – they lived in a very decent way.

Outside, the air is still quite sharp, Werner is fast asleep, spread out between two deckchairs, his position so dreadfully uncomfortable that she thinks he must have been drunk. Carefully, and without stopping in her walk, she has a look at him. Blond. She believes that to be properly convincing a man needs to be dark.

When she reaches the little lavatory house she releases the belt of her dressing gown and girds up her spirit. Inside, there is a powerful smell of Jeyes Fluid; well, that's something. There's a wide wooden throne reaching from wall to wall, with a candlestick and some magazines scattered on it, also the bottle of Jeyes and a Flit pump for insects. She has already seen one of those at Speck's. The throne stands over an abyss in which, mercifully, you can see nothing, even with the door open and the light flooding in. She shuts the door and locks the latch. There is a matchbox beside the candlestick but it is empty – well, she came to Africa to get experience. And to throw open a richer world to her brother, though who knows if he'll want it, whatever it is, this supposed richer world of hers. Where does Mathew go, for a lavatory? She knows enough by now to be sure that this little house and its pitch-dark pit are an all-white amenity, and a great relief comes over her when she is able to get up, open the door, and leave it. The exclusive little house seems to stand for everything she hates most. On the way back she hears a rustling in the red-flowered shrubs, but sees nothing. A rat, perhaps, or a snake. She hurries on along the path. Werner has disappeared. She can hear voices from inside the house, then the door on to the veranda opens and Mathew steps out, smiling when he sees her; a broad smile, welcoming, and so strong that she feels quite protected by it, whatever happens.

'Breakfast now, madam.' Their smiles without words meet and join, like the sunlight reaching through a window to the paler light waiting indoors.

Six

AUTHORITY BEGETS PARTIALITY, so all teachers and pastors and
doctors have their favourites. Since Mathew grew up and went away
to do work so far beneath him, Peter has been Douglas's pet pupil.
He sees in Peter the lightness of spirit which he wishes he could find
more of in himself. It makes Peter easy to teach and influence, and
therefore useful. He is quick, and unintimidated by that great
thunder that lives in the sky, the law of custom. That is why he's
willing to act as Douglas's interpreter for the language of the drums,
though naturally he tells Douglas no more than he thinks it right for
him to know.

'What were the drums saying last night, Peter?' They are walking
back in the shade of the jacarandas from the field where the boys
play, under the burning sun, their own wild version of cricket.

'When last night?'

'After supper.'

'Perhaps I was asleep then after supper.'

This is normal. Peter doesn't want his services taken for granted.
'Was it about the lady who came the day before yesterday?'

'Why you took her back to Gatooma, Doctor? You should keep
her here.' The only pupil Douglas has ever had whose English was

97

better than Peter's was Mathew. And the sad thing is that when these boys go away to work, they must pretend to be less fluent and less educated. Otherwise the jobs go to boys who don't need to pretend.

'What did the drums say about it?'

'They tell the men in that compound there where Mathew works.'

'Tell them what?'

'That she come to look at our village to chase the people away from her land to the lowveld.'

'I'm sure she would never do that.'

'But now the drums say she is gone to the farm of Boss Chance.'

'Well?'

'That boss is always making mines on his farm and always not finding any gold in them at all.' Douglas knows what's coming. He has known, and kept silent, for years. 'There is plenty, plenty of gold in the hill under our village.'

'Yes.'

'So you should bring that lady back here to the Mission and keep her.'

'You know I can't do that, Peter.'

'You far too long and no wife, Dr Douglas, no damn good for you,' Peter says, and skips away neatly, in time.

This cannot go on, this hiding from each other. Obviously Mathew knows. Miss West, he said, quite clearly. They must speak, they must find the words that connect, but he will never do it, left to himself. It would be insolence, she guesses that. The shadow of that horrible word on this lovely land. So it's up to her to make the first move.

After an almost silent breakfast with Anne, Briony hangs about the veranda alone, hoping Mathew will come. He must know where she is, he must be as eager as she is to recognise and be recognised, be together, belong. She waits and he doesn't come. She thinks she can hear him humming and singing and muttering some folk strain back there in the kitchen zone, while he works. Surely he can't be happy, doing that?

Harry, however, does appear. He emerges from the bedroom quarters looking spruce in clean, well-ironed khaki trousers and shirt, his face gleaming as if the iron had been passed over that too. His black hair is meticulously parted and the scalp under the parting is as spruce as the rest of him. He breathes good health, male vigour, authority, a good night's sleep. Briony wonders what has become of Werner. He probably has a blinding headache and a rotten taste in his mouth.

'I'm taking you out for a ride this morning,' Harry announces. 'You'll see, this country should be viewed from the back of a horse. It gives you a different idea. You are all right on a horse? You're sure? I don't want to find myself picking up the pretty pieces.' He laughs heartily.

'If the horse is nice and quiet.'

'Quiet as the New Forest, and I'll keep my eye on you.' He looks down at her quite kindly, probably measuring her up for the degree of protection she may require. But there's more than just that in his expression, now. There's the beginning of the familiar look you meet on every road, in a country lane, at your solicitor's office . . . 'You'd better put on some trousers. Have you had breakfast? I always make an early start. This is a farm and work is supposed to be going on here, but if I'm not on deck to crack the whip it doesn't.' He turns away and shouts something in the direction of the nearest trees. A man comes running out from them. As Briony goes off to the cottage for her trousers she can hear a loud, excited conversation between Harry and the man, with plenty of laughter and what she suspects is swearing, by the emphasis. Two men laughing and shouting, but the definite impression, somehow, that one of them is laughing to please, the other to show that he is pleased. Which is which? She turns to see. It seems to her that Harry is the man trying to please. He must be one of those men who like to be loved by the people, men or women, who have to obey them.

When she gets back, he is looking impatient, tapping his leg with the leather switch he carries. Over his other arm are the saddles. 'Right,' he says, in that way of indicating that there are many more important things in his world than waiting for a woman to decide when she's ready. 'Follow me.' He now has a couple of dogs trailing him, large dogs with a ridge of hair down the spine, standing up like a toothbrush. 'They're lion dogs,' Harry says without further explanation. The dogs look dangerous but are actually very gentle. One of them pushes his muzzle into Briony's hand and tries to get between her legs. 'That's what they do if you meet a lion. Terrified,' Harry says.

'Where are your stables?' It seems a reasonable question, though she only asks it because the situation is making her nervous again. Harry turns his head, laughing as he strides forward on his long legs.

'You don't have stables on a simple African farm,' he says, 'you have huts for horses. But we're going to have to catch them first. They're on the polo field.'

This turns out to take a long time and a lot of energy because the horses treat it as a game which with superior guile they are going to win. By the time it's over and both horses are tied up to the wooden fence surrounding their vast, burned-up polo enclosure, Briony feels hot and rather cross. If Harry has all those dozens, or hundreds – she really has no idea which – of men working for him on the farm, couldn't some of them have done this? She catches herself up short – she's starting to react like those women at Speck's Hotel.

He seems to read her thought. 'Africans still fear the horse,' he says. 'We've been using them for centuries but they haven't. They see it like they see the white man's dog, as an enemy. Another oppressive advantage – guns, horses, alcohol, dogs. We stole their land to ride about on with our guns and dogs. The Romans did much the same.'

She is surprised. She hadn't thought that Harry would be likely to express himself like that. Rome, of course, is a flattering comparison that simplifies everything. 'But they have dogs of their own for hunting, I've seen some. And there was the electric man who killed the leopard.'

'They think we treat ours like domestic deities.' He is saddling the horse she is to ride. It's a grey mare, only a bit higher than the average New Forest pony and much lighter. During the capture operation it showed itself particularly obstinate and unaccommodating, more so than Harry's far bigger horse Xerxes, a kind of equine juggernaut. Briony feels prejudiced against the mare, as if its obduracy was due to knowing it was to be mounted by a woman. It must have had a bad relationship with Anne. 'Up you get. Here we ride with a snaffle. I hate all curbs in life.'

'So do I.'

'Another point in common. We'll walk first, then try a trot. Xerxes and I will go in front, your mare will follow where we go. I warn you, Xerxes does not trot discreetly in well-bred silence, though he is a thoroughbred horse.'

Leaving the polo ground, they break into the promised trot, through the long dry grass, among the sparse trees, to the ringing sound of Xerxes's endless flatulence. It costs Briony nothing, busy learning the ways of the mare, to ignore it. The dogs run ahead, often looking back for reassurance. If this is a farm, where is the cultivated land? Where are the cattle and sheep? She feels she is riding through a country exactly the same as it must have been when mankind first stood upright. There's no track, they are simply trotting along through the middle of nowhere. Briony has quite changed her mind about the mare by now; she has a light, airy gait and rhythm and there is confidence, a growing bond between them like a good augury in this early-morning light and untouched landscape. Part of the beauty of the New Forest is the freedom from enclosures, but this – is boundless.

'You just say when you're ready to try a canter,' Harry says, turning his head towards her. He rides with long stirrups for his long legs, and an ease so natural it's hard to think of him back on the ground, separated from Xerxes.

'Not yet.' Looking ahead and around among the trees, she imagines the animals hidden there, watching as the horses pass, scratching a living in the bush. She's not sure why, but she feels another plot, another ground of liberty gained.

'Look there,' Harry says, stopping in front of her and holding out his hand to catch the mare's bridle, 'buffalo. There.' He has lowered his voice as he points through a clearing. Nothing moves. Brown forms merge and overlap so you distinguish nothing. 'See them? They used to be all over the place. Extremely dangerous animals. We shot a lot and drove them off. We'd better make ourselves scarce; they can charge without provocation.' He swings Xerxes round, still holding the mare's bridle, and they move quickly away among the trees. 'I don't mind saying, you sit that mare quite nicely.'

It is getting hot. There's the smell, almost familiar now, of burning earth and animals and something sharp and spicy, like grilled pepper. The muscles on the insides of Briony's thighs are aching but she feels happy, and free. As well as the ache, there's a glow.

'You should have a hat,' Harry says. They have stopped at the edge of the forest where only a sea of dry grass spreads out in front, undulating in the heated light, stretching far away to the foot of a hill. 'Have mine.' He passes his hat, a brown felt item, rather crushed, creased, and stained. 'I should have thought of it. The sun will be right overhead in half an hour.'

She is touched, and tries the hat in spite of the stains. 'It's much too big. It'll fall off.'

'Hold on with one hand, you can easily manage the rein with the other. I can't have you down with sunstroke.'

Which way is his mood taking him now? The same man who has a bonfire lit on the floor inches from his wife's chair is worrying about Briony and the rays of heat. She sneaks a look at him from under the brim of his hat. He is out in the open with that sun full on him; he faces it, head up, at attention on the back of Xerxes. There's something exalted about his expression and Briony feels a bit awed. She tries to check the awe. It may be Harry she is in awe of, in that foolish way she associates, from reading about it, with virgins. That wouldn't do; he's too erratic for a virgin to trust. She feels a shiver pass through her, under the shade of the big tree, and urges the mare forward until the two horses are side by side. Harry's leg bumps against hers, glancingly, a contact closed as soon as open. He is staring at her.

'Do you realise what you're looking at, over there?'

The heat now is creating a shimmer over the heads of the grasses, the sea is dissolving, the air and earth fused into a shifting, molten whole. 'I don't think I'm looking at anything definite,' Briony says, accurately.

'Your hill. There.' He points with his switch.

'It's a long way,' Briony says, not committing herself.

'Shall we ride over?'

It's tempting. To ride far away from the Chance house – with this man she thought she hated, yesterday – tempting and stupid. 'I rather think I'd like to go back, please.'

'I expect you would.' He must know she's afraid and he despises her for it. Come to that, she despises herself. All the same, simple prudence . . . and there's plenty of time. 'You're going to have to make up your mind what to do about it, you know. It's valuable land, there's gold under it.'

'Actually I really do rather need to go back,' she says.

That was a mistake. Harry roars with laughter. 'Oh, I see.' He dismounts and takes hold of the mare's bridle. 'You have miles of elephant grass before you. I'll hold the mare and Xerxes and I will wait patiently. But don't go too far, there could be a leopard. Look out for snakes and I'll look the other way.' He laughs again.

Men, with their little advantage, think that women are always at the mercy of their bladder. Briony kicks into the mare's flanks and the mare, startled by this show of wilfulness, leaps away from Harry's hold and into the long grass. The hat goes flying. Briony knows they're out of control and it's only a matter of time. She can hear Harry shouting something behind her. Then he shouts it louder.

'Let go!'

She doesn't need to. She can feel herself out of the saddle, out of the stirrups, in the air, then hitting the ground. The top of the grass is far above her in a gothic nave of stems and fronds, and the dry smell of roots and earth fills her head like a rush of blood. She has a pain in her shoulder. In a moment Harry is there, stooping down anxiously with both hands held out towards her. 'Are you hurt?'

'I think the grass acted as a cushion.' He helps her up, holding her by the elbows. Then his hands drop lower and his arms go slowly round her waist. He is drawing her closer, quite gently; she can feel him against her. 'Please, not now,' she says.

'That sounds like promise of melting snow to me,' Harry says, letting her go just as slowly and gently. 'Here, hold on to Xerxes while I catch that bloody mare. You fell quite neatly, for a first time. You're not a horseman till after the third fall. Stand by his head and don't let him play you up.' While she waits with Xerxes, the dogs push lovingly against her legs. Maybe they scent a lion in the grass.

It is only when the house is already in view through the trees that she thinks of Werner. She had better say something, otherwise it might seem that she's kept deceitfully quiet about it. That's part of life's injustice and has to be accepted. 'I met your manager in the night.' she says. 'He said I was sleeping in his room.'

'Oh, pay no attention to von Hippel, he's mad. A crazy German on the run. Didn't you lock the door?'

'I think he spent the rest of the night on the veranda.'

'I expect he did. He often does. He goes out to get drunk.'

'In Gatooma?' Why does she ask? What does she care? Pure curiosity, that's what.

'He goes to Chakari. It's nearer and there's a bar where he can buy an African woman.'

There. She asked for it, with her curiosity, but she can't keep a feeling of revulsion, a feeling she disapproves on principle, out of her mind. So that's what Werner was coming back from, to find his bed occupied. Think of Mother Shitofo. Was she bought? Surely not, surely Father didn't go to a bar in Chakari for that. 'What does he manage for you, between visits to the bar?'

'He doesn't know much about farming but he knows how to make himself obeyed. I'm too soft with the men but Werner isn't. He doesn't distinguish between men and oxen; the same whip does for both.' His voice is sad.

Briony feels a kind of horror and retraction in her own flesh, as if Mathew could be touched with Werner's whip. 'Aren't there any laws against that?' she asks furiously.

'Oh, there are. But the men don't dare appeal to them. They get even rougher treatment at the police station. You should see Lieutenant Pienaar. And they need the work to pay their hut tax, otherwise Pienaar and the government come and burn down their villages.'

'Does Werner pay the government any taxes?' Briony asks as they reach the front of the house. She would like to add, 'Do you?' She dismounts and hands the reins to Harry. She is sick with anger. He is as bad as Werner. Isn't it collusion if you let your manager go around attacking people with a whip? She needs to hurry along the avenue of flowering shrubs to the little house at the back, she feels so sick. 'Why isn't he in Germany? What's he here for?'

'I suspect Werner's a spy, or else he had to flee the fatherland because they were after him for his sins. One must sympathise with sins.' Harry's neighing laughter follows her along, yet she's sure that he is not a fundamentally bad man. She must believe that because she wants to believe it now, wants to so badly.

The farm compound swarms with women and children. Procreation continues, ignoring hut tax, eviction, hunger; and with such pitiable results: the children are underfed but pot-bellied. The women are slaves to conception and the death rate, the men are slaves to the hut tax and the farmer. Beer at night in the compound is the solace, as whisky and a woman at Chakari help Werner forget, for a few hours, the disgrace of exile. Or help him think it's the fatherland's loss. Each man carries his scar, visible or hidden. What could Harry's be, secure in his family, seated on his estate, blessed year round by the sun and with Xerxes and Mathew to serve him? He still doesn't look happy. He gives off that air of unrequited longing like a boy, commander though he may be.

The men from the compound are here and waiting for their pay, the women in the background, waiting too. There must be a natural law about a man's pay – he gets it, it will be paid to no one else, but he doesn't need it for himself. European men controlling the purse-strings have lost touch with nature. The fruit of labour is for the woman, it's she who needs it. The man just needs his beer, his meals, and the other thing, and the woman takes care of it all.

Harry sits behind a table in the open, on the veranda, with Werner beside him and the little cotton bags of cash lined up in front of them. Harry is leaning back in his chair, tipping it up, with his feet on the table, cleaning a rifle and smoking a cigarette and with a glass of whisky on the floor within reach. One of the men, like a foreman, stands at the head of the veranda steps and calls out names. Briony, curious and ashamed of it, watches from a window, keeping back out of sight, she hopes. One by one the men come to the table. She has no idea how much they get paid, but it seems to be a few coins. The men look neither happy nor unhappy about it. The women behind them look a lot happier, laughing and stamping their feet, the babies on their backs bobbing up and down. A perfect life for a baby, next best thing to being actually inside the mother. The money probably goes on the women's bright cotton dresses, their bangles and beads. No one wears shoes, toes spread out to take purchase in the African earth. Harry told her that everyone in farm compounds has free food, so what else is there, here in the wild, for men to spend money on? If you think about it, money in these conditions is an adornment, and that is exactly what the women use it for.

Are the house servants going to be called up in the same way as these half-naked men, publicly, like prisoners? Briony steps back from the window. She can't watch Mathew walk up the veranda steps and hold out his hand for coins. It would be worse, far worse than if she did it herself.

Suddenly from outside there's the sound of angry voices, argument, shouting. She thinks she can recognise Mathew's voice, rather high and hoarse, among the others. She is frightened for the first time since she came down the steps of the train to the earth of Gatooma station, feeling she is going to witness something violent and foreign. She retreats further from the window but in doing so puts herself in the line of sight through the open door. Mathew is standing in front of the table, beside an old man. Mathew is speaking, in English.

'He misses two days because he's sick. He works here four years, now. He works hard.'

Werner's voice, rough, guttural and contemptuous, comes from beyond Briony's field of vision. 'No work, no pay. He is weak, too old, no good. He has his money. Now he goes. Go, no good old man. Get out.' The old man is muttering something inaudibly. 'What does he say?' Werner's voice rises. 'I say tell him footsack or I hit him with this.'

'No,' Mathew says loudly, 'he is an old man. You a young one. Commander Chance is the boss, not you.'

Briony runs through the door on to the veranda. She knows what is about to happen. Harry is still oiling his rifle, or whatever it is he's doing with it, like a boy's toy. She shakes him by the shoulder. 'Stop it, stop them, please,' she says, the same words she used in Gatooma.

It all happens very fast. Werner is round in front of the table and he hits Mathew on the side of the face with his closed fist. Then, after a flurry of movement, Werner is on the ground. There is a cry of consternation and fear from the crowd of women and men, a distressed muttering and sighing. Some of them turn and run. Mathew is standing there as if nothing has happened, still and crisp in his white shirt and trousers, while Werner gets to his feet.

'Now then,' Harry orders in a loud voice. He has put his rifle on the ground, taken his feet off the table, and now he stands, taller than all the rest. 'That's more than enough. Get away, the lot of you. We'll finish pay in the morning.' He speaks a few words of Shona and smiles encouragingly at the old man and all the others who are still waiting and watching. 'All good friends in the morning,' he says, and Mathew translates in a firm voice. 'Go off and have a beer drink.' The remaining men laugh; their teeth flash to greet the familiar message. 'A good long beer drink. We'll hear the drums all night,' Harry says happily. He turns to Werner. 'Go easy, Werner, for Christ's sake; if you want to hit someone, hit an equal.'

An equal? The old man is still waiting with his unsteady hand held out, the fingers curled back. Harry takes some coins from the cotton bag without counting them, and puts them into the outstretched hand. 'Get off with you now,' he says.

'You give him more than he earn,' Mathew objects.

'Good God, man,' says Harry, 'what do you want me to do? If it's more, he can save the shillings up and buy another wife. I don't want fights here in front of the house.' Harry sounds as if in some odd way he depends on Mathew's opinion and didn't notice Werner ending up on the floor. Or decided not to notice it. Mathew speaks to the old man, touches his shoulder, turns him gently away so he can follow the others, shuffling after them, stirring the dust, like a lame dog.

Briony is sure, after only a short time in this land, that a black man who puts a white man on the ground, whatever the provocation, does not go unpunished, and that the laws of punishment here are private laws. The courts must be few and far between. What man of any colour, here in this little kingdom, is going to take his complaints to God knows what magistrate hundreds of miles away? Still less, what woman? But probably a woman doesn't have such things as complaints. Think of Anne and the bonfire.

Now is not the time to think about any of it. Harry has marched away with his rifle and no one asks a man with a rifle where he's going; the gun makes the mission. Werner is inside, in the sitting room, with the whisky bottle in his hand. Is it an illusion, or do the purple scars throb on his cheek while his eyes roll about in an exaggerated fashion? Briony suspects he has been drinking since this morning. 'God in heaven,' he shouts, 'those peasants should be whipped in their place.' He doesn't really mean it, this is a German joke. They're supposed to have no sense of humour but here's an example. 'Have some whisky, gracious lady,' he says, offering the bottle.

'I have never drunk whisky,' Briony says.

'Drink some now. It will warm the ice maiden.'

'No thank you.' Werner may be 'amusing', as Anne would say, but Briony doesn't much like being alone with him. However, the memory of Mathew with Werner on the ground in front of him is vivid and alarming. She must try to discover what Werner is thinking. She doesn't have to wait long.

'You saw the servant? No? He answered insolently.' In fact

Mathew did more than that. He knocked Werner down, but Werner may hope she didn't see it. 'I know how to punish insolence. I will shoot this butler, this house boy.' Werner laughs loudly. 'Soon. Very soon. Please sit here, next to me.' He smiles and pats the cushions on the sofa.

She sits. The fact is that although he makes her nervous with his scars and his hysteria, she finds him less revolting as a man than she thinks she should. Beneath the blond Aryan skin that everyone's been hearing about for years is some dark presence. It's the opposite of Harry, whose secret, she believes, is a fair heart in a dark shell. Maybe, Briony thinks, when she is no longer a virgin – when that day comes – she will see men in a less dramatic light. For now, Werner is the knave of spades who bullies defenceless black people and holds theories of racial supremacy. But so do most of the white people here. She is sure that Harry, if forced to admit it, would say that the men he seems to get on with so well, protect, pay, provide for, are his inferiors by race. If she was to be absolutely honest, she might even have to—

'I will ask you something,' Werner says. He makes no attempt to approach nearer on the long sofa. He holds himself upright, with a stiff elegance. 'You have visited the little house? Please forgive this question.'

'Yes, I have.'

'It is not a very nice arrangement for . . . white people. Do you not think?'

'I'm afraid I don't know what you mean.'

'I mean we must walk in the outside to go to it. We can be seen. Everyone else goes to the bush. Like the animals. But this is not what I wish to say.' Now he does lean a little closer. 'You found it . . . correct . . . safe?'

This is anything but amusing. She is only sitting here with Werner in order to discover his intentions towards Mathew, if possible, certainly not to learn his strange tastes. 'It seems all right, for the African wild,' she says carefully.

'This is not any African wild. This is a part of little England.' The contempt in his voice is like a slap in the face. 'But I warn you. In one way that little house is not a piece of little England. Two days ago I go there and what do I see? A snake. A huge great dangerous snake, all steel muscles curled up on the seat I wish to use. The snake raises its head as I come in. Next, it raises all the rest of itself, like . . . Aladdin from his lamp.'

'You mean the genie. Whatever did you do?'

'I shoot it. twice. Dead. Like I will soon shoot the house boy. The snake falls down into the black pit so I can be relieved. If you have a strong torch, you must look in, you will still see it there. It is not covered in just three days. But so, be awfully careful. Always take a gun every time you go to the little house, and a torch. The insolent house boy will soon also be at the bottom of that pit.' She had thought of his eyes as hazel. They are green, distinctly green, and the light in them is a crazy one. She plunges deeper into it to see what's really there, and she thinks she does see – he is only pretending to be crazy, because it amuses him. It serves some purpose of his. He is sane but his mind is dark and deep as the contents of the pit.

At least there's another woman here. Briony feels the need of one and tries to find her. What does Anne do, all day long? Couldn't they become friends, or at least somehow allies? Doesn't she run the household? Doesn't she need help – with growing herbs, or mending sheets, or putting eggs in isinglass, or something? There are no children now, she doesn't ride. Where does she spend her time? Briony approaches the door which she thinks must lead to Anne's bedroom, and knocks gently. Nothing happens. She knocks again.

The house is silent, the men have gone back outside, she can hear voices and dogs barking a long way off. So they must be out there

111

doing whatever farmers and their managers do, in the early evening. Ordering people about, probably, working up a terrific thirst. Briony opens the door a few inches. The room beyond is in darkness. Now she can hear a sort of sighing, almost sobbing, from in there. A more or less continuous plaint of unhappiness, she thinks.

'Mrs Chance?'

'Who is that, for heaven's sake?' There is no more sobbing and the voice is sharp.

'Me, Briony.' Who else could Anne suppose it might be? Everyone on this farm, or estate, or whatever it should be called, seems to be out of touch with reality; or too closely in touch with the strange reality of this high, dry land and a bit mad as a result.

'You may come in.' Anne sounds as if she is speaking to a child of an earlier generation. She was probably brought up by a nanny and governesses and has no experience at the receiving end of close parenthood. Her own children won't have any either. 'But I can't see you there.'

Briony feels her way towards a window whose outline shows faintly grey in the dark. 'Would you like me to draw the curtain back?'

'No, no. I have a migraine. No light, whatever happens. What do you want?'

'I wondered if you needed any sort of help. If I could be . . .' Be what? Free to ask some of the many questions going round and round in her head? Or just reassured and made safe?

'Oh yes, oh yes, I do.' There is another sob, a small series of sobs in the darkness. 'Come and sit here with me on the bed.' Briony is guided forward by the voice until she can feel the mosquito net. Isn't it only at night that mosquitoes are a risk? Perhaps Anne just feels safer like that in there, like a bird in the cage it knows. 'Push the net away and sit down.'

'Have you taken an aspirin or anything for your headache? Would you like some water?'

'Nothing works for my dreadful heads, nothing,' Anne says in a voice in which Briony distinctly picks up the note of satisfaction. So these headaches are a weapon, or a defence. 'How old are you, Briony?'

'I'm twenty-three.'

'Have you a lover?'

'No, as a matter of fact, not.'

'I thought so. I can tell you they're a dreadful nuisance, even the best of them. And then there are always accidents. And one gets pregnant.' Is that what's wrong with her? Of course.

'Would you like to have more children?' Briony asks. For herself, the idea of children exerts no particular pull, but others may be different.

'Are you mad? More children? Haven't you seen what he's like?' For a woman with a migraine, Anne is sounding pretty energetic now she has something to be indignant about. 'But I'm going to have to do something. And very soon too. You could draw the curtain back just a little. Just a few inches.' When Briony has done this she turns back to the bed. Anne is out of it. She wears a long silk dressing gown with a swansdown collar, and a vision of Fortnum and Mason's shop, which she has never seen, swims into Briony's mind, all feathers and silk and gilding. A pearl necklace nestles among the swansdown like a string of tiny eggs.

'Are you feeling better?'

Anne laughs. 'Come on, let's have a gin, just you and me.' There is a wicker sofa at the foot of the bed and Anne lowers herself on to it carefully, like a fragile object. 'The gin's in that wardrobe. We won't bother about water. Mother's ruin. Just what I need, at the moment and in the circs.'

As usual out here, everything seems to be moving very fast. It's as if the sun burns away all intermediate stages so you progress in dizzying fashion from one crisis to the next. A few minutes ago it was

Werner and his green eyes, now it's Anne and her medical gin. But Briony has a feeling, even if uninformed, that gin alone isn't going to do the trick for Anne, not if her body already knows about bearing children. She has an alarming presentiment. Anne is going to need help.

'Be a saint and fetch a couple of tooth mugs from the bathroom. It's through that door.'

Gin undiluted is certainly a new experience, to be taken with caution. Of course quite soon caution is going to be out of the window. Briony can feel her small stock of caution give way already, like shifting sand under the feet, after just a couple of sips.

'You're a little godsend,' Anne says. 'I knew it the minute I set eyes on you.'

That wasn't at all the impression Briony had at the time. What Anne is referring to here is the help she is going to need when the gin fails. 'I was afraid as you hadn't invited me yourself you might find me rather in the way.'

'Nonsense, darling,' Anne says. 'I want you to stay and stay. You have no idea what it's like being the only woman in a set-up like this. When they come out here, Englishmen forget about being gentlemen. And Germans don't have to forget it. Pour us out a bit more. And do please stay just as long as you feel like. We can do all sorts of things together, we can be friends. I have no friends. Men say it's impossible, what do you think? They say we don't know what it means. D'you *like* men?' Briony doesn't answer the question. What does Anne mean by like? 'Obviously you don't know yet. Do you shoot, at least? I've got a rifle, we can take turns, it's the greatest fun. There are lots of buck, you can pick them off from the veranda in the evening sometimes. I almost never go out in the sun, I have the thinnest of skins.'

It certainly is very white. Does she really mean it, in among all that, about staying? Or is it only until she doesn't need help any more? A gruesome picture forms in Briony's mind of what this help is likely to be. She's far from sure that she will be up to it. 'I've never killed an animal,' she says primly, and regrets it at once.

Anne laughs. 'But how priceless. You eat them, don't you?'

'I don't like blood sports.'

Anne's laughter dies away. 'Don't talk to me about blood, I never want to hear the awful stuff mentioned again.' The light outside is dying, against a deep red sky which shows like a stain between the curtains. Perhaps it's the dying light that makes Anne look so tragic now. Briony feels really sorry for her, trapped by what is going on invisibly inside her body. 'But now you're here, darling, I feel so much safer. You will stay and . . . and be a moral support, won't you?'

They both understand what she means. Briony holds out a hand and Anne takes it. They are allies. Briony needs to stay for as long as it takes to get to know Mathew, and learn to understand his situation; Anne needs her at least until she has managed to bring off her home-made abortion.

It seems they always change for dinner. 'Put on something simple, I expect that's what you've got,' Anne said. She was quite right. Briony has one plain cotton frock, rather a nice one actually, having left most of her luggage at Gatooma. Well, she can have a wash, anyway. The bathroom is between Anne's bedroom and Harry's dressing room, at which Briony steals a glimpse. Ivory hairbrushes, polished boots, a wall case full of guns. She shivers. In the bathroom there's a huge bath on legs and a wood-fired geyser for hot water. As it isn't lit Briony manages with cold. 'If I were you,' Anne said, 'I should go to the little house, that is if you need to, darling, before nightfall. Afterwards you're safer with the potty.' Briony has taken this advice too.

Night falls here as fast as the lights go down in a theatre. Now it's pitch dark as she vacates the bathroom, and she must cross over to the cottage to change. There is someone standing there in the blackness, holding a lamp. He turns. It is Mathew.

'No electric in your room, madam. Take this.' He holds the lamp towards her. 'And be careful.'

'About what?' She knows the answer already.

'Boss Werner.'

'Yes.' She takes the lamp from him, holding it up so she can see his face and he sees hers. 'Will you come in with me, please?'

'No time.'

'Please.'

'If you want, madam.'

They enter the cottage, pass through the outer room and into the bedroom. The curtains are drawn, the net is in place, the bed turned down. Briony's heart is pounding and her throat feels tight as if a cord is drawn round it. 'Your mother was too often afraid of things. Try not to be afraid of anything, it's a perfect waste of life,' Father used to say.

'You know who I am, don't you?' Briony says, facing Mathew with the paraffin lamp still held high between them so the moving light licks across the black surface of his face and the insipid, colourless surface of hers.

'Yes, madam.' His tone of voice is level, cool. There is no cord drawn round his throat. Of course, he's a man, in charge of his emotions, and a missionary boy, raised, hardened, on Bible dramas.

Seven

SHE HAS NO idea how or where to begin. The inequalities are so absurd: he is older than her, stronger than her, in his own land; and he is a male enigma, which gives an advantage you can't overcome. She, however, has to take the initiative. Hers is the master race here. Compared to him, she is free and rich, she doesn't need a pass to go along the track to Gatooma, she has a kind of power. He is a servant.

'Our father,' she begins, haltingly. 'Father remembered you.'

'He talk to you of me?'

'No. But I know he wanted me to find you.'

'How do you know this, madam?'

'For heaven's sake, Mathew, don't say madam. It makes me feel terrible.'

'Yes.' Does he mean by yes that it should make her feel terrible, because it is terrible? She thinks so. 'Reverend West leaved a message?'

She looks quickly at him and away again. He mustn't think that she, a woman, is trying to penetrate his thought. But is he secretly making fun of her with his pidgin English? There is no sign of mockery in his wide eyes, as far as she can tell. He looks reserved and defensive, like someone sheltering his self-esteem from expected

117

blows. Briony decides it is time to get away from Father. He isn't going to help, and anyway she is here because she wants to be, nothing to do with him really. But she will have just one more try first. 'I'm sure Father loved you,' she says, despising herself.

'Love me? A father here is not the same. With a son, a father is just one man and one more man. He doesn't run away down the Zambezi and not come back. Unless down the Zambezi he get killed.'

They are sitting on the bed with the mosquito net crushed behind them on to the sheet, their weight pulling the net down from its hook, up there among the spiders under the thatch roof. Mathew didn't want to sit down but she insisted. His feet are planted on the ground in front of him.

'Yes.' Her turn to be monosyllabic. What else is there to say? Well, there must be something better than that. 'I expect he wished he knew you better.'

'He never know the ignorant black child, your father. He only seen it.'

That may be quite true, and Briony has not come to Africa to argue for Father and his conscience. 'Dr Cathcart says you should have gone to university.'

'Dr Douglas is very proud of his good pupils,' Mathew says, smiling in a way that tells Briony she has got round his defence. 'But good pupils who read Shakespeare with Dr Douglas and speak well don't find work with white men here.'

'You can speak well with me. We speak the same.'

'Yes. Except you don't speak Shona.'

'Not yet.'

'You think you stay long enough to learn?'

'I have seen Mrs Shitofo,' Briony says.

'That poor woman,' Mathew says. A moment ago he sounded bossy, like an elder brother; now his defences are back. 'You should leave that poor woman alone.'

She had not, could not have calculated in advance the degree of bitterness she hears in his voice. She thinks back to the village on the hill, her slice of Africa. The children there, with only Douglas to see them through the diseases of African childhood, will grow up to equality with their parents, if what Mathew says is right. That certainly seems strangely different. Something else to learn about and weigh up, like the animals and the night sky. All the same, just what right has Mathew to be so high and mighty with her? She knows, of course, what he thinks his right is: it's because she is a woman, a sister. It is time for a more assertive approach. 'Mrs Shitofo lives in a kind of loose box. She says you never go and see her. I think she's unhappy.'

'I will get a pass and go to the Mission and send her back to the village.' At least he knows how to make up his mind on the spot.

'Suppose that isn't what she wants?'

'It is what I will do. She is old. You ask an old woman what she wants, she talks for two days.'

Obviously, no progress in their relationship can be made by discussing the fate of parents. Briony is pleased about that, in a way; it means they are on their own with each other. Sitting so close to him on the edge of the bed, her senses take him in. There is a faint, herby aroma like hay, enticing and warm. She can only hope her own is as good to him. She looks sideways at Mathew in the wavering light and sees that he's looking at her too, and smiling, so it must be all right. Tears come into her eyes. It is all right. But she knows that if she touched him, he would recoil. How sad that is.

'Don't cry, please,' Mathew says. Very slowly, very gently, he puts out a hand and lowers it on to hers. The quick under his fingernails is pink, vulnerable. An unexpected happiness, something entirely new, fills her. He has taken an initiative at last. She holds Mathew's hand between the palms and fingers of hers, holds on to it as if it was life itself.

★ ★ ★

'Werner, you're tight,' Anne says at dinner. Briony can tell that Anne likes Werner. It suddenly comes to her, watching them all, that Anne is a woman who is very keen on men. She looks at them the way they are said to look at women – as objects. You can see her registering her own physical reactions as she considers the man in front of her, close to her. Briony feels rather shocked, but not unpleasantly. She hadn't till now seen this as the kind of secret life a woman could decently have. Of course, it may not be all that decent. Have Werner and Anne . . .? If so, and Anne is pregnant, who . . .? Werner is dressed tonight in what looks like a white uniform, buttoned up to the neck and with the insignia removed, as if he has been cashiered. Now she thinks of it, what will become of him in an English Crown Colony after this time of waiting and ultimatums? What was it the captain of the *Edinburgh Castle* said that night with the telegram in his hand? 'Let us hope and pray it will not be war.' But perhaps after all, being a gentleman among gentlemen, Werner will not be put to too much inconvenience.

'Werner's no more tight than I am,' Harry says.

'You're both tight as drums,' Anne says.

In Anne's place, Briony would be a lot more careful. Does she want another fire lit on the floor under her? But of course she isn't, and can't put herself, and shouldn't imagine herself in Anne's place. Their kind – English or German, men or women – they have their ways which are almost as strange to her as the ways of life in the compound. With Mathew, Briony feels the barriers have almost gone. She may be wrong, but she feels it. With Harry and Anne and Werner there always will be an invisible barrier because of how they see her, someone from another category. When they're nice, they haven't forgotten it. And when they're horrid, they will be horrid in that particular way to make her feel she deserves it, just for coming among them.

It seems to be venison they're eating, strong in taste and fibre. Mathew has on his old tennis shoes, well whitened, and moves quietly about pouring wine and somehow creating around him, to Briony's satisfaction, an aura of distant, pointed superiority, like a star. The red wine is South African and Harry says it's quite decent, whatever that means. Briony finds it inky but doesn't say so. She watches as Anne's teeth turn bluish, glass by glass.

She turns to Anne and asks politely, not caring what the answer is, 'Did you shoot this?'

'Yes, I did, darling. From the veranda. But tomorrow you and I, we'll go off into the shade of the bush and see what we can see, it's the greatest fun. You'll be blooded.' Forgetting all about her dread of the word, Anne laughs much louder than seems wise.

Harry is restless at his end of the table. He picks up a piece of venison in his fingers and tears it with his strong teeth, then wipes his hands on the white linen napkin, throwing it on to the table when he's done. He empties his wine glass. It seems to Briony that he has been watching her, and knows that she is aware of it. 'I don't want you walking off into the bush with our guest,' he says. 'I have other plans.'

'Have you?' Anne says. 'What are your other plans, if one may ask?'

'One may. I want to show her the mines.'

'Ah,' Werner says. Until now he has been shovelling venison into his rosebud mouth as if it was the first serious meal he's been given in this English house. Perhaps in his part of central Europe one eats nothing else. 'The mines. So. I will come.'

'You will remain here in charge of work on the farm, Werner,' Harry says, quite mildly.

'Your farm – no work ever is done on it. Because you, my dear Harry, are an Englishman. You will not allow the methods which, I tell you, only will get some work done here.'

121

'Where are the mines? Are they gold mines?' Briony asks.

'They are. Old ones. Long disused. The Shona people mined the gold for centuries but they couldn't go down below the water table. They hadn't invented the pump. They didn't know about the Archimedean screw – as practised in advanced societies.' Only Werner laughs at this and it may even not be a laugh. A bit of venison could have gone down the wrong way. 'Those mines are on your land.'

There is a silence as this sinks in.

'I didn't know you had any land,' Anne says sharply. 'How do you come to have it? Women don't own land here. It isn't done.'

'You are right, gracious lady. This is not a woman's country,' Werner agrees.

'My father bought it years and years ago,' Briony says, trying to make it sound careless and unimportant and of little value.

'I pour madam some wine,' Mathew says close behind her. Something dry in his voice puts a chill on the conversation. More than that, it freezes it. Are the others thinking, as she is, that when the Shona worked their mines the land belonged to no one and to all, to their children down to the last generation? Is that what Mathew is thinking, and does his thought strike into theirs?

Briony turns half round to him. 'No thank you,' she says, and smiles.

Now it is Werner who is watching her, and also watching Mathew. No one could doubt the meaning of his look – this is a young woman of the dominant race smiling at an insolent native in such a way as to encourage him to think he is not an object. But the next moment Werner is laughing. His green eyes close almost into slits with laughter. He claps Mathew in the small of the back, stretching a long arm over his chair. 'Mathew and I, Werner von Hippel, we are the best friends, isn't this so? What are a few knocks between good friends?' he says.

'Okay, Boss Werner, all okay,' Mathew says, though nothing could be less okay. The polite pidgin lie breaks Briony's heart. She can feel the tears well up behind her eyes, not for the lie in itself, for Mathew's need to smile and lie.

'I don't think it is,' she says.

'Shut up, darling,' Anne says. It's a serious warning, not a sign that Anne is annoyed by the conversation. It means, it must mean, that in this land for men the clock is back to the days when women took care what they said, and kept quiet if they had anything other than the banal or the tender to offer. Anne herself forgets the rule sometimes, and gets a fire lit under her. Briony looks round at Harry, involuntarily. He is miles away, black eyes lost in some zone before him, invisible to all but himself. She feels a twinge of jealousy and anger about this private zone. He seems to fill it so completely, like a badger in its sett, all on his own.

'I'd rather go shooting with you tomorrow than go to see the mine with Commander Chance,' she says. Actually, this is not true. The thought of the mine thrills her; not because, according to him, it's hers, but because a mine seems an entry into the heart of things – and what other reason? Because she would like to go riding again with Harry. She has the scent of the bush, the man, in her nostrils, sitting here with unfinished venison and undrunk inky wine waiting in front of her.

Her remark brings Harry sharply back to present life. 'What rot,' he says. 'Anne can't hit a barn door at twenty feet. You won't learn about shooting from her. If you want to shoot, I'll teach you straight away. And tomorrow morning we'll ride out to look at those mines of yours. Clear all this away. I've done.' He stands up and comes close to her chair. 'Come on with me now, do.'

'But I haven't quite finished.' Briony looks at Anne, who lifts her shoulders in a slight, elegant movement that draws attention to their chalky whiteness against the navy-blue linen of this evening's dress.

'We'll eat our pudding afterwards. Mathew will leave it for us on the table,' Harry says, and takes Briony's arm above the elbow. 'I'll show you how to handle a gun. After dusk's the time, and in an hour there'll be a full moon.'

'Leave her alone,' Anne says.

He is pulling gently upwards on her arm. It's a difficult situation. Should she stay where she is, and become a dead weight? Or stand and give the impression of willingness? Still undecided, she rises, caught in the crossfire between respect for people's married dues and her own wrongful wishes.

'Do you mind too much . . .?' she says to Anne.

'I will shoot with you also,' Werner cries, springing up. 'We will take pot shots at peasants, like in the old, good days.'

'Sit down and keep Anne company, Werner,' Harry says. He looks for a moment at the two of them, his gaze seeming to sweep up and bury whatever possibilities they represent, together or apart. 'There's the brandy, on the sideboard. Help yourself. Better drink here than in the bar at Chakari. And better woman.'

Mathew, as Harry says this, is passing through the door into the kitchen. Briony feels shame for him and for herself. For him because of what Harry has just said and for herself because of the attraction that makes her stand and yield and follow Harry wherever it is he wishes to go, and her to follow. Briony has come into the open with herself. She didn't know it until now, but she has this feeling . . . compliant and revolted together. And wishful. Uncertainly but intensely wishful.

The huge moon breaking the horizon threatens the world like an approaching planet. You can see everything quite clearly at two hundred yards. Briony can make out the thinnest branches of trees beside the cattle grid, and of other trees beyond it.

'There's a vlei where the buffalo come down to drink at night,'

Harry says. 'Hold the torch. We won't need it, but just in case. Shine it on the ground in front of you but keep the beam down.'

'What is a vlei, please?'

'A stretch of shallow water, vague in extent, brackish in content. Too brackish for mankind; the wells are safer.' There it is again – a different kind of intelligence struggling for some outlet through pedantic-sounding definitions. It may be one of the things that attract her.

'And why do I shine the torch on the ground in front of me? Oh, I know, Commander. Ankles and snakes.'

'Right, Master West.'

That must be a compliment in its way. This man was at the Battle of Jutland as a boy of sixteen, remember, Douglas said so. So she is promoted to be someone he can order about in the most natural way. She is thrilled. She feels slightly silly, but still thrilled. Harry laughs, a low and rather intimate laugh. Silliness shared is exciting at some childish but important level.

They walk in silence for what seems a long time, close together, a sleeve sometimes brushing a sleeve. 'We must keep very quiet. Buffalo have no sense of fun. They attack on sight.'

'Perhaps that's their fun.'

'Here we are. Now lie down on your stomach and keep even quieter.'

Their station is between two trees growing close together on a small mound of earth and rock. The vlei, a shallow, irregular silver saucer with high grass surrounding it, seeming distant in the rusty moonlight, is spread out before and below them. The air is full of the sound of frogs, sleepless insects, night birds, laughing dogs. Harry's elbow is almost touching hers, and if he moves, they do touch. His rifle rests on the other forearm, the butt under his armpit. What is going to happen if buffalo do actually appear and charge? Rise and run behind the trees, or what? Would buffalo charge through the vlei? No, of course not. They're perfectly safe here. They're just going to shoot at some innocent animals slaking their thirst, from the security of a post far off across the water. It doesn't seem very heroic, to Briony, imagining how it was at Jutland with the shells whistling back and forth. After a time, she can't help it, she feels restless, there is an insect crawling across her back. Her feet itch in the tennis shoes she was ordered to put on.

'For Christ's sake, will you keep still. They're coming,' Harry whispers. 'Look. To the left of that big tree.'

There are some hunched dark shapes, close together and a little behind the tree on the far side of the vlei, moving stealthily to the water's edge. Harry waits, dead still, for a long time. Now the leading animal has lowered its head to the water. Presumably a bull. Where drink is concerned, the male generally seems to get first go. Harry's elbow nudges hers. 'Take the rifle,' he whispers, and with slow movements passes it towards her, on to her outstretched arm, draws the butt into her shoulder. All the animals are now at the water. 'Put your cheek against the stock, here. Look along the sights.'

She can see the nearest sight and just make out the one on the end of the barrel. Beyond that, all is an unfocused blur. 'I can't see anything.'

'Concentrate. Keep your eye steady. The line between your left elbow and the stock of the gun must be rigid. Spread your fingers round it but not over the top or you'll never see anything.' He leans over her, his hands are on her arm, fixing it to the ground, and on her fist, curling the fingers securely about the rifle stock. 'Now can you see them?'

'Just about.'

'Put your index inside the trigger guard.' She does so, feeling the cold metal between the first and second joint of her finger. 'Now, pull the butt hard into your shoulder.' She can feel him checking for himself the execution of this order. His touch is gentle. 'When you fire, there'll be a strong kick. If you've never done it before it will feel violent. The important thing is to pull the rifle hard back into you; that reduces the kick.'

The rifle is quite a light one; it feels to her almost friendly, smooth to the touch. It gives off an agreeable smell of oil, and metal and wood, and leather and brandy. But she is expected to shoot the thing at one of those poor animals on the far side of the water. However dangerous they may be, Briony feels it's wrong. But if she doesn't do it, Harry will despise her and take no further interest in her; there's the dilemma. The thought is too hard to bear.

'Aim just below the eye. Buffaloes have a horny excrescence on the forehead capable of deflecting a bullet.' At least this is an apprentice-ship, not mere slaughter. She's being taught something and that means she's taken seriously. 'We don't want a wounded animal roaming round the place. Shoot to kill.'

The leading animals have made way for the lesser fry to edge forward from behind them. The whole group stands out clearly in the strong moonlight, African creatures peacefully seeing to their needs.

'Don't pull at the trigger. Squeeze it. Just a light squeeze. The least jerk at your end sends the bullet miles off at the other.'

Briony takes aim at the biggest animal in the middle. The bead is centred in the sight. At that moment he raises his head into the air above him, and the animals at the water raise theirs. They look as tense, as ready to panic and vanish as Briony feels herself.

'Ready?' Harry whispers. 'Fire.' The word of command comes in a firm, low voice. Briony squeezes the trigger, feels a sharp pain in both eardrums and a violent blow in the shoulder. She can see nothing whatever in front of her – water, moon, buffaloes, the whole scene has been blasted away. The rifle lies cradled in her arms and against her aching shoulder like a child. 'You hit him but you didn't kill him. I think the horn on his brow saved him. I told you, aim below the eye.'

'I couldn't see the poor bloody eye,' Briony says, shaken.

'Oh, I like that,' Harry says.

'Where are they? Did they go?'

'Did you expect them to wait while you had another try?'

'I'm glad they've gone. Do you think he'll be all right?'

She has hardly noticed, till now, that his arm lies across her back. Probably he put it there to steady her against the kick of the rifle. However, she can feel pressure from his fingers on her own upper arm, right round the other side of her from his centre of gravity, so she knows that a good deal of Harry's bulk, which she can't see from where she is, still lying on her stomach and holding the rifle, is above her.

'I must say I do find you absolutely delicious,' Harry says. 'Do I think he'll be all right?' He laughs. 'Do you realise how many millions of buffalo there are in Africa?' He seems to be closer now and he is taking the rifle from her hands, laying it on the ground on the far side of him; not removing his other arm or reducing its pressure, firm, nearly coercive, on her back. 'Turn this way.'

Is this, after all, no more than what was supposed to happen? All that was foreseen from the start and nothing else? Briony turns on her side. Their bodies, from head to foot, are touching. As far as her feet, anyway. All after that is a void, as if nothing beyond this area of new sensation counts in the world. This *is* the world, this being one with another and no longer alone. Her own movements, and Harry's, are not willed, they flow from necessity. The taste of his mouth is part of the taste of hers.

But it's a moment that can't last like that. She knows it must carry over to become a moment of a different kind, or be broken off. She wants it to go on, and on, but not be different. She hasn't yet felt her way clearly forward into that difference. There are two rhythms at work here, one of them the rhythm of an active man with nothing to lose and, now she thinks of it, quite a bit of drink inside him; the other of a young woman anxious about herself and her body and feeling guilty on account of the wife at home in whose house she's a guest. She draws her head back, cautiously, fearfully also. Harry Chance is not the boy Jock on the *Edinburgh Castle*, he's a man used to his own way, to an extent unusual even for a man, and he is going to get angry. 'I do think we really ought to go back,' she murmurs.

'Why? You're not cold? You don't feel cold.' Harry's hands travel about, reassuring him of the correctness of his impression, she supposes.

'Please, Commander Chance, let me go.'

'Don't you like me, Miss West?'

Briony laughs. 'Oh, I do. Quite.' It seems so stupid, then, to insist on returning to the house. But enjoying the feel of him alongside her – enclosing her practically – doesn't make her feel any safer. You must be able to choose, and consent, or you're nothing. 'Still, I really think . . .'

He's surprisingly good about it, considering what an awful man her imagination took him for – awful, dark and devastating. In fact, he is evidently that rare thing, a gentleman, in dealing with a reluctant woman. He is already on his feet, holding out a hand to pull her up. She feels, besides relief, a touch of disappointment. Will he remember what it was like? Will there be another time? There shouldn't be, of course, because of Anne, and his children, and Briony's own sense of responsibility, feeble as it is. But she hopes there will be. He deserves it, in a way, for being patient and showing he's not a base creature after all.

'Well, you nearly scored a buffalo,' Harry says, and picks up the fallen rifle. A cloud of bats swarms from the tree they were under and zigzags away towards the moon. On the long walk back, his arm occasionally rests a moment on her shoulder, as if guiding an animal to safe enclosure pending further use and pleasure.

★　★　★

129

The telephone rings its coded call. Briony is alone in the big sitting room, Anne having one of her migraine headaches to let her off the demands of reality, few as they are. The men are out on the farm, giving orders, harvesting or creating out of dust the fertile tilth of cultivation; anyway doing those terrific farming kind of things. Briony goes through into the office, where the telephone hangs on a wall behind the desk where accounts are vaguely, inaccurately kept. Yesterday Harry asked her to have a look at them, leaning close as she did so, and she could see how badly a secretary is needed to clear up the disorder. It could give her some plausible reason for staying, not that anyone, so far, is questioning her presence. The telephone code system is laid out on a sheet of paper pinned to the wall beside the instrument. Her eye runs quickly down it. There are about thirty subscribers on the exchange and she thinks the code being called is the Mission. Briony lifts the ear-phone. The comfort is in knowing that she certainly won't be the only eavesdropper on the conversation.

Douglas's voice, dredged up from the back of his throat, is unmistakable. 'Well, Commissioner,' he is slowly saying, 'every other subscriber on the line will be waiting like me to hear what you want to come out to the Mission to see me for.'

'It's a matter of land occupation, Reverend Cathcart.'

'Yes?'

'The native settlement on the hill owned by the Mission. You are well aware of the provisions of the Act of 1930, I'm sure,' says the other voice. It is a voice with an accent unfamiliar to Briony, a bit like the woman at Speck's but much more so, with flattened, foreshortened vowels and a slightly nasal sound. Someone whose first language is not English, possibly. She may have heard something like it on the train, winding its way slowly across the South African veld, among the ostriches. The conductor, or some other official, spoke like that.

'Yes?' Douglas is not helping this other man. He is trying to get him to spell out, for all the eavesdroppers to hear, what exactly his business over land occupation is. Douglas is trying to shame some-body, or perhaps everybody. After all, missionaries must be in the business of guilt, or what are they for, in the end? It may even be part of why she feels she needs him as soon as she hears his voice.

'They apply to the Mission same as everyone else,' the Com-missioner says. 'I will come out in the morning. Ten o'clock suit you?'

'As you like.'

'Can you get the headman of the village too? Or must we go and see him? It makes no difference. Those people have to shift off white-owned land. It's the law. They should have cleared out by the end of 1937.' The Commissioner sounds defiant. 'I think you'll have to see it our way, Reverend,' he says. Doubtfully. Threateningly, too. He must hate missionaries, and fear them. A woman doesn't have to be long in Africa to understand why; he hates them because a missionary has the Africans on his side, and fears them because he has God on his side too. Men carry the values of the playground to the grave.

'It would be right to go and see him. We should respect the dignity of a headman. He is chief of a community of two or three hundred people and a more important man than you or me.'

'Ach, don't give me that talk of Africans and dignity and respect. You, I must respect. But otherwise I sooner respect the animals in the bush.' Afrikaner, that's what they call that accent. Briony remembers Harry's contempt for the one who was busy flogging the native in the street of Gatooma.

'Come earlier than that, before the sun gets high. It's quite a walk,' Douglas says. 'Come at eight. And you know and I know that law you mentioned has been amended by Parliament. The time limit's 1941 now.'

'I'll bring Pienaar along with me. The natives know it means business when they see him around. Pienaar, he isn't the type to hold his hand waiting for amendments.' There is an angry click in the earpiece, followed by another.

Briony needs help. The Commissioner and this famous Pienaar are going to inspect her land, knowing nothing about her, evidently believing the land belongs to the Mission, and they are going to order the inhabitants out of their homes. She won't allow that, but how does she go about stopping it? Perhaps she should talk to Mathew. Suddenly the gulf between her perception of what it means to own the hill, and his that the hill can never be owned by anyone, ever, seems too great to bridge. Not this morning. Then she remembers that Mathew's day off is today. He won't be leaning over her at the dinner table and saying, 'Wine, madam?' in that way that upsets her. He will have shed his tennis shoes and departed, like an antelope, into the forest, by forest paths, running, racing to the Mission to see to Mrs Shitofo and her complaints of unhappiness. Impatient no doubt, but like a gentleman is impatient, with politeness.

His absence leaves her friendless. She sits in the chair behind the desk where the accounts pile up in a hopeless, neglected manner. Because with people like the Chances, there is always money in the background, plenty of it – trusts, marriage settlements, rich fathers in England. Briony thinks back to the conversation overheard a minute ago. Something in it, she feels sure, offers a key. Something she noted at the back of her mind. Significant, not to be forgotten. Yes, there it is: 'white-owned land'.

A happy release occurs in her, almost physical it's so gratifying and simple. Several birds with one stone, a single solution to several problems in the air. Mathew must become the owner of the hill as Father surely wanted. She will need a lawyer. Though Mathew had a white man for a father, he is not white, therefore the hill will no longer be white-owned land. It will be a fiction, but a good one. How good? Isn't it saying that Mathew, whose skin might just as well have been white or something in between, will be the saviour of the village on the hill because his face, and the rest of him, is black? Isn't this thinking the same way, in a sense, as the Afrikaner Commissioner? Is it impossible in this land to be generous? Generous? Who is she to think herself generous? The hill, since the beginning, belongs to the people who live and die on it.

The telephone rings again. Briony looks at the code sheet, running her finger down the names. While she's still doing it, the ring is repeated. She has found it. It is the code for here. She lifts the earpiece, gingerly, off the hook. 'Hallo?'

'I would like to speak to Miss West, please.' Douglas's voice, she's sure.

'Briony speaking.'

'I thought so. Were you far away?'

'No. I was standing here.'

'Yes. Then I expect you overheard my talk a couple of minutes ago?'

'Yes, I did. And I've had an idea.'

'You had better not say here and now what it is.'

'No. But I must see you. Only I don't know how I can get there.'

'Mathew came today. He has taken his mother away.'

'I'll ask Commander Chance to bring me.'

'Take care what you . . .'

'Oh, I will.'

As she hangs up, Briony hears a sound behind her, and looks round. Anne is standing in the doorway, watching. She wears a kimono in red and purple and gold, enough to give anyone a migraine, Briony thinks, and has a handkerchief to her nose. She breathes in deeply. It must be soaked in something to clear her head.

'Who was that?'

'It was Dr Cathcart.'

'That old maid. What did he want?'

'He wanted to speak to me.'

'What about?'

'I think it must be something to do with the piece of land—'

'I see.' Anne is looking hard at her, but with the handkerchief half over her eyes, occasionally wiping them. 'Did you enjoy taking a pot shot at the buffalo last night?' she asks.

There is something barbed about the question. 'Yes, I did, rather,' Briony admits. She hasn't really earned the embarrassment she feels, so it must be guilty wishes that produce it. 'But I'm glad I missed.'

'You may not go on missing. There has to be a first time for everything. Any blood sport.'

Briony decides to say nothing in answer to this. What is there to say, anyway? The meaning is obvious. Surely, Harry wouldn't have told . . . no. Unless, of course, he wanted to light another fire, so to speak, under his wife, to smoke her out. The situation is more complicated even than she thought. What, for example, did Anne and Werner do after she and Harry went out under the moon with the rifle? Say good night, discuss the international news? Or what?

'I wonder if Commander Chance would very kindly drive me over to the Mission this evening? Do you think I can ask him?'

'I'm sure you can,' Anne says, 'but he can't. He has to be here.' Briony is not a person of sufficient importance to be told why he must be here. It's very easy, talking to Anne, to know your place in the scale of importance. Voice, eyes, movement of the hand with the handkerchief, all have a way of showing it. 'Werner can take you, he'll be pleased to. We spoke of you last night. He finds you charming. A real English miss; he's never seen one before, naturally enough. Tell him to take you now.' There's a change in the impression Anne is making on her. She seems more deeply wrapped in her kimono, as if she has a secret pleasure to hide in there with her. Is she wearing anything under that kimono?

'I suppose I'll have to ask him. But he's out somewhere on the farm, with . . .'

'No he isn't. He's here.' Anne turns. 'Werner,' she calls. 'Werner!' When he appears behind her at the door of the office, which is almost at once, it is impossible to know from which direction he came. From one of the rooms, obviously, but which one? 'The English miss needs someone to drive her to Marimari. You know the way? Take the Ford. Come straight back and don't stop to get drunk at Chakari.' These orders are given in a way that seems to Briony, deeply ignorant of such adult games, somehow suggestive of play-acting, as though it's Anne's turn to be king of the castle. 'Besides, you may not need to stop off there this time. Just think what that would be like.' She glances from Werner to Briony and back again. 'See to your passenger properly.'

Werner is an appalling driver. He crashes the Ford truck along in low gear with the engine screaming and makes no attempt to avoid the deep potholes or fallen branches, or the baboons which, knowing nothing about the dangers of the road, swing and amble across in front of the Ford or sit in the middle of the track removing insects from each other's ears. In fact, Werner aims at them.

'Please, don't do that,' Briony pleads.

'These are only monkeys. They feel nothing.'

She tries to control herself. There is an unusually violent jolt over a deep hole in the road and her head hits the metal side of the cab. 'They feel just as much as you. Or more, probably.'

'Yes, I also feel. I feel sadness. I am chased away from the fatherland because of this soft heart.'

Briony doesn't believe a word of it. Harry says Werner is a spy. So he pretends to have been thrown out of Germany when in fact he probably left on account of debts, or some more sordid cause. 'How did you get those scars, Werner?' she asks. She feels there's no need for delicacy with him. He's probably very proud of them.

'It is by *die Mensur*.'

'What's that?'

'We fight other students with swords. The feet do not move. This is to show one is a man.'

'How perfectly ridiculous,' Briony rashly says.

'So? You think this? How perfectly English.' She looks quickly at him. The scars on his cheek throb angrily and his face is flushed. He says nothing more for the rest of the ride to the Mission; neither does she, regretting that she didn't start saying nothing rather sooner. A man you don't know well is an alarming animal, if angered when he's driving.

Douglas has taken her into the chapel, obviously to get her away from Werner. 'This is the only place on the Mission where you can have a private talk,' he tells her. The chapel is built of corrugated iron and inside is like an oven. He doesn't seem to mind that, but Briony starts to sweat at once, as soon as the door closes behind them. They sit on a polished dark-wood bench in the light falling through two clear-glass pointed windows. Briony is not much at ease in ecclesiastical buildings; they seem to make a claim for penitence that your innocent state cannot sincerely meet, that's what she thinks.

'I've had a brilliant idea,' she starts straight in. 'We'll get a lawyer and Mathew will be made owner of the land. Then the people can go on living there, and hunting and having their children in peace. And Mrs Shitofo need never be disturbed again.' She feels suddenly happy in spite of the sweat and the penitential atmosphere. 'Anyway, I'm sure it's what my father wanted, really.'

'But he didn't do it, and I'll tell you why. Because he couldn't. Land apportioned for white ownership cannot be sold to people of African race.'

'I'm not talking about selling it. I'm going to give it.'

136

Douglas is silent for a time. Perhaps he's praying. Briony is embarrassed and dare not look to see. 'I must check the Act and the map of European-apportioned land. I'm not sure. There may be a way, I'm not sure.' He is silent again, not moving either. Briony turns to look at him. He is trembling, slightly, as if he were cold here in this oven.

So the true Africans are not only turned off the land of their ancestors, they can't even buy it if they have the means because it's white land, defined by the Act. 'I can pay a lawyer for advice, you know. It can't cost so very much.' She can feel mounting in herself that armoured wall of defiance that Father so often deplored. He thought it unfeminine, perhaps. 'Where is your map?' Against the back wall of the chapel is a bookcase with drawers underneath. 'Is it there?'

Douglas doesn't answer this question directly. 'I think you should reflect,' he says. 'You know, in many ways the Apportionment Act is in the natives' best interests. I hate to say it, but I must admit that. Under the Act, they can call a huge part of this country their own, and continue their old way of life on it. Without the Act, they would be driven off, sooner or later. If not by the English settlers, then by the South Africans, who are much rougher people.'

'You are going to tell me the English are gentlemen.'

There is another long silence. 'Who is that German?' Douglas asks. When she has explained, he says, 'Be careful of him. Try and understand the way things are.' He sounds painstakingly patient, as an impatient teacher often sounds. 'There are a lot of people in Africa who have nothing to lose, and above all, with no tie here. At least the Land Apportionment Act helps tie the Europeans who want to own land to the land they own, and to the law. This German is one of those who own nothing and belong nowhere. They're dangerous. Whatever you do, don't let him know about . . . Mathew.'

'Mathew?'

'And you, for heaven's sake. Try and understand what you're doing. Our work here is to protect, not provoke and antagonise.' There are tears in his eyes; they swim in them, and a flush reaches up to the lined surface of his face. 'You can't know,' he says. 'There's so much you can't know. The people here are fine, free people, and like anyone else, they can turn savage.'

What she does know is that Douglas is a man living without a woman. Would he speak so passionately to another man, or speak in a more measured way? The question is its own answer. Briony feels a long way from Southampton, with these men and their ceaseless agitation in restless bodies under the African sun, even the missionary.

'You see, Briony, the great lie isn't burned into these people that I like to call mine.'

Briony looks at Douglas with new interest. What did Anne say? That old maid. Well, a passionate old maid. 'What great lie?' she asks.

He gazes out of the disturbance in his own eyes to the calm of hers, as if trying to guess whether or not the truth is safe with her. He raises a hand to his face and partly covers his mouth. The hand is trembling. 'They can't be persuaded of the truth of the idea of original sin,' he says, 'and their scepticism is very catching.'

'Oh, I see. Yes, I understand. And I'll be very careful with Werner,' Briony says, going back for safety to the point of departure. Isn't original sin really Adam's particular problem? And of course if a pastor starts calling it the great lie, it means his belief has crumbled, and she knows what happens then. The man is lost. Once again she doesn't know quite why, but she doesn't want to lose Dr Cathcart. 'What about that map?'

'I don't need it. I can tell you without it.'

She is not surprised; she thought all along he was only playing for time with that talk of a map while he made up his mind whether to trust her or not. Now she knows more about him than probably anyone else does, or could. Like Father, he has lost his faith as he has grown to love the African people, and it seems obvious to her that it is the inevitable result. Faith is held in place by what surrounds it; surrounded and shaken by Africa, little faiths would dwindle like curls of smoke into the sky. She feels both flattered and alarmed that this lonely man trusted her with his secret on such short acquaintance. It's true, of course, that he once saw her in her cradle. 'Well?'

'The land your father bought was named as part of the Undetermined Area. I think he managed to arrange to get it included. The government in 1925 needed the support of the missionaries. Now they don't think they need us so much. They've moved far to the right.'

'What is it undetermined about?'

'It means that this hill, this particular land, could only be bought from the government by a European, but unlike the rest of the reserved land it could be transferred, though not by sale, to an African, and then become part of the Native Area.'

'So he meant Mathew to have it.'

'I think so,' Douglas agrees. 'And that's one of the reasons we've never done anything to turn the people off it. The other is that we shelter our friends. And it's why the Native Commissioner is coming to see me tomorrow. They must know about your arrival here.' He pauses. 'May I ask, have you written any postcard, any letter?'

'Yes.'

'The posts are watched. The hotels cooperate in that.'

'We need a lawyer,' Briony repeats. The Land Apportionment Act and the Native Commissioner and the government loom over her mind like fog moving in from the sea. If her letter to Jo has been read – the fog gets thicker still. Douglas is a steady beacon, but one lightship is not enough. A lawyer carries armaments as well.

'I will find one,' Douglas says. 'In fact I know one.'

139

'What will you say to the Native Commissioner?'

Douglas's laugh is not humorous but bitter and angry-sounding. 'The Native Commissioner and I have private business and I think you can believe he will do what I tell him, in the end.'

An awful curiosity fills Briony's consciousness. What can Douglas possibly have in the way of private business? Has he a Mrs Shitofo of his own tucked away somewhere? But how would that give him any hold over the Commissioner? The opposite would be more likely. While she is still thinking about it, there is a loud, insistent knocking on the chapel door. Douglas calls out something in that language which is dark and rhythmical as the night drums. The answer comes back in a boy's light voice. Briony thinks she makes out the word 'Mathew'.

Eight

THE MOUNTED POLICEMAN is a dreaded figure. With revolver and whip he moves through the pathless forest, turning up anywhere, any time, from behind some great teak or mopane tree, shouting words of command and arrest. There is one now out on the open ground in front of the Mission buildings. As his horse turns restlessly about, so the policeman's gaze shifts constantly, striking terror into the minds of the boys who stand on the naked earth in the late-afternoon sun. The long black whip hanging from his wrist moves restlessly too, alive as the horse impatient for work.

Douglas, unhurried, walks over. Werner is already there, leaning against one of the brick pillars that support the veranda roof, and behind him is Mathew, dressed not in white with tennis shoes but in the same lifeless, defeated, shapeless cotton shorts and shirt that the men in Gatooma wear, the conquered men. His head is bowed, he is studying his bare feet on the cement floor. Douglas stops and turns back to Briony, who is waiting at the chapel door, unsure which way to go.

'You had better come, I think,' Douglas says.

The policeman sits his horse with the ease and touch of display to match his physique. He is a well-made young man in ironed khakis

141

and polished belt and boots, and when he catches sight of Briony, he puffs up like a frog with conceit. He even smiles in her direction.

'Well, Reverend,' he calls out in his strong, manly voice, 'there's a native here with no pass. He isn't one of yours. What d'you say about that?'

Douglas, with Briony now beside him, has stopped some yards away from horse and rider. He looks round at Mathew. 'You mean that man there?'

'That's him. I'm ready to run him into the station.' The horse performs a complete turn, raising and shaking its head. 'Stand, you bloody animal. I say stand.'

'I won't allow that,' Douglas says. 'That man was a boy here in the Mission.'

'Allow? How d'you stop it, Reverend?'

'The Native Commissioner with Lieutenant Pienaar will be here in the morning. I give him your name and make a complaint.'

'It was Piet Pienaar himself who sent me. Orders to check on all natives hanging spare around the place.' He reaches behind him to a coiled rope attached to the back of his saddle. 'With the end of this round his neck, I can trot this munt back to the station in record time, and Pienaar, he'll be happy as Larry.'

Mathew has not looked up as Briony hoped he would. She doesn't know how serious, or not, this threat is. A lot of what goes on here seems to be like a perverse sort of game, but the rope decides her. She takes a couple of steps nearer the horse's head and raises a hand towards it.

'Please, officer,' she says, 'we know the man. He works for Commander Chance.'

The police officer looks down on her with the delighted grin of a man being pleaded with. 'Friend of the Commander's, are you?'

'I'm a guest at his farm.'

'And what does this native do, at the farm?'

'He works in the house.'

'You mean house boy.'

'Yes,' Briony says. What else is there to say? How many miles is it to the station? What happens if a man led on the end of a rope falls while the horse trots on?

'Sorry, miss, Pass Laws apply. If this boy works at Chance's place, that's where he has to be. And he's here. With no pass.' He smiles at her again, more kindly, less arrogantly this time. 'You know, one native is much like another. You may have made a mistake. Come over here, you,' he shouts at Mathew in English. 'If he doesn't come, it's that he isn't a house boy and doesn't know English.' Mathew doesn't stir. 'See?'

'Please,' Briony says again. She doesn't want the tears to come, it would be a surrender. But they are there, ready.

The humiliation is spared her. Standing with her back to Mathew and the house, she has forgotten Werner. Now here he comes with his odd, stiff walk, and puts a hand up to the horse's neck. Briony quickly withdraws her own. 'This is a fine animal,' he says, 'and you, you are another fine animal.' The police officer is very young and he doesn't know how to take this compliment. A faint flush spreads under the tan of his face. Werner's scars perhaps seem to him like insignia of rank and certainly of experience.

'Who are you, sir?' he asks.

'I am Baron Werner von Hippel, manager to the Commander Chance. I will take the charge of this . . . what you call boy. Give me your rope for prisoners.'

The policeman looks doubtful. Chance is a commander and here is this baron chap working for him – these are people who are used to having their own way in the home and getting themselves obeyed outside it. The policeman looks at Douglas. At least he's someone familiar, even if only a missionary.

'Let him go. Next time he wants to come and see me he'll

remember to get a pass. He's a good Christian. I'm his friend and he's one of mine.'

'You'll be giving him his pass to heaven next, won't you, Reverend? They have pass laws to get their friends in up there all right, don't they?' The young man laughs at his joke, without offence. His laugh is like his voice – manly and a bit unsure. 'Okay. If the baron here guarantees to take him home and keeps an eye on him on the way.' He looks round at the truck. 'These jokers can jump off the back of a vehicle like that and vanish into the bush like a snake.'

'I say it already, I say again – give me this rope you have.' Werner's voice has risen.

'I'll do better than that, sir,' the police officer says. 'I'll lend you the handcuff. Commander Chance can drop it back at the station any time he likes.' He turns again to Douglas. 'Does that suit you, Dr Cathcart?'

'If it's the only way, yes.'

'And the young lady?' Decidedly, he wants his pound of flesh and all present must see that he is acting in the best manner in the execution of important duties.

Briony looks at Mathew. He has raised his head and he nods it, almost imperceptibly. She looks quickly at Werner. Werner is watching and he has seen; his green eyes are wide with an expression in which the surprise is only a pretence. Actually, you can read in it the satisfaction of a man whose suspicions have been confirmed. There is something between Mathew and Briony which there should not be between a black man and a white girl. An unthinkable complicity. 'Thank you, Officer. It will be all right,' Briony says.

'Quite sure?' What does he mean? He is looking from her to Werner. 'You going back together? Sure it's okay?'

'Oh yes, quite sure.'

Just as she climbs back into the truck, Douglas takes her hand and holds it firmly. 'When you need me, I'm here. Always.'

'I'll remember.'

He smiles, a hesitant smile full of feeling. 'Yes, please do.' He's a warm man, despite his dried-up appearance. She feels comforted by it, as the truck starts up.

Mathew is handcuffed to the metal rack which rises up behind the cab of the truck, so he must stand as they stagger along from pothole to ridge, in the fast-fading light. Standing, actually, is probably better than sitting. The leather of the seat is shiny and torn and a spring, or bit of one, sticks through and rips at Briony's bottom whenever the truck lurches and skids. Werner is humming, a thin sound from behind the teeth, a sound like a secret thought rising above the noise of the engine and the grinding of the gears. Only one headlight works, and by its dim radiance from time to time the hind parts of an animal can be seen vanishing into the trees.

'You are quite happy?' Werner asks, waving one hand at her so the gold ring with the opaque red stone in it that he wears on his little finger brushes against her face.

'Please watch the track,' Briony says, and he laughs his barking, harsh laugh. Through the window like a porthole in the back of the cab she can make out the gap between Mathew's shirt and his shorts. He looks too thin for comfort. All his strength and presence are concentrated in his face and head – the high-bridged nose, the wide mouth, the brow so serene you'd think that Africa had never been raped by the white man. The word uncoils, snakes, and strikes out in Briony's head. She feels suddenly alone and chained to the truck like Mathew, but more vulnerable, in spite of the handcuff holding him.

'I stop here one minute,' Werner says as the truck lurches to a halt in the middle of nowhere after a long, wearing progress during which no one has spoken. He turns off the headlight. 'I have the call of nature.' He climbs out and disappears into the blackness. Briony would like to ask Mathew if he is all right but for some reason she is afraid to. She can hear Werner whistling among the bushes, not some popular tune like 'Smoke Gets in Your Eyes', more complex and difficult, an air from Schubert, or someone. A minute later his tread is audible on leaves and branches, then it sounds as if he's moving them about on the ground, gathering them to light a bonfire. He has stopped whistling and is talking to himself in a mutter, like someone memorising an important message. The call of nature is not what's occupying him now.

'Please,' Briony calls out from the truck window, 'I would like to go back to Commander Chance's farm straight away.' Her voice sounds childish in her own ears.

'So?'

'Yes please.' It's stupid, but she feels afraid, here in the dark. The forest all around is far from empty. The animals in it are strange, large, and dangerous, and so may be the people, issuing in the night from their secret villages. Mathew is handcuffed to the grid above her head and Werner, about whose mental stability she has felt unsure since he first appeared behind the mosquito net, drunk and excited, could take it into his mind to go off and leave her. Earlier, she noticed a shotgun lying on the shelf behind the seat. She reaches up and feels for it. It has gone. Through the trees ahead the sky has begun to glow along the horizon. The moon must be just below it. Werner may have taken the gun in order to shoot something by the silvery light of the moon; he seems to hate baboons and he might think it good sport to shoot some as they come out to play. And in ten minutes the whole sky will be lit as the huge circle floats up from behind the earth.

'Get out from this truck,' Werner's voice says, unexpectedly close to her ear. The door on that side opens.

'Why?' There is a hand now on her arm.

146

'Get out.'

There is a heavy bang on the metal behind her head. 'What you doing there, boss?' Mathew's voice sounds urgent. 'Why you want her out of that truck for?'

Werner doesn't answer him. Why would he? Mathew can't move far. The hand on Briony's arm is now tight and hard as a handcuff. She is being pulled. To avoid falling, she pivots on the seat and puts her legs out, then quickly has her feet on the ground. Werner doesn't let go of her. Over his shoulder the first red segment of moon is above the horizon, visible through a gap in the trees. He has the shotgun in his left hand, lifted so it is aimed at the truck, at her, at Mathew behind her.

'Come here with me.'

He has made a bed of branches a few feet from the side of the track. Briony pulls away but the grip of his hand is too strong, far too strong for her.

'If the gracious lady wants to fight with me, she will get hurt, certainly,' he says. 'More hurt than she must.'

'Don't. Don't,' she says, feeling the hand at her skirt.

'Lie.'

What can she do? Struggle and scratch? Mathew is banging and crashing against the grid and the side of the truck, shouting something in a hoarse voice. After a minute or two of that, Werner will kill him with the shotgun. She sits on the pile of branches and makes no resistance when she feels herself pushed into the lying position. And none when the hand comes between her legs.

'You like me, I know this,' Werner says, speaking between breaths like a man on the run. 'You like the fine baron of the green eyes. You watch them. You want it.'

It is soon over. It's stupidly brutal and very brief. She is conscious of a weight, a sharp pain and a horrible sense of invasion, then Werner is away from her and standing up. Lying alone on the branches, Briony feels fouled, sore, and worthless. Something is dead. Mathew is still and silent now except for a rasping sound in his throat as he breathes. At least the two of them, Mathew and Briony, are still alive. This was an accident, a filthy little accident which doesn't rob you of your contempt. She goes back to the truck and climbs in, wishing now, hurt as she is, that Mathew would stop his noise. He wasn't the one penetrated. But even so, she understands. It is because he couldn't help her; the iron round his wrists made him less than a man while she was being made less than a woman of value. And then, too, it must be her fault. No one speaks now. When the engine has started and the truck moves forward again, Briony carefully uses her skirt to wipe away the blood or whatever it is that has trickled down the inside of her thigh. The moon is fully up; you can see for a hundred yards ahead. The light of the truck, pitching up and down with the ruts on the road, fades and shrinks and dies in this brilliance.

When they reach the farm there are no lights on. Werner hands her a key without speaking and disappears behind the house. She turns the key round and round in her hand. It is a small, flat key. Of course – the key to Mathew's handcuff. She gives it to him without looking at him.

'Wait,' he says.

'I'm in a hurry.'

'You take this.' He has put into her hand a folding knife with a wooden handle which she can see in the moonlight, nestling there like a cuttlefish shell off the beach. 'You keep this near you.'

Briony runs into the house, holding the knife tight in her hand. Now she needs water, rivers of cold water in that bath with the long clawed legs, to sluice out all that's been forced between her own.

Sleep doesn't come in its usual sweet, effortless way. Under the net, Briony lies on her back with arms stretched out as if crucified. Dead still. Her mind is empty of everything except that image of the single headlight bobbing up and down, like a child inventing a dance on its own before the age of dirt and guilt.

She must have given him some encouragement, by a smile too many, or a look too long into his green eyes. It must be her own fault, somehow. Such things only happen, between civilised people, because the woman has sent out an unconscious invitation, or a message of provocation received and translated by the man's unconscious. She has never read this anywhere but she knows it because the sense of blame building up in her tells her it's so. Briony tries to move her crucified limbs, to escape the judgement. They are too leaden to shift.

She knows what it was. She knows what she did, the message she sent. A flush seems to rise, slowly and then in a rush, in the dark under the mosquito net, from her feet to her scalp, as she recognises and accepts the part of blame due to her. It was because of Commander Chance – Harry. Think of the animals there in the forest. Think of the baboons, for example. If a female is aroused by a male and the moment is not . . . what's the word? . . . propitiously consummated – obviously the next male to come along senses how the land lies. That was the message the German baron's unconscious decoded – the scent and lie of the land. For the first time, Briony feels a spring of tears well up and over, and feels it run down her cheeks. The gift her nature was getting ready to offer is forfeit to the thief, and the frost.

She finds she can turn and fold her arms about her, and draw her legs up against her stomach. The foetal position, they say. A new dread comes in where only blame was, a moment ago – supposing . . . no . . . it was over too soon, surely . . . and after all, not so far in, she thinks . . . but still supposing? And she went straight to the bathroom and washed and washed and went on even when Anne banged on the door – but the invisible worm works fast.

And she is alone in Rhodesia. Douglas in his strange way, diffident and impulsive, is her only friend, but hardly for this. Within a month, she will know. But she won't know what to do, all the same, and then there'll be only Anne to turn to if the worst comes to the worst, and she certainly doesn't feel very sure of Anne. No more has been said about Anne's need of an abortion. Briony suspects that of being just another manoeuvre, juggling with myth for the sake of some kind of power. Where is Mathew, now? Her worst feelings are for him, the impotent witness, as if it was a violence against him more than her. She thinks back. Werner saw something, guessed, smelled something out between Mathew and her. A familiarity. He did what he did to punish a familiarity he couldn't tolerate.

No, she can't accept it. Werner must have been victim of a compulsive attraction, it's the only bearable explanation. Without it, she is reduced even further. She sits up, pulls a corner of the net free, finds the paraffin lamp in the dark on the table near the bed and lights it. Next to the lamp is a Flit spray which you operate by pumping a wooden handle in and out, aiming the gun all round the room and with special attention to the corners. The smell is not unpleasant, though fatal, they say, to mosquitoes.

No, that's wrong too; it had nothing to do with compulsive attraction. It was totally impersonal. Only a man could be as impersonal as that. She was not a *being* to him, she was a gesture. A terrible word comes into her head – she was no more than a gold-pit in the crease of a hill; a hole in the earth.

She must read something, anything. She picks up *A Guide to Rhodesia*. There is a chair with a wicker seat, cool under her when she sits. She finds the place where she last left off reading, about the Matabele Rebellion.

There is no evidence to show that the rule of the British South Africa Company was harsh or cruel, or that the settlers

150

ill-treated the natives. Native Commissioners were stationed all over the country ... missionaries too, have testified to the generally kind treatment of the Kaffirs by the white population. The rebellion, therefore, cannot be said to have been caused by any cruelty towards the natives.

... the climax was hastened by three definite circumstances. The first of these was a matter of superstition. The religion of the Matabele is based on spirit worship; and witchcraft and prophetic oracles exercise a powerful influence over the native mind. Just before the rebellion the voice of a spirit was said to be heard making utterances from a cave in the Matopo hills ... and prophesied that the white men would be wiped off the face of Matabeleland. A total eclipse of the sun had just taken place, and this was a sign that the white man's blood would be shed. The second of the circumstances referred to was the withdrawal of the whole of the white police force ... and the white inhabitants being in the minds of the Matabele defenceless, the moment for striking a blow had come.

Striking a blow. She lets the book fall on to her knee. The story it tells, the explanations, the excuses, are all part of a man's view of the actions that count. If it had been an eclipse of the moon, the sign it gave would have been different, things might have turned out otherwise – without the unequal, gruesome battles of rifle and Maxim gun against assegai, not so many women and children massacred, perhaps no villages put to the torch. But the angry sun is always king and loves these things.

Sleep, at last, is approaching, six hours flowing like smoke from the dark corners of the room, the friend she needs. Briony turns the little wheel of the paraffin lamp so it flickers and dies too, then manages to crawl back into bed in the dark while the image of pillow and sheets is still on the retina of her mind's eye. The air is charged with Flit, the mosquito net hangs loose, it's a warm night. Harry told her that quite soon the nights will be hot, too hot to sleep indoors. Do mosquitoes fear the stars? Or does Flit work even out in the . . .

Douglas has an unwelcome but not unexpected visitor. His wife. She has long wanted and begged for a divorce. However, she is the one in the wrong. And Douglas's principles do not allow him to go to a court and accuse his wife of adultery; his principles, or his pride, definitely prevent it. They sit in the chapel under the roasting corrugated iron, with the lawyer who, as agreed through the post (above all not over the telephone), is to advise them.

Mrs Cathcart rises from her knees. The prayer she has been offering up was a long one. It needed to be. She is a sinner who means to go on sinning. She lives, Douglas has been told, with a rich man in Johannesburg, or at least in the next-door house to him. Douglas has never asked for information and she has never asked for money. Her dress is made of silk, her scent is probably French. All Douglas's pain and disgust – faint but revived – can't prevent his body from reacting to her in the old familiar way. Not actually so familiar, now that there's something new, a fresh, clean element in his lonely imagination.

'Your wife is well aware that she has let you and the Mission down, Dr Cathcart,' the lawyer says.

'Only the Mission matters.'

'You mean in the eyes of God?'

It isn't actually what Douglas means. He means in his own eyes. 'Of course.'

'But for the eyes of the law, she is more than ready to take the blame.'

'I blame no one. It's a hard life, here.'

'Then perhaps you would consider the necessary legal steps to liberate you both? The process is so much simpler in the absence of children.'

That, of course, was the difficulty. She didn't want them. In fact, she shouldn't have any; she was made by nature to be some fool's decoration. And what a fool he was, to bring a woman like that to the heart of the highveld, where women do most of the work and wear bright cotton, not shot silk. Douglas's thoughts go to the connection of Mrs Shitofo and Dr West. That, if you can free yourself from the old, narrow ideas, was beautiful. His body's reaction, the futile urge, has subsided. He looks at Mrs Cathcart and the lawyer in turn. They are hanging there, suspended on his next words, and she doesn't look so proud of herself in scent and silks now, in her apologetic, hopeful submission. That makes Douglas feel more cooperative. And since the bitter day when after many smaller betrayals she first went off, he has learned a lot from his beloved Africans, those people unpuritanical by nature but who seem respectful of Puritans – perhaps because they respect anything so difficult as to be fairly thought impossible. Or perhaps because of the magical powers the pure store up, unlike everyone else. Well, as it happens, Douglas has had enough of that kind of respect. He only comes into the chapel nowadays when he needs to have a private conversation. A light has gone out in his firmament; but low down on the horizon is the early hint of another, more human, more within reach. Faith has burned away, but there is movement in the ashes. In place of the expensive silk from Johannesburg he sees the cotton frock bought by Miss West in Gatooma.

'I agree,' he says. 'We will free ourselves while there's still life in us.'

His wife gives him a hard look. 'You got yourself interested in something on the side, Douglas?' she asks in her characteristic vulgar manner.

'You should be grateful if I had.'

'I am.'

The lawyer clears his throat. 'It's an oven, in here,' he says. He turns to Douglas. 'Mrs Cathcart asks for nothing and is willing to play the guilty party.'

'I should think so,' Douglas says grimly. 'And it's no play.'

'Then the case will come up in the South African court in about a month from now. This meeting, we're all agreed, never took place. No one knows Mrs Cathcart came here. No collusion, in other words.'

'That's all right with me,' Mrs Cathcart says.

'You won't be staying here, whatever you do, will you?' the lawyer says.

'I don't think there's a spare place for me under Douglas's thatch,' she says, and laughs her vulgar laugh that Douglas liked so much, once. 'You can drop me in Gatooma.' Just before she climbs into the lawyer's car she turns her head and smiles at Douglas a last time.

'Whoever can she be, out in this hole?' she asks. She jerks her head in the direction of the surrounding forest. 'Not one of . . .?'

Douglas gives no answer. His mind is empty. A pure, echoing vacuum.

Werner hasn't appeared at meals for several days. Harry says there's a lot of work on the farm at the moment and at night, of course, there is the bar at Chakari. Briony has caught sight of him a couple of times in the distance, always moving the other way. It makes her still more afraid of him; her body shrinks into itself at the distant sight of him. A lurking animal is likeliest to strike.

At first, she thought she must get away from the farm, but that didn't last long. She found that too much of her was tied up here, too many questions, about experience, about herself. Now she knows it's only here that the answers will come, one way or another. In the New Forest and at Hythe, not even questions ever came. The lake of emotions she contained remained flat as a mill-pond, without ripple or reflection but filling up all the time. Now the emotions are whipped into a tide, streaming this way and that, blind and fierce. Perhaps it's not so much Werner she's afraid of, with his flash of lust, as herself, and the long anger building up.

There is no one to share either fear or anger with. The questions and the guilty shame are secret. On the very first day . . . after . . . in the early morning, she saw Anne and Werner together, talking. They were out on the area of grass known as the lawn, a space about the size of a tennis court but round and with flower beds full of zinnias in every colour of the rainbow. Ghastly, actually. They were talking low, with the sort of brief exchange like telegrams that only people who understand one another well can safely use. Briony knew at once for sure what she already suspected, that it would be no good talking to Anne; and mercifully ten days later she found she wasn't pregnant. A copious flux, as if the body rejected the outrage on it. The emotional tide eased a little. She didn't need to see a doctor, though in fact even a doctor to talk to would have been better than nothing. Relief makes her feel more kindly about Anne – perhaps it wasn't a neurotic manoeuvre hinting at abortion that evening which now seems so long ago, just premenstrual fears.

And then, Harry Chance. There the tide runs and runs again. He goes about the lands on his horse, Xerxes, his long legs reaching straight down to distant stirrups, his head with its coating of black hair under the felt hat with the broad silk ribbon. Briony once picked the hat off a chair in the sitting room and looked inside. 'Lock & Co, St James's Street', the label said. Her heart swelled within her. Now she knew something really personal about him; she could imagine St James's Street and the men more or less like Harry going in and out of the premises of Lock & Co, ducking their heads at the lintel and then making their way to their clubs to drink whisky and make bets. But none of them his equal, on Xerxes, with his long legs.

When he looks at her now, it's a new wound. He looks with patient

but determined longing, like a dog. And what held her back before –
the hesitation, the hanging on to the questionable virgin's gift like
the chancy pearl in an oyster – has gone; but she can't tell him that,
not even with her eyes. The reason would be enough to devalue her
fatally in his, where she would see it, because of course the woman is
responsible, in the end. She provokes, by definition. She arouses. She
has mainly herself to blame for whatever befalls her.

With Mathew, she exchanges glances without words. She is sure
that what he will read in her glance corresponds to what she can
easily read in his – pity. They are both under a burden of injustice.
Mathew has had his country stolen from him, and she her gift. She
thinks back to Mrs van Breda on the *Edinburgh Castle*, warning her to
be careful in Africa. Mrs van Breda is someone she could perhaps
have spoken to now, because she is worldly. Anne may be worldly
too, though Babs was less sly. But there is no way of finding her.
Briony understands to the full what it means to be thrown back on
your own devices.

There is a circular swimming-pool built up like a giant chamber pot
from the ground and Harry has decided it's time to fill it. All the
water on the farm is pumped from wells, the nearest river, the
Nyabongwe, being three miles away and dried up and full of frightful
bilharzia when it rains. The amount of shouting that seems to be
needed to get the water pumped in sufficient quantities to fill the
pool is prodigious. Listening to it from the veranda, Briony realises
that much of it is a joke; Harry shouts so much, and threatens and
waves his fists, because he knows this country belongs to the Shona,
the Zezuru people, and he feels, no doubt without actually working it
out, that clowning and pretence make it somehow less of an outrage
in their eyes and his own. That is what's good about him, in spite of
everything that isn't. She watches and listens, fascinated. He seems
quite fluent even if the same words are often repeated. Those will be

swear words, no doubt, because men like them, whatever their language or race. Now he has stopped shouting and joking and is walking towards her. She wishes she had left the veranda before he noticed her. She feels her own presence, in her clean, cool clothes, like a stain on a sheet.

'Come and help,' he says. The smile that goes with this suggestion is strained, hardly a smile at all, and his eyes are unhappy. 'You can hang on to the hose.'

Briony gets up from the step she was sitting on. Dangling above her head from a beam of the veranda is a canvas sack full of boiled water. The magic of evaporation keeps it cool and Harry looks terribly hot, under his Lock headgear. She has a glass in her hand and fills it from the canvas sack and offers it.

'Do you know you haven't spoken a word to me for days?' he asks.

'Yes.'

'Why?'

There is no possible answer. Because she disgusts herself? Because she has grown too angry to speak in a steady voice to any man? He is standing close as he drinks the water, very close. She can smell him. The smell of horse and man and heat. The muscles of his throat contract and expand and she can hear the water go down. It's as if she is inside him. 'I wanted to,' she says.

'Well then?'

'Sorry.' Words seem less important, have less meaning, when your whole body sends out, can't help sending out and receiving, messages like this. Just the word, 'sorry', is a volume. She spares a guilty thought for Anne, and the thought becomes a lightning of revelation as she pictures Werner and Anne together, talking, their heads close. She knows, she's sure, it was Anne who planted the seed in Werner's imagination in the first place – 'think what that would be like . . . see to your passenger', Briony remembers her saying. Anne wanted him to do what he did. Why? The answer to that question also comes as a revelation. She wanted it because she already knew that Harry was in love with the victim.

'When?' Harry has taken off the hat and holds it towards her.

'Soon. Oh soon.' And when soon turns into now, he will find out that she has no pearl to give him. Well, why should she have? What right? Why? Only because she so longs to have it still for him.

'When, then?'

They insist, like that, questions, pressure, always. The whole world is run on the fuel of their insistence. 'I don't know,' Briony says.

'Oh, for Christ's sake.'

'Sorry. Honestly.' She is conscious of something being slowly restored to her, only a remnant of what once was, but as it returns she realises how till now she'd thought the whole of it stolen for ever. Power, is what is returning – to dispose of herself, withhold herself, choose. 'Not here.' She looks back at the windows of the house.

'Of course,' Harry says. 'No, of course not. I'll think of somewhere.' His brow knits under the Lock brim. The mouth covering prominent teeth is determined. He looks divinely reflective and he will certainly think of something. Oh yes. Briony is divided between laughter and . . . what? Anger, or disgust, with laughter overtaking it when she should be reflecting on consequences and how to avoid them. For the moment, she's safe. She doesn't say anything because they don't know one another well enough for the words that would convey to him the limiting condition of the time of the month, but he's no longer thinking of desire, she can see that; his body, his eyes, are less tense. He is working it out. He puts a hand on her arm, a long, brown hand with knuckles like knots. 'I have the message,' he says. 'Shall we give it a day or two?'

You'd think he was talking about a sailing or a tide or some reading on his sextant. Even so, nothing in her rises up against him. Suppose he was smoother, wouldn't that just be another way of keeping you in your place? She prefers the sextant and the knotty hand; she melts, foolishly, under it.

'I'll see,' she says. 'Perhaps I should really go back to the Mission. Dr Cathcart . . .' Briony allows herself a pious lie, 'really is the only friend I have in Africa.'

She sneaks a look at Harry. It is rewarding. His black eyes are moist. 'Nonsense, girl,' he says. 'You have me. I am your best friend here.' Need has turned to protection. Demand has become supply. Briony wonders if men criticise their behaviour, internally, as she is criticising hers. She knows she is exploiting his desire not only to meet her own, but as an antidote to the disgust which cannot be her fault. It's as if his desire will clean her, not soil her further. But she feels sure that men think of nothing but what goes on in their . . . well, their heads, where desires spring from – or should that be the heart? Either way, men, wanting something, think just of that. It's a mess, really. In nature there's no equality; nature is only brutal imperatives.

Mathew has something to say to her. He is refilling the canvas water-sacks on the veranda but watching her as she walks back from the swimming-pool. She must pay an urgent visit to the little house. The pool is full of icy-cold water and it will be days before she even thinks of getting into it, if she ever does. Her body feels more in need of cover than exposure, she feels she is liquefying under the influence of the moon's phases and her emotions' tides.

Mathew looks carefully around him before speaking. His movements, even when he is being distant, are fluently expressive, everything getting full value.

'This is a bad place,' he says in a low voice. 'You should go away and leave this bad place for ever.'

Briony has no need to think before answering. 'I can't,' she says.

He looks hard at her. When he's not smiling, his eyes are very hard. Mathew in that vein frightens her. 'Why can't you?'

'Because of you.'

He shakes his head. 'I'm no good for you,' he says. 'You are not African. Already Africa has hurt you. You will have more, much more hurt if you stay here.'

He has changed towards her, she can easily sense it. She is less in his eyes than she was. She thinks she understands that. Everything here is a war, a long, slow war, and everyone must move with it. The wounded are left behind, especially the women. 'I'm going to stay,' she says.

'Because of the Commander?'

'Because of you,' she says again. 'Because of Werner and you.' She sees suddenly that she has brought Mathew harm, not good. 'I know he'll try and kill you.'

Mathew shakes his head. 'I think it's because of the Commander, and that's how you'll be hurt. With him.' He turns away from her, starts to walk back into the house with the empty kettles for the boiled water, then stops. 'And the Baron. You think it's finished for you with just one time? Longer you stay on this farm and more times he will come. A man or a dog, he has it, he wants it again.'

'I will be very careful.'

'You get a gun, that's what you do. You have a knife, now you go to Gatooma and you buy a gun. And tomorrow, after breakfast. I tell you a few things.'

When he has passed through the door, Briony breaks into a run to reach the little house in time. In broad daylight there's no fear, whether of men or snakes, as inch by inch on her own horizon she feels a rim of bright daylight returning.

A letter has arrived, forwarded from Speck's to the Mission and on to here. Pencilled on the back of the envelope is a cross and the initial, D. The letter was first posted in London, W1.

Dear Briony,

Well! I must say, you of all people, a true spade for a brother! Actually, I've got three of them at home myself and I can tell you they're a pretty damn big nuisance for me more than anything else, and expensive for Dad to keep them in the style they want to be accustomed to. Fast cars, slow horses, and girls who stick like limpets.

But yours will be different, out there in the bush. A real man. Just don't get in your head that he'll be proud of having a little white sister. It's your old Jo telling you that.

Yesterday another boy asked me to marry him! What d'you think? That's the fifth, I've kept count. But I won't do it, I'm sticking with Dad till the real right one comes along. Have you lost your virginity yet, Briony, out there? Ages ago it was of course for me but I always thought you were going to be among the late starters.

Write again and tell me when you have, and how it was.

Love and best of luck, Jo.

The letter, a couple of days ago, would have made her laugh, it would have excited her. But she doesn't feel she knows Jo quite well enough to answer her question. How do you put shame into a letter to someone you haven't seen for more than two years? So Werner has done this too – he has wrung the neck of her correspondence with the one point of contact she had in the world away from the scene of the crime.

Nine

UNTIL THE DROUGHT breaks, trees seem to plead for water with bare arms stretched to the sky. Harry loves to say that there's an abundance of beautiful water, but a long way down. Now the pale leaf is on the mopane again, crawling with edible caterpillars they call worms; but all the rest of the forest is like bones in the desert. A bush fire rages some miles away and the delicious, destructive smell of smoke parches the air you breathe. Wherever a fire starts, animals go on the move, the quick ones going furthest and leaving last like the people at a party who have a car; but tortoises know when a fire is coming and they start their pitiful lumbering exodus well in advance of the first flames. Two days ago a huge one appeared overnight near the cattle grid, like a boulder fallen out of the darkness.

The wireless is on in Harry's office and Briony can hear it from outside. She is waiting for him and they're going riding. It is a broadcast from London being relayed from Salisbury, something to do with the Prime Minister, but she is not interested in prime ministers and she switches herself off while the sound continues without her. All of that belongs to the world she gave up with relief long, long ago after Father died. Until then, the wireless was always turned on in the house under the dripping cedars, poor Father ever hoping to receive short-wave broadcasts from Africa, from anywhere in Africa. Perhaps in his heart of hearts he never got over Mrs Shitofo.

One day Mathew told her some of the things he wanted her to know. He is less respectful than he used to be. She hated the respect because it was false and kept them apart, but she regrets it now, knowing why it's less – she is a damaged woman, she has lost value, not consciously, no of course not, but value goes behind that. And he knows that he is no longer the only reason, or even the main reason, for her presence here; he sees her for what they say women always are – moved by the tide of their feelings and too weak to swim against it.

'The white men tell lies,' Mathew said that day. 'If I am Dr West's boy I can say this, all right? I am half a white man. They think Africa is their home. They own Africa, they have maps of everywhere, the smallest village, except the ones they don't know about. But soon there will be no more room in the forest for all these white men and their women.' His eyes, African eyes when Mathew is living the African past, now gaze into the future. 'We have our own kings for hundreds of years and we don't need King George, who never comes here even once.' He smiles. 'You see, Dr West taught me some history.'

'I understand.'

'You can't understand.'

But she took Mathew's advice about one thing. She borrowed Anne's lightweight rifle and now keeps it, loaded, in her bedroom.

'What do you want it for, darling?' Anne asked. She had gone back to calling her darling, for a time.

'You don't come out any more and I'm going to shoot at targets on trees, to learn.'

'I expect Harry will teach you some lessons.' Nowadays Anne is getting a lot of migraines, and when Harry is out in the afternoons she draws the curtains of her bedroom and locks the door. Briony knows, because she once tried it, very gently. Locked tight.

Briony doesn't question – any more than they seem to – the situation they've settled into as if a hand of cards has been dealt round. That makes it sound too definite; it's more like the misty, clinging, elusive folds of a fallen mosquito net that you fight with though it's no adversary. You fight to control the net that clings to your contours like a lover.

She does go out with the rifle from time to time, down beyond the maze to the polo field. At one end is a fallen tree beside a huge ant hill, and that's what she practises shooting at. She finds it exciting. It's a freedom she would never have had at home – imagine a woman blazing away with a rifle in a field at Hythe! But now Hythe is not home any more. Nowhere is home. She is a woman without price, at large, turned loose like a scapegoat with the sores of her blemish.

The wireless has been switched off. That means Harry will come and find her soon and they will ride through the trees to the Baring farm. You can canter along the paths and it takes less than half an hour. The Barings are in England and Harry is supposed to be keeping an eye on the place.

'Josh Baring isn't a real farmer. Hasn't got land in the blood, he comes here to shoot big game. Calls his place a ranch. There's nothing over there to keep an eye on except the house boys, and they're all too busy copulating in the compound to do any work. The house is empty, it'll be our Rhodesian corner of paradise.' That's how Harry explained the situation after their first time, in the maze. The maze is between the house and the compound; Harry made it for the children, he says, but really it was an exercise for his own ingenuity. It's made of tightly bound mealie stalks in dense bundles seven feet high, held in place by stakes, so you can easily change the whole configuration by shifting a few bundles of mealies and hide from someone who thinks they know the way in. At the heart of it you're quite private; you can hear them wandering about, lost. That was how it happened with them the first time, on the ground, among the ants.

She was afraid, that first time, of being hurt again. She couldn't know how her own body would react, but he was very gentle and spoke the words of love you want to hear, however much or little they mean. He wanted their feelings and their pleasure to be the same, he said. Of course that could hardly be, but for Briony the intention, the tender intention, was everything. If he noticed, in his urgency, that she was not a virgin, he didn't let it show; and actually she knows that he did notice. There was an instant of surprise, and a wider smile, and a touch more urgency. But Harry is first and foremost a gentleman, after all.

The Barings must be rich. Their house is far more comfortable than the Chance house; there are water closets and a septic tank, for one thing, and it is on two floors, for another, which looks strange in Africa, with a staircase, as in Speck's Hotel. 'Judy Baring considers a house on one floor is a bungalow. She has no taste for Africa. Attractive little thing, though. Bit common.' Even when he says things like this, Briony's heart plays to the sound of his voice. It seems Judy was once Anne's great chum. And the bedroom Briony and Harry use has an electric fan and a huge double bed with a spring mattress; and various appliances in a drawer. Briony, for her part, trusts to luck and the bidet in Judy's bathroom. The Barings have no children, which is rather reassuring anyway. Harry says that the unsprung mattresses at his farm, made of hair, have to be opened up and teased out and unflattened every year by an old man who travels round from European farm to European farm (not to the Barings, though) to do only that. Briony is reminded of a poem she read at school – 'The Leech Gatherer', or something unpoetic like that. 'From pond to pond he roamed, from moor to moor', that's all she can remember, but it sounds a bit like the life of the Rhodesian mattress-teaser, scratching an unlikely living.

A bit after the limit of the polo ground is a huge muwanga tree with the small grave of the Chances' middle child under it. Harry raises his hat as he canters past it. The canter turns to a gallop for the last stretch to the Baring place, along an avenue of eucalyptus with peeling trunks and feathery branches, long curved leaves like blades scattered against the background of the sky. They tether the horses to a gate with a bucket of water on the ground between them, and run indoors. When she left England could she possibly, in her farthest fantasy, have ever imagined something like this? Her own nakedness which she had been so careful with, so chary of, making such happiness? At least for him. Because hers, even after these months of trial, still has a check on it. She cannot approve the fierceness of her enjoyment. She feels she should be ashamed of it, that her reactions ought to be more moderate than they are. She should shrink away, after Werner, but she doesn't. Casting back in her mind, she can't even feel the revulsion properly any longer. Either it has faded, or she wasn't truly revolted. It's as if the humiliation set her going, and you can't allow yourself to feel completely happy if that's your psychology, can you? She thinks of her mother, and shuts out the image.

Harry's legs make her laugh, inwardly. Out of the trousers, they are so straight and thin, yet very strong, and she knows he wishes they were thicker, like a rugby player's. In the Navy, he says, they called him ninepins. 'There was a midshipman in the *Lion* at Jutland called Molyneux killed on the deck beside me,' he told her once. 'Head blown clean off. Disappeared completely into thin air. All I saw was the end of his neck.'

Those experiences perhaps made him tougher, the thin, muscular, bony legs capable of galloping about the deck under German shells, but they also make him more seemingly callous, Briony has come to think. A pretence of callousness, rather. Fear of pain and death had to be suppressed, and sensitivity to others was supposed to go the same way because men are not sensitive and women – well, they're not to be taken too terribly seriously. Actually, he is extremely sensitive. He cannot bear that her skin be burnt by the sun or the inside of her thighs chafed by the stirrup leathers. He suffers agonies at the sight of the least bruise or blister on her body. 'Does it make it any better if I do this?' he asks, leaning down to the afflicted part so his head is below her.

Today doesn't seem to be going as hypnotically as usual. He is distracted so Briony feels like an outlet, not a passion, and she can't respond as an outlet; her desire has to be a reflection, an echo of his. Today the reflection isn't there and she feels reduced. The pollution from those short minutes with Werner returns in full force. It seems that only Harry's concentration on her can make her forget it.

'What's the matter?' he asks abruptly.

How can she say what the matter is? They are supposed to know. Their hands are supposed to find out. But it isn't a thing that hands could find out, it's in the heart, or somewhere. It's burned into the body memory. So she must give an elusive answer.

'You were thinking of something else,' she accuses.

'How could I?'

'I can tell.'

'What nonsense. It's impossible to tell what anyone's thinking,' Harry says manfully. It wasn't guessing what the other fellow was thinking that lost the Battle of Jutland, he has told her that himself, in humorous mood, showing the scars of his wound. Nothing to the wound of Midshipman Molyneux, though, thank God. Harry's is a long white scar on his left shoulder, at the back. And the wound left in his mind. Like that, they each of them have one.

'I know something's worrying you. Was it bad news on the wireless?' She tries hard to bring her mind back from Rhodesia, with its joys and fears, to Europe, where she knows things are not going well. If the word 'war' is spoken at the Chance farm, Anne suffers an immediate onset of migraine headache.

'My brother was killed in the Irish Guards in 1917,' she moans, as if that in itself rules out any further war. The word is spoken all the same. Harry and Werner laugh about it, like gentlemen before the engagement at Jutland.

'Has something bad happened?'

'I think it's coming,' Harry says. It never takes much for his mood to change, and now his mouth is drawn back hard, without opening, over the barrier of his teeth so that the lips are tight with unhappiness. Briony's heart dissolves. She thinks again of Midshipman Molyneux, headless in an iron floating grave. What if it were all to start again, the maiming and killing and separation?

'What do they say?' The fan above the bed revolves with a swish-swish like a horse's tail chasing off flies. Looking up, you can see the hub of the fan rock alarmingly from side to side as if the whole thing, like the map of Europe, is about to fall on you.

'The German army is massing near the border of the Danzig Corridor. We will mobilise.'

'You . . .?'

'The bloody Admiralty knows where to find me, and by God, they'll find me all right. The Admiralty is always number one at digging up the dugouts. That's why Baring went back; he isn't waiting for it, he's going to America where he's got cousins. And financial networks, for all I know.'

To Briony, all that is really just Harry's depression of the moment, and hardly surprising, considering Jutland. But she knows him, now. The mood will swing the other way so fast you feel dizzy with the oscillation. She lays a finger on his throat, runs it down the centre of his chest, slowly across the flat stomach. 'It may never happen, Commander,' she says.

'Oh it will, it will. And I'll never come back to Africa, and my loves, and you, and the farm.' His sorrow sounds so hopeless that she forgets her own, for what she was and what has been made of her.

Briony is aware for the first time of an element other than love in the way he folds her. He has often said it was love alone and she let herself believe that, because love is a remedy and faith absolves, so Father said until he lost his own. Today, Harry folds her with desperation as if for the first time ever – in Malta as a midshipman, say, or Port Said. And behind that, she can sense something else. He wants something else, a thing settled into his mind and which he says nothing about, like a hidden, shameful idea ruling you. She can see how it could be for a prostitute having to accommodate herself to an idea ruling in the back of a client's head, wanted for something other than herself. Wanted, if you can call it that, as a blank screen for the slides of a man's archaic fantasy. Before Werner, Briony could never have put herself into a poor prostitute's downtrodden shoes, but she can do it now, quite easily.

Suddenly, out of the blue, with his hand resting on her, he asks, 'Who was it?'

'It was your manager.'

'You must be a very modern girl, taking the manager before the boss,' Harry says sadly.

'It was a very old-fashioned rape.'

There is a pause. 'Yes, I thought as much. How terrible, terrible. Why did you never say anything?'

'I was too ashamed.'

'We'll get rid of the swine.' His voice shakes but she doesn't think he will. The awful thing is that he sounds as if he secretly prefers it that way. It leaves him sole master of the field; she has never gone willingly with anyone but him. But she is a woman and they are men. You have to accept nature or deny it, and Briony can't do that. She can only engage with him deeper, to hold and keep him.

Afterwards they walk slowly along between the eucalyptuses in the direction of home, leading the horses. 'We'll mount when we come to the bush,' Harry said when he handed her the rein. Apart from that, he doesn't say anything. He's as silent and distracted as if he'd forgotten all about what they have been doing. Love and its language are put away, but not on her side, oh no. She's the slave of his love. Without it, she is just the young woman who got herself raped between the Mission and the Chance farm.

'When d'you think the new war may start?' she asks. War seems unreal, far off, a thing for other people, not for lovers under the eucalyptus leaves. If only he would remember that and love her again. But you must never ask for it, it's like praying for rain. Rain and love must come on their own, in their own time.

'Within months – days, it doesn't matter. So soon it's the same thing.'

'Don't you care to go back to sea?' What a stupid question. If there's a war Harry won't be going to sea to enjoy it, he'll be going to get himself killed by the enemy.

But it makes him laugh for the first time that day. 'Actually I can manage the sea, but I loathe it. My friends and I, we were sent to Dartmouth because that was where George V sent his boys to be knocked about a bit. George V was a naval man. That's the only reason I was at Jutland – what was good enough for the King and his sons was good enough for us.'

Briony stays silent. The mare has its head over her shoulder, its mouth near her ear as they walk. She can smell the delicious breath and skin and hair of horse, and turning her head, she sees the great eyes a foot away from her own. No place for unhappiness in them. Unhappiness in the eyes only follows after human love. If he could just love her as he did, once more . . . The longing thought repeats itself, endlessly. They have reached the edge of the forest, where two paths divide in front of them among the trees. She can't remember which they came on and Harry hesitates as if he can't remember either, but he must know. She mounts and waits. The mare is hardly even restless, waiting too.

'We'll go this way,' he says at last, and even as he says it Briony knows it isn't the way they came. It leads off at a wide angle from the other path. It must go somewhere quite else than the farm but she won't question him; she must show trust, or love will never return. She leads the way along the new path at a trot, then at a canter as it widens out into a track, with Harry close behind. Soon he overtakes her, Xerxes charging heavily forward into the bush like cavalry in the Middle Ages, to the sound of his habitual flatulence booming through the forest in the quiet of the afternoon heat when all Africa sleeps. Except for the mad Commander, his horse and his wretch.

It's because of the unvarying heat and changeless sky that you don't notice how fast the afternoon sun drops towards the level of the higher hills in the distance. Now it hangs above the kopje in front of them as the track swings round. In an hour it will be dark. First, the brief bloody drama of the sunset; then, abruptly, the drama of the stars.

'This is it,' Harry says, his horse halted just in front of her and half turned her way.

'What is it?'

'The mine.'

At the foot of the granite kopje is a breach in the trees, and a deep open wound in the ground. Boulders on either side of it are like monuments before the burial place of kings. But if this is a mine, it would be slaves buried here; she has read the figures of deaths in the gold mines given in *A Guide to Rhodesia 1924*, and with allowance made for the understatement everywhere in that work where it's a question of the sufferings of the native population, she knows that half, at least, of the men working in gold mines died in gold mines. She mustn't say anything, though. He will never come back to her the way he was if she says anything. He will know her for a troublemaker like a turbulent sea and the last spark will go out.

'It isn't worked any more, is it?'

'Of course not, you can see that. It's half blocked up by trees.' He sounds impatient, but then his tone changes. 'Can you guess whose mine this is, my girl?'

Is that a glimmer of tenderness? Or mockery? 'I expect it's yours,' she says.

'No. This mine belongs to you. Have you forgotten I told you about it?'

There are no fences or posts to mark the end or beginning of anyone's property here. The idea of property seems absurd in the heart of Africa. They are in an overgrown clearing with giant ant heaps like red pyramids in the dying sun, standing among the surrounding trees before a hole in the earth which Harry says is hers. It makes no sense, it means nothing. Who owns the sand of the desert? The Jutland waves? Looking down, she sees a great black millipede, ten inches across, coiled up like an ammonite near the mare's off-side front hoof. She doesn't mean the mare to shift but it happens and the millipede, using the only defence it knew, is destroyed in a second. Briony can smell its strange death odour from the saddle – hydrocyanide, Harry told her it was.

'I'm glad no one goes down it any more, then, to get crushed.'

'Well they should,' Harry says. 'I've been down it and I know. This mine touches on an extremely rich quartz reef. Whoever was working it must have stopped very suddenly about fifty years ago, I'd say. They were probably attacked.'

'Why would they be attacked?'

'Because that kopje is a burial place. There's nothing more danger-ous than disturbing a burial place. I can understand that; my people are all buried in a vault in Yorkshire and I wouldn't want anyone digging holes under them, poor souls. Still, if . . . if there was a reef there . . .'

A vault. Briony thinks of Father under his plain stone, no cross, in the churchyard at Hythe. She should have scattered his ashes in the Solent, in the path of the Union Castle ships. A thought strikes her. 'Where's the village from here?'

'Round the other side of the kopje.'

So they are not so far from Douglas's comforting presence, and the Mission – home, to be painfully honest, of a better man. Her mind veers away from the painful thought. So this too was where Father staked a claim for Mathew; he must have known about the burials and the mine, and so must Mathew. Maybe this is where all the Chifodyas come for the last long rest. 'Is there something to mark the graves? I mean the burial place?'

'That big muwanga tree at the top. In this land you always bury important people under a tree. It's what I did with my poor girl; she was buried the African way.'

To the right of the hill, where the ground is level with the horizon, the flaming segment of setting sun shifts and flickers among the trees. The sky spreads every shade of colour imaginable and many more, between the gold of the mine and the black of night. 'Can we go up there and see?'

'Not now,' Harry says, and turns her horse's head with the tip of his riding crop. 'Home. We'll just make it before dark.'

'Don't hit the horse,' Briony says with an alarming presentiment.

'I never hit horses.' The riding crop slashes the air between them. 'It isn't necessary. They do what I want without it.'

Werner reappeared after a time, like a boy counting on long absence to erase all memory of his offence. Not after a decent interval, how could it be that? And not at lunch or dinner, not at first, but about

173

the place again. She saw him in the distance consulting with Harry, and then once near the swimming-pool, apparently in argument with Anne. Briony was too far to hear anything more than a murmur of voices, but the gestures were enough. What could they have to argue about, apart from the international situation, setting Aryan against Aryan, which is never mentioned in the dining room? Werner works for Harry, not for Anne. Of course, it's not a normal work relationship; these are people who recognise each other across any frontiers, they belong to a world one and indivisible. In their homeland they get buried in vaults, not in graves. So Anne and Werner could be arguing like brother and sister, but Briony doesn't think their relationship is close in that way. In another, yes. Anne's hand, hovering in the air between Werner's chest and his cheek, as if uncertain where to strike, said everything that need be said about them. They are lovers, and war will separate them.

The discovery brought back the anger and revulsion, almost forgotten during the time of physical love in the ease of the Baring bedroom, under the swish-swish of the turning fan. But Werner, this lover for Anne, who set him on and whom he can have any time when Harry is out of sight, did once apply himself to the task of raping Briony, and she knows why, of course – it was to teach her not to be familiar with an African, not to have secret relations with a black man. But her anger tells her that in this land the sweet track of revenge may be a simple path in the forest.

Werner gives Anne a stiff little bow, back straight, head lowered. You can practically hear his boots click and Briony would laugh if she didn't have other images of him. Now Anne is drifting back to the veranda, where Briony lies on a deckchair in the shade. Anne wears a big floppy hat and linen trousers, floppy too. Her hands float in a way that doesn't just suggest but demonstrates, by their whiteness and frailty, that they have never been employed for anything useful. She is taking the first careful step up on to the veranda.

'Resting, darling, from your exertions?' she says.

Briony springs up. You couldn't feel guiltier, in spite of what you know and have seen, if you'd stolen the woman's baby. She would offer Anne her help if there was anything to help her with, but the household seems to run itself without a woman's guiding hand. Mathew does everything and Harry occasionally issues some unnecessary, arbitrary stream of orders that Mathew pays not much attention to. 'Yes, Nkosi,' he says, nodding and beaming, and gets on with his work. She has never seen Anne do anything except arrange flowers, in other words the heads of zinnias, in a thin glass jar kept for the purpose on the dining-room table. 'I haven't been out riding today,' she says.

'Haven't you? You must miss it. You've improved a lot, you know. I was watching you go off with Harry. Does he put you over the jumps?' Anne lowers herself into the deckchair Briony has just vacated. 'He must be awfully pleased with your progress, he loves teaching women to ride. He tried to teach me but it wasn't a great success, I'm afraid. That gripping with the knees and rising in the stirrups . . .' It has the feel of a threat; Anne is looking at her from under the floppy brim, a wide-eyed, tactical, scrutinising, exploratory look. 'There's one thing I might give you a word of advice about, darling,' she says. Briony's nerves go tense and her fingers curl up in her closed fists. 'Be more careful about dealing with Mathew. I've sometimes seen you talking together. I don't think it's a very good idea. I love having you here, I don't mind how long you stay and if I did you'd have vanished long ago, but take my word for it, it's better to keep your distance from a native, however handsome he may be. In fact, particularly if he happens to be spectacularly handsome as my Mathew is.'

What does she man, *her* Mathew? For the first time, Briony is jealous of Anne and the prerogatives she claims without claiming them. The woman is a parasite. Africa has no place for women like her. No wonder Harry had that fire lit next to her chair on the first night long ago; he must see exactly how she is. In fact he must have the best of reasons to know what she really is. *My Mathew*. Does that mean the same – or something like – as it seems to mean with Werner? Surely not. And would Mathew . . .? No, he wouldn't. Yes . . . after all he's only a man and he might.

'I'll take more care,' Briony says.

'Sensible girl.' Anne says this in a kind of failing drawl, as if Briony has resolved not to smoke or drink for the new year. 'Be a saint and get me a pink gin from the dining room, will you? And before you ask, quite a big one. I'm cross with Werner.'

So there is after all something she can do to help. Pink gin. Even the smell of it makes her feel sick. She pours a large lashing of Plymouth into a tumbler, shakes the angostura bottle over it, and goes back on to the veranda. The water comes out of the sweating canvas sack hanging from the rafter, always deliciously cool.

'Half and half, and a lot less water,' Anne says, and laughs. Her laugh is a humourless gurgle, a sign of how inimitable she finds herself. 'Mathew knows just how I like it poured.'

'Well he isn't here and it's only me,' Briony says, handing over the tumbler.

Her tone of voice causes Anne to raise her eyes and give her another of those long looks. 'Yes, well, cheerio.' She takes a mouthful of the awful pink mixture. 'Why don't you get yourself something, darling? Ale or something? No?' Another mouthful. Like the first, it is sucked delicately, not to stain or dilute the lipstick. Anne sighs and relaxes in her chair, unwinding as if she's had a hard day to unwind from. 'Another thing, Briony. I want my rifle back, you've had it for ages and I saw a buck from my window yesterday. Will you be a dear girl and fetch it for me? Now that you spend your time riding I dare say you won't be doing static things like shooting at targets any more, will you?'

'Of course, Anne. I'll get it at once.' It's a release. She can leave the mistress of the house on her veranda with her gin, and then quite soon surely Harry will come back in the Ford truck and perhaps they will saddle the horses again . . . go out on the farm or into the forest, boundless as a shifting maze, endless as ideal love.

'And the cartridges, please, all the ones you haven't used. I gave you three boxes.'

'Of course.' It only strikes her as she crosses the dry ground to the cottage that Anne might actually want her left defenceless.

The rifle is not where she put it. She's quite sure, the last time, after cleaning it with the ramrod and pulling it through, she placed the gun sensibly in the wardrobe with her couple of dresses. It isn't there. She stands stock still in the silence, not knowing what to do. Then, from behind her, there is the little shuffling sound of tennis shoes moving on dusty concrete floor. She turns, frightened. Has Werner come for her again?

Of course not, he wears boots, not tennis shoes; this is Mathew. He is holding the rifle in front of him with both hands, in an awkward, unpractised way. They look at each other in silence, wondering. There is a bulge in the pocket of Mathew's immaculately creased trousers. The cartridges. He was taking the gun. Briony's heart gives a painful leap in her chest like an animal shot in flight. He was intending to steal the gun.

'Mrs Chance sent me for her rifle,' she says. She doesn't even address him by his first name. She feels confused, afraid, unsure of herself. Is this brother a thief? She can't believe it. Nor can she entirely believe, in her corrupted head and in this world where myth rules like the line of a hundred kings he comes from, that Mathew is truly her brother. She wants to, but she can't, not now. Something, some attitude, some colouring, has rubbed off on her from being so close to Harry, even if she's not sure just how close to him she really is, or he to her. Perhaps the hard, sad truth is that they're no closer than any of the other animals mating in the bush. But who can say that there's no love in that?

'I told you before, you English girl, you must go away from here and the bad things that must happen here. Go to Dr Douglas. You safe with Dr Douglas, that good man. Safe from bosses, and safe from me.'

'Can I have the rifle, please?'

Mathew shakes his head. 'Women and rifles, they don't go well.' He laughs and she is as amazed as ever by the strength of his teeth. Her own are still young and fairly white, but not like that. He has the teeth of a leopard in a tree. 'Same with Africans like me. Not allowed guns. The white law says we don't go together.'

'What do you want to do with it then? If it's forbidden, it's dangerous for you to have it. It's loaded, too.' She knows about Lieutenant Pienaar and the station at Chakari where offenders are taken and treated in ways too brutal for her to picture to herself. Especially him, probably all the worse because of his . . . of how he looks and what women like Anne think about that.

'You don't know anything now. You must go away, very soon. You know nothing. Nothing at all.' He approaches her, takes one hand off the rifle and puts it on her arm. The familiarity comforts her. Like the swinging of Harry's moods, her own had blocked out the idea of Mathew as brother; now, with this contact, it swings back, bringing a kind of fearful happiness. 'One day,' Mathew says, 'one of these days that are coming to us – you and me we will forget all the bad things between black and white and we are brothers again.'

'And sister.'

'Yes, and sister who doesn't see me with this gun.' Mathew turns away and slips smoothly and quickly as a snake out of the room, disappearing into the region of sheds and storerooms and kennels behind the house where he is the only master. He must have a sleeping cabin there like the one Mrs Shitofo was curled up in at the Mission, until he exercised his kingly authority and removed her to the village on the hill.

Briony returns to Anne on the veranda. 'I think I will have a glass of beer after all,' she says. 'It's getting hot.'

'You've put the rifle safely in my bedroom?' Anne asks sharply, as Briony goes back into the house to fetch the beer. Until she came to Rhodesia, she never drank beer in any circumstances. Some vague, ridiculous sense that ladies don't. Now, she has rather taken to it. It doesn't make you drunk, it doesn't affect your whole personality like gin or whisky, but it enhances the moment, or eases it. She drinks some before going out again.

'I'm sorry, Anne, I can't find it,' she says, returning with the glass in her hand.

'Don't be ridiculous. Of course you can find it. Where did you leave it? I heard you firing it a week ago, I'm sure. You silly fool, you don't think you left it out by the vlei, or on the polo ground? Why did I trust you with it?' Anne sounds agitated. Gin calms some moods and whips up others.

'I don't think so, I'm not sure, perhaps I did. I'd better go and look.'

'Of course you must go and look. Where is Werner? He must go with you. Where's Mathew? He must find Werner and you must go together.' Anne springs up from her deckchair. 'Don't you realise that every firearm must be guarded? I should never have let you use it. A gun in the hands of an African is a crime, and whoever lets an African get his hands on it is a criminal too, for the police. Harry will go mad with rage.'

'And it's your rifle,' Briony says with a touch of spite.

Anne hasn't heard. She is calling for Mathew inside the house.

Briony follows. Anne has gone to the dining room and there are voices. When Briony gets there Anne and Mathew are together, Mathew smiling, soothing, calm.

'Sure I find it soon, madam,' he says. 'I go to the polo field and the vlei with Madam Briony and we soon find your rifle. Don't worry.'

'Oh Mathew, you are wonderful. We won't tell the Commander.'

'No,' Mathew says, looking at Briony beyond. 'Not the Commander.'

'But wait until I find Baron Werner. He'll go with you. You know you mustn't carry a gun. Not even just back to the house.'

'Madam will carry it,' Mathew says. 'The baron boss, we don't need him.' When he speaks like that, offering no smile or soothing voice, he sounds and looks like a judge on the bench. You don't question him, and Anne doesn't do so now.

'Thank you, Mathew,' is all she says, quite humbly, Briony thinks.

They walk side by side, brother and sister, pale and dark, under a sun directly overhead, across the dusty polo field, and into the scrubby wood on the other side.

'We take our time,' Mathew says. 'Looking bloody hard in all the trees for the rifle of the Commander's woman.' He laughs. His arm brushes against her shoulder. 'For a white man, he's a good man with his bloody everything. But no good for you.'

'You've already said so.'

'In Africa, everything is said twice or three times. Four times if it's a woman.' He laughs again. He is excited about something.

What will she say to Anne when they get back? And to Harry, when he learns about it later from Anne, with all the hostile emphasis? Oddly, Briony thinks she has nothing to fear from Harry. He isn't going to decide that their little fling was only a little fling and now is over, and that Briony, committing the unforgivable stupidity of losing a rifle, had better be sent away at last. Why? Because he loves her in his fashion? Her heart breaks at the thought, but that isn't the reason. The reason is the mine. Harry wants it, she knows that. Perhaps it was always all he really wanted. She won't believe it but still her heart breaks again – while the heart lives, it can break as often as the bell can ring on its little platform above the polo ground, for the end of the chukka or the start of a new one.

But the heart breaking so often and regularly gives a certain resilience. It doesn't seem to break for quite so long.

There is some shade under the trees; not from the baobabs that carry their root systems in the air like bones, nor from the parched bush, but a big mopane spreads leaves and branches wide over a space with smooth granite rocks like benches. 'There's something we must talk about, Mathew,' Briony says. 'Let's sit down.'

He brushes the surface of one of the stones with his hand and then regally indicates the swept space. 'No scorpions, you can sit safe.' He is making fun of her, but also looking after her. As a damaged woman she has lost the claim to consideration, but because of Harry she has perhaps earned some of it back. It isn't how things should work, but she believes, and now with more experience she knows, that they work this way. The world runs in male channels of thought like a river between walls. Being Harry's lover restores to her a certain doubtful esteem, because Harry is the great man here, the owner, the boss, the Commander.

'You must sit down too.'

'I will.'

'Is Mrs Shitofo still in the village now?'

'Yes.'

'Were you born in that village, Mathew?'

'I don't know where I'm born. How do you, or anyone, know that? Your mother can drop you on a road, on a path, in a hut. The mother decides what she tells you later, about where you are born. And who is the father.'

There is no denying any of it. Briony has no sure idea of where she first saw the light of day. She thinks it was in Salisbury. She doesn't know. She has no memory of infancy in Rhodesia, only somewhere in the recesses of consciousness an apprehension of strong sun, mastering everything. A black sun. 'You know Dr Cathcart says that village is in danger.'

'Yes. The government must chase the people away into the bush, the parliament says so. That is white land, that village.'

'It's my land.'

Mathew looks at her for a long time before speaking. 'You are white. The Doctor is white, even if he is a father to the boys and the women and he learns to think black.'

'I told him I want to pass that land to you. He's going to find a lawyer to make sure we do it the right way.'

'The right way! The right way is this way – the day I want some of Africa, I take it.' Indignation is making him less of a Mission boy. 'I build a hut. I make some children. You can't give me part of Africa, that village of huts with my mother. You can't give me my mother.' Now his voice quietens, becomes more reasonable. He is still, in a way, making fun of her; he hasn't thought about this seriously, and suddenly she sees that the idea seems to him too fantastic to take seriously. Land-owning capitalism doesn't enter anywhere into his mind as a personal possibility, any more than into hers.

'I didn't mean that. I meant our father bought the land for you.'

Unprompted by any hint or indication from her of a desire for contact, he puts his hand firmly on hers, where it sits on her lap. It is a new, more authoritative familiarity that makes her feel happy. Here, at last, is love that you need not buy or beg for. 'No,' he says. 'He didn't know what he did. He stopped believing in god and he lost his way in the bush. This is what happened to Dr West.'

'Do you believe in a god, Mathew?'

'Not in Dr West's god, no more than him. That god is a white god with too few wives for a god of Africa.' He laughs heartily; the

182

wooden cross which he wears on a thong round his neck bounces up and down against his throat. He is making fun of the whole world. 'Dr West's god is for women. Here we must have one more like a man.'

'What shall I say to Anne about the rifle?'

'You forgot it here and some bloody African stole it. Some African bastard. And the cartridges, he stole those too.'

'What will he do with them, Mathew?'

'I told you all along, some bad things. Like Dr West's god. A god with plenty of wives has no time and is too tired to bother with all those bad things the Christians' god loves to do to poor weak people.'

'And you – have you any wives anywhere?'

'Mathew Shitofo is another one with no time left for having wives.'

Ten

ALMOST ANYONE WOULD say it was a social as much as a moral question. First of all, this is Anne's home and Anne doesn't want her here any more. Anne is furious about the rifle, mainly because it would be an indignity to have policemen on the farm and above all in the house. Perhaps she knows Lieutenant Pienaar and detests him from acquaintance as much as Briony does from repute. Second, Briony's reason for coming was Mathew and Mathew doesn't want her to remain any longer either. That leaves Harry, and the moral side of the question. Harry is determined she shall stay. The moral question turns into one of power. Perhaps that's what they do, left to themselves. In any case, though feeling some sense of old-fashioned shame, Briony hardly considers Anne to be on very solid ground morally speaking. No one here is, apart from Mathew. They have the particular standards of their world, and they judge each other and everyone else according to power principles, not ethical ones. In that way, their butterfly ancestors hung on well and are still hanging on, and not just in Africa. It doesn't seem that Werner had to leave Germany because the class he belongs to lost power; it didn't. He had to leave, Harry now says, because he gambled all his money away. Or got himself into something too dirty even for the Nazis. If he hadn't, presumably he would be there now, getting ready for the new war. Saluting Herr Hitler and wearing his *Mensur* scars like laurels.

'Prussians are very strict, you know,' Harry says. 'Werner is what you might call a bit of an outsider. They're far more brutal with outsiders than we are.' But that isn't why he lets Werner stay on. 'These are the last days of our world, his and mine,' Harry says, and Briony doesn't question that.

Anne, too, might not want to let Werner go. Maybe she's a woman who likes the scars of Junker brutality. Does Harry have any idea about Werner and Anne? Is there anything to have ideas about, or has Briony imagined it all? Is it her own guilt, blaming Anne so she can go on being in love with Harry as she is, angrily, hungrily? If the moral question for them turns into power, for her it gets washed away by emotions, not truly shared, she thinks, by Harry, and she isn't so blind she doesn't understand that. The reasons he won't let her go are the war, and the mine, and the desire which like a thirst she knows easily how to slake. Very well, she will be careful about all three; especially the mine. Being not honestly loved for herself but only desired, needed, gambled on – the mine is her strongest card. Desire, after all, is less personal in action than peacetime lovers would have you believe.

Werner has finally taken his place at the dinner table, next to hers. His behaviour is easy and natural, as though nothing out of the ordinary has ever happened. Before sitting down he tries to kiss her hand; as he lifts it to his mouth in that patronising gesture, his own hand gently supporting hers from below, she pulls it away. He ignores the rebuff. Of course for him anyway it was little or nothing, what happened out there in the bush, and so soon forgotten – *trinken und lachen*. Now he's making Harry laugh with his German accent; they're like boys who know that when they get out into the playing field, or whatever it is, they will quite naturally resume the battles of yesteryear where they left off. Meanwhile they laugh loudly and too much, and at nothing at all. Harry doesn't say anything about the Danzig Corridor. Perhaps it wouldn't suit a gentleman to do so any more than to accuse another of being a rotter and a rapist, until you decide to shoot him down in a ditch, and even then he would still be a gentleman from birth.

Werner claims, with parodies of terror, to have met another snake on the seat of the privy. 'Ach, I go no more to your little house,' he shouts, banging the table in his joy. 'I want not the cobra bite in the bottom.'

'Enough scars down the baronial cheeks already, Werner?' Harry says.

Werner is beside himself at this. 'For the future, I take my baron's cheeks and my pistol into the trees. After the tennis court where no one goes when it is not tennis time.'

'Thank you, that will do,' Anne says. She sounds cool and absent. She doesn't fear snakes, she told Briony so once when they were still on good terms. Harmless, timid things, she said. 'It's men who're afraid of them because they're so alike,' she said. Perhaps, like Briony, she doesn't care for the jokes and all the laughter with the threats behind them, like trees casting an ever longer shadow as the days pass and the dark night comes with its shells and bombs and barbed wire.

Werner's knee brushes against Briony's under the table. His legs must be wide apart to do that, like hers when he took her. It means that touch of his knee is deliberate. She shrinks into a narrower space. With Harry it's love, the requital of the senses; what happened with Werner is really not so important, not now, in this world of the open forest where you let yourself leap like an antelope. But he did hurt her, and that matters, as every burned child knows.

Standing behind, Mathew leans forward to take her empty plate.

'Soon finish now, madam,' he says, almost in a whisper.

'Yes, thank you,' she says, and hears a slight sound like the sketch of a laugh.

'What are you saying there, Mathew?' Anne asks. Sometimes she speaks to him as if he were sitting at the table with them; at others she mentions his name in some context or other as though he isn't in the room at all.

'Guinea fowl tonight,' Mathew says. 'Poor bugger boil a long time in white wine.'

'Oh good,' Harry says. 'Wheel him in.'

'Mathew is getting more like my father's butler Holden every day,' Anne says brightly. 'Holden is forever muttering something incomprehensible. He orates at Speaker's Corner on his day off. Holden is head of his own private religion. We'll have Mathew orating about religion to our groans before you know where you are, won't we, Mathew?'

He isn't there to answer. He has gone like a hospital orderly to fetch the body of the guinea fowl. From experience, Briony knows it will take a lot of cutting and an age of chewing before you can swallow any of it, so thank God for young teeth. She shifts her chair further away from Werner's. The scars are on her side of his face and the sensation that was perhaps pity when she first saw them is now tinged with pleasure. She is shocked by herself. She is seeing the marks on his face as if they were weals left by a whip on a body that deserved it. But the shock passes. The proximity of his knee under the table sheltered by the white damask cloth reminds her that Werner's body does deserve scarring. More than it has yet received.

But some time under the stars, or at first light it might have been, alongside a path and beneath the great sky, Werner gets the scar he deserves. The body is not found for three days. There is only Harry to give orders to the men, and that means getting up at five and spending all day riding about the farm when he has other things to think about. Werner's disappearance is a bloody nuisance, he says. Women trouble, he says. Of course. What else? But Briony, who heard the shot fired in the dawn, puts two and two together and believes it was not women trouble, at least not the way Harry means. It was something like punishment and it makes her afraid. There is such a lot of punishment waiting in the wings already.

Naturally, it's Mathew who reports finding the remains beyond the tennis court, quite a way into the bush. The sand has to be rolled and marked and Mathew is in charge of the boys who do it – real boys, about nine or ten years old. He shouts at them for being lazy and bad at it as the white lines wander across the court, he shouts much louder and more harshly than Harry, but the boys revere Mathew because he was educated at the Mission. They know he can write, it is said he drinks the remains of the white men's drinks when they are too drunk to finish them, he talks easily with the boss's women. Someone, no one is sure who, and now no one will admit it, has seen him with the last, the greatest of forbidden things, a white man's gun. And there behind an ant heap and screened by young fresh leaves of banana, he has stumbled on the remains. They bring Werner into the house in the dressing gown he was wearing, pulled up to cover his face. The sun is going down and the whole sky and all the air are blood red. Werner has been cleanly shot in the back of the neck.

'He was in a squatting position,' Harry says. 'Neat job, apparently. He just squatted a bit closer. I'll miss him, in a way. I'm going to miss his jokes, specially the times when he didn't know he was being funny.'

'Do shut up, you're being horribly obtuse,' Anne says. 'Don't you see what it means?'

'What does it mean?'

'The rifle, the police, the magistrates, or whoever it is. Everyone being questioned for hours.' She is quite cold, quite detached. Briony can see, in the back of Anne's deep blue eye, a void. Something has been taken from her; certainly not love, but something to do with taste, something she cared for on account of the taste it had. 'Searches everywhere. They'll pull your compound to pieces. And the maze.'

Harry is thinking about this. He looks towards Anne at the other end of the table – lunch takes place at the usual time, murder or no murder – with an expression of disdain in his eyes. But nothing is more vulnerable, Briony decides, than black-brown eyes; they can hide nothing. Blue or grey ones are better liars. 'I'm not so sure,' he says at last.

'But obviously,' Anne says with a shrug. 'What else? I don't want them taking the servants away. The house won't run without Mathew.'

Harry waits until Mathew is no longer in the room, then gets up and shuts the door to the kitchen quarters. 'I've thought,' he says, as if this was an entirely original activity, inaugurated by himself. Briony loves him all the more. 'Who knows anything about Werner? I advertised for a manager and he turned up. I took him because . . . well, because he was the first one I've ever had who was a gentleman. One could sit at the same table with him. But of course he was a scoundrel really. Even the German Consulate know nothing about him, he told me so. He was in Africa because Germany wouldn't have him, that's what he claimed. So if he was a spy or an agent provocateur sent to stir rebellion they won't want anything to do with him now he's dead. No need to say anything to anyone. In a few weeks we'll be at war with them and then, frankly, who gives a damn for one German baron more or less?' He has finished. It's true he's been thinking quickly; in fact, he has thought it through from start to finish. Perhaps the Navy teaches you to do that under pain of the plank.

'There are hundreds of natives in the compound. They know about him,' Anne says. 'And then there's . . .' She sketches a movement of her hand towards Briony.

'The compound will never talk, that's where the rifle must be. They'll bury it and they won't want it dug up. It was only stolen for Werner because he was a bit too free with his fists and his riding crop. If you do that they get you in the end, and so they should. As for . . .' In his turn, he indicates Briony, near him. 'Discreet as a nun, aren't you, angel?'

The effort of thought has been too much for him. The careless words slipped out.

'I see, a nun,' says Anne. Her eye is less void than it was a minute ago. The careless words must make her feel isolated, here with the two of them and no Werner any more. Perhaps for the first time she misses her children and wishes they were somewhere closer than their schools in the northern hemisphere. And there's a pinpoint of anger in her eye, too. 'What are you going to do about the body?'

'That's just what I'm thinking about now.'

'Werner had a sister, did you think of that? She ought to be told.'

'No, I didn't know. He never mentioned it. You must have had more confidences with him than I ever did.'

'She lives in a castle in Bavaria.'

'Well I suggest we leave her undisturbed in her Bavarian *Schloss*. Before you can get a letter to her we'll be at war.'

'I leave everything to you,' Anne says finally. 'But get it done quickly, please. In this heat . . .'

When Mathew returns with the pudding, Harry says to him, 'When the moon gets up, you and me, we carry the German boss out into the bush. We never hear any more about him, understand, Mathew?'

'Understood, Nkosi,' Mathew says. 'Vultures leave white bones of black man or white man, same thing in the end.'

'Correct,' Harry says. 'Send everyone else back to the compound.'

Briony feels afraid of what Anne may do next. Perhaps that's why she follows her to her room. She knows that an angry woman is dangerous and she would rather see just how dangerous she is, even with a woman's limited possibilities in this man's country, than wait and find out when she isn't expecting it. Should she knock? Or go straight in? She goes straight in.

'What do you want?' Anne says.

'I feel to blame.'

'You are to blame. When you came here I thought you were a little fool, but an innocent little fool. You aren't.'

'I was, you know, until Werner.' There is a silence. She was provoked into saying that and it may have the wrong effect. Even if she already knew, Anne could be jealous because Werner, the cause, is gone.

'No you weren't. You were a little cock-teaser, quite a smart one, considering.'

Mrs van Breda used that expression too. It isn't one you hear in Hythe, but these women have been around the world. Briony wonders how much truth there is in the accusation. That kind of teasing can obviously go on below the surface of the mind. Perhaps, she thinks for the umpteenth time, it was all her own fault, what happened, the violence and sharp pain and humiliation beside the forest track; and the degrading, the unjust degrading in the eyes of Mathew, because Mathew, consciously or not, must really think it was her fault too. 'Well, Mrs Chance,' Briony says, lashing back, 'I don't tease any more. I've learned how to deliver. It's like carrying water to a parched tree.'

Anne laughs, throwing her head back and opening her mouth wide. She has a rather narrow jaw so the last, uneven teeth seem embedded in the dark. 'If you care to think of it like that – but which of you was the tree?' She isn't laughing any more. She is studying her hands, the long fingers, the useless fingernails, polished to a point, here in the heart of Africa. 'With Harry . . .' She hesitates a moment, looks up at Briony and then quickly looks away. 'Do you . . . I mean, were . . . the poor roots watered?'

This is some sort of odd appeal, Briony decides. The woman has been alone here among men for a long time; she needs them, exploits them, and fears them, and now there has been a murder in their midst. When Briony thinks of how it must be to live here, a lone woman among men, she can see herself going to pieces too. Socially, women create everything, but not in isolation. Other women, whatever the rivalries, are indispensable. 'You mean for me?'

'Yes, darling, that's just what I do mean.'

'Not always.'

'Ever?'

'Oh yes.' Briony feels shame at being asked these questions, and still more shame in answering them. Would it be less if she could truthfully say, as Anne no doubt hoped she would, that she never enjoyed it? The roots never irrigated? But that would denigrate the man; she loves him, and never more than here and now, as she makes this claim more for his sake than her own. 'Wonderful, sometimes, actually.'

'Well all I can say is you must know how to manage pretty well for yourself.' The anger is back. It might have been better to say never and neutralise the anger, but it would have denied her one experience of love and admitted that between Harry and Werner, between one man and another, there's no real difference. And it isn't true, it isn't true. A flush is rising from her neck to her face, she can feel its progress. 'I expect you're lying, but anyway, you do know he doesn't think about you when he's doing it, don't you? You don't imagine that, do you? He thinks about himself. He pictures himself up there, the conquering hero riding a woman instead of that farting old Xerxes. That's what goes on in Harry's head while you lie all on your own under him with your romantic thoughts. Little fool. Even a cock-teaser has to grow up some day.' Briony is feeling a bit sick, all of a sudden. She feels dirty again, as after Werner. It isn't the words Anne uses that degrade, it's the experience of relish, and disgust, behind them. 'It's all lies, we lie and they lie. But we pretend it's true and they don't have to.' Anne is in front of the long mirror, which stands opposite the foot of the double bed. She is slowly getting undressed. She wears a silk petticoat with lace at the hem and breast. Anne never goes in the sun uncovered; her limbs are white, glowing white, and as fleshy as you would expect in someone who does nothing to exercise them, outside the bedroom. She looks over her shoulder at Briony. 'Undo me, darling,' she says.

'Undo what?'

'What d'you think, you idiot?'

Briony is quite near the door. There are things here which she understands while not understanding them in action. Anne is unhappy, forlorn, and her body is full of longing, but Briony cannot undo her. Undoing the way she means needs a minimum of coopera-tive desire, say, and Briony hasn't the minimum, even. It needs an admission that women can do for each other what men are often too self-concerned and urgent to bother about. Even Harting didn't go that far. For Briony, another woman's body is foreign ground, blank, even if admired. The door is half open now and her hand is on the latch. Anne has dropped the petticoat to the floor. Fully dressed, her appearance is deceptive, she looks frail due to her performance of a woman never entirely free from woman's pain. Naked, she doesn't look frail at all. She looks as if she could create the embryos for an entire race without help. The idea shoots into Briony's head that if there is indeed going to be a war, Anne will be wasted here. She is an asset her country needs, back at home. 'I'm sorry,' Briony says.

'You're a disappointment,' Anne says, and Briony, perversely, feels it.

'If you don't mind,' she says as she slips out, 'I have a telephone call to make.'

'I have no one to ring any more,' Anne moans, statuesque before her mirror like Narcissus, 'and no one to ring me.' There are real tears on her cheeks. 'Werner was my friend, you know. Please tell Mathew to bring me something – a cup of tea or something. I don't want to be alone. Don't leave me alone with them, Briony.'

She isn't a danger because her anger is too volatile and her sorrow too real. She can scratch and wound, but not plan anything mortal; put the idea of rape into a man's mind but not hatch some deep-laid scheme of revenge in her own. She would forget why she started long before she reached the sticking point because her own image in the long mirror is her occupation. Anne is not going to denounce Mathew to the policeman Pienaar when he comes, if he comes, to enquire about the disappearance of the German baron. Briony decides to put Anne out of her mind and certainly not tell Mathew to take her a cup of tea, or anything else. Mathew, who is always telling her to leave this bad place, should leave it himself before he is corrupted and starts to lay white women on the ground among the ants, if he hasn't already. For herself, Briony feels that the corruption of the Chance household raises her up, in a sense, from where she was thrown by Werner, but Mathew it can only pull down. There is, after all, a difference between Mathew and her. She won't name it to herself, but it's there to be seen. It is wrong, it doesn't match her feelings, it's only part of her estimate of reality, yet it's real.

She winds the telephone handle for Douglas but he doesn't answer. Several other subscribers lift the ear-piece, but no one speaks. Only eavesdropping ghosts inhabit the silent line. She needs Douglas now and she can't reach him. He said he would always be there, he should be there like a rock or tree, he should be waiting to be needed. Grass-fire love is one thing; the trees still stand afterwards when it's burned itself out.

The drums have not been silent. Peter pretends to have slept through them as there are things it's safer for a boy not to know, but Douglas is already warned of the death at the Chance farm by a runner sent to the Mission from the kopje before first light. Such a thing has never happened before, so it must be the authority of Mrs Shitofo, daughter of the Chifodya line, that lies behind it. Now Douglas is on his way, driving as fast along the forest track as his old Ford will let him, crashing violently across the potholes and ridges. Every couple of miles he has to stop and top up the steaming, boiling radiator. In the harsh loneliness of his private thoughts he knows that these events must have something to do with Mathew and Briony and their relationship. The only two people who mean anything to him – apart from the children at the Mission, the people on the hill, the women who come to him for help – are in trouble and he wants to reach the farm before Lieutenant Pienaar. The drums announced that the death was over a woman. Not a black woman, that would hardly be reported by drum, it's so common. Therefore a white woman, therefore Briony. He has reached a better stretch of road and he drives the accelerator to the floor, the dust behind the wheels rising in a reddish cloud to the height of the treetops.

Douglas has never been in the least at ease with the Chances. He doesn't know them well; they have called at the Mission twice in ten years, the Anglican padre in Gatooma knows them no better than he does. They are probably pagans, or even Catholics. Douglas no longer cares. He is a kind of halting pagan himself. His difficulty with the Chances is exacerbated by the fact that Mrs Chance and the woman who is soon to cease being Mrs Cathcart got to know each other some years ago in Salisbury, and hit it off pretty well. They used to meet in Meikle's Hotel bar for gins and gossip, at the very time when Mrs Cathcart was being most adulterous. In fact about the time she abandoned the Mission and Douglas to their own devices and moved into a flat in Salisbury with – no, he will not go down that road. Actually it was the

Gatooma Native Commissioner, for weekends, which now gives Douglas a certain leverage on him when there are contentious issues at stake. How could he ever have expected Barbara, with her high spirits and her overwhelming sex appeal, to settle down with a missionary in the drought-stricken bush? A man married to his faith and his task and his school? Well, now the wife and the faith are up in smoke. The task and the school, and the people on the hill – they remain. And still need him. That he must believe.

The Ford is rumbling at high speed over the cattle grid. The Chance house is spread before him. The way the whole thing is laid out, the sweep of the buildings, residence, stables, offices in confident, natural hierarchy among the occasional trees standing gracefully in attendance, is like an English manor in a climate of paradise, Douglas thinks, not a farm. He himself was brought up on a farm, beyond the spreading outskirts of Liverpool. There were plenty of manorial oases in that world. The thought of Briony in this one makes him feel unaccountably, miserably angry.

Mathew is watering the zinnias in his immaculate white uniform. As Douglas gets out of the Ford, he strides forward. They shake hands, Mathew placing his left hand on Douglas's forearm, trustingly. Douglas believes he is the only white man in this part of the country who ever shakes hands with an African, but actually he's wrong about that. Whenever Harry Chance has been away for more than a night he shakes hands with Mathew on his return; he salutes first, as if boarding a ship, then offers his hand. Mathew considers it a joke and takes it in good part.

'Everyone all in that swimming-pool with the tadpoles,' Mathew says. He laughs, the skin round his eyes creasing up at the outer edges as if the laughter of his mouth, so frank and easy, has pulled the whole front of his face round towards the back. 'Big white fish in a small pond. You hot, Doctor?'

Douglas has no intention of going to the pool. He stirs his

shoulders uneasily under the damp khaki shirt. He is afraid of swimming-pools. He remembers calling once on the Barings and finding them naked beside theirs, shut off from the rest of Africa by a high wall. The memory hurts. He knows he is a man not gifted for joy. Mathew has stopped laughing and now he looks wary. Douglas recalls what he is here for, dismissing the vision of the naked Barings. 'I must talk to you, Mathew. Where can we go?'

'This crazy garden is always the best place. Zinnia flowers see no evil hear no evil speak no evil, just look horrible.' He is laughing again, but Douglas is in no mood to join in. There is an unnatural round lawn between the flower beds, watered every night by natives who know nothing of English lawns and probably think this is a propitiatory circle to honour the Chance ancestors. They're right, in a way. Douglas sits down on it because the fresh green looks cool, and crosses his legs under him. He wishes that Mathew would sit too, but knows that of course he won't. There are his white trousers for one thing, and his status for another. He keeps shreds of natural dignity by standing when a white man, even a missionary, lets go of his by sitting on the ground.

'Who has been killed?'

'Boss Werner.'

'Who killed him?'

Mathew puts up a hand to the wooden cross at his throat. 'God sent an angel with a rifle and bullets.'

'Was it you, Mathew?'

'I am an angel then?'

So it was. Douglas is not really surprised. Ever since Briony came to the Chance farm, he was sure there would be bloodshed. The clash of wills and race and sex was bound to come to this. 'Does she know?'

'Madam Chance?'

'No. You know who I mean.'

197

'I think she knows.'

Never lie, whatever happens, that is Mathew, that was always Mathew. Kill, perhaps, but not lie. Probably the same ethic as Chance's in the end, intrinsic for the regal African, drummed in at Dartmouth to the gentleman. Douglas is less sure of his own, as if there may be something missing to it – the commandments in Exodus have nothing to say about lying. 'It's dangerous for both of you. The drums speak and whoever can hear, knows. How long before the mounted police come?'

'Drum secrets, they don't hear them at the police station. No one comes. And if they come, the Commander sends them away.'

'He knows too?'

'The Commander and me, we took the baron a long long way into the bush.'

Mathew must trust him absolutely, to tell him all this. Douglas never doubted the trust but he feels flattered all the same because Mathew is so obviously a better man than any of them, and dangerous, as good men tend to be. Now Mathew leans down to speak emphatically, confidentially, near to Douglas's ear. 'You, Dr Douglas, you must take her right away from here. You always teaching the boys duty – that is your duty. Take her from the Commander, no good for her.'

'You mean Briony West?'

Mathew doesn't answer the absurd question. Who else could he mean? Douglas only asked it because he wanted Mathew to acknowledge, in some way, the shared truth that Briony is their responsibility. If Dr West in his heart made no distinctions, his children should make none in theirs, nor any denial either. But Mathew nods, and something like an affirmative light in his eye gives Douglas the answer he wanted. The Englishwoman is accepted, she is included. 'It's for her I shot Boss Werner in the back of his stiff neck.'

198

'For God's sake, Mathew, don't say it, even to me in the open air.'

'He was a criminal man with her.'

'Yes.' Why pretend? Such things happen in Africa, as elsewhere. More here, perhaps, because people feel freer. The vast forest pushes the laws back to the faraway outer edge of this free world. Poor Briony. Douglas's pity is real and deep, but compared to the permanence of the injury it doesn't occupy him for long. He recognises the fact with surprise. It must be because he doesn't think of Briony as tainted by what happened to her, any more than by some contagion that her youthful health and strength would quickly throw off. And also because love cures injuries and he's now so strongly conscious of his own. If she will let him, he will make it all right. And then, too, he has been here so long and seen so much between men and women – in a way, her relations with Chance upset him more than the criminal German.

'But the bad things here, they not over, not yet,' Mathew says.

If an African says something like that and you have any experience, you take it seriously, very seriously. Time, here, is not like European time. It can accelerate suddenly so the future arrives before you've drawn breath in the present. 'I'll tell her to come back to the Mission with me.'

'That's right, Dr Douglas, you do that.'

'Please be careful, Mathew. You can always trust me to say nothing. But you know what happens in police stations and prisons. Plenty of men don't come back from them.'

'Over there now is the Commander coming back from the swimming-pool.'

Chance is striding towards them on his long thin legs. He wears a towelling dressing gown and tennis shoes like Mathew's, only newer. 'What's your name for him?' Douglas asks, smiling.

'The one who laughs and walk on sticks.'

'Does he know?'

'Oh yes,' Mathew says, laughing himself. 'He laughs and laughs about that.'

It's almost enough to make you quite like the man, Douglas thinks, until the sound of Chance's voice reaches him.

They are seated in the office. Chance has his feet up on the table so the dressing gown falls back beyond his knees. Douglas shifts his chair a bit further to one side. Men like Chance make him feel somehow less than truly physical, as if his flesh and its responses are clothing borrowed from the cupboard of his betters.

'Have a whisky, Cathcart. You look as if you need one. Help yourself, over there. I never drink in the afternoon.'

Douglas, actually, would like a whisky. What he has to do here, take Briony away from Chance whether she likes it or not, is going to need courage. Rather more than he has on hand. But with Chance implying that only inferiors drink in the afternoon, he cannot accept. 'No thank you.'

Chance lowers his feet to the floor, gets up and fetches a glass of whisky himself for Douglas. 'Here. Come on, you're done in. You know what's happened, don't you?'

It's humiliating, but Douglas takes the glass thankfully and drinks. The unaccustomed whisky immediately warms his spirits and rises from his gut to his head. Like that, the entire system is alerted – to decision, carelessness; he soon starts to feel almost as if he'd been born himself into the Chance world, the careless world. On a bookshelf in the corner is a photograph of an old man in robes, holding under his arm some ludicrous sort of glorious, pompous headgear. Douglas, whose long years of service in a Crown Colony have ended by making him a republican, recalls that the poor stammering King was recently crowned at Westminster. 'A member of the family?' Chance nods. Whisky emboldens Douglas further. 'I've come to take Miss West back to the Mission with me. I don't think this is a very safe place for her. She's an inexperienced girl. You and Mrs Chance and your German manager all belong to a world with its own values, and they're not those of—'

'For Christ's sake, Cathcart, stop talking nonsense. Briony's perfectly all right here with me. My wife likes having her around. She's . . .' Chance seems to search for the right word, 'like a companion for Anne. You know how women are.'

'No,' Douglas says, 'I don't. But I do know the dangers that can face them in Africa. That's why I think she would be safer at the Mission.'

'Is that your wife's opinion also?'

'My wife left the Mission quite some time ago. I think you knew that. I'm divorcing her.'

'And your idea is to take Briony away with you? She'll be all that much safer where there are no other white women at all?'

Douglas sees he may have underestimated Chance. The man is not the fool you might think, in spite of the naval voice and the Coronation photograph. He looks quite cool, watching Douglas from the other side of the long, narrow writing table, hands joined in front of him, enjoying himself, not like a man taken in an adulterous relation with a young girl in his own house. Of course with people like these, what you do in your own house is different. They have a long history behind them. Douglas is conscious of having none. His own dates from the death of belief, and that's too recent to create a habit of freedom; in fact he's hardly aware that freedom is within him. 'Miss West – Briony has told me she wants to consult a lawyer. I have one coming to the Mission tomorrow morning.'

'About your divorce? Or is it about the steps you need to take in order to conform to the Land Apportionment Act? Like clearing that hill of natives?'

'The hill is not the property of the Mission.'

'I know whose property it is. But it's the Mission protecting the people on it from eviction.'

'No one is trying to evict them,' Douglas says. 'Not the owner. Not us. And not the Native Commissioner because the Act doesn't give him the power.'

'Who, according to you, does it give the power to?'

'Just the owner.'

'Yes. With the legal obligation to exercise it.'

'There's no time limit set by the Act of 1930.'

Chance leans forward. 'There is now. They passed an Amendment. The time limit is 1941. The first of January 1941.'

Douglas smiles. 'I know. But by 1941, Commander Chance, you will be at sea if what they say on the wireless is true. You will have other things to worry about than a raw Rhodesian hill. You'll be fighting for your country again.' He knows that from the security of his non-combatant status he has won the argument. It is inglorious but gratifying. He can feel the tension peel off him like a skin.

'Let's ask Briony, shall we?' Chance says, taking his feet off the table. The way he says her first name would make Douglas despair, if he didn't know that despair in Africa can blow away like smoke in the night.

She reads in their eyes what's going on, as they come towards her along the path between the zinnias, followed by Mathew with a tray of glasses. She stops under the shade of an acacia tree and puts her thin blue and white spotted cotton frock over the wet bathing dress. They look as if they need all their attention available to them. Something is to be decided.

Anne is still in the swimming-pool, going slowly round and round with her long, beautiful legs opening and lazily closing behind her. Briony has decided she can't bear to watch them a minute longer, and so she has started back to the house on her own. The men are still fifty yards away from the tree and she watches them walk. How they stride, the lords of the earth! Every footfall a claim. And as each leg comes forward all the male machinery – muscles, and the rest – announces how one half of humanity rules and the other passively endures – one quarter, rather, the white male quarter. Briony, however, has no intention of enduring so passively; she is going to watch, and wait, and see how love turns out.

Odd, that she should have this feeling of fondness for them, all three. Even Douglas with his glasses, and his shirt buttoned up to the neck. Then Mathew, immaculate, enigmatic, withdrawn. Of course he's a servant and there are conventions; but he withholds from her, he gives very little, he doesn't trust himself. He can't or won't leap the barrier. She signals, she calls, Mathew stays obstinately in the shadow, watching and waiting too.

And Harry – Briony tries to stem the flow of foolish yearning. Time moves on and men are rotten, a few hours, a day or two, and they show it. Women change their clothes and men their commitments. She should change hers. She can see in front of her, walking over the dust between the zinnias, the objects of her affection or love. Who would have thought that Douglas would ever be among them, and why is he? Because he's truthful. Perhaps she has affection only because she feels pity for the truth. She should be harder, much harder, even with Mathew. But with Harry she can't be hard, there's the answer to everything. Her feelings drown judgement merely as she watches him reach her side and feels him touch her arm.

'Cathcart and I have been talking about you,' he says.

Briony wishes she could blush, even slightly, with surprised modesty. But she can't because she knew that was what they were talking about. 'Saying what?' she asks in a voice meant to sound hard as Anne's.

Harry must have noticed it. He turns to Douglas. 'Better say your piece now, Cathcart.' Then to Mathew, 'Put the tray down here under the tree. We'll sit on the ground.' There's lime juice in a bottle, and gin, and a jug of water, and two tumblers, one containing what looks like whisky. Harry passes this to Douglas and pours out lime juice and water for Briony. How does he know without asking that she doesn't want something stronger? Because she's a girl. Life is made up of these little humiliations. In the same way, he no longer asks whether or not she feels like a ride over to the Baring place. He just says, 'Come on, we're off,' or something of the sort, and she, like a seaman, obeys. But unlike a seaman, she loves to obey. Without words, she pits her will against his and yields with a little shameful thrill of pleasure each time. Leaving a sift of resentment accumulating like sand in an hourglass.

'Miss West ... Briony,' Douglas begins uncomfortably, 'I am wondering if you will agree to return with me to the Mission? You could give us valuable help in many ways. There's always so much that needs doing, for the children and the old people and the sick. Everyone old enough to remember your father would be happy if you were there, and you told me you wanted to be useful to the people your father loved.' He seems out of breath by the time this speech is finished.

Did she say all that? She has no recollection of ever saying, or feeling, that she wanted to be useful to anyone but Mathew. But one should, one should. All the same, usefulness, however worthy in itself, is not part of why she came to Africa. She came from selfish West motives, and they haven't yet been satisfied. Other more selfish reasons have taken over, and injuries she didn't have before she landed. She looks up at Mathew, standing in splendid isolation in full sun, glowing, statuesque, stern. He nods. That is why he is still there instead of going back to the house and his occupations. As a rule, he never waits in the presence of his employers a moment longer than he must. He serves, and expresses his contempt by disappearing.

Now, like Harry and Douglas, he has his reasons for staying, his man's will to impose.

'It's very kind of you, Douglas,' Briony begins. The close attention in all their eyes switches off. They think she's going to dither politely and pretend not to know what this is all about. They believe her female insecurity will get the better of such powers of decision as she may have, and then they will be left with having to put pressure on her while she resists, for the sake of resisting. Well, let them think it. There are three of them and one of her. 'Of course I would like to return to the Mission very much.' Their eyes bore into her. 'But I don't feel I ought to leave Mrs Chance.' This shameful pretext comes to her at the last moment, but in a way it's true. Anne, whatever her reasons were, begged not to be left alone among heartless men, and they're all by nature heartless. Heart is something they have to cultivate, like Douglas, or do without.

Under the acacia branches there is a long silence. The insects are asleep in the glare of the afternoon. No gliding hawk in search of snakes sails across the naked heat of the sky. And not one of these men was thinking about poor Anne. She may not deserve it, but Briony thinks about her. She is more solitary, to Briony's mind, than anyone she has ever seen before. Anne is like a message in a bottle thrown over the side of a sinking lifeboat saying simply, I'm not worth sailing off your course for, but help.

'Madam coming now to us from the swimming-pool,' Mathew says. And there indeed she is, walking slowly in her low-cut bathing dress, coming towards them gracefully, languidly, well aware of the audience – even this boring audience – so that each pace is a plotted step. But it is exactly people like that who need help when things go wrong. The mirror is their only view on the world. The distress they feel is all they see, reflected, repeated, doubled.

Douglas has stumbled to his feet. A crude question enters Briony's mind, watching him. He has lost his faith, so how long is it since he . . . was with a woman? His expression now is pitiful, full of want and shame and the demands of good manners. So it's been a long time, obviously, and as she now knows, if she didn't consciously know it before, men can't do without for very long or something goes haywire; there must be some outlet, it's as necessary and can be as disconnected as a cough or a sneeze. What do they know about love, ruled like that by mere needs? Or even understand about it at a remove? But perhaps, all the same, Douglas with his clumsy shame does understand something, and more than Harry for all his easy, sensual frankness. Which reaction do you prefer, in the long run – easy, vain frankness or gentle, clumsy shame? Perhaps the one that's closest to your own. Briony has always thought of herself as clumsy.

'Anne would hate to lose you,' Harry says while Anne is still just out of earshot. 'She needs a bit of female company.' Mathew turns to go back to the house. 'Don't go yet, Mathew. We may need you.'

'What you need me for?' Harry doesn't answer.

What indeed could Mathew be needed for? The drinks are poured, the bottles are there on the tray if they want more, there's no other service, out here under the acacia, that Mathew could do for any of them. It must mean that Harry doesn't want Mathew waiting out of sight to catch Douglas on his way back to the Ford. It must mean, it can only mean, that in a way Harry is afraid of Mathew, of what he could do and of what he thinks, and of the old alliance between the missionary and his pupil – because Harry fears they both want the same thing, to get Briony away from him. He is suspicious, now, of her relations with Mathew, as Werner was, though more vaguely, having affection for them both – affection going over into love. By the time Anne reaches the group Briony feels even more sorry for her. It's Briony, not Anne, that everyone here is interested in, one way or another. That may be flattering, but alarming too. She is a long way from the silly girl who crossed the equator on the *Edinburgh Castle* and she's not sure she can manage the situation she finds herself in, despite herself. Despite herself? Is that really quite right?

Too late to worry about it now that Anne is among them. The way she gives Douglas her hand, drawing her towel in closer about her and keeping her elbow close to her side because she is only half dressed, actually makes her seem quite naked. Douglas is red under the dark brown of his face and his eyes search desperately for rescue inside himself where he won't find it. Everyone here is the victim of desire but Douglas seems doubly unfortunate; he is like the muwanga tree over the grave of Harry's little girl who died of malaria; he grows without grace or culture, unselected, heavy, lopsided, but his branches connect the earth to the quiet of the sky. The idea of God that sent him here, to succour the people, has died in him, but he stays with them because he doesn't need it. Father left because he did. Briony apprehends with a sense of shock and grief that Douglas is a much better man. It is, in fact, her first moment of true grief. Until now, death seemed unimportant because it took nothing away from Father, in her mind, but now, in a moment's insight, it has taken almost everything. Sitting on the dry grass among the parched trees, she feels as if all the famous Rhodesian water table has risen in her alone so she is flooded with tears. They feel cooler on her cheeks than the lime juice and water, lukewarm now, in her glass.

'Oh, I say,' Harry says. The solicitude in his voice announces loud and clear everything that anyone could wish to know about their relations, while it tells Briony, for her part, that he views her – tenderly, of course, tenderly as you could hope for – as a kind of necessary child. Sudden weeping reveals her weakness, but also her necessity. A woman so unexpectedly distressed is a woman crying out to be made use of. If only she need not judge him as sharply as that. She loves him, after all, with an aching, lonely, wounded love, accepting the crumbs that fall. Why judge, what good can it do? 'Don't be upset. Cathcart isn't going to take you away. I won't let him.'

'Won't you?' Anne says.

Another silence falls. Briony doesn't think it's up to her to break it. The question has been decided without her saying anything much; her sad flush of tears was enough. Now Mathew is offering her a straw hat, a floppy thing which she has seen on Anne's head and which he must have brought out into the garden with the drinks tray. 'Madam take too much sun,' he says. 'Mashona sun burns. Smoke goes in the head by the eyes.' He lowers his voice as he leans over her. 'But no crying ever put out African fires.'

Eleven

'I'M SORRY,' BRIONY says. She puts out her hand and lightly touches his, which is gripping the steering wheel. Does she mean sorry for him? You should never let yourself feel sorry for a man you like, it cuts him down. He can feel sorry for you in his funny way that you needn't take too seriously, but not you for him. There's a balance to be respected. You both benefit and no one is made less.

'Just turn the telephone handle and I'll come for you. Everyone will know, but who cares?' Douglas, with the regret that cries out loud in his eyes, seems to have grown more positive than she thought he ever would be. He has reached the point of not caring.

'I'll remember.'

'It wasn't the only thing I came here to tell you.'

It's boiling hot, standing next to the metal of the Ford in full sun. And there may be, almost certainly are, watching eyes behind her on the veranda. She walks round the other side and opens the door. 'I'll come with you as far as the jacarandas by the cattle grid,' she says. As the Ford goes lurching off she has the little sharp satisfaction of seeing Harry jump off the veranda and run after them. 'Hurry up, Douglas,' she says, and puts her hand on his again, but just for a second. Not thinking about it.

Beyond the cattle grid the Ford draws up under the trees. Harry, of course, hasn't followed; he was acting on impulse and must have turned back almost at once to his cooling gin and lime. From the branches of the jacaranda above, a vervet monkey is throwing nuts, or fruit, or twigs down at the Ford below, its black face and white whiskers drawn back into a sneer like a small, pickled Mashona ancient. Briony thinks of the village on the hill and the little chief reigning there in peace, over other ancients, and children, and the community of grown women. Where were all the young men, when she and Douglas called? Out doing manly things, presumably. Felling and hewing and stumping and hunting. Or were they working for slave wages down a white man's mine? The Cam and Motor near Gatooma, for instance?

'The lawyer came over to see me. I talked to him about your land.'

'Was that what he came for?'

'Well, no. I have to divorce.'

'You have to?'

'I want to.' He could quite well tell her to mind her own business but he hasn't. She understands the reason, she won't think about it, but she knows, she knew from the moment she touched his hand. And she thinks again of Mrs van Breda and her good advice.

'Well?'

'There's been an amendment to the Land Act. At first it seemed it was to make things easier for Africans in the European area. But it doesn't, unless they're contracted labourers, and even then their women and children can get thrown off. But if an African has what this lawyer calls a possessory right, he goes. The same for a village or any other community. They go. No legal argument about it. It's what the amendment to the Act says, and that's what the magistrate does.' The rage in Douglas's voice is alarming. All the fury of righteousness is there. If she had anything to do with him, Briony would try to – what? – wean him off righteousness and rages, that's what.

'Well, I see,' she says, not seeing, and waits.

'Then you know you mustn't think any more about making over that land to Mathew. If you did, the Native Commissioner would get the word from the Land Registry and fetch in the mounted police, and those people would be driven off into the bush like animals before the flames. With the divorce going through I lose my hold on him.'

'Was he involved?' She shouldn't have asked that. It's vulgar curiosity to ask about a man's divorce if your relations with him are delicate enough already.

'Let's say I could have made trouble for him higher up. And I don't mean in the sky, I mean the Governor's office.' So a missionary is not above a bit of blackmail and leverage.

'But if I do nothing – what then?'

'You're the owner. Under the amendment you can let them stay at least until 1941. And God knows what will happen by 1941. They may be able to stay for ever. If war comes . . . and it's coming – it's up to you.' Douglas, sweating beside her on the leather seat of the Ford in his frustration, gives a painful smile full of undeclared longing. 'You're the mistress of their fate. And not just theirs.' Briony knows what Mrs van Breda would say, that this is a good man of mature years, not a boy, and not a hardened naval adventurer. Teasing him even unintentionally is cruel and wrong.

'I'll be careful, I will,' she says, thinking of the gold mine now. 'It's the other people I should think of, not myself.'

'That's the first time I've heard you sound like a daughter of the manse,' Douglas Cathcart says, and they laugh together in a new feeling of ease. As she's climbing out of the high-up front seat of the old Ford, he suddenly leans across and grazes the bare tip of her shoulder with his closed lips. Neither of them says anything.

The news from England is sombre and the Chances have decided to give a party. 'It's months since I've seen anyone,' Anne complains. She also claims to be worried about her two children at their expensive English schools. 'I feel frightened. Don't you think you should send for them?' she asks Harry in a failing voice.

'No,' he says. 'There may not be time.' She doesn't argue. It's as if having brought the children into the world she regards them as classed in the inventory of their father's belongings, and should he decide to deposit them thousands of miles away and not want them back, well, at least they're far from the womb, a part of her body for which she obviously has little regard, and henceforth would rather keep closed and blank as an album in which you have never had the heart to fix any permanent photograph.

The Barings are on their way back to sell their farm, so they've announced, and Harry no longer rides over there with Briony. They go to the ancient gold mine instead. There's a wooden shack beside the entrance to the workings. The circumstances of their love have turned sordid but Briony hardly notices it. It's enough to be alone with him, far away from whatever can remind her of the transience of affairs and the ulterior character of most men's motives. In fact, no site could be more ill-fated to love than the gold mine, as it turns out.

But meanwhile, often in their absence, the organisation for the party is going ahead. Anne spends a lot of time on the telephone and Mathew a lot of time avoiding her and the flow of instructions coming from her. She has no idea who is coming and who isn't, nor what to give them, nor what to do with them when they arrive. She just wants to see someone other than Harry and Briony and the ghost of Werner.

A red-haired policeman came over one day, a few weeks after Werner's disappearance. Harry sat with him on the veranda and they drank several gins together. Briony watched them from inside the house, not hiding, the windows and door wide open. The police officer was friendly, respectful, smiling, and you could see that he hated Harry like poison but would never dare do anything to make trouble for him. Harry is probably on first-name terms with the Governor. The Prime Minister is someone whom Harry would treat with polite condescension because the Prime Minister is a doctor by profession and you can't be a gentleman by profession.

Briony sympathises utterly with the police officer over this, but Harry is her weakness, her necessity. She goes out on to the veranda and sits quietly some yards away in the background. She wants to know what they're talking about, and whatever it is, they're unlikely to stop talking about it merely on account of the presence of a girl.

'You know what they are,' Harry is saying. 'Devious buggers. He was probably gathering information about British officers on the reserve in these parts. He'll have hopped back over the border into German South-West. That border – anyone can walk over it in the night.'

'Or the day,' the officer agrees, and empties his gin.

'Another?'

'I don't mind.'

Harry pours it. Briony knows, watching him, that in spite of the police officer's agreement, he doesn't consider the situation entirely safe. Jutland has taught him caution, perhaps. 'You're in no hurry, are you, Pienaar?' So that's who this is. 'We're having a party. Why not stay on? You can stop a couple of nights. My wife will organise you a bed. What d'you say?'

'I don't mind,' Pienaar says again. 'Or I'll get back to Gatooma and come out again for your party.' He's making it clear that he is not to be bought by an Englishman's hospitality. Watching him discreetly, Briony knows what would buy Pienaar; his price is bursting out of his khaki uniform. 'I'll report your man left without a word and probably made for the border. No one seems to have seen him in Gatooma. Did he have his own car?'

'No.'

'And he didn't steal one? Or a horse?'

'Nothing. Except my wife's rifle and a few rounds.'

'Then he went on foot through the bush. He'd need the rifle. I still better have a word with your head boy. Routine questions for my report.'

'I'll call Mathew. He works in the house and he knows everything that goes on.'

'Speak English, I dare say?'

'Very good English.'

'I don't care for natives who speak English. They get ideas.'

'He's a very intelligent man.'

'There's no such bladdy thing with them. You mean boy, anyway.' The resentment and dislike sound clear and loud through the Lieutenant's neutral, rasping voice. He hates black people and he hates English naval officers pretty well equally. Harry must be able to hear it, but he doesn't react. He gets up and goes into the house for Mathew, calling him as he passes through the insect net hanging in the doorway.

Pienaar swivels in his chair and stares at Briony in the shadows. 'Did you know this missing German baron, young lady?'

'I hardly saw him. He was always out on the lands.'

'And what would you be doing here, then? No children about the place for a governess, that I can see.'

'I'm on a visit.'

'Name?' He has become decidedly more brisk now that Harry isn't present. The resentment must be mixed with a dose of fear. Of course a lieutenant, whatever his powers, is lower than commander – hierarchy, always hierarchy with men; even Douglas speaks of Father with that little bit of awe and resentment, as if he were his father too, in a sense.

She will give nothing more than is strictly demanded. 'West.'

'First name?' Pienaar has opened a notebook on one knee, with the gin glass on the other. His knees are hard and reddish brown with freckles, his legs hairy, and his shorts short. Perhaps he enjoys asking women a lot of questions in an abrupt voice.

'Briony. What's yours, Lieutenant?'

'Piet.' He smiles at her in a way that shows how stupid it was to ask the question. The sun beats down on the thatch of the veranda roof, and in the heat you can feel lasciviousness crawl and lash about like a snake in a pit. 'You got a pal back in England you sometimes confide in?'

'Here's Mathew,' Harry announces in his big, carrying voice. 'Mathew, Lieutenant Pienaar would like to ask you about the baron.'

'Not like,' Pienaar says. 'Intends. You, you come out here on to the open ground with me.' Mathew follows him, serene in natural superiority. How infuriating that must be to Pienaar, if he notices it. And seeing them together in the glaring light, over there with no shade, you see the superiority confirmed. Pienaar is short, broad, and coarse. Mathew, behind him, is like a kudu next to a warthog.

'Mathew'll throw him off the scent all right,' Harry says quietly, with a low laugh. Whenever she finds herself near him like this in a public place and therefore unable to touch him, she feels the same – as if they can't touch because something is wrong with her. She's a gift refused because it shouldn't decently be offered. Yet she knows that this is not what he thinks or feels. If a woman offers herself it's an offer and what Harry feels is that decency doesn't come into it anywhere. A gentleman has standards to uphold and duty to perform, and if that coincides with his desires, well, he's lucky.

'Do we go riding this afternoon?' Briony asks.

'I don't want to leave this policeman alone around the place, sticking his nose in anywhere he pleases.'

'Get him drunk. He'll go to sleep in the sun.'

Harry looks at her with what she hopes is respect. 'It's much the best thing to do,' he says.

★ ★ ★

And he does it. An hour later, Pienaar is spread about a deckchair in the shade of the veranda, legs apart, mouth open, freckled face red. What on earth does it matter if he knows about Jo? Briony named no names when she wrote the African brother story to Jo. It doesn't matter at all.

'He's out for the count, stupid bugger,' Harry says. 'Can't take his gin. And Anne's safely shut up with her migraine. Let's go. We'll ride to the mine for a golden legover before they declare war on us all.'

'Is that the name you had for it in the Navy?'

'It's the politer one.'

'What will happen to me after that?' His silence shows that he hasn't given his mind to it, not that he doesn't care.

This time, they cut through the eucalyptus plantations where the open track allows them to gallop. The gallop is doubly exciting across the shadows of trees falling over the track, light and shade flashing before your eyes fixed on the approaching distance. Briony knows that no ride in her life will ever be as good as this one. At the end of the plantation is a low closed gate which Harry, ahead on Xerxes, takes without looking back. She has never jumped a gate before and there isn't time to waver. She must jump it or fall. She leans well forward with her hands down and the mare does the rest. It's a flight, like a moment of requited love. And he doesn't even look round, but canters on ahead between the trees whose branches here grow across the narrow path, swiping at you as you go.

It was never so good before – not even under the Barings' rhythmical fan. Here in the shack she crosses into a territory where the ghost of Werner and the humiliation and anger have no entry. Where hurt was, delight has coiled and settled like a cat in the sun. But Harry can't love her for ever and she mustn't expect it. Oh, she can imagine it all right – if she lets herself – here or in England, with no war, no claims, just her and him, settled like two cats. No. She didn't come to Africa for that. She tells herself that she can't love Harry either, not with the right kind of love, the kind that returns year on year as a crop from the soil. Yet this new happiness *must* somehow be for lovers who love. Surely. Surely it must – a thing so good *must* be good in itself.

'Thank you, thank you,' she says.

'Couldn't have managed much without you,' Harry says, looking up at her. That of course is his way of emotional side-stepping. Even so, love receives a small jolt and delight a check. He owed it to her to make the pretence of having nothing to side-step. Love is ruffled, that's all.

'May the gold seam under you be rich and happy, and run for ever,' Briony says. Harry doesn't care to be made fun of. He looks at her suspiciously. But her eyes must reassure him, so wide open and giving and, after all, so grateful, with a gratitude which is at least half real. She gets off him and lies back on her spread-out clothes with her head resting on his arm. It must be proof of a gentleman that he's willing to be underneath with his back, not yours, on the prickly hard ground. Yet that still is no proof of love. If only love mattered less – what is it, after all? In hard reality, nothing; but the real is not the category at issue. In the category of what is, love, and the belief in it, are everything.

'This shack and the mine didn't make anyone happy. Mines are bad places. A lot of poor men died in them under the rocks and for some of them it must have been a release. Conditions were grim. They worked under the whip. This must be the first good thing that ever happened here.'

'How horrible,' Briony says. She shudders to suppress the knowledge because she wants to come here again as often as the weeks still left before war allow – weeks crushed into days and hours.

'But I do happen to know the reef's a splendid one. No one's been

217

near it for years. It's only twenty feet down and the gold stands out on it like the veins in my arm.' She looks at the blue veins under the tanned surface of his inner arm. She touches the surface with her fingertip and the muscle tightens. Apart from the veins, it is all hard under there, like the stone of the reef that fell in on the miners.

Harry says nothing more for a minute, as if turning something over in his mind. She waits, lying quite still with her eyes fixed on the corner of sky visible through the filthy smashed glass of the window. The sky has the whitish haze of smoke with the ardent African blue behind it. She knows he will soon speak again because there's something he wants, and she knows what it is, but she won't admit it as she couldn't admit that Werner didn't want her for herself. She won't, she can't. Then, she must, because the obvious is breaking in as tanks break into the Sudetenland – Harry makes love here because he wants the mine for himself, and she knows she'll let him have it. The land can't be given to Mathew, Douglas was definite about that, the mine is only a hole in the side of the hill; and she, poor clown, she cannot do without the show, the physical show of Harry's love, whatever its motive. She isn't even prepared to try doing without it.

'You know, my girl, these workings deserve to be reopened. There's a fortune in there.'

'Oh, is there?'

'For the taking. I could bring fifty men, a hundred men over from the compound, drop the farm work, cut a path for a waggon and the donkey engine – you don't know what that is, do you? It's the two-stroke engine for crushing the rock we'll get out – and before war has time to raise its ugly head again we'll be breaking the bank at Monte Carlo.'

'But when it comes you won't be here to do it all.'

'Before then I'll have sold the concession to the Cam and Motor Mines over near Gatooma.'

'Don't you mean I will have sold it?'

Harry turns his head, puts his mouth on hers, and leaves it there for a long time. 'Yes, that is what I mean, of course.'

'And you'll be gone.'

'By then it won't matter any more. I'll have had what I want. I can go to the bottom of the sea knowing I've had it.'

She knows what he means because she is in him. He isn't really talking about gold, or the price to Cam and Motor, or his love affair with her. He's talking about his love affair with the African earth. She understands. He will enter the soul of Africa by the mine. For some, the gold under the brown surface is the stuff of Africa itself and gain is secondary. What Cam and Motor actually pay for the concession is beside the point. The point for Harry is to go back to the sea he hates, and the war he dreads, and perhaps the death he is ready for, with a vital desire satisfied at the last.

Briony wonders how men react, inside them, when they know that the woman with her head on their arm has a rotten motive. The two perspectives are so different. For them, probably not tortured by this need to *consume* the love of the other, motives may be less important. They tell so many lies about them, so automatically, so innocently almost. And what they want is only a part. She knows she's a fool, women are fools because their feelings make fools of them. But she sees what he has in mind. He will dig out a big sample of gold-bearing rock and claim that the mine is on the march towards a great fortune, and if she thinks, even for half a day, of refusing, what then? Why then she will read in his eyes the truth she knows but never wants to see laid out – that their relations are for this, and if this fails, the relations fail, all fails. She can see the concession already in Harry's pocket, slipped into the khaki trousers folded up under his head.

'I don't want the people to have to move off the hill, whatever happens,' Briony says.

'Your old people are safe as the huts they squat in. Leave all that to me.'

Under so many eyes, a moment alone with Mathew is almost impossible, because the eyes would hate to see it and they're very watchful. Briony feels herself suspect. In the end she finds him in the little house, scrubbing the wooden throne with Jeyes and sharp sand for the white people's ease. She decides to tackle him head on.

'You're always telling me to go away,' she says, her hand on his wrist so the scrubbing ceases. 'I want you to leave here too.'

'You want? The white sister comes from England and tells me what she wants? So if I leave the Commander, what do I do then?'

'You could work for Douglas. Teach the boys. You could . . .' She doesn't know. She has no idea. She came to Rhodesia with love and good hopes; love has been sold into slavery and the hopes seem less pure, the ideas less right than they did while the prow of the *Edinburgh Castle* turned the ocean blue into foam and froth under the southern stars. 'Please, Mathew, let's leave here together and find some way . . . to live properly.' He doesn't answer but only moves his head slowly like an eland troubled by flies.

The party is going to be sooner than anyone thinks. Anne, in an absolutely unprecedented burst of energy, has driven herself to Salisbury and is rounding up some old friends there. She rings to say so. She's staying the night away. She will be back, with the old friends, about lunch time tomorrow.

'Who are they?' Harry asks.

'Better not say on the line,' Anne says. Then she raises her voice and speaks distinctly. 'We're not inviting every bloody busybody in the neighbourhood. But the Barings are back, as I expect you know.'

'Meanwhile you've gone off leaving us here without a car.'

220

'Us? You've got the horses, haven't you?'

'I don't like how Anne's being,' Harry says later. 'She's up to something. It happens about once every five or six years.' He laughs, his high, neighing laugh like a call to Xerxes. 'We'd better be on the look-out.'

Briony is never not on the look-out for Anne. She believes she has her measure by now. It's simple enough – Anne is a neurotic woman whose weakness is her strength. She's like a pool in the forest which you think stagnant because its surface is opaque with decaying matter; and when you turn back the next day it's running over, soaking, spreading, sapping. Or she is the triple mirror in her darkened bedroom, never more blank than when she's in front of it. 'Did she say if she's enjoying herself in Salisbury?'

'She's stopping at Meikle's so she's bound to enjoy herself. She'll be much the prettiest woman in the bar there.' A bar full of sex-starved bachelor farmers and assistant farmers – or don't the assistants go into Meikle's? – but Anne won't be interested in any of those. In this country there are fairly few of the kind of people she would be interested in, but one or two all the same. Briony knows this because she has had a look at the list of telephone numbers outside the Gatooma subscriber area, marked with Anne's blue pencil. The poshest people live in the east of the country where the climate and landscape remind them of Scotland at its best. They have ranches, not farms, unlike Harry, who prides himself on working the land when not playing polo or committing adultery with whoever comes along. Adultery without love. No, not just with whoever, not quite without love, that's unjust. It's self-defence, the futile method of denying what you long for so that not having it will hurt less. But adultery without the title deed of love is a fair enough description. And God knows these people believe in title deeds. Lack of them is what allows you to drive native Africans off the good land of their forebears and away into the wilderness where the soil is easily turned

221

because, being so thin, it's not worth turning.

So it looks as if Anne may be returning to the party with a few of the kind of people Briony fears and was taught at Harting to despise, if she could. There's the name of a Scottish island with 'Duke of' beside it in brackets, among others of that ilk, on the telephone list. How are you supposed to talk to someone like that? Well, she probably won't be required to. If he's a real one, and if he comes, he won't be wasting his time chatting to Harry's latest, just waiting to be cast off.

'Where will all these people sleep?' Briony asks.

Harry gives his Xerxes laugh again. 'At a Rhodesian party, no one sleeps anywhere. They occasionally lie down but they don't sleep. Don't count too much on the lock on your bedroom door. You'd better stay up. You'll see. Keep near me. It may get a bit rough.'

Twelve

THERE ARE PAPER lanterns strung along the jacaranda branches, and others lurking like Chinese spies half hidden among the zinnias. But soon the full moon, still dull on the smoky horizon, will be so high and bright you will hardly see the candlelight behind the gaudy paper. Anne brought the lanterns from Salisbury for the occasion. As soon as she got back, alone, she set about preparing the party with fierce determination, as if it was to be far more mayhem than pleasure.

It seems to Briony that Anne looks at her now even more critically than before she went to Salisbury, as though something new and worse has come to light. Briony offers to help with the lanterns but Anne doesn't hear her. She knows that here you don't help with anything unless specifically instructed, the danger for a white person to avoid at any cost being that of seeming to offer to share the task of an African, in the very least detail. If an African servant's duty requires him to blow out a candle, hold your breath until he's done it on his own. So all she can do now is hang about waiting for something to begin, and hope that when it does it won't be too alarming, such as humiliating party games, or Harry being drunk, because when he's drunk he's dangerous, as when he

223

had that fire lit next to Anne at dinner.

Briony wanders off towards the swimming-pool. The sun is sinking in a red flood across the sky. The black water of the pool seems to be lapping over its rim with blood. The red earth is saturated with it; if you leaned down and clutched a handful and squeezed, it would ooze between the fingers. Over beyond the far side of the pool a boy is leading a few goats somewhere – or are they leading him? There are six or seven yellow-eyed animals, and the boy, and they're like a native tune, they're like the surge from the earth at the African spring. Or they are only the dust that shifts when you think about it and settles back into nothing as soon as you don't. Where does he come from, this boy, so casually wandering across Harry's farm like a tortoise? Where is he going, how far? If only she knew some Shona and could ask him. She learned ages ago a few words and phrases of what they call here 'kitchen kaffir', but she's so ashamed of the name and the mixture it refers to that she has never tried using any of them, and she isn't starting on this boy. His features are so clear and his bearing so straight that for all she knows he may be, like Mathew, the descendant of a hundred kings buried under the ground she stands on. If she can't use his language, she will say nothing. They stare at each other in silence, but appreciatively, across the backs of the goats. It looks as if he has reached the same conclusion as her. Then he smiles. The whites of his eyes compete with that of his teeth in an almost blinding display of well-being against the backdrop of earth and sky, bloody as a battlefield.

Briony smiles back. The exchange of smiles makes her feel happy, like telegrams of good news. This boy and her, they share the cradle of humanity. The moment can't last, of course. The boy lowers his eyes because he has been taught never to look insolently at a white woman. A sullen expression comes on to his face and he calls sharply to the goats, which have begun to wander all over the place as goats do at the first sign of potential anarchy, such as symptoms of human

224

happiness. After a moment of reorganisation, the little herd and the goatherd drift away among the trees and into the blood-red grass. He must have some kind of musical instrument with him that she didn't notice. A rapid series of notes, sounded and resounded across a narrow range, lightly metallic, with a rhythm that varies, so it seems to her, according to the boy's proximity to the nearest forest tree as if in a game of hide-and-seek, follows behind him while he disappears into the gathering dusk and is lost, as his music diminishes, echoes, and fades away. She wonders if he will still be playing when at last he reaches his village in the dark. Perhaps the musical instrument is for beguiling leopards so they leave the goats and him to go their ways in peace.

On the wide space in front of the veranda, among the lanterns, the guests are gathering. The sound of their voices, the clinking of glasses, the harsh laughter, make quite a different kind of noise. It's the sound of the white man and his woman drinking white gin forbidden to the black man. Never mind the black woman; she is forbidden black drinks too. She suffers, if she must suffer, without antidote. Well, Briony has no intention of doing without one. She's beginning to feel reckless already, and defiant. She sees Mathew, cold and withdrawn as an executioner above the heads of the guests, with a jug of something in his hand, and makes her way over to him.

'We don't talk tonight,' he says.

'What do you mean, Mathew?'

'Stay away from me.'

'Why?'

He looks at her with contempt, over the big glass jug full of what looks like fruit cup. 'Why? Because I work. The house boy has work to do. And people see. Even drunk white people see a lot. Much more than you think. Drunk white eyes watch black men like they see the lion in the little hole on the end of their rifle.'

225

'Don't talk so much about rifles,' Briony says. She doesn't like Mathew's mood. And her own, what about that? Inside her, she feels a vengeful resentment rising. She knows she is not going to be able to check it; she must either go away somewhere and make a scene all on her own, or make one where it will do her most harm, in public, in front of all these people who belong to the same world, in her eyes, as Werner von Hippel. And the longer she leaves it, the more she will want it to be in public and not harmlessly alone, because anger, like love, seeks an object. She looks round to see what Harry is up to. Mathew she already has at hand, towering over her in his threatening mood. She is afraid of what is behind his eyes, but after all, he's only her brother. 'Give me some of that drink you've got in your jug. And don't be so cross.' She smiles at him because although she's cross herself, that is what instinct tells her to do. Smile, disarm. Then you can do more of what you want.

Harry is in the dusty centre of the open space between the trees and the house, receiving guests. If this was England, it would be the carriage sweep he's on, and he looks as if he thinks it is. He's talking to the newest arrivals, just stepped out of their car, a big Packard. No one has English cars here, Harry says, because the ground clearance isn't enough. It's the kind of silly detail that love preserves in memory like a valentine. Harry kisses the woman, rather distantly, then puts a hand on the man's shoulder. He may well detest them as he's told Briony he detests most of the English settlers round here, whom he considers either parasites if poor like Douglas, or loafers if rich like the Barings. But Douglas isn't a parasitic settler, he's a good, needed man, and Briony rocks him and his need in the bosom of her thoughts. 'They come out to Africa to grab an easy fortune or squander one,' Harry says. Which is he doing himself? Briony, a silent landowner among all these noisy ones, thinks of her mine under the hill, the gold in it and the people above. Holding the tumbler filled with fruit cup to fortify her against shyness, she goes towards the group of guests, because Harry is with them and she needs his protection from these people who are Anne's friends. Or is it herself and her anger she needs protection from?

'Josh Baring shot a lioness from his own bedroom window,' Harry is saying in the high, nervous voice he uses when he wishes everyone would go away and leave him alone because he has something on his mind. 'She was wandering across to his stables to help herself to dinner.'

'I won't ever believe Baring hit a haystack at twenty paces,' the man says.

'He killed the lioness. Got the skin by his bed.'

'She must have had a heart attack. Bang bang. Drop dead. Barings foreclose.' Everyone within earshot laughs loudly. Too loudly and too long, even allowing for the lashings of gin in the fruit cup. Briony concludes that this must be the possible Scottish duke. The louder you laugh, the more likely you are to be favourably noticed. She examines him curiously, if it is him, from behind the shelter of her raised tumbler. He is a rather good-looking small man with a big head and an expression of wondrous patience and calm. Well, he can no doubt afford patience. No one would presume to inconvenience him once it's known who they're dealing with. 'Baring, from what I've heard, could no more shoot a lion than a missionary, and he'd do better bringing down missionaries,' he says in his deliberate, slow, deep voice. 'With what we have here I wish him best of luck.'

'I don't see how he could shoot anything, not even a missionary, from his bedroom window,' Briony says in a loud, trembling voice of fury. 'All you can see from there's the back wall of the squash court.' There is a silence all around among the lanterns. She looks at Harry. His mouth is drawn back, not laughing but uncovering his teeth in the way she knows. He is looking forward to trouble. She has brought it on herself, as Father would say.

'And this is . . .?'

227

'Young Briony West. Her father ran the Marimari place years ago over near Gatooma.'

'I see.' The unlikely duke leans forward a little without offering a hand. 'It seems quite a long way from the Mission near Gatooma to the Barings' bedroom window.'

'Perhaps not as far as you think, Ian,' says the woman who arrived with him and who has been watching the last moments of the sunset over the jacarandas from under her wide-brimmed, green, flowery cotton hat, through her huge dark glasses. She turns back from the contemplation. Briony hasn't specially noticed her till now, among all these new, alarming people. The pink silk trousers she wears, with wide bottoms, like a clown's pyjamas, ring a bell, an alarm bell, startling and persistent. Briony leans forward to read the identity through the shield of dark glass. It is Mrs van Breda.

'Remember me all right?' she says in her raw-edged voice, inspecting Briony from head to toe.

'You know each other?' Harry asks, surprised. 'But where . . . how could you?'

The chatter, which had started up again, dies down. Everyone is watching, everyone knows that Briony is the girl who Harry, to use his expression, has legover with. She wishes she could tell them, worthless though they are, and before they're too drunk to take the message in, that love like hers, so deep and sacrificial, is beautiful, not sordid, not shaming at all. 'Mrs van Breda was aboard the *Edinburgh Castle* with me,' she says.

There's another silent pause, then a burst of laughter round about. 'So that's the flag of convenience you fly under, Barbara,' someone shouts.

'But this is Barbara Cathcart. Douglas Cathcart's . . .' Harry says.

'Oh no. Oh no . . .' The earth moves under Briony's feet and a dizzy calculation goes on in her head. It's unbelievable. Babs – or Barbara – is so vulgar and Douglas so unlikely as the husband of someone as blatant and physical as she is. It makes you see Douglas in a very different light. At some time in the past he was blatant too, with Barbara, coupled and physical as brutes in the bush, though not for long, presumably. Barbara found the high-up South African official and did whatever was necessary to earn all those jewelled rings, and the First Class cabin on the *Edinburgh Castle*. And to get on Christian-name terms with a Scottish duke, too. All Briony's self-righteous anger has faded, and fear, urgent fear, fills its place. Barbara knows too much. Briony can't look her in the eye; she turns away hoping to lose herself quickly among the other guests in the cloud of gin. She can only hope that soon all identities, and pasts, and secrets will fuse and shift elusively as shadows cast in dying light.

'So how's that famous quest of yours, Briony?' Barbara calls in a voice like a foghorn, following her. 'You found the dusky Dr Livingstone? Or did you give up? Anne tells me you've taken to riding in a big way. You canter over to the Baring place? Not all alone through the bush, I dare say?'

Harry is beside Briony now, his hand on her arm. It's what she wanted so badly but it makes her still more afraid. Women like Barbara can read the contact of others – the fears, the secrets – like a flayed skin nailed out on a plank. The little duke gives out a deep, manly laugh. 'Well done, Harry, good luck,' he says. 'But I hear the Barings are back, not that one knows them. Too bad for you. Bad luck.'

'It's a wide-open land, Ian,' Harry says.

'It is indeedy,' Barbara agrees, 'as Ian knows all right.' She jabs him in the side with her elbow, laughing. Her elbow, actually, is at the level of his chest. Could they have . . . but of course. Briony creates a picture of them based on her memory of Barbara sunbathing aboard the *Edinburgh Castle* – bronze breasts and thighs swaddling the little man in an envelope of flesh. Perhaps the emeralds and all the rest came from him, not from Colonel van Breda, always supposing he exists. 'What d'you make of it, Ian?' Looking up, Briony sees that Barbara and Ian are both watching her with hot eyes as if they can not only see her rolling about with Harry, but read the raping images of Werner stored at the back of her head, and exactly what happened to him afterwards. She looks quickly across to where Mathew was last standing. He is coming towards them with a tray of glasses. Ian leans forward to peer at Briony more closely, his gaze dropping down from her face to the top hem of her cotton dress.

Harry's hold on her arm has tightened. 'Off my turf, Ian,' he says.

'Still whipping the bounds, Harry?'

What is it about them? They are all so . . . just look at them. Whatever it is, they glow with it as they gulp their drinks in the lanternlight; they are young, they are strong, compared to the poor of the world and the Africans of the villages round about, they are rich, unimaginably rich. Even the men who work, like Harry, can drop work the moment a hunt or a pursuit makes it look like something unworthy of the class they adorn. There – the word is spoken. She knows from listening to Anne and Harry that nothing is so despised as viewing them and their friends through the lens of class. From below, that is.

Mathew has reached Barbara's side and is standing over her with his tray. Her arms are naked to the shoulder, her breasts even more abundant under the loose pink silk blouse than Briony remembers them by the canvas swimming-tank. Does he need to stand quite so close, with the tray and his black glow? Barbara looks up at him, they watch each other for a moment, then both look away.

'You can fill my glass,' she says.

'Yes, madam.'

'And you can fetch me my scarf from the veranda, over there on that chair.'

'Yes, madam.'

If only he would stop repeating that awful formula. Briony knows, she can hear, the depth of contempt it hides. If anyone else hears it there will be trouble. Especially if Barbara does.

'And be quick about it,' Barbara says. 'My arms are getting cold.'

Ian puts his hands round them and massages vigorously. 'You need rubbing down with straw, my dear,' he says.

'The horse huts are behind the house,' Harry shouts, to general laughter.

Briony breaks free from him and them and walks back towards the veranda. She knows that Harry and Ian and the others think about as well of Barbara as Mathew does, for different reasons. They consider her a superior tart; Mathew sees her as an insolent woman who should be kept on all fours in a hut. He's only a man after all, with a man's bad ideas. How on earth could Douglas, of all people . . .? Because of the bronze thighs and breasts, obviously. Even Douglas's tight hold over instinct can loosen, that's how it must have been. Poor Douglas. The awful little duke understands women better than him, how to assess them, buy them, drop them.

'Don't let Mrs Cathcart see you looking at her,' Briony tells Mathew as she passes him on his way back with the tartan scarf.

'I don't look at any white woman.'

'Yes you do.'

'Only to fill their glass.'

'And to think what you'd do with them.'

'A sister does not speak like that,' Mathew mutters with as much dignity as he can.

'I'm only a half-sister, and anyway I watch you. Mrs Cathcart is dangerous.'

'I told you before, bad things happen here. And now worse. That – woman, she knew me, she recognise me. You go back to the Mission quick.'

'Mathew,' Harry shouts from far over among the trees and the magic lanterns. 'Mrs Cathcart wants her scarf.'

'Poor Dr Douglas, with that animal to divorce,' Mathew says, and at these words an image of Douglas, penitentially labouring under his burden of loving decency, fills Briony's mind. It's the image of something clean, and she feels that if only it came closer still it would wash away all the shame she feels with these people, in her situation, here at the Chance farm with a lover who wants her and wants her but has no real love to give. But as suddenly as it came, the image fades and fails and she is left where she was.

Anne is holding court in the dining room. There are several women, obviously wives a lot less stimulating than Barbara, and a couple of elderly men sitting down and looking, the way elderly men do, as if struck amidships somewhere below the water line. The phrase is enough to reawaken in Briony a longing to be beside the Commander in the gold mine shack instead of among hostile people too white for a black land. Or is the hostility hers? She realises that she thinks of no one, not even of Douglas a moment ago, failing her as he faded from imagination, without a surge of aggression. Where's the famous love in all that? The deficit of love must be Werner's legacy to her.

Yet this very afternoon, in the little office among the accounts she was supposed to sort out, she has signed a letter of concession of the mining rights. Love can ask no better, surely. And she knows, all through and all over her, that she has done something wrong, though she cannot know with what consequences. Only that when her eye falls on Mathew, she feels bad. And afraid. Afraid of Mathew, of the power behind him in the forest, growing in the hills.

'Briony,' Anne calls. 'Come over here. This is our young friend what Harry brought to keep me company, with the children away, poor angels. But she's been taking the toll of the men like nobody's business, haven't you, darling, you clever thing? First poor Werner, who vanished in despair; now stupid old Harry.' There's no escape, everyone knows. But also, no one condemns. They are salacious but they don't think any the worse of you for giving them something to chew on. How could they? The solecisms that matter to them are social, not moral. An African brother would of course be the ultimate solecism, the unforgivable; Briony, ringed by dangers she can do nothing to avoid, feels a growing recklessness. Perhaps it's the gin, or perhaps it's just doing and thinking as these people do and think – or perhaps both. If Douglas was only here he would tell her the right way to be herself. 'You wouldn't think it to look at her, would you? Hugo? Would you?' Anne cries.

'Seems quite a serious young thing,' the one called Hugo says. 'Looks like a governess. Of course in my day, governesses were something . . .'

'Oh yes,' Anne says, 'she's serious all right. And I know why, now.'

Hugo is out of his chair and sidling round the table towards Briony. It's like the approach of an octopus skirting a rock. 'Come out looking for a decent husband, have you? Young ones are no good at all. Let you down every time. Go running after whores like Barbara Cathcart, that's what. Fix sights on a well-established land-owning man with trust funds back home, that's what a sensible young woman does in Rhodesia these days, with a war in the offing. Young fellers going off to get killed. What's yer first name, d'you say?'

'One lives and learns, in Rhodesia,' Briony says, edging away, but too late. He has her by the elbow in a horny grip. Short of making a scene she is caught, and a scene is what she wants above all to avoid, with Barbara watching out for it.

'We'll go out under the moon and have a closer look at those magic lanterns, you and me,' Hugo says, half leading, half driving her across the veranda and down the steps. 'Don't you let a chap like Harry monopolise you, my dear. He's a terror with the women. Always was. Burns them up like a packet of fags and tosses the ends away. Don't let him do it. You're a nice young girl and you come from a different world, as I can see. Half the women out here are whores and the other half turn sour.' He is breathing heavily and now he's more hanging on to her arm than controlling it like a tiller as he did before. Briony has a reluctant look at him. He is not a good colour.

'Are you all right?' she asks.

'All right? I'm a damned sight more all right than most of the people here. Look at Ian Mull. Ghastly little fairy. Highest rainfall in the British isles, no wonder he's so wet. Needs a nanny like that Cathcart woman. Only came into the Mull thing just the other day because all his distant cousins got themselves killed in the trenches. Title went sideways, have to go sideways again after him, I shouldn't wonder. Little bugger'll never get a son, hasn't got the balls on him . . .' The voice is down to a mutter, like a drum in the rain.

'Does he live on the island then?'

'Live on it? He owns the bloody thing, shouldn't wonder. And welcome. Let's stop here a minute. I need something to sit on.' Hugo looks creakily around him. No help is in sight.

'I'll go and fetch you a chair . . .'

'Make sure you come back,' Hugo says, 'or I'll catch you and take you into one of the bedrooms and show you what happens to girls who don't obey orders.' Behind her, Briony can hear him gently hum and grind what is left of his teeth as she hurries away. Hurrying away seems to be something you have to get good at in the Crown Colony.

The empty Plymouth Gin bottles are piling up on the veranda and the candles have burned out in the lanterns. The moon is at the zenith and so is the noise of voices, laughter, crashing glass. From the direction of the compound, if you can hear yourself think, comes the sound of drums. Harry said earlier on that there was to be a beer drink below decks tonight, matching the gin drink. That was what he said. Usually when there's a beer drink in the compound, there is trouble. But tonight, the trouble could be right here at home. Briony, feeling a bit drunk herself, senses it coming.

Since the passage with Hugo – whatever became of him, by the way? Did he pass out, or pass away, or forget all about her as she tried to about him? – she has had increasingly ephemeral and inconsequent dealings with a number of other male guests, all showing more or less keenness to carry her off into one of the bedrooms and teach her a lesson. Every time, she has made good her escape. It's enough to make you suspect they aren't serious. In a haze, she thinks she knows the reason why. Everyone is aware that she is Harry's latest; everyone would like to take her off him; but no one really believes he can. It isn't exactly flattering, yet to be the property, even without title deed, of the leading attractive male gives you a role in the Rhodesian pantomime. Briony makes her way to where the unemptied gin bottles still stand, and pours herself some more.

'Too much drink,' Mathew says sternly from his station behind the table.

'What about in the compound? Isn't drink flowing there? It sounds like it.' As soon as she says this, even in her poor condition awash in fruit cup, she knows it was a bad thing to say to Mathew. Douglas would never say anything so stupid. Mathew doesn't live in the compound.

'Not for women.'

'Oh you and your ideas about women and what they can do and what they mustn't do – I'm sorry, I shouldn't have said . . .' Her train of thought seems to lose itself in the sand. Is there sand at Plymouth? It's on the coast, isn't it? There must be.

'Dr Cathcart, he wouldn't like to see you like this.'

'Like what?'

'Drunk.'

She isn't drunk, she can't be, it's just his dictatorial prejudice. However, it's true that her head is turning in rather an unpleasant way and her legs, though tingling and restless and full of go, feel a bit shaky. She leans against the table. Mathew comes round from the other side of it and stands close. Once again, she's aware of his smoky odour like a jute sack sewn up, dry, preserved, and the long wiry strength of his body. And, overwhelmingly, of a longing for their true relationship to be open and recognised so she can have someone who is in some way her own, growing in the same soil with her, side by side, roots entwined, locked, embraced. So that she can feel less afraid. She looks up at Mathew, the arm she was supporting herself on by the table top seems to buckle under his gaze from another planet, and she knows she's going because she hears the retching noise – then the noise turns to a roar.

'But I *saw* him. He picked her up.' 'Why didn't one of the men . . .?' 'A boy, carrying a white woman like that . . . holding her . . . I ask you . . .' The voices are shrill and angry but each protest fizzles out like a squib. Gin does that, it ignites but dampens the squib. Briony has this reflection as she lies on the sofa in the sitting room with Mathew still there, above her.

'You okay, madam?' he asks.

'Not very,' Briony mumbles thickly. 'I think I'm going to be sick.'

'You control yourself,' Mathew says.

The crowd of people seems to dissolve and re-form in front of her, swaying, sinking and rising like the mast of the *Edinburgh Castle* against the Atlantic sky. Now she makes out Barbara Cathcart . . . and disgusting old Hugo . . . and Ian carrying a paper lantern – and Harry. Thank God, Harry is here now. He leans over her, grinning. He must have jumped in the swimming-pool with some woman or other; his clothes are dripping.

'You'll be all right in a minute. Head going round a bit?'

She expected something better than that. Where was love, to watch over her? Where was he? But it's no good expecting. When he's sober, he's kind and considerate and makes sure his pleasure is her pleasure too, as far as that can be, between such unequal lovers. All the same, he wasn't there when she fell, and he hasn't been there much during the hour or two of her drinking unaccustomed amounts of gin. She resents that, furiously. He should have been there. If he had, she wouldn't feel so peculiar now. 'Lucky for me Mathew was by to pick me off the floor. If I'd had to wait on your . . . but I didn't. There was a proper man there.' She raises a hand to take Mathew's. He quickly steps back, but Harry has already turned on him as their hands meet.

'Don't touch the women in my house, Mathew, keep yourself to yourself,' he says in a rough, loud voice. They are face to face and close together, carved black and white like chess pieces. In their own way, the way of men, they're friends and they understand each other, but now Briony, with her love and her anger, has managed to come between them. Loving and angry, she has achieved that bitter result.

Mathew, even to her eye, is staring now with hostile insolence. 'Hm,' he says.

Without warning, Harry's right arm uncoils and his fist strikes at the side of Mathew's head, making a dull, thick sound like a stone knocking against a tree. 'There. Know your place and don't look at me like that. Now take those empty bottles away.'

Briony rises from the sofa, sobered by fury she didn't know was left in her. The blow to Mathew's head has released it. 'He helped me. All you do is get drunk with all these awful people and then hit him for helping me. Where were you? How could you hit Mathew? Oh, how could you?' She believes Harry is asking himself the same question. He has hit his friend, he looks sorry, sad, and afraid of what the fist has unleashed.

And now – oh God – the inevitable is about to happen, like the flux of the calendar. She is going to burst into wretched tears as if she'd learned nothing, in Africa, about being hard; and here they come.

237

Tears never tell the truth, they lie about the balance of distress and anger. But above the sound in her ears of breaking water is the sound of scattered laughter, all about. The guests can see her, through the mist of Plymouth Gin, for what she is – a girl from a world not theirs, less up to it, not as steady and stoical as a girl of their own world would be; and above all, not careful, too familiar with the natives. But then none of these women, and none of the women of these men, have been raped in the bush by someone like Werner. Or have they? Rape – who draws the line, and where? Who knows? In this wonderful country, dust and fire soon rub out the lines. Except those a black man must never cross or they'll wreck him for good, these heroes of Jutland.

'Don't cry, girl,' Harry says in a voice which she can interpret at once. He's pleased that she's crying, she deserves to cry; he has forgotten that he was on the verge of tears himself for the loss of his friend. All he remembers is that this is a party and every party needs a victim. It amuses him to let her be the victim because he can pick her up later from where she will be fallen. Briony swears not to be a victim and never, ever to drink another glass of Plymouth Gin; she will insist on beer, or wine, or . . . 'Here. Steady, girl. Hold on to my hand.' He's still laughing at her like the others; he's worth no more than they are.

She pushes his outstretched hand away. 'You hit him for helping me.' She can feel the tears dry up.

'He's my servant and I give a friendly knock on the head where I want to, here.'

'It's against the law.'

'You don't know what you're talking about. The law is the Master and Servant Act passed under Good Queen Bess, God bless her memory.' There's more laughter. It's a fine thing to be living where Tudor law still runs. Better than in the old country, where you have to watch your step.

'It was cowardly.' There is a sudden silence as if blasphemy has been uttered. Mathew has his back to the scene, he's bent double picking up bottles and discarded glasses from the ground, piling them on to his tray. The recently elevated Duke of Mull, half his size, is behind him. He raises a foot, looks round to see that everyone is watching, plants the foot on Mathew's backside and gives a push with all the weight he can muster behind it. Mathew pitches forward on to the ground, his hands breaking his fall. He is there on all fours among the broken glass like an animal. The excited, drunken laughter rises up all around. Someone cheers. 'Carry on, Ian,' someone else shouts. 'Don't leave it at that.'

'Stop this now,' Harry orders, his voice thickened and slurred and slow, but it's too late, the party has switched victims. They are howling for their due.

Ian steps closer to Mathew on the ground and raises his foot again, holding it in the air as if this is part of a measure in a reel. He's the social lion, he can roar, or lie down, and the party waits, eyes wide, breath held.

He lowers the foot. 'Suppose we drop his breeks,' he cries. 'There's a little sjambok on the back seat of my car. The ladies like a bit of sport. Am I right, Barbara?'

Disgusting Hugo, eyes starting from his head, beats a rhythm with his feet on the wooden floor of the veranda. If he's drumming a message, it reaches Briony all right, it floods her. They want to humiliate Mathew still more. The fact that they'll hurt him is not what matters, because a man expects a certain amount of hurt as he lives his life. Hurt passes, but not humiliation. It touches those around him too. The humiliation and the Plymouth Gin and the nausea and dizziness all melt and fuse and flash inside her. She throws herself at the tormenting Ian Mull, her hands on the large face adorning the small neat body, scratching it with the point of her mother's diamond ring. He makes a shrill, angry sound like a magpie.

'Get up, Mathew,' Briony says, turning back to him. Even turning round makes her feel unsteady. When he's up, she takes his hand and holds it close to her breast, to steady herself.

There has been a drastic fall in temperature; lanterns held high have been lowered, glasses have been spilt on the ground in consternation, faces display the tincture of shame that excitement had masked. Even Harry, so ever-ready, stands there gaping, arms hanging, no laughter yet formed up to be run out on deck.

There's one exception, though, someone whose temperature hasn't fallen; on the contrary. It's Mrs van Breda – Barbara Cathcart. Whether she gives a damn or not for Ian's scratched cheek, Briony can never know. She always afterwards suspects not. Barbara's reaction is to do with background. Barbara is South African. Every woman in South Africa is brought up to be afraid of native Africans, real Africans, and the horrible things they can do . . .

'I see,' she calls out in her penetrating voice with the flattened accent from down south. 'So this is him, is it, your half-brother you came to find, Briony? The reverend pastor's black mark at that Marimari slum? I remember him all right. A teacher's boy.' She comes up and peers at Ian's bleeding face. 'It's nothing,' she says, then turns back to Briony. 'I'm sorry for you now, girl. Women like you end up hanging round the mines. Munts pay anything for a white woman who's past caring. They haven't much but what they've got may be enough for you – twopence, a tickey; you'll just be an open hole for the next shift down.'

Mathew, upright with Briony beside him and still holding his arm right against herself like a branch in a flood, looks deliberately around at the white audience; slowly, as if waiting for a silence still more complete that the one that followed Briony's attack and Barbara's announcement. There's the unexpected sound of a car arriving, a late guest, then the engine is cut off. Finally, while the long silence lasts, he speaks in his always surprisingly high, hoarse voice. 'It is no fault of madam,' he says. 'Dr West, he's punished where he is for what he did. All of us unjust will be punished.' He looks at Harry. 'The Commander too one day.'

Lieutenant Pienaar, who has just walked over to join the party, is smiling in the background.

Thirteen

THE FIRST OF September and still no rain. Heat rises like smoke off the parched lands, the sky is grey with it, the sun is a masked fire falling on your head and arms and scorching the delicate skin of your face.

Mathew has run away. Last night – or was it already this morning? – Harry ordered him to his quarters. Harry was like a man struck on the head with a blunt instrument. His stammer silenced him for a full minute after Mathew's last words, then at last he brought something forth.

'Get out,' he said. 'Go away. I was wrong to knock you, but clear out of here.' He turned to Briony. 'How could I know? I wouldn't have touched him.' Did he mean, 'or you'?

Anyway, Mathew took him at his word, and when the surviving guests crawl from their resting places he is no longer there but somewhere in the forest with the other free animals. A young man raised with his feet on earth can cover a lot of ground in a few hours, like an antelope fleeing the white domain. Mathew, Briony feels sure, is miles away. She knows that in the bush the life of villages continues as if the white domain didn't exist, except when horses carrying the hated mounted police pass among the trees. And a man can hide so

242

easily. The drums tell him when horses are coming. The villages are unconnected by roads or telephone wires but the drum is faster and surer than either. Go well, Mathew, the lands will be yours, live on for ever.

Earlier, waking behind the locked door of her bedroom with a frightful headache, Briony wept for Mathew and Father and herself. What will happen now? What will Harry do with her, what love, or semblance of love, can he give to damaged goods, marked at Customs with the stroke of the tar brush?

She must do as Mathew told her, fly to the Mission. Douglas must come for her. She hasn't the smallest doubt about him; the moment she telephones he will set out in his ramshackle Ford. Why? Because – the terrible headache and accompanying nausea and guilt enforce total honesty – she knows that Douglas wants her for herself. He doesn't need her for any mine. Total honesty takes her a step further along the road. Better to be wanted by Douglas than end up the way Barbara said – because who else here will ever want her? Briony knows that Harry will turn her away in the end; by the time war comes, once he's entered into possession of the shaft and the mine, and the soul of the red earth, Harry will send her away, like Mathew. And not another white man in this gentleman's land will have anything to do with her after that. The poisoned word will run like the bilharzia fluke through water. She gets herself dressed, slowly packs her belongings into the two cases she came with. It must be the headache that prevents her from fitting them all back in, though nothing has been added since she arrived. She starts again, thinking of the punishment Mathew declared like a judge that they must all expect to suffer, his prophecy from the secret book of Africa. At last she closes the suitcases and staggers over to the main house to telephone.

No sign of life anywhere. Bottles and glasses and filled ashtrays lie about where they fell. Already, at the sight of them, she knows

Mathew has gone. She goes into the kitchen to make herself a cup of tea. No one – plates unwashed, dishes unscraped. She knew he was gone the moment she first opened her eyes, she knew it before that, in her sleep. Lieutenant Pienaar's smile told what lay ahead. Mathew would run and Pienaar follow, leaving her the time to get away, and the time to be caught again.

There's a page of blue-lined writing paper on the kitchen table. She knows it's meant for her but if she reads it now, someone may come in and find her doing it. She quickly tucks it into the pocket of her cotton dress, cut like an apron. There is no question of making any tea; the stove burns wood and it's out. The whole house, the entire Chance way of life, is about to fall into pieces, because Mathew, Harry's friend, Anne's – what? attendant, follower? – was the pillar holding it up. Briony runs from Mathew's headquarters, her heart dead as the fire in the kitchen stove, and through the dining room smelling of human digestion gone horribly wrong. At least there may still be some pure water hanging in the canvas sacks from the rafters out on the veranda.

Here and there is a body flung about a chair like fallen wounded past medical care. Nothing stirs. If there's a feather's worth of breath in any of them, it's in abeyance. The water bottles are empty but there's some fruit juice in a jug which Briony sniffs for the faintest trace of Plymouth Gin, enough to kill her on the spot. It seems all right. The taste of Rose's lime juice and water, bitter and sweet and synthetic, tells her that one day everything will more or less fall into place again, and quite soon she begins to feel marginally better. An empty Rose's bottle happens to be standing on the table beside the jug, the label showing a butler paternally pouring a glass of the contents. It is too much for her in her present state. She bursts into tears, despising herself, pitying herself, hoping to wash away the awful throb in her head.

Ian Mull's car, which she noticed yesterday evening because of the coronet painted on the door, is no longer there. What pretension, anyway. Who cares what his station in life is? Well, the other white men, of course, even Harry, because rank counts with them. The car has gone and with luck Barbara will have gone with it. She liked Barbara, ages ago, on the *Edinburgh Castle*, she admired her for being rich and free, but it turns out she isn't so free after all; violent fears lock her in and the pigment of skin stains her mind. And if she's in the middle of a divorce from poor Douglas she's hardly rich. Briony walks out past the trampled flower beds in the direction of the swimming-pool. As there's not a living soul in sight she might even get in and float for a minute under the veiled sun.

When she reaches it she sits on a plank bench in the thatched summer house where waiting tennis players make jokes in loud voices about players on the court. Anne has a way of raising her left leg while serving underhand with her right arm which provokes a lot of hilarity, though not from Harry.

Briony takes the blue page from her pocket.

B. West

Go right away from here now before flames. Not wait like the tortoise

M.

Drums will say when you gone. Then I know.

Bad things soon.

He has said it before, but this time it's a threat – Mathew is going to come back. Sitting in the thatched summer house by the tennis court she thinks of the unseen people ready for the day, for one of these days, soon or far. In the compounds and mines is a servile population paid with a pittance and driven to work for the white man because of the Hut Tax. Douglas's deepest indignation is roused by the Hut Tax; she used to think, before she knew and respected him better, that it

245

took the empty place of sin in his mind as the thing to hate. But beyond those eucalyptus trees planted in lines, far the other side of the polo ground and Harry's fences and the boundaries drawn in the earth, are armies, peoples, of men and women waiting in the forest, slaves to no one and camouflaged against rocks and the bark of trees. When they move, this world, this thatched isle, will drown in its own blood. And perhaps it will be Mathew who brings them.

She must find Harry, she doesn't know why, she has no idea what to tell him or what he can do, but she needs to find him. She is afraid, more for him and the farm than for herself, more afraid of the armies in the forest than of the coming war – so far away, it seems. And he's still her lover, though she knows by now that not only women with their hopeless faults but men too are ruled by motives as mixed as a deadly cocktail. Harry will reject her because she is Mathew's sister – a thing he could never have imagined – and he will take her back again because he still wants her; and he won't let her go, because of the mine. She might take it into her silly head to rescind the letter of concession and Cam and Motor wouldn't care for that, she can hear him thinking. She runs from the summer house with Mathew's blue paper crumpled like a litmus in her fist.

Harry is nowhere. Some of the guests are groaning and stirring but no one is upright. He must be in bed with Anne – well, isn't that where he should be, in theory? Anne is like a spider; one day when she's finished she'll make a meal of him. Their bedroom window is round the corner of the building from the veranda and there's no one to see Briony approach it quietly and look in. The curtains are drawn but there's a gap between them through which she can see the two big beds side by side, touching. Harry has only to roll from one to the other – he needn't put a foot to the ground if he feels like visiting the spider. The light from the window falls on to Harry's half. His bed is empty now, the bedclothes not even folded back, so he didn't sleep there. Where did he sleep?

Now Briony can make out Anne's bed more distinctly, with two people in it. Outrage swells her breast. He is betraying her with his own wife. She puts her face closer to the glass and peers hard into the semi-darkness. Anne is on her side, facing away from the window, her hair spread out on the pillow, but the hair covering the other head is not dark hair, it's red. Who has red hair? Not Ian, and anyway he is already gone. Not Hugo, who has hardly any at all. This is a young man. Briony casts about and catches the right memory. This can only be Lieutenant Pienaar, the late arrival. Obviously Anne was waiting for him, expecting him, or else she took to him like earth to lightning. She must know that Harry has gone away somewhere, she must have known that he was going, and when. He told her, and she has profited by it like this.

Briony returns, as quietly as she came, to the veranda. She's thirsty again, even more thirsty, and there's a boy filling the water sacks from a kettle. Not a boy. She has slipped into the shameful local vocabulary. A man.

'Where is Mathew?' she asks.

He looks at her with unfriendly eyes, yellowish rims surrounding the inscrutable black centres. He shakes his head and mutters something she doesn't understand, then turns away and goes back towards the kitchen. She feels more alone now than in all her life.

The new-boiled water in the canvas sack hasn't cooled yet and the mixture of Rose's and warm water leaves her feeling thirstier than ever. The sky above the trees to the south is milky, like a day when mist builds up far out to sea and then rolls slowly in towards the coast, but hot, and with that smell of burning in the still air, more like fire storm than mist.

There's only one thing left to do, and that is to ring Douglas. She should have done it sooner, at once, when she regained consciousness, but she let herself get distracted by fears for her love, then by jealousy, finally by the tormenting thirst. She swallows the last of the

247

warm mixture because you must drink to live, and then walks slowly though the big sitting room and into Harry's office where the telephone is.

It is in use. A red-haired head, turned away from the door, is bent close over the mouthpiece as if its owner has his tongue down the opening. Hearing her, Pienaar swings round: '. . . half a dozen men out here double quick,' he is saying. As he hooks the earphone to the wall they watch each other. He seems more interested in her than before; he is considering her. Briony can't read him; his eyes are strangers, their surfaces hard and so opaque that you can hardly imagine how they see anything, but they certainly do, you can tell that because what they do show is a weighing up, as if each eye is a pan attached to an accurate scales in the head behind it. 'Yaa?' he says.

'I wanted to use the telephone.'

'Who did you want to ring?'

'I want to talk to Dr Cathcart.'

'You call him a doctor, do you? You know he's no more a bladdy doctor than I am. The missionaries have ruled long enough over half the country like . . .' He doesn't find the right word for the missionaries' rule. 'Teaching munts to read and write.' He is inspecting her from head to toe. 'What's this paper you have there in your hand?'

'It's nothing.'

'Give it here to me.' Before she has time to refuse he has advanced on her and taken her wrist. She can feel the strength in his fingers as they prise hers open and confiscate Mathew's blue paper. 'We need a long talk, you and me, Miss Briny West,' Pienaar says. He says it like that – briny. His smile is the smile of a man who enjoys long talks with the helpless.

'I must ring Douglas . . . please let me.' How bitterly, absolutely she despises herself for pleading with him. Before Werner, she believes, she would never have pleaded with a man. She had an ascendancy over Father that increased as he went downhill, but helplessness and superior force are things you learn about, here.

'We'll be seeing, as to that.' He has let go of her wrist and is reading the note. He takes his time about it; his smiling lips move as if reading doesn't come easily to him, but that's only an illusion. The sense of the message is being weighed. 'Stay where you are just now.' Slowly, enjoying it, he sits down in Harry's chair behind the table littered untidily with farm accounts and invoices and letters from England, all jumbled up and dropped at the point where Harry lost interest in them. What Harry needs is a real secretary, but of course he would seduce her and then she would stop being real.

Briony attempts to pull herself together. She is thinking rubbish because her emotions are in a mess. The men who matter have disappeared and she's cornered by Pienaar like a rabbit down a hole. But Douglas hasn't disappeared, after all. He's at the other end of the line from that instrument hanging on the wall. For the first time, the thought of him is better comfort than the thought of Harry – no, it always was more comfortable, but now her need is greater and she sees him more clearly so her need increases his strength and value. She remembers his mouth, momentarily on her shoulder; a gesture that seems to declare allegiance but actually creates it, in a woman's mind. Briony needs no romantic fiction to tell her that.

'Sit down, Miss West.' Pienaar points at the hard chair drawn into the table opposite him. He spreads Mathew's sheet of blue paper out carefully on the table in front of him, smoothing the folds, straightening the edges, as if carrying out on it some painful minor operation without benefit of anaesthetic. Briony pulls her chair out and sits.

'I must talk to Douglas Cathcart,' she says, more firmly. 'I demand to talk to him.' The demand sounds silly in her own ears, let alone his.

'I better explain your situation a bit to you, Miss West. I'm here on duty, I'm making enquiries and my enquiries bring me to you. You being officially questioned, here. I'll let you know when, and if, you free to use the phone. Till then, please limit your remarks to answering my questions.' Pienaar takes a packet of cigarettes from the breast pocket of his khaki shirt and lights one, using the lighter on Harry's desk. Also on the desk is a silver ornament in the form of a zebra, about a foot long, with a hinged tail. When the tail is raised and lowered a cigarette is shot out from the zebra's rear end. Pienaar operates the tail several times, laughing like a schoolboy while the tobacco droppings pile up on to the litter on the table. Briony has never found this toy very amusing and she doesn't smile. 'Nice little item for a commander's idle moments, isn't this?' Pienaar says, and works it a couple of times more.

'I thought you said you were here on duty,' Briony says. She knows she should be careful, she knows it. 'Your temper, Briony,' Father would say, 'do watch your temper.' But now temper, once a girl's failing, has become the woman's strength.

'That's correct.' Pienaar blows his smoke in a slow, thin jet across the table towards her. He wants her angry, that's what it is.

'Were you already on duty an hour ago?'

Pienaar doesn't answer this. He picks up the blue paper. 'So this servant Mathew has run for it,' he says. 'Where would he go, without a pass? Back to the Mission? Is this why you're so keen on talking to Cathcart?'

'I don't know anything about it.'

'But you know plenty about Mathew.'

'I know Commander Chance sets a lot of store by him. They trust each other.'

'You mean they did, till you come along. And now Commander Chance isn't here to confirm or deny what you say. We don't know when he will be. There's been a lot of disappearing done round this farm lately, which is not so unusual. Europeans come to Rhodesia to disappear, like the German manager who was here till a short while ago. What became of him? Didn't you wonder?'

'It wasn't my business to wonder about him. I'm a guest here.'

'Mrs Chance says you got quite friendly with him.'

'No.'

'No? Did he give you trouble?'

'I hardly saw him.'

'That doesn't just square with what Mrs Chance says.'

His voice sounds quite gentle and reflective as he smokes away but Briony is beginning to feel more afraid. She knows there are two different sorts of white people; politeness requires that you don't make a distinction based on social background, so-called, but now that difference is a threat. Lieutenant Pienaar is of the same sort as Barbara, he speaks like her, the hardness in his eyes resembles the hardness in hers, they were both educated in South Africa, not in England, obviously. And Barbara's reaction on learning about Mathew, aboard the *Edinburgh Castle*, would be the same as Pienaar's reaction in the middle of the African forest to a white girl with a black brother – hatred and fear. The image of Werner swims into her mind, his scars throbbing, his eyes hard as theirs. They hate her for Mathew and she is alone with them. She is shut in a hot room with a man who smells of sweat, she is under Lieutenant Pienaar. He isn't sweating now, though; in fact he looks quite cool for a man with a red complexion. The sweat he smells of must come from what he was doing an hour ago when he wasn't so cool. At once, she thinks of how he might be, with a woman. It's a question of how tempered by gentleness a man is. Pienaar wouldn't be very tempered, instinct tells her.

Suddenly, he stands and turns to the window, opens it and roars something in Shona in the direction of the kitchen, then after a long delay the new servant appears, standing barefoot in the dust outside. Pienaar gives him an order in a violent voice like a man commanding a gang of stupid oxen. 'He brings us some tea,' he says, turning back into the room.

He is watching Briony again. Does that hardness on the surface of his eyes cover up stupidity behind them, or is it, on the contrary, a cover for intelligence, which a white police officer in this part of the world does well to hide? Apparent intelligence is unpopular with people like the guests at last night's party. Harry seldom lets his own show in public. 'I don't think that boy Mathew runs to the Mission at all. Even the Mission couldn't hide him. But I'd like you to call Cathcart and ask just the same.' He gestures with his head at the telephone hanging behind him. 'Just that.' He taps on the table top in front of him with the end of his police officer's black cane. 'Go on.'

It's a relief to be released from the hard chair. Douglas answers almost at once.

'It's me, Briony.'

'Are you all right, Briony?'

'Yes thank you, Douglas, I'm all right.' There's a pause in which she can hear the tapping of Pienaar's stick on the table. 'I'm to ask you if Mathew is there.'

'You're to ask? You're told to ask?'

'Is he?'

'Has he left the farm then?'

'Yes.'

'Mathew hasn't been seen here at all.'

'That's all I need to know,' Briony says.

'I understand.'

Now the tapping sound comes from the door, the servant pushing against it with his tray, which he lays on the table in silence. As he turns to go, Pienaar knocks a heap of letters off the surface to the floor and the man bends to pick them up. Taking his time, Pienaar raises his stick and hits him a forceful blow on the back. The sound is sickening. The man straightens himself silently but as fast as if struck by a snake, and when he looks at Briony, his yellow-rimmed eyes are full of hate. His hatred is for Mathew and Father as well as for the blow with the cane. In the compound they hate what happened at the Mission, they hate it even more fiercely than Whites like Barbara because it was one of their women, Mrs Shitofo, the Chifodya heiress, who was taken, degraded, and abandoned.

'Why did you do that?' Briony cries in despair. 'Why?'

'Another time I give him an order he'll be quicker about it. A cut across the backside is the way to get what you want from a native round here.'

'This is a gentleman's house, not a police station.'

'Ach yaa,' Pienaar says. 'A gentleman's house, like the Mission in your pa's time. Except he wasn't such a gentleman, preaching the monogamy he didn't practise to the kaffirs. You pour me that tea.' Why does she do it? No male under interrogation would be ordered to pour out the Lieutenant's tea. She does it by reflex. Even Pienaar can confine her in a role as he confines her to the hard chair she sits on. 'Monogamy to kaffirs – might as well preach to the baboons on a kopje. You know what a kopje is? It's a nipple on the land. But did the missionary marry his baboon? Oh no. He waited for the right English miss. Did you know a female baboon can conceive from a man? The result is something you wouldn't want to see.' He drinks his tea comfortably, contentedly.

The terrible thing about this is that some of what he says and implies is right – Father didn't have the courage of his indulgences. It makes Briony all the angrier. 'Was monogamy what I saw through Mrs Chance's bedroom window an hour ago?'

Now Pienaar is laughing at her; he's pleased she's angry, it's what he wanted. 'So we watch at windows when the Commander isn't home?' he says. 'When we're not out riding? Or firing Mrs Chance's rifle on the polo ground?' He is playing again with the silver zebra toy, watching its back end closely as the cigarettes shoot out. From beyond the closed door and the big sitting room, from the veranda perhaps, or the garden the other side, the sound of voices, shouts, cars started up, laughter of the stricken sort that follows waking to headache, nausea and shame. Even those guests might know shame as they depart. Soon the rumbling of the last car to pass over the cattle grid dies away. Awful as they were, Briony feels helpless without them. At least they would have – no they wouldn't, they would do nothing. She is finally alone here between Pienaar and his hatreds, and the people of the compound and theirs. Otherwise, there's only Anne, who, Briony believes, hates everybody. Pienaar doesn't know that yet, but when Anne is finished with him, she will swallow anything left and eject it the same way as the silver zebra with the cigarettes.

'We better take a walk out to that polo ground, you and me, Miss Briny, just now,' Pienaar says.

From outside comes the noise of horses approaching fast, men dismounting – a few words exchanged – then tying up to the rail just below the office window. There's a trough there, it's where Harry ties Xerxes when he comes back to the house to fetch something forgotten, say something left unsaid, complete some sentence broken off halfway through when something new caught his interest – another future, another woman, another mine. The policemen's horses are drinking now, in long draughts, giving that sound of refreshment deeper even than the feel of cool water running down your own throat. Pienaar opens the window again and leans out. 'Just the two of you?' he says. 'I asked for half a dozen. Where's the rest?'

Briony doesn't hear the answer, spoken low and in an urgent tone of voice.

'I see. Come in here, both of you.' Pienaar swings round to the table. He remains standing, leaning forward, propped on his fists planted in among the bills and invoices, looking down on Briony from a couple of feet away and giving the strong impression that he has a lot more to say to her. How does a ginger-haired, freckled man like that manage under this sun? The skin of his face apart from the freckled areas is red, not angry red – brick colour. Some of it you could put down to abundant health, evident also in the muscular column of his neck, and some of it, perhaps, to excitement. She lets her eyes flicker downward and away. Yes, the situation seems to please him. She thinks of Werner and the single-handed power that pleased him too. She must think . . . think hard of some defence, some way to protect herself; and she remembers the knife Mathew gave her which seemed so childish, so pitiful then. Now it doesn't.

'I must go to my room for a moment.' She moves her legs restlessly and looks away from him in embarrassment. 'I need to.'

'Yes? You sure? Then I better come with you.'

They meet the two policemen coming in. They are both black. Harry says that black policemen are much more feared than white ones; they do things that even Pienaar and his like would shrink from, according to him. These two watch Briony go past them, with hostile eyes behind which you can imagine any horror. Can you really? Aren't they just two young policemen who have accepted the uniform because life in the bush had so little to offer them?

'Wait there,' Pienaar tells them, indicating with his cane the patch of cement floor just inside the door.

In the bedroom, he doesn't take his eyes off her while she goes to the chest of drawers and pretends to take something from it. 'You could look the other way,' she says. 'A gentleman would be ashamed not to.'

For the first time he shows a more human sign, his eyes flicker. 'Okay,' he says and turns his back.

Briony squats in the corner behind the bed. In a drawer of the little cupboard with the chamber pot, Mathew's razor-like knife is waiting. Straightening up, she has it already under her skirt. You can learn, from rape, so it isn't after all a totally sterile experience. You know how to time your attack and where to aim for the best if you have to.

'All right,' she says, 'thank you.'

Back in the office Pienaar listens to the report of the native policemen, of which Briony understands nothing. If only she had picked up some Shona, but she had other occupations, she was too busy with love. And for what? She was using love to treat a wound, that's what.

'Get out there and ride the boundary,' Pienaar says in English. 'The others join you when I've seen them. No one goes back to the station before I say. Understood?'

'Understand, baas,' the two men say in unison. English isn't their language and anyone could hear in their voices how they don't bind themselves with the colonial word.

Pienaar must know that. 'Look out if I get any slacking off you,' he says, and smacks the table in front of him sharply with his cane, scattering the papers and making the zebra jump on its silver base.

His car is a blue Chevrolet sedan, frightening to get into, as if its dedicated use is to carry victims, particularly female ones, from the scene of arrest to the grim cells at Gatooma Police Station. Yet oddly, since the moment when he turned his back in the bedroom, Lieutenant Pienaar seems less fearsome to her. The seats are of leather and you hardly hear the engine as they race across the polo ground and come to a stop behind the makeshift platform where the chukka bell hangs. Pienaar turns towards her on his leather seat. 'I want you to show me just where you left Mrs Chance's rifle.'

'Yes,' Briony says. The less she says the better. They get out of the Chevrolet and start across the field. As she walks, she can feel the haft of the knife rub against her waist. If she veers left or right, he must follow. At the far end of the field is the giant ant hill, monstrous mounds and crumbling spires and secrets, like that crazy cathedral she saw on a school holiday in Barcelona. She leads the way to it.

'You thought you'd shoot a buck, here?' Pienaar says.

'From behind the ant hill.'

'You were alone?'

'Mrs Chance had a migraine that evening.'

'Usually you went out together?'

'Sometimes.' He has information from the other side and it's no good making anything up. Answers must be the minimum.

'Where was Mathew?'

'As far as I know, in the house. Looking after Mrs Chance.' She shouldn't have said that. She's too quick, too easily surprised.

'The kaffir looked after Anne?'

'I don't know anything about that.'

'I think you do.' They're behind the ant hill, out of sight of the polo ground and with the dense forest within yards. 'Lie down and let me see how you waited for the game to show. Here, take this for the gun.' He passes her his sinister black stick. 'Go on.' He is challenging her; the relationship has passed beyond interrogation and into the realm of play, the sort of ugly play where a woman submits, and then may get hurt. Briony lies on the dust the far side of the ant hill, with the stick in her arms like a rifle. She settles into the earth, aware of Pienaar looking down on her, on her back; at her legs, below the limit of the loose cotton skirt.

'I lay down here,' she says. She turns her head to look up at him. 'Like this.' She aims the stick in the direction of the bush, holding the little leather handle against her shoulder. 'Just like this.'

Briony knows what she's doing, and the risk. She gives the hint of a smile. She is playing too, at a game of mastery and repetition, but now the real mastery is on her side; she can so easily make this young man lose his self-control, she has that power and she has the knife. The scene with Werner may be played again but with a razor-sharp knife this time in her hand, and the sight of the enemy shrunken and withdrawn.

He doesn't need much provoking. An hour or two ago he was in bed with Anne, but he's young, and he likes his work. Now he's crouched forward with his hands on his knees. 'Did you see any game?'

'Not that time.'

'How long did you wait?' His mouth is half open and he's breathing through it.

'Not long. I'm not sure. The ants – you know, they get under your clothes—'

'So you got up and ran from the ants in your pants, leaving the rifle behind?' Now in a swift movement he is kneeling next to her, his hands down below in front of him. Briony twists her body the other way like a fish, and while he is still fumbling with his belt and buttons she has the knife in her hand, the blade out. Pienaar is as quick as she is. A man is supposed to react like lightning to protect that part of himself and his mind must be as quick as all the rest of him. He's already sitting back on his heels, out of reach, and laughing at her, but this is a different laugh, not insulting, a laugh of real amusement.

'Well, you a fast one, Miss Briny, I can respect that, you thought you'd make me forget I'm on duty, and by God you damn near did. I suppose you thought you and your Commander would complain to the Governor? Well you don't have to. You a pretty girl and it's a shame. Now give us that knife over.' He holds out his hand for it, a hand at the end of a long, strong, red arm.

It's another humiliation; but one for him too. She's seen what she wanted to see. He is back in control now, of himself, of his strength, which is five times hers. Briony hands over the knife, sitting on her heels as she does but with the end of her skirt as tightly tucked in under her shins as possible.

'This is a kaffir weapon. Where did you get it?'

'It was . . . it belongs to Commander Chance.'

He is turning it over, inspecting the wooden handle. 'I see a M burned in with a hot iron here. I can see them doing it, squatting round their fire in the bush. H would be Chance's initial, wouldn't it?'

Briony doesn't answer. What is there she can say? He won't hurt her now because in his own way he has decided to respect her; she is game, and therefore no longer fair game. She tries instead to scan the future. It looks as smoky and obscure as the horizon just above the top of the forest trees before her, and with a smell of burning stronger than usual. She lifts her head that way into the slight movement of air. Surely that smoke above the trees has thickened and darkened in the last half-hour?

Pienaar, watching for new tricks, follows the direction of her gaze and sees it too. 'My, that's a big bush fire over there,' he says. With an easy motion he rises, then stretches out a hand to help her up. 'That's the Mission, over that way. We want to get there fast.' It's as if they've passed through some danger together and come out the other side with a kind of understanding, almost an alliance for now which you would never have thought possible. He leads the way back to the Chevrolet without watching behind him to see what she's doing. As she follows, she remembers that he has left his black stick lying on the earth, the far side of the ant hill.

'You forgot your cane back there,' she says, 'just the same as me and the rifle.'

As they bump and lurch at speed across the polo ground one of the mounted policemen comes cantering towards them, then pulls the horse back clumsily in the way Harry would hate, with a curb. Pienaar sticks his head out of the window and the man delivers an excited report which goes on for some minutes. He hands down something to Pienaar, who only nods, starts up again and drives on.

'They found a body in the bush,' he says. 'Bones picked bare white by the vultures. But there was a ring on it. This ring.' He holds out his left hand. He has Werner's ring with the dark opaque stone on his own third finger, between the second and third joint. 'Recognise it?

Yes? Give you a turn? I thought so. They should never have left it on the body, you agree, Miss Briny? You know the only way you get a ring off the finger of a stiff? You bust the finger backwards. P'raps this killer didn't just have the balls for the job. What d'you think about that?'

Fourteen

MOST BUSH FIRES start from lightning strikes, but there's been no storm. The sky has stayed quite clear, apart from smoke-drift, for months. So this one has some other explanation. There's a hot, light breeze from the north and the flames advance through bone-dry vegetation at a leisurely, deadly pace, towards the kopje and the village on the farther slope. In the middle of Africa you can do almost nothing to fight with nature, you have no weapon against it, you are an ant without even the organisation of an army. You dash hither and hither as the flames march on, your heart breaking for the people and animals that must burn.

The village is Douglas's child. For years he has sheltered it from the colonial administration and the lawyers and policemen who wanted it emptied and destroyed, but now the fire will do their work for them. He is facing the fire, he's beating at it with branches, shouting at the Mission boys to hold a line against the advance, seeing them one by one give up and sneak away. His face and arms are blackened, his hands blistered and burned, his back breaking like his heart. Then he sees that Peter has not sneaked away but is coming towards him across the ash where the fire has passed and done its work. As always, Peter looks as if he rises above the situation.

'We know who start this fire,' he says.

Does it matter? Anyone, anything can start a fire at the back end of a drought. 'Who?'

'That boss where Mathew works.'

'Someone saw him?'

'Yes. I saw him. And I follow him. He start another one the other side of the kopje.'

A boy like Peter shouldn't have the example of educated violence thrust under his nose; a new generation should have a new chance. But Douglas knows how minds work, have always worked here. 'Is it because of the gold?'

'You know what it because of, Dr Douglas. The gold, and the lady that is Mathew's sister. Everyone at that farm knows all about that now. And Mathew's boss,' Peter goes on, becoming garrulous, with smoke and fire all around, because obviously this is the interesting point, 'very very sick about his woman has a black brother.'

'That's enough, Peter, enough for us. We must go to the village.'

'Better go to the farm and fetch that woman, Dr Douglas. You don't ask her what she want, you take her back and keep her for yourself. After, that's what she want.'

No amount of missionary teaching will change the mental habit of boys here. Their mental habit is closer to instinct, and it isn't teaching that can change that, only fear. Here is Peter, aged fourteen, telling him what an instinctive man should do; and of course, in a way, he's right. Douglas remembers his student reading, and what sense he could make of it. It's how Freud said we should learn to be – in touch with instinct. Chance, with his passions loose as cannon, acts as if he's pretty well in touch as he is.

But where can the people of the village, victims of Chance's passions, go? Will they crowd to the Mission? He doesn't think so. The Mission was their protector but the god of the missionaries disapproved and sent this fire. The people will disperse in the forest, homeless, waterless, penniless, and within a few weeks they will have been rounded up and herded to the reserves, where the land is no good. Their cattle and dogs and goats will die on the way, and many of their children, too.

Douglas accepts exhaustion and defeat and sits on a fallen tree. The advancing front of the fire is ten minutes away. In his flask there remains half a cup of warm water, which he offers to Peter, but Peter shakes his head and Douglas drinks it to the last drop. They must get away now from the fire or be swallowed like the small animals too slow to escape, the tortoises too late to start trundling through the grass to safety. Peter, like the salamander, may be immune to the flames; but as for Douglas, he knows he'll be baked in the shell of his inner self – that self he knows capable of love, with rights to love in return, the self which has never found full expression and longs for it. He rises from the tree and starts to stumble and run on his clumsy long legs and his blistered, roasting feet towards the other side of the kopje, along the thorny track he knows so well.

'Come back, Doctor, you going to burn like heretics,' Peter shouts. But there's one old person in the village even less able than a tortoise to flee from the onrush of the fire. Mrs Shitofo deserves better of the late Dr West's god than that.

'I could be your friend. You going to need one,' Pienaar says in his warm voice. 'We could work well, you and me.'

'I have Dr Cathcart for a friend,' Briony says. It's true, however, that Pienaar would be both a more powerful friend in need, and – she shamefully admits to herself, because she's learned about honesty in these questions – in his horrible way a more ... a more masterful one. His arm on the steering wheel a few inches from her is dressed with short gingery hairs, and is very strong. What is the matter with her? Does she want a master, another commander over her like this brutish Rhodesian policeman?

'I can tell you like me,' Pienaar says.

'I don't like you,' Briony says, 'but I have to answer your questions.'

'You certainly do,' Pienaar agrees. 'You dead right there.' They drive on a bit in silence. The car has a powerful engine and good springing so all you hear is a hum and from time to time the crash of a stone thrown up from the track against the metal under you. 'See that hill? That's where the fire is. There's a lot of old gold workings under that hill. They say there's a terrific reef there, man.' Perhaps he isn't thinking of her as a woman at all. Women don't get information, in his world. They get questions and orders and blame and brutal intercourse. 'I wouldn't mind owning that hill,' he adds. She won't ask him why, she won't ask anything. She's sure he knows, anyway, who owns it. 'If that's my hill, I drive the kaffirs off and open up the reef.' His tone is conversational, unofficial. 'Will I tell you why drive them off? Because that's where they bury their chiefs. Soon as you start working the reef it's the Matabele Rebellion all over again, you dynamiting into the last resting place of their big daddy.' He laughs like a schoolboy. 'We wouldn't take long putting it down but it costs some white lives. Your friend Cathcart, for one. The Mission is number one place they go to boil someone alive for their supper.' He laughs again, his simple, youthful laugh.

'No one's going to drive them off,' Briony says. 'It's my hill.'

'That's what I thought. Some joker lit a fire just the same. Wonder who. Who'd you think is going to do a thing like that, Miss Briny?'

She knows, of course. She knew as soon as the first tall flames above the tree tops became visible from the road. She won't admit it in her heart, she defends her heart, but in her head she knows that this fire isn't only to clear the way for work on the mine; this fire is much more: it's Harry putting his friendship with Mathew such as it could be – true, more real than his acquaintance with the neighbours he despises – into the flames like a love letter. It's the bonfire of brotherhood, black and white. She thought, after Werner, that hers was the great right to anger, but others can be angry too. Harry is angry because she slept with him over and over and never said that Mathew, the house boy, was her own brother. Was that because she feared to lose the master she needs? Is she no better than that, bringing disaster with her from over the seas and making it worse by spreading her possessive, secret, woman's lust? While now, inside her, a new disaster may be preparing itself? Because she's three weeks overdue, another thing she's been shutting her mind against.

Pienaar is apparently still in conversational mood, even though they're nearly arrived at the Mission and the air is thick with smoke and the ash of leaves carried on the light wind. 'You people, you soon going back to war,' he says. 'You ever listen to the wireless? No? Then Piet Pienaar can tell you something you don't know. The British government's given an ultimatum to the Nazis to get out of Poland, or somewhere. They won't. They tough, those Nazis. They don't listen to nancies in London or nervous types like your friend Commander Chance. And it's going to take you longer with them than us with the Matabele Rebellion.' The boyish laugh explodes again. 'I tell you something else – in South Africa, we don't think those Nazis so bad. They know who needs to be boss – men with ginger hair like Piet Pienaar. God gave the world to Adam. Was he a baboon?' The Chevrolet sedan bumps across the cattle grid at the entrance to the Mission. 'I'm asking you here, did God present the earth and the gold reefs under it, and Rhodesia, the most beautiful land in the whole world, to a bunch of baboons?' He is deliberately swinging the car about to hit the deepest corrugations in the track. 'I'm asking you. Did he?'

'There are animals and people burning up all round the hill,' Briony says. She won't cry for them nor cry out for him. She will not.

'A bush fire, that's something a British commander can start, but he can't command it to stop, not in Southern Rhodesia, not even if he wanted to. Which I reckon he bladdy doesn't, because if he did want, he doesn't drive off his farm in the early hours with twenty gallons of petrol in tins, man.' Pienaar, who for a perverse moment she'd let herself stop hating as he deserves, has put all her fears into words. She knew, but she wanted to go on hiding from the knowledge. Now she can't. Where is Douglas? Her little universe of love is in flames like a Zeppelin in the sky and she needs Douglas because he's all that's left of the solid world; Harting didn't teach her to recognise it, but she has at least learned something on her own – Douglas is strong because he's good, and the other way about.

You can just bear to look at the sun; overhead through the thickening cloud it's now nothing but an intense, swirling white globe. Around the Mission, figures loom and run and disappear, shouts carry across from the edge of the forest and the calls of animals in distress ring out from the hill and from further off still. A covey of francolins, the last lagging bird with feathers alight, trying to follow, breaks noisily from the smoke and streams like a tidal rip across the sandy earth of the Mission precinct. The buck have speed on their side and will escape but the small slow animals of the undergrowth will go up in smoke. At least the people of the village, understanding fire, have surely dispersed in time, leaving their huts and pots, their only claim on the face of the earth, to the flames.

Briony is running towards the thickest part of the smoke. She can hear Pienaar pounding behind her. If he wanted to overtake and arrest her, he could; he doesn't because he likes the play, knowing that a spurt, an arm stretched out and he could stop her. She can imagine him watching her legs and arms as she runs – a girl running always amuses a man, like that. But very soon the air is too thick with smoke to run in it any more, it hurts the lungs and gives a sharp alarming pain about the heart. Anyway, where is she running to? No wonder Pienaar laughs, striding easily after her. She halts in the fringe of big trees fifty yards into the smoke, near the carved teak post marking the path to the village.

'Who you waiting for just here?' Pienaar asks, laughter cruelly audible in his voice.

'Dr Cathcart.'

'You sure? Not the Commander with his petrol tin?'

She feels soiled, fouled – not from the smoke and the ashy soot falling out of the sky, rising from the ground into shoes and clothes, but from the petrol tin, and the man carrying it, the man who will soon go to war leaving behind him a wife, and children, and a stupid, yearning, pregnant girl.

'I'm sure,' she says.

There are boys coming back out of the fire in twos and threes, limping on bare feet, sheltering behind trees from Dr Cathcart's powerful god because they've disobeyed him. They ran away from the fire and left him to fight alone. As they catch sight of Pienaar in his uniform they seem to dissolve like cigarette smoke into thin air, passing clouds. Briony calls out to one she thinks she knows.

'Where's the Doctor? Where's Peter?'

'They go into the village,' the boy answers. He has stopped running, he's halted like a shot partridge and stands near Briony as though she can protect him from the Lieutenant.

But she can't. Pienaar takes the boy by the arm. 'You run back just now and find Dr Cathcart and say him come here quick.' Pienaar repeats the order in Shona. He gives the boy a bang on the side of the head to speed him on his way and the boy vanishes again into the smoke. 'He won't do it,' Pienaar says, 'but I'll catch up with him later.' He laughs joyously at the disaster taking place all around. 'It'll be a pleasure. I'm like the mills of God, that's me.' He recites in a sing-song voice: '*Gottesmühlen mahlen langsam, mahlen aber trefflich klein.*' His laugh now sounds like a song chanted in his own ears. 'The Germans'll win this war and then there won't be any more British commanders lording it round here.'

Briony, unable to bear standing still near him any more, starts off on the path into the forest. She knows one thing for sure – if Pienaar chases and catches her, he won't rape her, and for a reason other than the fire all round. He likes to tease and torment and bully, but he respects her like a sister. Well, she supposes sisters get some sort of respect, though as an only child she knows very little about it. They ought to, and among gentlemen, they do, that's what she thinks she believes. Pienaar isn't a gentleman but he's a man, and she believes that some instinct has risen to the surface and told him to keep his hands off her.

Making a slow way through the shifting smoke on the narrow path ahead is the tall figure of a man carrying something towards her. She stops. What will she do if it's Harry? Her heart, irresponsible, lifts. Then falls back again. It can't be. He'd have thrown the container for his petrol away long ago. Covering his tracks by removing the evidence is something Harry would never bother with, and of course it isn't. The stumbling figure is close now. It is Douglas, followed by Peter. Douglas is carrying someone light and wasted, their rags and hanging limbs like a scarecrow demolished by a dust devil as it spins. Briony goes towards him with arms held out. He stops in his tracks as she approaches him – are her arms for him, or for the burden he carries? She can see the doubt on the features, always hesitant, of his smoke-blackened face, and she's doubtful herself. It's one of those heartfelt gestures undreamed of in the organised mind. The what? She is there, she's face to face with Douglas and her arms reach out to him. Then, just as her heart fell back, her arms fall. Between her and him is his burden. She looks down at it. She thinks of a broken wooden toy, a figure of jointed sticks with limbs bending in all directions like a clown's. This figure in Douglas's arms is as disjointed as that, but it's Mrs Shitofo.

'She's dead,' Douglas says.

'Not burned?'

'No. The smoke. They left her. I expect they waited and then left.' From his voice she thinks he too has inhaled too much smoke. It is rough and hoarse and painful to hear and his words are indistinct.

'Well now, Doctor,' Pienaar says, catching up in his own time, enjoying himself. 'Got a body there? Dirty work out in the bush? One of your own? No medicines for bush burns?'

Briony turns to face him. He is laughing, an old black woman stifled to death by smoke is a joke to him, and Douglas's despair an even better one; laughing and enjoying himself like that, he's off duty, when on duty he doesn't laugh. So what she's about to do is not assault on a police officer, it's a natural gesture between a woman and a man and will speak for itself. She swings her right forearm and hits his mouth with the back of her hand, the sharp little diamond scratching his lip so the dark blood runs out of it and down his chin. The blood looks black against his red-haired white man's skin.

'Briony!' Douglas says, shocked, sounding just like Father, who was never more than slightly shocked, actually, when she jumped the rails as he called it. As a matter of fact she believed he secretly liked it. This suspicion now transfers itself to Douglas. He must know all he needs to know about Pienaar but of course he can't hit him himself. Missionaries have to get their way by more devious and peaceful methods, they must be patient, and as if to prove it, Peter vanishes.

'You're bleeding,' Briony says, and offers Pienaar her rag of a handkerchief.

'And you just a bladdy scratchy cat,' Pienaar says, taking it from her and wiping his mouth and chin. He doesn't sound really angry. There's a kind of twisted grin on his face. Maybe he likes that sort of thing. Hidden in the hulk of any sadistic bully can be found the opposite type of pleasure. How disgusting and awful.

Douglas stumbles on past them with the hanging remnant of Mrs Shitofo. On the forest tracks you're not bound by limits or laws, you can turn your back on the cleared land and you're disconnected from the world. That's why Douglas lurches on in silence. However, he's walking now towards the cleared land and the limits where he will have to speak, because Pienaar is following close. After all, a man carrying a dead body, even a black one, asks for investigation. Briony brings up the rear, smoke in her lungs and grief in the space where she supposes the heart must lie, somewhere above where the new, uninvited life burrows on in her, like Harry in his mine. Now Harry and Mathew, for so long companions in their own way, are enemies for ever. Mrs Shitofo is killed by the petrol cans and the fire and nothing can change that. Even the Rhodesian forest won't be enough to contain them both. Which needs her more? Which should she work for, as far as a woman can? Is she needed at all by anyone, other than the burrowing life inside?

'You need to sit down, Briony,' Douglas says at the door of the Mission house, looking hard at her. 'You're done in.' He looks seriously done in himself. 'Peter, where are you? We need you.'

Pienaar answers the first of her questions for her. Inside the Mission, he demands the whereabouts of the telephone, and while Douglas lays out Mrs Shitofo's remains on a table in the entrance room of the Mission house, Briony can hear Pienaar giving orders down the line.

'Get more men over to the Chance place. What? Mounted men, of course. And a truck. And three or four on foot. I want the farm circled and patrols in the bush all round. The missing man's armed with a stolen rifle.'

Douglas is watching over Mrs Shitofo laid on the table, his lips moving from distress or just his own exhaustion, which he hasn't noticed yet. Briony knows it is distress, and what it means; Douglas's loss of faith deprives him of the words he would have spoken to relieve his sorrow. The old woman was his protected guest, in a way.

She stood for his endless love of Africa and for the harm even a good man like Father can do by coming here. She was Mathew's mother, and Douglas loves Mathew too because he believes him upright as a spear planted in the ground, and grieves on his account.

'I can't pray,' Douglas says, looking at her with eyes reddened by the fire.

'No,' Briony says. 'You give your life instead.'

'I can't do that alone.'

Briony turns away, not to reject him but because men are always saying these things in that headstrong manner and expecting you to answer, somehow, anyhow, without thinking. It's because they really believe that women don't think. Or don't need to, being guided by mysteries. But it isn't like that, a woman needs time to reflect and set all passion aside and work things out. Unless she has the bad luck to be in love, of course, with someone else, in which case it's humanly, femininely impossible.

'I'm sorry about Barbara,' Briony says. 'I've seen her, I know her, I'm sorry.'

'Don't be,' Douglas says. 'African women' – he waves a hand over Mrs Shitofo – 'they never regret things. This old woman lived. You can't call what Barbara does living.'

Pienaar is back from the telephone. He looks pleased with himself and the blood on his chin has dried up. He has given a lot of orders and for him orders given and obeyed are oxygen. But that turns out not to be what he's so pleased about. 'I got news for you,' he says. 'Mr Adolf Hitler, he pisses good and strong on the ultimatum from London. My young sub picked it up on the wireless a minute ago. You people got a war on your hands.' There is a long silence through which a faint humming comes from the back of Pienaar's throat. 'Any other bodies up on the hill?' he asks cheerfully.

'No,' Douglas says.

'You sure? These bladdy munts use fires to get rid of people they don't want around, you know that, don't you, Dr Cathcart, eh? Didn't you know that, already?'

Douglas looks up. 'Listen, Pienaar,' he says in a reasonable tone. 'Just listen to me for a moment. You're a young man and you've still time to learn respect for people. Stop using the word munt. Stop kicking men and women around because you have a gun and a sjambok and they haven't. One day they'll come at you with the fire, not the sjambok, and fire hurts a lot worse. This woman' – he waves a hand over Mrs Shitofo – 'was the daughter of a chief. The people who live here under my protection . . .' Douglas's voice is growing weaker. 'You could turn yourself into a decent man but you still behave like a . . .'

'Go on, say it,' Briony urges. 'It'll do you good, and me too. And him.'

Douglas looks at her and smiles, making creases in the sweat and caked ash of his face. 'I forget the right word, but it was a strong one for a missionary.'

'I get it,' Pienaar says. He claps Douglas on the shoulder. 'You roundabout, you British people, but I get it. Well I promise you, I won't be bothering your boys here on the Mission. I was brought up Dutch Reformed and I respect what you do – except teaching the ka . . . the natives to read and write, I don't go with that. So this old woman was a chief's daughter? Not a headman, a chief?'

'Yes.'

'Why did she live just here?'

'She always has, since a child.'

'No husband?'

'No.'

'Children?'

'Possibly.'

'Who?'

'I don't know,' Douglas says.

272

The lie is too obvious. 'She should be covered over,' Briony says. 'Is there a sheet?'

'You do, you know,' Pienaar says. 'Withholding information from a police officer in course of enquiry. I can run you both into the station in Gatooma.'

'Tell him, Douglas,' Briony says.

'She was the mother of Mathew.'

'Chance's house boy?'

'Yes.'

Pienaar laughs, rocking about on his feet as if here is the joke to see him through to the end of the year. 'So this,' he says in the end, turning to Briony, 'this . . . would be your stepmother, in a way? I get a scratch mouth from a girl with a kaffir stepmother? I'll pay you off, girl, don't you worry.'

'I don't.' She isn't afraid of Pienaar, not for herself, anyway. 'I want to stay here with you at the Mission if you'll let me,' she tells Douglas.

'Oh no, Miss Briny,' Pienaar says. 'Oh no indeed. You coming back with me to the Chance place. I haven't finished with you yet, not at all. Actually, I'll be needing you, just now.'

'Are you arresting her?' Douglas asks. 'Take care, Lieutenant.'

'Care? Who for? You? Chance? She's going to help me with enquiries, that's all.'

'You a bit burned, Dr Douglas,' says Peter, reappearing from the back of the house with a sheet to cover Mrs Shitofo. 'You come to the dispensary now.'

Douglas is huddled on the end of a bench next to the bare feet of Mrs Shitofo, hanging twisted over the edge of the table. 'I hold you responsible for Miss West's well-being,' he says in a low voice, and puts his head in his charred hands.

'Else you'll complain to the member of Parliament? The Bishop of Salisbury? You men here, you part of the London Missionary Society,

273

right? The Bishop doesn't much love the London Missionary Society, I've heard. And MPs, they don't love the Bishop, and the Native Commissioner, he doesn't much love you. But you love Miss Briny. So I'm taking her away.'

Pienaar takes Briony's arm in a firm grip. 'I'm not worried about the fire and how it got going,' he says. 'A man has a party at his house and drinks a bit and gets excited and goes off with a few of his friends – if gentlemen like that start a fire, it isn't the concern of the police. The fire's in the bush, not on another gentleman's farm. What my job is, it's catching any kaffir carrying a stolen rifle used already to kill a white man.' He leads Briony towards the Chevrolet sedan and pushes her into the leather seat. 'So long now, Dr Cathcart,' he says. 'Get Miss Briny's stepmother underground fast as you can. You got a couple hours before the flies lay eggs on her. And if that Mathew boy turns up, tell him I'm holding his orphan sister safe and sound.'

Fifteen

SO NOW SHE'S become a prisoner on the farm where for a few months – they seem days – she believed she'd won a woman's uncertain happiness. The future was open, for the good reason that she didn't think about it; it was vague and warm and still a long way off, like the summer rainstorm you hope will stop on the far side of the hill. Because how could she ever explain Mathew to Harry? She couldn't. What happened was bound to happen. And with three weeks overdue turning into four . . . five – how will she one day explain him to Harry's child?

At first she's too afraid to come out of her bedroom. It is Anne who comes for her. 'I can't have you dying of starvation in here,' Anne says, 'that would be going too far.' She seems energetic, for her; Briony's plight is interesting, in fact more interesting than Anne knows. She looks Briony up and down. 'You need a bath. Come over to the house.' When they get there she locks the bathroom door and turns on the taps. The wood blaze inside the geyser is burning brightly and there's a jar of bath salts with a Harrods label on it. Why is Anne making herself pleasant? 'You poor thing,' she says, 'you're miles out of your depth. Things always go wrong at Rhodesian parties, that's what they're for, we'd all go mad without them. You

275

know,' she continues, sprinkling the salts generously into the bath, 'what annoyed me was you keeping it all a secret. No one really cares a hoot what your father did – lots of men do it. Mathew's the one who suffers the consequences, not you. Did you think of that? If you'd come into the open Harry would have kept off you and Werner would be alive and Mathew would still be here to look after us. I put it down to your upbringing. Progressive education didn't teach you how to be a wily woman, and your mother probably didn't even have an idea. Women have to finesse – oh, of course, you don't play bridge . . .'

'I'm sorry,' Briony says miserably.

'Well now we're stuck with you because Pienaar says so and we must make the best of it. Have a good bath, put on some clean clothes, cheer up and come to the dining room in twenty minutes.' Just before she closes the door behind her she adds, 'Africa teaches you everything, even how to put up with the unbearable people you have to meet there.'

'I am sorry.' But, reduced though she is, Briony doesn't believe that Harry would have kept off. He wouldn't have had reason to be as angry as he is, and he might have managed to keep some kind of detachment, but he would still have come on because he couldn't help himself. She's seen him come and she knows that. She looks at her reflection in the mirror when she gets out of the bath. Her arms and legs are brown, her middle part is pinkish from the hot water, and well covered; her face is white as chalk.

Lunch is silent and Briony eats almost nothing. The dish is guinea fowl with all the shot trapped near the surface because guinea fowl are tough as tyre rubber. Naturally Harry has heard on the wireless about the expiring ultimatum, and Josh Baring, who is also on the Navy list, has had a wire from his cousin in the government. 'I'm heading back for the good old USA,' he told Harry on the telephone so everyone in the district knows, 'to spread alarm and despondency in the national interest. We have to get those Yanks in, cost what it may.'

'On clover for the duration,' says Harry, who swings, as always, between excitement and the deepest gloom. He shouts orders at the head farm boy but no longer rides over the farm to see if they're carried out. He stands on the veranda, staring across his lands, and the despair on his face makes Briony want to fold him into her. At other moments she would like to stifle him as Mrs Shitofo stifled in the smoke. But in any case he turns away from her, stubbornly withdrawn like a madman. Perhaps he knows, in the way these things get known between people though nothing's said, that her love, the servile love of an ignorant girl, is changing. But not to indifference – as strong, but not the same.

Since the party he drinks a lot of gin, all day. Briony doesn't believe he sleeps with Anne now, but she doesn't know where he does sleep. Certainly nowhere near her, either. She longs for him, for how he once was with her, condemning him for what he did. Her feelings are still turning over and over, like seaweed in a strong tide. If he came, she would open to him, but he doesn't. And there's so little time; this world of the masters of everything is coming to an end with terrifying speed. Josh Baring has already flown away in his monoplane to Beira, to catch a ship to South America.

'Not such a bloody fool, Josh,' Harry mutters over the guinea fowl. 'A rat but not a bloody fool like some of us. This is disgusting.' He pushes the plate away. 'How I miss Mathew, after all.'

'You shouldn't have fired him then,' Anne says.

'Or anything else,' Briony murmurs, speaking for the first time. No one notices.

Lieutenant Pienaar showed himself in true colours when he got her back here; he forgot all about being her friend. That, no doubt, was for when he was off duty. Duty is the male excuse for capriciousness. The world is full of women persecuted by male duty but Briony cannot condemn Pienaar like Harry, because Harry, she has loved.

'You will stay here under the eye of Mrs Chance until I say you go,' Pienaar told her as they alighted from the Chevrolet.

'Why must I stay here?'

'You mean to say you not pleased? I thought you and Chance . . .'

'Mrs Chance told you that?'

'Maybe.'

'In her bed?'

'Everyone knows everything. Just pick up the phone . . .'

'So why?'

'I don't need to give you an answer. You got yourself mixed up in a racial trouble, girl. But I'll tell you just the same. That boy Mathew, he's going to come back here looking around. For you. For a Shona, his sister is something he doesn't leave behind for someone else. You never heard of lobolo, that's sure. Lobolo is the price of a woman. And when the white people round here don't look after one of their women any more because she's gone wrong – you heard what Mrs Cathcart said – she ends up round the mines. For a white woman, it's going to be a big, big, big lobolo. So Mathew comes back just now to look after you, I'm sure of that. And you stop here, and no monkey tricks, I make bladdy sure of that too.'

Naturally, what Pienaar says is utter, rabid nonsense, but she must find some way to warn Mathew. Pienaar's men, dressed in ordinary clothes as if left over from the party, are on constant patrol – sometimes near the house, at others hidden by the trees or spread out in the bush beyond the cattle fences. The farm, Briony knows, is six thousand acres in all and only a few hundred of them stumped and cultivated, so through all the rest a man could slip as easily as a snake. The patrols must move, day and night. She thinks there's probably an

278

inner and an outer patrol, turning in concentric circles about the land.

The drums have been silent since she got back and she has longed for their rhythms in the sleepless nights. During one of them, she realised that the drums – of course – should be used to warn Mathew. She seeks out the new servant, finding him in the kitchen and closing the door tight shut behind her.

'Please tell Mathew Shitofo something.' She approaches the table in the centre of the kitchen and beats out a kind of rhythm on it with her fists. 'Drums? Understand?' The man looks at her without expression. 'To tell Mathew.' His eyes are hostile, it seems to her; there is a particular coldness expressed by African eyes, so cold it chills you inside. 'Please, do you understand? I'm sorry I don't speak Shona. It's for Mathew. There are policemen here, waiting for him on the farm, hidden.'

The man seems to relax very slightly. He moves his head in a way that could signify assent.

'Tell Mathew not to come back here. I will find him one day. He must not come here. The police will take him because of the German boss. You understand?'

Now the man laughs. He says nothing, but he laughs, shaking his head, and then turns away to get on with his work of chopping chickens for the awful soup that will be served up tonight. She doesn't know how to interpret this. She thinks he knows something which he wouldn't tell her even if they had a language in common. His eyes and his laugh and his turned, broad back are an African rejection of her, they're his refusal. Perhaps, because they were seen together, he considers her as Werner's woman. He may have totally misinterpreted her clumsy attempt to communicate; or he may not. Surely a man like that, working in the house, must know a few words of English?

Perhaps what it is is that this man won't lie to her. When white people say that Africans lie, it's because they want to hear only a particular, fitting version of things, and anything else is perversion, ignorance and calumny. He won't lie to her, because he won't send the message of warning to Mathew, and he won't send it because the people in the compound want Mathew to come. She's sure of it now. They expect him and they must know all about the policemen in the bush, they know about everything that moves. Mathew, like the Messiah whose coming they teach about in the Mission, is awaited.

Briony returns to her bedroom feeling even more afraid, if possible. She wishes she hadn't understood so easily, so quickly that something is going to happen on this farm. What did Mathew say when he told her to go away? – 'Bad things soon, here', and now the bad things will arrive at any moment. She should say something to someone, but what, and to whom? That she has an intuition of danger? Tell Anne that? Or Pienaar? He would love it, and Anne would just look through her in the way she has. 'Africa teaches you everything,' she would say again.

And Harry? Where *is* Harry? The fire on the hill still burns in Briony's breast and the man who set it is still desired, of course he's desired, but hated as you hate the idolised when they fail you, even if you knew they were only the clay grown tall. He's not in the house or she would have smelt his presence there with the sharpened senses of her changing love – the habit of desire so hard to shake off, so centred, for a woman, on one object. She thinks she knows where he may be. She has seen him before now in his black mood, talking to himself, striding along towards the horse huts where in hot weather Xerxes shelters. Xerxes, at times like that, is his friend and confidant, he speaks his sorrows into the horse's nostrils and both of them slip into a magic calm. Xerxes doesn't know sorrow but he knows the odour of need and Harry puts his arm about the big horse's neck as his complaints die slowly away into a whisper. Almost furtively, a prisoner dragging guilt like a chain, Briony makes her way to the horse huts.

And he is there, his head against Xerxes' shoulder like a boy grieving for a lost dog, though the lion dogs are there too, curled up in the dust. Xerxes stands patiently, giving whatever it's his secret to give, one hoof, from time to time, scratching the ground of his loose box, stirring it as though comfort comes from the soil. Tears rise to Briony's eyes for the childishness of the tall man, for the past, for being weeks overdue and without help. But she must talk to him.

'Harry. Harry . . .' The words cost her an effort but he doesn't lift his face from Xerxes' neck. 'I need to tell you . . .' She can't go any further. He won't turn. But she must. She can't say that Mathew is coming and that the compound is only waiting for him to light the fires. Before the death of Mrs Shitofo perhaps she could have told him, but not now. Fire avenges fire. 'You burned my hill,' she breaks out. It's not what she means, she means that Mathew's mother is dead, but that seems to be another truth she can't bring out.

He shrugs, not in contempt or carelessness but in a sort of despair. 'Those people had to go. The Native Commissioner wouldn't ask them to clear off politely.'

'You were only thinking of the mine.' Love, like a metal bathed in acid, alters its nature as the hours pass. 'Mathew's mother lives there.'

'Not any more.' He is combing Xerxes' tail now, eyes withdrawn and mouth set. He must know what's coming.

'She died in the smoke.'

He looks at her without speaking, his whole expression one of anger and something else too, which may be shame. 'That was very wrong,' he says in the end.

What use, what good now telling him that she's overdue, and soon not overdue but definitely, sworn pregnant? The Chamberlain ultimatum has expired, war isn't any longer on the horizon, it's at the door, and one more rash, impregnated girl can't fight the Admiralty. Harry will go back to sea. But she must leave him first, she must, so it will hurt her less badly. 'All these policemen all over the farm – that's very wrong too. If you told Pienaar you were taking me to Salisbury he couldn't forbid it. You'd be rid of me and the police would go away; they're only here because of me.'

The strange, wide gap between his eyebrows is as bland and unfurrowed as ever. His eyes, when he's unhappy, retreat into the dark. 'Because of you?'

'Indirectly,' Briony says.

'Because of you indirectly?'

He's trying to show her how little she's worth. If he'd had a house boy's black sister as mistress, that would have been quite all right. It's the mixture that degrades. Yet Mathew and Harry, actually, are alike in one respect, they both know from birth that they're head and shoulders above the men around them. And bad luck for whoever gets in the way.

'I'm the bait.'

'I see.' What does he think he sees? Some still more degrading prospect? 'We'll be at war tomorrow,' Harry says. 'All those policemen will be recalled. You won't be bait for anything.'

'Tomorrow?'

'September the third. The dream of peace ends and Xerxes loses me.' So final.

'And do we lose you?'

'We?'

Suppose she tells him now? Will it change him? Will he somehow take care of her and his child in her? How can he? He will only do what she can't bear to see or hear – deny the child too.

'I meant me.'

For the first time, he touches her. His hand is on hers, which somehow without her knowing it has come to rest on the broad acreage of Xerxes' flank. Harry's mood is swinging the other way, like those violent tidal currents round Spithead and the Solent.

'You know I have to go, I'm on the reserve, I'm a dug-out.' He takes her arm and pulls her gently against him. 'I won't forget. Never. I'll remember when I'm at sea and always think of the Baring place and the shack at the gold mine.'

He's returning from his mute withdrawal. His arms go round her. Oh it's so easy. For her, for him, here in the stall where it won't be for the first time, with gestures and signs they both know well. Xerxes must know them by now too – he hangs his head and studies the stirred earth and straw by his off-side fore hoof. The dogs whine.

It's over – not just the moment – the story, the alchemy. You should never make love when rage and hate have eaten into the metal of your former feelings. For Briony it was like being hired by a stranger, because in themselves they're dead to each other. She thinks of how it may be for him, her nature makes her think of it. Perhaps when he's sailing into harbour at Portsmouth, or Gibraltar, the life will flow back into what was once so good. He stands, turning away from her as he buttons his trousers.

'So. That's that – September the third, and the balloon goes up. The curtain falls on peace and love, such as they were,' he says. 'Just twenty years between wars, that's what they left us for our youth.'

It's too late – too late for both of them, for all of them. She can't pity him now, and he has stolen the pity she could feel for the other men who must die. 'That's that,' he says. By what sort of right does *he* say the curtain falls on love? Revulsion against him rises to spread until there's nothing else, and before Harry has time to knot the tie he wears instead of a belt, Briony has left him and gone from Xerxes' thatched hut for the last time.

But out in the open she stops a moment, and looks back at him. 'I suppose you know Pienaar jumps in and out of bed with Anne, don't you?'

Half turned, Harry raises an arm in front of his face. 'Well? What difference does it make? You think I'd run away? We don't run away.

283

You really belong in another world; you talk like the world you came out of.' Xerxes snorts, lifts and lowers his head, breaks wind.

Now she can only watch, knowing that Pienaar will catch his prey. She may belong in another world but she's not so naive as to imagine that here in Rhodesia the courts demand the strictest proof against a black man accused of murdering a white one, and when caught, the prey will be sacrificed. If she had a trace of the faith lost by Father, she would send up a prayer. But there's no one to receive it. If Douglas came – if only he would – she could believe in something, at least – the rock and the tree. But why should he come? She has given him nothing to hope for, he isn't a youth to hang about under a woman's windows. Douglas is a loser in love, anyone can see that, as he's a loser in faith. Being a rock is his one rough charm. He won't come.

The sun is going down, red light floods the rooms of the house, drains away as soon as the last corner is filled. Sunset here is like a malarial fever, you wait for it to pass. Waiting, she feels a desire to talk to Anne one more time, perhaps because the woman's an enigma to her. Anne has no consistent feelings, or perhaps no feelings at all, only manners and tastes. Briony often wishes that she herself had fewer feelings and more manners but her condition is inherent and it defines her. A woman without feelings is like a hermaphrodite, a freak in a circus, an object of pity and curiosity. Or an acrobat with no gender but many partners. She taps on Anne's bedroom door, wondering who will open it. How would Pienaar's ginger hair look on the pillow in the red light of sunset?

'Come in.'

'I wanted to thank you,' Briony begins with the door only half open. 'Oh, I'm sorry.' Anne is lying naked on the bed and there is nothing at all hermaphrodite about her.

'Sit down.' There's no sign of anyone else. 'You can pass me that petticoat.' She slips it over her with the grace and speed you learn from long practice of undressing and dressing again in a hurry, remaining elegant, cool and always out of the top drawer. 'Thank me for what? For Harry? Are you giving him back? I would really rather you'd returned with my Mathew, then we'd have better service and fewer, quite frankly, of all these boring balls-ups on the farm.'

'Is Lieutenant Pienaar one of those?'

Anne laughs. 'In a manner of speaking.' She goes to one of the long windows that open on to a private veranda all of her own on this side of the house, and draws back the curtains. The red light floods in. The long window is open as if someone has just passed through it. 'Crude, but not so very boring.'

'I wanted to say sorry, too, for stopping on in your house when you hoped I'd leave. And of course now I can't.'

Perhaps that's just enough good manners for Anne. She smiles. 'When I was a girl I had my mother to tell me how awfully stupid I was. I paid no attention but I suppose some of it, I don't know, a bit, took root or something. You were brought up by a man and we know how hopeless they are. It's not really my business and I expect we'll never see one another again, but I feel I ought to tell you – your weakness isn't just sex, as I thought it was. It's sex with sickly sentiment, that's what makes you so vulnerable. Well,' Anne says after a pause in which Briony has found nothing to say, 'we'll all be leaving for good with the war. I must go to my children, who need me.' She says this with her head half turned and inclined towards the ground, eyes tragically downcast. You'd think that nothing but her duties here had held her back from joining them at their schools in England all these months. Does she believe in it, or is it a sort of joke which someone in her own world would appreciate at once? Impossible to tell. But Briony at least knows that Anne is glad to have this chapter of life, written in blood thousands of miles from civilisation, closed at last. Thank the war for that.

'I hoped you might kindly ask Lieutenant Pienaar to let us all go away from the farm at once. Tonight. I think we should. I know we should . . .'

'I don't see that I need his permission to leave. Or Harry's, actually.' Now she's putting on her linen dress, blue and white, shipped out from Fortnum's, Briony has seen the label. 'So why would I ask him?'

'Because you know he's ordered me to stay here till further notice.'

'No, I mean why in a hurry?' Anne raises her eyes to study Briony standing there, a bit awkwardly as usual, before her. Her eyes go up and down. 'Are you ill?' Understanding seems to dawn. 'Oh, I do see. You silly little fool. Didn't you have a Dutch cap, or even a douche? Did you expect Harry to take care of it? Didn't you know that men like Harry don't think it's up to them?' Now Anne is peering at her in an excited way. Her eyes are bright. 'Get rid of it. It's the only thing to do. I can tell you how to set about things, in fact I can help.' She laughs. 'Out here in Africa in the middle of nowhere one learns, as I told you. How far on are you? It's important to know.'

What she's suggesting is of course a possibility. Briony hasn't thought of it because what she thinks of is love, she's love's servant, messenger and agent, and there's no part for any of those in an abortion. Her arms hang by her sides and she wraps them in imagination round her lonely womb. 'I couldn't do it.'

'What a pity you didn't get yourself deflowered in England before you came out here to the land of the lords of creation,' Anne says, laughing again. 'Then poor Werner couldn't have taken you by surprise.'

From the window Briony can see the open space between the house and the first trees, and beyond that the free bush which seems to advance like a silent army, wading through the flood of the sunset. 'I think we're all in real danger of getting caught by surprise here soon,' she says. 'That's what I'm so afraid of.'

'It's what Pienaar is for,' Anne replies; she sits at her dressing table before the triple mirror, picks up her double rope of pearls and hangs it round her neck, the tips of her fingers turning the pearls, running over them as if each one plays a note in her secret ear. 'To catch murderers and deal with them, even the best of them. Remember, it's too late for any hysterics about love then.'

Briony has never heard her speak that word before; perhaps there's feeling somewhere in her after all. But it's too late for that too; the time has gone, this is the time for doing something, thinking of something to do, daring to do it.

'Take my advice,' Anne says. 'Forget about running away, shut yourself in your bedroom and lock the door.' She laughs more gently to herself, then adds, with one of those flashes of kindness like a marsh light that come to her from time to time and disappear as fast as they came, 'You know, if there's one line here in Africa you can't cross it's between them and us. Men may breed across it because they're brutes, but socially one can't go over and I think you're still trying to. But you can't. Anyway, your country needs you. You could train to be a nurse, or something suitable like that. Let's just make sure we don't sail home on the same ship, I'm sure it would be better not to. Mine's usually the *Windsor Castle*, of course. Harry will be on a destroyer, I expect, and God knows that'll be suitable enough.'

It's hard to believe anyone needs her, or ever needed her, let alone her country. And which country is it? Perhaps that's not the right question. If she's pregnant, and now she's sure she is, she has to give birth somewhere, and what use then will her country have for her, any country? She'll be a burden for two. For the moment, she's bolted into her bedroom, but beyond and outside it is an open land. The night is silent, indoors. In the open the sounds of life never sleep, but these walls are built thick, to keep the heat out and because Harry, who built them, comes from a northern house with walls six feet through, so he claims. But what Harry claims has no more hold on her now. Is that so? No more *rights*, is what she means. Claims, yes, for repayment in kind. His true claim is the burned-out hill and the trace of Mrs Shitofo and the dead fire in Briony's breast.

This is the third night with no moon. Stars all the sharper, sharp as spurs, but under the trees an almost total darkness. She saw it – ages ago, it seems now, though it was only two days – when Pienaar finally turned off the lights of the Chevrolet and the engine, in front of the blind windows of the house.

'Sleep tight,' he said, not touching her. 'You know your way. I know mine.'

'I can't see.'

'You a cat, Briny,' he said, 'and the only thing cats get lost in is mazes.'

Yes, indeed. She gets off the end of the bed where she's been crouched, longing for some useful thought in place of all that woman's dirge about dying love. Of course, yes, the precious maze, outward show, like a leopard's spots, of Harry's character – his manic maze, inflammable as possible. Commotion there, between the house and the compound, will bring everyone running; and her hill, the mine, the Mission are all on the other side, along the other way – Mathew's way.

Then, perhaps, he will be able to come and she'll know at last how to help him. Mathew needs friends – against Pienaar, and prison, and the unthinkable rope. He can hide, but he needs more – an ally beyond that line which they say no one can cross. Briony turns down the flame of her paraffin lamp and blows it out, then unbolts the door; outside, she waits for her sight to get used to the blackness and give her some grey outlines under the stars; the maze is some way after the little house where Werner had his last encounter with the snake. The lamp swings against her leg as she feels her way round the side of Harry's thick walls. The paraffin level is nearly full. That silent house boy has seen to it, as if he knew what she was going to need – not boy, man.

The door of the little house is open and the usual smell of Jeyes leaks into the night; the maze is a hundred yards further on. She's wearing solid shoes, her toes safely contained, not spread out. She will learn to go barefoot and carry her child on her back if only she may stay in Africa, but not tonight. Through the dim grey in front of her she can see the tall, striped sides of bound mealie stalks like palisades. The middle is the place, the heart, it will take longer for anyone to reach, far longer. She enters the circular maze with a feeling like reverence.

There are no drums tonight again, no singing, so no beer drink and no fights. Fear seems to wrap the compound and the Chance empire in silence, as if the fears in Europe have travelled over the wires across oceans. Everyone waits. Briony feels her way round the blind alleys, the short circuits of Harry's ingenious puzzle. She was sure, before entering it, that she knew the way, after all the half-hours spent playing in this maze since that first time. Like the sort of silly girl despised by Anne. Even if you know it, it takes ten minutes to get in, assuming no one has tampered with the barriers as Harry likes to do when making love to the wrong woman in the heart of things. Briony stumbles on in the dark, the paraffin in her lamp sloshing noisily against its galvanised sides. She knows now the only thing left for her to do.

The bound and piled mealie stalks go up faster than she expected; she'd thought there would be moisture still in the fibres to delay the fire, but there isn't, and as soon as she puts the match to the paraffin there's a plume of flames above her. She abandons the lamp and turns to run. The flames leap across the blind alleys and the short circuits and there's crackling and a series of short sharp explosions which intensify and grow. Something in the mealie stalks is behaving like gunpowder. Briony runs, bumping against the walls of the maze, but is she running the right way? In a maze, it's dangerous to run; you need your wits, and if you're trying to find your way out, you need back-to-front map-reading skill. She hasn't much left of any of that, with the burning, exploding stalks behind her, ahead of her; and it's getting hot, terribly hot in the blind alleys. She must be somewhere near the exit, she must be, by now, she's been running and stumbling for ages in the growing heat. But each time she comes to a blank wall of mealies, lashed impenetrably together with wire by powerful hands and too tall for her to scramble over. It's as if Anne's casually malignant spirit is working ahead to shift the barriers. Desperate, Briony shouts for help and her voice fades and loses itself in the roar of the flames and the lion dogs' barking.

Douglas hears the ringing code which he knows is for the police station in Chakari. He doesn't trust Pienaar. He has almost never before lifted the receiver for someone else's call, but now he does. Pienaar is at the Chance farm, and if anyone is calling the station it's likely to be him. Anyway, everyone else will be listening too; the news from Europe has blown away the last barriers of discretion, frail as they were.

He hears Pienaar's unmistakable voice with the flattened vowels. 'We got a fire out here. Bring every man you got. Most of mine are out in the bush with orders to stay there and I can't call them back in the dark.'

'You didn't think of taking a couple of rockets with you?' asks the man at the station, obviously not unhappy to catch Pienaar out in a professional oversight.

'Do what I say. And get your backside off that chair so I kick it when I see you. In twenty minutes.'

'What's burning?' the other man asks.

'The whole bladdy surroundings,' Pienaar says.

'Not the house?'

'Not yet. Wait. I can hear some of my men coming in. And horses. You people, you don't obey simple orders.'

Douglas thinks he understands what has happened. There has been a beer drink in the compound and a fight and someone has gone mad. It's not so unusual. The people have been deprived of their land and so they fight over what's left to them – the women. But the difference this time is that Briony is held by Pienaar at the Chance farm and when a compound bursts into flames everyone anywhere near is in danger. Douglas doesn't hesitate a moment. He tells Peter that he's going out in the car.

'It too dark,' the boy says.

'I have to go.'

Peter looks at him kindly. They all know Douglas is lonely. 'You find women here at home,' he says. 'These women round the Mission, they love you.'

'Thank you, Peter,' Douglas says. 'I've told you often before that marriage is . . .' He cannot go on. This boy's ideas on the subject are worth so much more than his. 'I'm going out to find Briony West.'

'You right, Doctor,' the boy says. 'She like a sister for you.'

'Oh no she isn't.'

'You quite right,' Peter says again, 'a sister is only a woman. And I'll come with you for filling up the radiator. I'm a useful boy, Dr Douglas.' Douglas is glad of the company as well as the usefulness. Alone, he would be afraid of his own feelings even more than of the fire and the policemen ahead. After the first stop for topping up the radiator, Peter takes the bull by the horns. 'You love that woman, Doctor,' he says.

Faced with it like that, Douglas has the obvious reaction. 'Maybe, yes, I do, but I don't know why.'

Peter laughs so loudly that even the noise of the engine is almost drowned out. 'You too English, Dr Douglas, wanting reasons. I tell you why. No reason. You just in love, man.'

There's someone there, she can sense it even through the fearful noise, someone who moves quietly. She shouts again because she's lost, every alley blind and her skin burning.

The man calls something – two or three words – in Shona. Not Pienaar then. Pienaar she knows, but what thanks will this man expect? She shouts back.

He appears, calmly, round the mealie barrier. It's the new servant, laughing at her, as before. 'Madam come, come here,' he says in English, beckoning her with a movement of his whole arm. Is it her he's laughing at? The fire doesn't seem to frighten him at all; he looks in his element among the flames and smoke. He holds out a hand; no hand has ever seemed so welcome, and she hangs on hard to it.

Outside the maze he deliberately open his hand to let hers go. She knows – she knows. A native mustn't touch a white woman. She tries to hold on but he withdraws and the two hands lose each other. 'Mathew come.' He smiles. His smile, seen in the light of the flames, is like – like what could it be? It isn't *like* something or other. It *is* forgiving; African forgiveness, undeserved.

'I understand.'

'Polo field. Find you.'

'Yes, I know.'

'Police boss . . .' He gestures towards the main house, where there's a confused sound of shouts and the neighing of a horse, answered by another from farther off. 'Now. I say you do bloody now.' That's what has so often been said to him.

Briony touches his shoulder, hard under the spotless white servant's shirt, as she goes. She will learn to speak Shona like her mother tongue, she will, she must. She will.

★ ★ ★

She crouches under the primitive platform built long ago for the polo judge and the chukka bell. A few yards in front of your eyes you see nothing, but the sky glows and throbs like a bruise. She hears a horse go by, two horses, men speaking in low voices, heading across the ground and towards the house. She waits, her eyes slowly gathering more of the grey outlines in the dark till she thinks she can even see the forms of trees at the far end of the field. Or are they sleeping animals? She feels glad of the platform above and around her.

Nothing stirs anywhere. She can make out the trees quite clearly now. The stars, through a gap in the planks above her head, are frozen to the black of the sky.

'Briony? You?' It's a whisper from behind her. A less grey bulk shifts in the dark.

'Mathew?'

'Yes.' He wears only a pair of black shorts, and is carrying something, loaded in a sack. 'Why you here?'

'The farm's full of policemen everywhere, to catch you. I set fire to the maze so they'd ride in from the lands to the house.' Is he listening to her?

'I told you, go to Dr Douglas.'

'Pienaar kept me here. They found the body.'

'I know.'

'He knows you had the rifle. He suspects me too.'

'I told you, Briony, plenty more bad stuff on the way here.' He isn't whispering any more but speaking in a low, hard voice. 'You know how to drive a car?'

'Yes, just.'

'You steal the Commander's car while those men keep busy with your fire. You drive to the Mission. If you don't want Dr Douglas, don't make the man unhappy. Catch the train to Cape Town in

Gatooma in the morning – six o'clock. You go back to England.' He has taken hold of her arm. His voice is not so hard but more intense, much more, and she knows he's near to tears. She leans into him. Just at this moment, he is all she has. 'Come with me in the car,' she says. 'Wait here. I'll drive over the field with the lights out. With Douglas we'll hide you and . . . he'll know what to do.'

'I have work.'

Briony puts a hand up to touch his face. She has never been so close to him before. His face is smooth, the flesh behind the skin fills it. She lowers the hand. 'What work?'

'Burning work.' Mathew is holding both her arms; he controls her now, he's in charge of the distance between them, he doesn't reject her, but draws her towards him. She brought herself innocently, naively to Africa believing she could help him, and now, because of her, he's a man on the run; he will be on the run all his days, he will never have a home and a family. No one can tell if they're truly brother and sister, but still he doesn't reject her as Harry did. She knows Mathew may even love her; he must, because they're young and her own love goes out to him. There's a current running here in the first light of day, and they're only, after all, like the first man and woman, who were brother and sister too, in a sense. Surely he has a right to this?

'I'll help you do whatever you have to do,' Briony says. His arms are almost round her. She knows he won't refuse her. Neither of them will refuse the other anything.

The blaze has spread to the horse huts, leaping from explosive mealies to dried grass and from there to the thatch. Out in front of the house the fluctuating glow from the other side of the steep roof lets you see well enough. There's no sign of anyone. Three horses are tethered to the jacarandas by the cattle grid, heads hanging as if asleep. A fire over there doesn't trouble them. Everyone, presumably, is trying to fight it while patient horses rest and wait.

'They can do nothing with your fire,' Mathew says, 'but you hear the Commander?' Mathew puts on a parody of the voice. ' "No such word as can't in the Navy." Just one thing, in the Navy they have more water. The Navy is not a Rhodesian farm or a Shona village. I know, at the Mission we read picture books – *The War at Sea*. Soon he gets plenty more war at sea. All the war he wants. All the fire.'

'I don't want Xerxes or the dogs to burn,' Briony says.

'Xerxes, that big windbag – the Commander will take care of him. Even before Mrs Chance.'

Mathew is talkative. He's excited, and his grip on his emotions has relaxed. It's obvious why. Mathew, so made for love, has no previous experience of it; here with Briony is probably the first time, as it may be the last. But his excitement and his new ease worry her, because work like this needs a cool head. Her hand is still in his; she first tightens the fingers, then draws her hand away. She has given what she had to give and no name need ever be put on it. 'You must be quick. Pienaar will send someone back to watch the house.'

They're in front of the veranda. Anywhere – behind a tree, a pillar, at a window – there could be someone looking out. Mathew doesn't seem aware of it, he has gone beyond the sense of danger, doing what he was determined to do. Perhaps it was like that for the boys at Jutland. He puts the sack on the veranda and pulls out a tin and a bundle of rags, holding the rags up, showing them to Briony.

'These, you see these – Mrs Shitofo's clothes.'

'Don't talk, Mathew, it's too late. Be quick,' she says again.

'The Commander – before he treats me well, shake hands old chap, ask me what I think about everything, teach him so he speak some pure Shona, and I love him. But in Africa even a commander pays.' He's busy soaking a rag in petrol and scattering petrol around the foot of the brick pillars that support the long roof over the veranda. 'You see, Briony?' When he uses her name his voice is soft.

'You burn the maze, Mathew burns the house. Now you a real African because all bad things in Africa, you pay for them. Boss Werner paid. I must pay too.'

'No. We'll go away, in the car.'

'You go. I pay. Now bring that tin.'

Mathew lights the first soaked torch and throws it up on to the thatched roof. Now everything must happen fast. He strides along the veranda, Briony following. When she looks back she sees a long thin flame like a snake twist and run on the thatch. Mathew throws another rag torch, higher up this time, then moves on towards the corner of the house and Anne's private veranda at the side. He moves as if all this is part of a dance; his movements seem ritual like the movements of a priest. He has ignited the thatch above Anne's apartments. Smoke from the roof rises high over the house and the flames lash upward in the draught of air.

'It's enough, Mathew, stop. They'll come. Mrs Chance is inside.'

'Mrs Shitofo was inside,' Mathew says, and there's no answer to that.

The heat is intense. The sky is alight and there are running figures everywhere, black and white in the red light of the fire, shouting above the noise. Within herself Briony is aware, she thinks she's aware, of the next life stirring. Mathew can live for these moments now; men like Harry, midshipmen, lived at Jutland for the moments then; but a woman has the next life in her. Men live for action, and women for life. She has retreated from the heat and the angry light to the jacarandas by the cattle grid. She notices she's still holding the empty petrol tin and lets it drop. Mathew has no more to do here; Pienaar is surely one of those figures dashing about and shouting orders, and where is Mathew in all that? Perhaps there's still a chance.

She can see him standing by Pienaar's Chevrolet, over near the path to the swimming-pool. It's the only car in sight; Harry's must be round the back by the horse huts, between the fire of the house and the fire of the maze. She thinks again of gentle Xerxes, and the mare. May they be saved, as Mathew said. He has opened the bonnet of the Chevrolet, he's placing his last petrol-soaked rags, and now he starts running towards her. The Chevrolet explodes in flames with a delayed blast that reaches her ears like a knock with a closed fist.

Why did he do that? She was supposed to steal the car, that was his plan. Why? He runs like an antelope, dogs following, his feet hardly touch the ground. But why? Because they decide for themselves and she is a woman, and this time a woman without an alternative plan; she's an African sister, made for waiting.

Mathew is bleeding heavily from a wound on his neck, red and black, startling, frightening. 'You're hurt.'

'No,' he says. 'No real hurt.' Blood runs in a stream down his arm and across his chest. One of the dogs stands to him.

'Oh Mathew,' Briony says in despair. She knows why he did it – Pienaar's Chevrolet was like the enemy at Jutland. She puts a hand on her stomach. 'They'll catch you.'

'Never mind, I shall kill some first,' Mathew says. He smiles his great smile, which is the mocking of Africa for invasion and empire. 'One man, one life. You, Briony, you carry life to' – he gestures at her hand still laid on her belly – 'to give it back so Dr West has a grandson. Not the black son he better forget up there.'

Behind her, the policemen's horses tethered to the jacarandas are restless. They were sleeping, the fire and the noise have disturbed them and their eyes roll indignantly. The sky above the trees, near the horizon, is beginning to lighten. A pale, thin line of light with no flames.

'You take the horse, that small one,' Mathew says. 'I tell you so many times and women don't listen, go to Dr Douglas. Quick, double quick. From the polo ground, you—'

'I know the way.'

'Go now.'

'Come with me.'

'I don't ride horses,' Mathew says. He unties the smaller of the two horses and picks up a saddle from the ground under the tree. 'You put this on like the Commander showed you, I hold the bloody horse.'

Briony obeys. Her fingers fumble with the buckles. She is only one more of all the women sent away with their precious wombs full or empty, for another time. Mathew helps her into the saddle, his hand on the inside of her thigh, then he leads the horse gently through the gate beside the cattle grid and out on to the open land.

'Goodbye, sister,' he says. He's like a torn standard, with his red and black bloody streamers in this light. 'Dr West, he taught me everything. To be a man, only not to be a son. And not how you be a brother with only that little love a brother allowed. Now you go, like I'm always telling you.' He taps the horse on the rump. 'Giddup. Giddup. Ho! Oh yes. Go!'

The horse is bigger than the mare she's used to, and so far up from the ground she feels unsure. She keeps holding it in against its will and they advance along the track at a walking pace. The horse, probably thirsty, is eager to get on. She can recall no well or trough before the polo ground where there's a rainwater butt, certainly bone dry now. The roar of the fires behind them fades slowly as they progress among the trees, and the horse, in spite of her, breaks into a determined trot. Briony thinks of her clothes and few belongings going up in flames in the cottage with all the rest. There wasn't anything important among them. She has nothing important except inside her, no other salvage, as the trot turns into a canter.

They're at the edge of the polo ground. It can't be long before the theft of this horse is discovered, and the other one, with a policeman mounted, will chase after her, pounding, crushing, much faster than she can go. The polo ground is flat and smooth and clear of obstacles; its limits and all the gold-brown canopy of the forest beyond are now flushed and visible in the first light, and the track that goes the right way for the Mission is at the far end. She gives the horse its head, digs in her knees and heels, hangs on with both hands holding the reins close to the animal's neck. Not textbook horseman-ship, but here, on the flat and in the open, not much can go wrong except falling off. The horse accelerates at a terrifying speed. They're galloping headlong across the dusty grass and the bare patches of earth, past the platform and bell, racing for the track into the forest. Hanging on hard, she can't rein back; if she tried, the horse would ignore her. It's a horse used to the legs of a man about it, it's in flight, it hardly seems to touch the ground. It's exhilarating, you can only die once, and when they reach the narrow track, with danger of pursuit left behind, the horse will calm itself and surely tire and she will regain control.

But that doesn't happen. This horse isn't flying, it's bolting. On the track between the trees it seems to bolt even faster as twigs sharp as birches tear at Briony's face and arms and at the horse, driving it on. The mopane trees in leaf, the flame trees in flower, the elephantine baobabs, flash past her. She knows she must fall. If she survives, she will continue on foot. She believes this horse, alive under her like a child, is really only playing; it's excited and frightened by the fires, and when she falls it will stop and wait for her. But she's too afraid to throw herself off. Excited, and frightened as the horse.

Ahead, the track turns sharply to the right up the short, steep side of a kopje. Surely the animal will slow, she'll be able to pull it in, they will unwind together and everything will be all right, excitement and fear forgotten. Not the future though, never the future, because that unwinds at its own sweet will.

They take the bend. Briony's left foot loses the stirrup and flails about behind her. The sharp slope is in front, the lighter eastern sky lifting ahead between the trees. And crashing down the slope towards them, filling the track as it swerves from side to side and followed by the usual cloud of dust, is a car with its lights full on in the dawn.

As she falls, Briony knows the horse is going to be hurt because there's no time for horse or car to stop. She feels nothing, at first, when she hits the ground. A kind of peace, perhaps, a return to earth; and in a final flash, a coming home. Above the wheel of the careering car she has time to recognise Douglas's anxious, determined, set face – the man so much more generous of spirit than the God he mourns – and beside him that funny black Mission boy who laughs at everything. That's good, that's very good, she thinks, just as the pain runs through her.

Afterword

THE SHONA AND Ndebele people were sympathetic about the distant war, when they heard of it, because their own bloody wars live unfaded in the collective memory. But this new war was a long, long way off. Some families of English people departed; others stayed. Admiralty, for the inhabitants of a landlocked country, had no real meaning, but it was known that men like Harry, and Baring, and Ian Mull had all been summoned by some remote and almighty power which they couldn't disobey. The Ndebele in particular respected that, the feudal levy being part of their culture and rooted in all the codes of virility.

Douglas wasn't summoned by any power because he was over age, at forty-five. Anyway, a chaplain to the forces who had lost his faith would be less use than a missionary who at least had not lost his love. What the London Missionary Society would think about that, no one knew, and no one cared. The boys at the Marimari Mission and the women seeking protection knew what to think. They needed him here.

And now he wasn't alone any longer, which was a relief to everyone. Especially Peter, who felt responsible. 'You don't let her go to any hospital, Doctor,' he said when they got Briony back. 'They kill you in hospitals.'

'She's badly hurt.'

'Only her back,' Peter said. 'She don't move, it mend and in twenty thirty days okay again. There in Gatooma hospital you lose her for ever.'

Douglas, unable to bear the thought, let himself be convinced and Peter did a great deal of the nursing. He was, of course, much less timid about the physical side of things than Douglas would be. 'You going to marry this woman, Doctor,' he said. 'Not any job for you going behind her before the wedding day.' Douglas tried to join easily in Peter's joyful laughter at this statement of custom, but knew that due to emotional tension, he'd failed. But he sat long hours with Briony, who had a lot of pain in the night which she bore more or less stoically.

'Douglas . . .' she said one morning as dawn showed behind the mosquito nets; then took hold of the large brown hand that lay on the edge of her sheet and hung on to it like a log in the flood. 'I must tell you – I know how you feel and you need to know – I think I'm pregnant.' She tried to withdraw her hand but he held on to it fast.

'How long? Not from . . .?'

'No. From Harry.' After a silence she said, 'I'm sure.' Then, 'I should try to go back to England.'

'When you can walk, you might. Land up there with no one and a baby,' Douglas said. 'Or you could both stay here with me and wait for a sign from Mathew. When he makes one he's going to need help.' It was almost the first time in his life that he had resorted to subterfuge in a good cause.

'Oh yes,' Briony said. 'Thank you, Douglas, you're . . .' She searched her vocabulary and came up with the very word that Anne might have used. 'You're a saint.'

Mathew ran with his wound into the forest, and on to the Tribal Trust Lands. He was caught a year later, near the frontier into

Portuguese East, where he would have been safe. But he would also have been alone and useless to his own people. Perhaps he wished, really, to be caught, a man of two races, to serve some symbolic purpose to both of them. They brought him back to prison in Bulawayo and after many months put him on trial for the murder of a German, a man from the country they were at war with.

After preliminary hearings before magistrates, the case came to the attention of Chief Justice Tredgold, who could see at a glance, as he later declared, that delicate issues were involved. He invited prosecuting and defending counsel to lunch at the Bulawayo Club, two minutes' walk from his court. As to defending counsel, he had no serious worry because the young man was a junior in his own chambers. 'Who's backing your brief, Sinclair?' he asked, just for the form.

'The Marimari Mission, Judge.'

Tredgold turned to prosecuting counsel. 'There's a decent Paarl Hock on the list here. That suit you, Centlivres, eh? We'll have a couple of bottles, then.'

Chief Justice Tredgold let it be understood that he would like this case to be dealt with, to pass through the judicial calendar, with discretion and dispatch. 'If not, Centlivres, the rainy season will be on us and you won't get in any shooting out there at Matusadona where you have all those thousands of acres.'

'How do you propose to hurry it through, Tredgold?' asked Centlivres, who had been his contemporary at the bar.

'I'll tell you. We'll have another of these first.' Counsel, numbed by Paarl Hock, waited to be told something – whatever it was – which almost seemed to concern them no longer. 'I intend to hasten the proceedings by questioning witnesses myself. Get through the whole blessed thing in half the time. You agree, Centlivres? Brandy?'

Walking back to chambers, the Chief Justice put his arm through that of young Sinclair. 'In my experience, African homicides make far the most attractive prisoners. They're ordinarily warmer by nature and free from the meaner depravities. But a white jury is going to hang this chap,' he said. 'Take a word of advice. Get him to plead guilty, then we don't need a jury. People have better things to do, with a war just on and their sons going away.'

Briony was not allowed to see Mathew in prison but Douglas, as his religious adviser, was admitted with counsel the day before the trial.

'I'm going to leave the talking to you, but don't say too much,' counsel advised. 'There's always someone listening, in these holes.'

'Does the judge know what to expect?' Douglas asked.

'No. We'll take him by surprise.'

Mathew looked unhurt but terribly thin. 'You all right, Mathew?' Douglas asked.

'They going to string me up, Doctor,' Mathew answered, and laughed.

'I've a message for you from Briony.'

'She with you at the Mission?'

'Yes.'

'Then she made up her mind.'

'The way she likes to. Now listen. Her message is, plead guilty to the judge. And remember the Chance party, whatever she means by that. I can't say any more.'

'They going to string me up anyway. You ever hear of a black boy not getting that for killing a white man?'

'You'll do it?'

'You know I nearly always do what you say, Dr Douglas.'

The birth was a difficult one. The child was a boy. Briony was walking again by then, but with less of the old spring in her step, and the pain in her back so bad that at times she could hardly lift the baby from its cot. Seeing Douglas with it in his arms, she knew that there would have to be more of them, or she would fail in her woman's contract. When he was at work away from the house she watched for his return, as at the end of a sleepless night you look for first light.

'When you going to marry that man?' Peter, her great ally, asked.

'He still isn't divorced.'

'I don't mean church sort of marrying.'

'Oh, that's happened already,' Briony answered, laughing.

'And no one think of telling me before now,' Peter said reproachfully.

'You didn't ask.'

'Me, I mind my business.'

'It's time you found a girl for yourself, Peter.'

'Girls – plenty of those when I want. Make them happy like the Doctor make you,' Peter said with lofty dignity, and left Briony alone with the baby and the pain in her back.

The case of R. v. Shitofo, Mathew, came up in April 1941 before Tredgold, C.J., at the Bulawayo Assize. Tredgold's elder son, a pilot in the Royal Air Force, was shot down and killed over the south coast of distant England a few days before. The judge looked unusually severe, even for him. Mathew pleaded guilty and the jury for that day was dismissed back to their farms and shops. The eminent judge considered Mathew across the well of the court, standing between two policemen in the accused's box. 'Give the man a bench to sit on,' he said.

When counsel on both sides had told the story and endeavoured to analyse its elements until Chief Justice Tredgold could have torn his robes with impatience, he turned to Sinclair. 'Any extenuating argument, Mr Sinclair?'

'I call Miss Briony West,' Sinclair said, somewhat nervously, and after the customary altercation between counsel Briony was sworn. Tredgold watched her curiously, and so did all the other men in this hot, all-male courtroom.

'What have you got to tell us that we don't already know, Miss West?' Tredgold asked, cutting short Sinclair's carefully prepared examination.

Briony was grateful for this and smiled at him. There was at once an almost tangible relief in the atmosphere of the court. The judge, receiving this luminous smile full on, looked in spite of his private grief as if something pleasant had happened to him in a waking dream.

'Mathew is my brother,' she said.

'Your brother?'

'Yes. My father was head of the Marimari Mission, and Mathew's mother . . . received him and comforted him and gave him a boy.'

It takes a lot to startle a judge, and this story, even if the avowal was unexpected, was by no means enough to shake him. 'We may expect too much of the missionaries,' Tredgold said, 'and there's the result. But this man's being your half-brother doesn't seem to me to help him.'

'He was protecting me from a second rape when he killed Baron von Hippel.'

This time, the Chief Justice was startled. 'A second rape, you say?'

Briony told the story in a low voice, leaving nothing out. At the end she said, 'Baron von Hippel followed me to the tennis court that night. He was drunk.'

'Why did you go to the tennis court after dark?'

'I was going to meet Mr Shitofo. We could never talk alone in the daytime.'

'Was he there to meet you?'

'Baron von Hippel arrived first. That was when he tried to rape me again.'

'If he had already raped you as you told us, why did you stay on at the farm where he worked?'

'I was in love with Commander Chance.'

Tredgold, C.J. knew how the world went round. 'Your love for Commander Chance, who I understand has left the country with his family and is on active service, was it consummated?'

'Oh yes.'

'Was it not him that you expected to meet by the tennis court?'

'Oh no, we went out riding when we wanted . . .'

'The Commander knew that Shitofo was your brother?'

'No one knew.'

'And no one can prove it,' the judge said grimly. The court, roasting under the afternoon sun that beat down on the tiled roof above, was silent and still for several minutes. 'So Shitofo came on this scene, armed with a stolen rifle?'

'He wanted to protect me and he broke the law to do it.'

'This sounds to me like a trap deliberately laid for the dead man to walk into.'

'Some men,' Briony said in a louder voice, 'treat every woman as a trap.'

'So you wish the court to believe that Shitofo shot von Hippel and then hid the body so that you could continue your affair with Chance?'

'No. He wanted me to return to the Marimari Mission where he and I could have met and I would be safe to give birth and there would be no shame in being brother and sister.'

'You were pregnant? By which man?'

'Commander Chance is the father of my child.'

'Does he know?'

'No. And he won't hear of it from me.'

At this point, defending counsel asked for time to consult the accused. On the court's return, he announced that the accused begged to be permitted to change his plea to not guilty.

'I don't see we have any choice in the matter,' Tredgold said.

In his judgement, the Chief Justice said that any decent man would have acted as the accused apparently had acted; that the witness was a brave woman; that he hoped for himself and his own children – here he hesitated for a moment – to live long enough to see a society in Rhodesia where the sibling circumstances of Miss West and Mathew Shitofo would be no matter of shame; and that Shitofo would go to prison for one year, including the six months he had already spent there, for illegal possession of a firearm. The temperature in the courtroom was by then about 105 degrees Fahrenheit.

'I think you perjured yourself quite a bit today, Briony,' Douglas said in the Ford on the return journey to Marimari.

'Don't be such an old Puritan. The only thing that matters is that Mathew doesn't have a rope round his neck,' Briony said, and because she was so much younger and he wanted to believe the same thing and wished the world to move on, he supposed she must be right.

The papers made a brief fuss about the case, and at the Mission they noticed a falling-off in social support from among the settler community, even after Douglas's divorce came through and the position of 'that woman' living with him was regularised. But the Mission didn't need the settler community, it wasn't there for that.

When Mathew came out, Douglas met him at the gates. A crowd of young Africans had gathered. No one raised a hand or fist, but there was some singing and rhythmical stamping in the dust of the road outside the prison.

'Who are they?' Douglas asked.

'Poor boys hoping their children to one day rule their own land,' Mathew said in a voice which Douglas hardly recognised.

Douglas took the main road north out of Bulawayo to Gwelo.

'Where you going, Doctor?'

'Marimari.'

'No. I must go to the mines at Filabusi. You write me a pass and put me on the road there. I walk it in a day.'

'Briony is waiting for you, Mathew.'

Douglas looked quickly away from the road ahead to see, if he could, what Mathew was thinking. It was not difficult to read. Europeans have professionals, in a long tradition, to do their acting for them. In Africa, the drama of persons is more naked and direct. Mathew's face, his eyes, were the speaking picture of a man who has once – once is enough – broken a taboo.

'Better for Briony and me . . .' in spite of everything, he smiled as he spoke the name, 'we love at a distance, you understand, Dr Douglas?'

'Yes, I think I do.'

Briony understood too. It was part of the male system whereby a woman – any woman – always loses, this self-denying ordinance of Mathew's. But she accepted it. He had chosen the mines because it was surely out of the mines that a new kingdom, like the old Great Zimbabwe, would rise. After a time, she heard that he had migrated from Filabusi to Cam and Motor at Gatooma. There was talk of a movement among the men called the Watch Tower, and Douglas obtained permission to meet the organisers, because it was feared all round that the Watch Tower was going to end in a bloody massacre. Cam and Motor, to whom Briony had always refused to sell a mining concession on her hill, tried to keep in with Reverend Cathcart and his lady.

The organiser was Mathew. He sat with Douglas in the comparative comfort of the mine offices, with a fan overhead and beer and sandwiches provided by the management. Douglas tried to warn Mathew about the danger he might be putting himself in through illegal trade union activity.

'I know,' Mathew said. His face was less thin than when he came out of prison, but also harder, more brutal even, as if what he saw every day in the mines had changed his nature.

'They'll send you back to prison at the slightest excuse. You're a marked man, you know that, Mathew.'

'You haven't seen what happens in the mines.'

'I can imagine it.'

'No, you can't imagine it. The only human beings in the mine compound are the prostitutes. And they're the dirtiest prostitutes in the land.'

Douglas's old protective instinct asserted itself, even though he had two children of his own now at the Mission. 'Be careful, Mathew – disease . . .'

Mathew laughed, without humour. 'There are plenty diseases in the mines. We all die from some of them.'

'Commander Chance was killed in the war. They gave him a medal, afterwards.'

Mathew laughed again, this time with genuine amusement. 'That man, he didn't need medals. Anything that man did, it was because he wanted it. So if he's killed in your war, he wanted that too.'

The uprising at Cam and Motor was historic, violent, and short-lived. The Watch Tower men were gunned down by the police, under the command of Major Pienaar from Salisbury, within twenty-four hours of occupying the mine offices and appropriating the cash found in the safes there. For a time, Briony mourned Mathew though no one reported his death, and Douglas's mourning took the form of guilt that he, as Mathew's father in the way of disinterested affection, the way that counts, and his brother-in-law too, had failed him, failed to talk him out of it.

Then one day long afterwards, when their children were almost old enough to go to school in Gatooma, Briony and Douglas had the visit of an old pupil, Peter. He came on the bus, along the treacherous strips of road from Salisbury to Gatooma, and then walked. In Salisbury, he cleaned the floors of a school for white children before they arrived for the day's education; children who spoke English less well and who would never see life as lucidly as he did – but Peter's plight is another story. Douglas greeted him with open arms, held him hard and inspected him.

'How many children you got now, Doctor?' Peter asked.

'And you, how many, without bothering your head to get married?'

'Children, they wonderful things sent from God, but they also a bladdy nuisance,' Peter said.

'I know, I brought you up,' Douglas said.

'You never use a stick on us, Dr Douglas. That's wrong. You want peace and quiet, you use a stick.'

'Nonsense,' Douglas said stoutly. He was already afraid that all this jocularity screened some piece of bad news that Peter was terrified to impart. 'It makes me happy to see you, Peter, whatever you've come for. Briony will be very happy too. Come in the house, now.'

But the news Peter brought wasn't so bad. In fact it was good, wonderfully good, in a way. Mathew was still alive. He was over the border in Mozambique.

'What is he doing there?' Douglas asked, though he knew the answer already.

'They work so one day the earth is for everyone,' Peter said, with tears of despair in his eyes.

'With guns?'

'Yes, with guns.'

Peter returned to Salisbury and life went on as before, more or less. Briony knew that she would never see Mathew again, but he lived, and his ideal – whatever the violence of the methods – was the ideal that was in her heart too, and in Douglas's. Whether it would still be in their children's hearts, who could say? Ideals change more than appetites because they are secreted first in the head, not the genetic apparatus.

'I regret nothing,' Briony said. 'I helped him do things he might never have done without me – be a murderer, and a revolutionary, and a free man. At least,' she said, laughing at herself and the world, 'I gave him love and stopped him being a servant. A West can only be the servant of love.'

It is some time after this, one night when the air is crisp and clean and the branches bare and the drums pattering away in the distance, that she begins to put down, line by line in an exercise book, how she came to be here, and what it was, and is, that kept her.